EVERYONE WANTS TO KNOW

EVERY- ONE WANTS TO KNOW

Kelly Loy Gilbert

SIMON & SCHUSTER BFYR

NEW YORK | LONDON | TORONTO | SYDNEY | NEW DELHI

SIMON & SCHUSTER BFYR

An imprint of Simon & Schuster Children's Publishing Division
1230 Avenue of the Americas, New York, New York 10020
SIMON & SCHUSTER BOOKS FOR YOUNG READERS
and related marks are trademarks of Simon & Schuster, Inc.
For information about special discounts for bulk purchases, please contact Simon &
Schuster Special Sales at 1-866-506-1949 or business@simonandschuster.com.
The Simon & Schuster Speakers Bureau can bring authors to your live event.
For more information or to book an event, contact the Simon & Schuster Speakers
Bureau at 1-866-248-3049 or visit our website at www.simonspeakers.com.
Interior design by Hilary Zarycky
The text for this book was set in Baskerville.
Manufactured in the United States of America
First Edition
2 4 6 8 10 9 7 5 3 1
CIP data for this book is available from the Library of Congress.
ISBN 9781665901369
ISBN 9781665901383 (ebook)

For my grandparents
and all the ancestors I never met

EVERYONE WANTS TO KNOW

PROLOGUE

ere's the opening scene: an old wood-shingled Craftsman house with huge windows looking out over the Northern California coast. Along the bottom of the screen the title flashes: *Lo and Behold*, the name of our family's reality show. The camera pans slowly through the modern-looking kitchen, which is bright and clean except for a cutting board with lemons and chopped fresh herbs and shallots: dinner in progress. We pan over the view from the kitchen windows of the sun setting in pastel layers above the water, over a trio of guitars hanging artfully on the wall in the hallway, to where the five of us kids are playing in a stylish, neutral living room. We're also wearing neutral clothes, which people assume is our style but actually is a contractual point with the network, which wants sponsored items to pop against the background and which does not want to give any nonpaying brands free airtime. Skye is nine, and Atticus and I are seven, and we're playing dim sum.

How dim sum works is Wrangell, age sixteen, and Jamison, age seventeen, arrange the three of us into different dim sum dishes. Skye and Atticus and I curl up in a row, on a blanket, and Jamison drapes the rest of the blanket over the top of us: we're shrimp inside cheung fun! We curl up again (more shrimp), each on our own blanket this time, and Jamison crimps the blankets around us: we're har gow! The three of us are shrieking with laughter. Our parents sit nearby on the vintage wood-framed couch, our dad gently playing the acoustic guitar resting in his lap while our mother pages through some sheet music. They are young and attractive, Asian in what Wrangell once referred to as a kind of Disney look; Asian*ish*. Our dad has tattoos partially showing under his shirtsleeve. When they hear us laughing, they look over and smile, then lean in to kiss each other. It is, objectively speaking, wholesome and really cute, somehow both relatable and aspirational, the idealized version of the life you always wanted.

That's our brand. Or at least, that used to be our brand.

It's fake, yes—there were about eight more people in the room, between the producer, Shelley, and all the filming crew, and it was before we'd gotten proficient at navigating around the huge boom mic and all the equipment, and Atticus and I kept bumping into things. Also, neither of our parents has cooked dinner in probably ten years. And it wasn't, in fact, a spontaneous moment. Shelley had seen us playing dim sum and loved it so much she called our parents over to come be in the shot, and we had to film probably twenty takes.

But it's also, in some essential way, not fake. We filmed that first season on faith. It was hard, even for the credulous seven-year-old I was, to imagine that the pandemonium and drudgery of filming were going to be worth anything. The house chaotic during the day, the hours we spent shooting and reshooting because Shelley had some narrative she wanted, then the too-quiet nights with the house emptied out—this was going to build somewhere? Our parents were tense with worry that this would all be a flop; Wrangell was constantly irritated at all the disruption and demands. And maybe we hadn't learned yet to believe in ourselves. We still felt like we had a lot to prove. So we weren't expecting very much.

And then Shelley showed us that intro scene. It would be our opening credits, she explained, our weekly reintroduction to an audience we all hoped would come to love us. She started the clip and there we were, that same living room transformed somehow on screen, and right away I think we all knew. I still sometimes go back and watch it whenever I want to remember what it felt like to know you were at the beginning of something magic. And I still think, all these years later, that that moment, crafted as it was, is also a time capsule of the best of us: We were together, we were happy. We were going to be big.

CHAPTER ONE

Our sister Skye, the person I'm closest to in all the world besides my twin brother, Atticus, graduates from high school at the end of Atticus's and my sophomore year, and the whole Lo family shows up for the occasion, of course. We Los are all about family first.

There are nine of us, counting Jamison's husband, Andrew, and their baby daughter, Sonnet. It's the first time the whole family has all descended on Rearden in years, and I'm hyperconscious of us in a way I'm usually not at school. For the most part, we're old news here, but today for graduation it's a parade of everybody's cousins and aunts and uncles and family friends, random people who are going to spend the whole ceremony trying to pretend they aren't taking pictures of us or debating whether or not to come say hi—someone's aunt already stopped our mom on the walk up to the field—and I don't want it to look like we're full of ourselves. My friends always tell me I'm just normal, which, isn't that all anybody wants?

I am dreading Skye leaving. Being the youngest has always felt to me like a procession of absences, all of them tumbling over one another to reach you: little parts of your heart parceled out to San Diego with Jamison or San Francisco/God knows where else with Wrangell.

But today we're all here, so I'm happy. The graduation is on the field, overlooking the bluffs, and it's gorgeous today, perfect June weather—the sky pale blue, the coastal pines and cypresses the kind of vibrant green that makes me wonder how people live anywhere but coastal California. At heart I am perpetually a ten-year-old still scheming about who's going to sit next to whom, and I sit next to Jamison so I can hold Sonnet for as much of the ceremony as she'll let me. Sonnet is almost a year and a half. Jamie's dressed her in the most perfect tiny jumpsuit in blue and yellow, Rearden's school colors, and I spend the whole first part of the ceremony hunting for pieces of grass or clover, or things in my purse Sonnet might be interested in, little things she can pluck from my palm to inspect, Jamison watching us like a hawk to make sure I don't let Sonnet put anything in her mouth. Atticus, who is universally beloved in a way that both gratifies and rankles me, sits next to our dad, on the end because he's surrounded by classmates who also want to sit by him. Wrangell sits on my other side, badgering me with questions about my life at school. Half the time Wrangell ghosts you, but when he's there and in a good mood, there's not a more magnetic person in the world. He's solo today, which is unusual, because his MO is to show up to important family events with a girl who seems wildly into him, whom we then never see or hear about again. He's carrying an almost comically huge bouquet of ruffled, peach-colored roses for Skye that's probably not sustainable, but that's the kind of thing only Skye and Jamison and our mom would get crap for. There's always been a double standard. Ava and Lauren, our mom's assistant and publicist, are both here too, sitting on the other end of the row next to our mom.

After graduation is over, we're going to lunch, because my

parents have an announcement. Our dad is huge on ceremony, and my guess is that it's about where we're going to go in September for our birthday. Our most sacred family tradition, the thing that weaves us together as a family and the thing I treasure most in life, is that every year on my and Atticus's birthday the whole family goes on a trip together. Even after Jamison and Wrangell moved out, they still made sure to never miss it. Our birthday trips are some of my best memories: swimming in the Aegean right after Atticus and I learned how, Jamison telling us she was pregnant at high tea in Hong Kong. Barcelona knitting us even closer after everything fell apart on our book tour. This year I'm hoping for a big city, somewhere we haven't yet been. Tangier, maybe, or Cairo.

As the processional music starts, our dad and Atticus are talking, and I murmur, "Shh." The last thing we need is someone's angry video showing up online. *The Los were dicks during my niece's graduation!*

"I'm just saying," Atticus says, lowering his voice by probably a single decibel, "I think studying or trying to get good grades, for me, would be unethical."

"Unethical," our dad says, amused. "That's a new one."

"I think it would be an inaccurate representation of who I am."

"You could *make* it an accurate representation of who you are," our dad says. "Imagine that, huh?"

This is where, normally, our mom would jump in to tell Atticus to think more carefully about his future, to remind him that the typical pro volleyball player makes (she looked this up) a median salary of less than $50,000 a year. Atticus has always been hell-bent on becoming a pro volleyball player. Our father likes prestige: Ivy League schools, TED Talks. He's always wanted Atticus to parlay his volleyball into a scholarship somewhere like Dartmouth or

UPenn. Our mother is eminently practical and wants Atticus to do what she thinks would be most stable financially, which is to work on branding and influencing partnerships instead, like our three older siblings.

Our mom seems distracted, though, and has the whole time we've been here—tight lipped and short tempered, keeping to herself. She doesn't jump in to remind him about volleyball salaries.

"You don't expect me to believe you studied in school," Atticus says, grinning. "You're a Bible college dropout, so—"

Our dad socks him lightly on the thigh. "I had an Asian dad, so yes, I studied. You guys don't know how good you have it. Anyway, Atticus, you're always reading. Why don't you read what you have to read for school?"

"Atticus only likes books that make him look pretentious," I whisper, which is true: philosophy, psychology. On the way here he made me listen to excerpts from an audiobook about how everything we know about the history of humankind is wrong, from a particularly excruciating chapter about grain farming.

Atticus laughs. "Touché. I get it from Dad."

"You're grounded," our dad says immediately. "Starting now. All summer. Give you some adversity to write about on your college essay."

They both laugh, which makes them look like twins. Most of us don't look very much alike, but Atticus is a carbon copy of our dad. They have an incredibly similar face—people always comment on it—and they work out together all the time, and from behind you could mistake them for each other. And beyond that, their minds work the same way. One of the soundtracks of my life is the clink and murmur of them up late in Atticus's room next door, lifting weights and talking about whether our generation will be more Marxist than our dad's or whether free-solo mountain climbing is morally acceptable or how to endure in the face of the climate crisis. I am always up for a good discussion, but after a while I want to talk about other things, preferably people. The two of them, though, can keep going forever. I often think that if they'd met in another context, not father and son, they would've immediately become friends.

They finally quiet as the seniors begin walking across the stage to collect their diplomas, Atticus whistling for basically everyone. Skye asked me to get some pictures and videos she can post later, and I have her camera ready on my lap, my phone ready in my hand. We all explode in cheers and screams when it's her turn to walk across the stage. At school, like everywhere, Skye is beloved. Wrangell said once that there's probably not a more likable person you can put on your screen multiple times a day, though people will find reasons to hate anybody. She laughs, waving at us. I take a long video and then quickly switch the camera, zooming in and trying to get a good shot. She told me it doesn't matter how they come out, that she has shoots planned for any actually important pictures, but I don't want to mess it up.

After the ceremony is over, Skye takes approximately seven million pictures with basically everyone in her class, while Jamison looks around and says things like, "I am so glad I'm not in high school anymore," and Andrew says, "Wow, yeah, really," and Wrangell laughs and says he'd do it all again. Jamison lets me take Sonnet to show off to my friends, and everyone crowds around us in a circle and coos over her until she gets shy and buries her face in my shoulder, nuzzling against me—best moment of my year—and

Jamison materializes to take her back. Our mom stays in her seat, talking quietly to Ava and Lauren and typing into her phone, until Skye's finally done taking pictures and we all pile into the waiting cars to go to lunch.

I ride with Jamison and Andrew and Sonnet and Skye, me and Skye pleasantly squished in the back around Sonnet's car seat.

"So are you stoked for Texas, Skye?" Andrew says. "You're going to have to get really into football."

Skye laughs. "I'm nervous!" she says. "I mean, it seemed like the smart move, right?" She signed a lucrative deal with Baylor to go there; she'll post about going, doing all the normal college things. She's had some impressive collaborations, but it's the single biggest deal she's signed so far—basketball star money. (Leagues above pro volleyball money.) "But then every now and then I remember I'm . . . moving to Texas? And I'm not sure what I'm even doing?"

"No, it was smart," Jamison agrees. "It's a really good opportunity. I think you made the right choice."

"It's been so long since I've had to actually meet new people. I bet I'm socially deficient."

We've been at Rearden since sixth grade for Skye, fourth grade for me and Atticus. "Yeah, but people always love you," I say. "They'll love you there, too. Maybe there will be a bunch of hot guys."

"At least one!" Skye says, laughing. "I don't need a bunch! Just one is plenty!"

"Just not *too* hot," I tease, letting Sonnet play with the zipper on my purse. "Right, Sonnet? We don't want Skye to fall in love with Texas. We Los have California in our blood."

You're Not Famous: A Snark Site

ynf.com/forums/LoFamily

calendulateam, 11:46:13 am PST: Uhhhhh I'm a florist and are those Juliet roses in Skye's bouquet? Because if so she's carrying literally thousands?? of dollars??? worth of flowers in her arms???? For a high school graduation?????????? She seriously could not disgust me more.

gatsby11, 11:47:12 am PST: truly so incredibly on brand for the Los to act like Skye's *high school graduation* is soooo special and unique and interesting and needs to be broadcast to the world

Luca isn't the kind of place where anyone from the restaurant would fawn over us, which is how I know our father didn't pick it, and something about the energy feels off as soon as we sit down. I try to push my trepidation aside. We all make toasts to Skye. Sonnet tries a sip of sparkling water and makes a face of pure, unmitigated betrayal. Andrew gets it on video and we rewatch it probably a dozen times, and I laugh so hard my stomach hurts.

Our parents don't, though; they seem disconnected. We order a few plates of calamari, and prosciutto and melon, and the shaved zucchini salad, which comes with a sprinkle of herbs and spirals of lemon zest and bright shocks of flowers and looks like art. I take a picture of the plate. Wrangell tells a story about some cocky guy at his gym who tried to swim to Alcatraz on a dare.

"So then they have to send the literal coast guard to pick his ass up, and he tries to convince everyone it's because he saw this pod of sharks, and then he's telling the story and this other girl at the gym goes, *Actually, I'm a marine biologist and you are full of shit.*"

Jamison covers Sonnet's ears at the last word, but we're all laughing, except our parents. Our mom asks the waiter for a glass of wine and then, when it comes, drinks the whole thing in one long gulp. Atticus and I exchange a look. We all get Asian glow when we drink—none of us got those genes from our white relatives—and our mother avoids it whenever possible. Wrangell tells another story about a friend adopting an incontinent pit bull.

"So what's the big announcement?" I say. "Is this about where we're going this year?"

Our dad clears his throat, then he looks to our mom. She makes a short, barking laugh.

"No, this is all you," she says. "You're the one who wanted this. Don't look to me for help."

He works his jaw. "All right," he says finally. "Okay, everyone, we have some news we wanted to share with you. Ah, first of all, let me just say that we love you all very much, and—"

"Oh my God," Jamison says, sitting up straighter, "are you getting a divorce?"

I expect him to laugh. They have always been almost irritatingly devoted to each other, *What an absurd idea! No way in hell.* But then our mother starts crying, and our dad sucks in a long breath, and Wrangell snaps, "Oh, you are fucking kidding me," and then balls up his napkin and shoves his chair back from the table and I can't breathe.

"First of all, no one's getting a divorce," our dad says. "We're very much still married. But in the last few years—it's been a period of real growth and introspection for us, for both of us, for all of us, really, because I know you've all been doing your own growth and your own work too. And there comes a point when you need to step back and reevaluate, and—"

"Reevaluate what?" Atticus says.

"All of it. Everything. All the levers on all the systems. This has been a long time coming," our dad says as our mother stares, stone faced, in the direction of the kitchen. "We're very proud of everything we've built, which is this family, obviously, and also the podcast, and the conferences, and the albums, and *Lo and Behold* and everything we've done—but how do you find who you are under capitalism? Are we just a means of producing? We need the space to get back in touch with ourselves. We need to—"

"Oh my God," Wrangell says. "You're blaming this on *capitalism?* You own fucking *NFTs.*"

"Okay, so like—what's happening, then?" Atticus says. "You're taking time apart, or what? Who's living where?"

"Oh yes!" our mom says, whirling around to face our father with a terrifying, vicious smile. "Tell them who's living where. Where are you living, Nathan?"

Our dad blinks at his water a long time, then drinks a sip. "Well," he says, "I've temporarily rented a place in Brooklyn."

Jamison laughs aloud, reaching up to rub her forehead with her fingertips. "Great. Okay."

"So your father will be moving out," our mother says, turning to face me and Atticus. "You're still in school, but your father—"

"But Brooklyn is awesome," our dad says. "You'll come visit, obviously, and—"

"Just *awesome,*" our mom says, her voice like ice. "Just really so, so, so awesome."

Skye reaches out and grabs my hand. I can't feel my face. Around me there's commotion and noise, and none of it pierces me. I am floating in some different world. My whole body is stiff. I

make myself pick up my other hand, reach for Atticus. I need to feel
him solid and real against me. He lets me take his hand, and I can
tell from his expression he isn't going to say anything else tonight;
whatever he thinks, he will keep it to himself; he will be steady and
good-natured and calm. There's a reason everyone likes him.

"I want to be abundantly clear that this is not in any way a reflec-
tion on our love for the five of you," our dad says. "We are still a
family. Everything is the same. We just need to all hold space for this
period in our lives where we're figuring out how things need to look
going forward. Sometimes to strengthen something, you have to pull
it apart, and that's what we need to do right now in our relationship."

"Have you even tried counseling?" Skye says. "Have you
even—I mean, moving to *Brooklyn* is so drastic, and—maybe counseling would—"

"The world belongs to the drastic," our dad says. "Change
is hard. Change is uncomfortable. But without change there's no
growth. And it'll be a challenge for all of us, yes, but you know what,
I believe in us. I believe in the ways we can rise to the occasion. We
think this is the best path forward."

Our mother sets her water down harder than necessary. "No,
don't you dare put this on me. There's no 'we' here. Your father is
leaving me," she says loudly, to no one in particular. "He's decided
he isn't *happy.*"

Skye is crying. Wrangell stands up.

"This is fucked," he says. "This was a fucking ambush. And this
is Skye's fucking graduation lunch, and this is how you want her to
remember it? She's a kid. You two are toxic people, and you know
what, frankly, do whatever you're going to do. Who cares. You've
already ruined our lives."

People magazine

LO FAMILY ON THE ROCKS! FANS DEVASTATED AFTER MELISSA, NATHAN LO SPLIT

STINSON BEACH, CALIF.—Nathan and Melissa Lo, popular influencers and former reality stars of TLC's *Lo and Behold*, have announced a temporary separation. The couple say they are taking time to work to be the best versions of themselves.

Nathan Lo is the executive producer and host of the podcast *Rise*. Melissa Lo is the author of *Own Your Life*, which has sold over 1.5 million copies. *Lo and Behold*, which chronicled the couple's exploits as musicians and parents to five, ran for four seasons.

The couple's upcoming conference, Rise Together, has been postponed.

Fans are reeling at the news.

"It really makes you wonder what's been happening behind the scenes," says Karen Liccardi, 44, of McKinney, Texas. "I consider myself pretty up on the Los, but I had zero idea they were even struggling."

Liccardi, who has given copies of *Own Your Life* to family and friends as gifts and moderates a Facebook group for fans of the Lo family, says she and five friends purchased Rise Together tickets in March.

"This is devastating news, honestly," Liccardi says. "I just hope there's no one else in the picture. Assuming they really are trying to work things out, if anyone can do it, it's them."

Reps for the couple released a statement, saying, "We are so grateful for the ways our community has supported and uplifted us in this time. We remain committed to each other and to the family we've built together."

The couple share five children: Jamison Lo, 26, the face of popular momfluencer account @SonnetAndMe; style influencer Wrangell Lo,

25, who has released several lines of menswear; YouTuber Skye Lo, 18, brand ambassador for Glossier and, recently, Baylor University; Atticus Lo, 16, who is a nationally ranked volleyball player; and Honor Lo, who is also 16 and Atticus's twin.

CHAPTER TWO

"The thing about Jamie and Wrangell," Atticus says, heaving some of his dumbbells up and down, "is that they just constantly expect the worst from Mom and Dad. I mean, yeah, I think this sucks, I think it feels really shitty, but is it a catastrophe? I don't think I'm there yet. I mean, maybe they really do just need some space and then they'll be fine again. Don't you ever want space from them? People get exhausting after a while. They in particular get exhausting after not even a while."

"So you don't think it's time to freak out yet," I say.

"No, I really don't."

"Are you going to say that to Jamison? Because Jamison is definitely freaking out."

He grins. "No, because the other thing about Wrangell and Jamison is that to them, we're always going to be eleven years old. Also, she's probably mostly freaking out because this is a headache for her. Whereas for you, Skye, the people who follow you care, like, four percent as much about your parents."

He sets the weights down. He and Skye and I are in my room. I'm at my desk, at my clay-making station, mindlessly kneading together a ball of translucent clay and one of deep blue. We've made it through most of the rest of the day, our phones overheated from a zillion alerts. Jamison's back in San Diego already and has been messaging almost nonstop, telling us whom she has and hasn't given any kind of statement to. Wrangell's gone silent. Our dad has been everywhere—the kitchen, the living room, the yard, the staircase—talking on his phone to seemingly everyone but us, but none of us has so much as seen our mother since we all left the restaurant.

"Do you think Mom's okay?" Skye says. "You guys haven't talked to her, right?"

"No. I don't know what to even say to her," I say. "*Sorry your husband is leaving you*? What do you say?"

"Yeah, I guess it really depends on where she's at emotionally," Skye says. "Which is anyone's guess. She hasn't done any interviews, right? Is she talking to Dad or, like, Jamison? Or is she just totally MIA?"

"I'm sure she's at least talking to Lauren and Ava," I say. "If she weren't, that would be genuinely alarming, but I think we'd hear. They'd tell Dad."

"I mean, I guess it would be alarming, but also, who knows," Atticus says. "For all we know she's like, *Yeah, leave town and get out of my face.*"

"I really doubt that," I say. "She was so mad at lunch."

"Right, that's what I'm saying. She was mad."

"Okay, but she was mad because he's leaving!" I say. "Because he's, like, breaking her heart. Wouldn't you be super hurt? Aren't you hurt?"

"She's probably not around because she doesn't want to see him leave," Skye says. "That's probably what I'd do, I guess. Just hide so I didn't have to watch it happen."

"Skye, no, ew," Atticus says. "You aren't allowed to make me feel bad for Mom." His relationship with our mother has always been a little more fraught—our mother isn't someone who just lets you be. Love to her is molding people into their most successful, promising selves. "You're going to make me side with her."

"Well, we are siding with her in that this is stupid," I say. "What does he think he's accomplishing by leaving? You never accomplish anything by leaving. Did Dad talk to you about any of this, Atticus?" If he's been talking to anyone, it would be Atticus.

"No, not at all. That's why I kind of think—I don't know, maybe it's just super naive, but that's why even though Wrangell and Jamie were, like, instantly freaking out about a divorce, I don't really think it's going to go there. They probably just have some shit to work out and then it'll be fine."

"The things he was saying about reevaluating sounded pretty ominous."

"Did they? Or is that just how he talks? He's probably just bored. He just needs to try some new diet or new workout or something. Dad's whole thing is integrity and commitment and 'We're Los,' all that. I just don't think he'd actually go through with anything that drastic. I think they're just having a rough patch. Which happens."

"I wish I were as calm as you."

He laughs. "Yeah, you know what, I wish that too. Like, in general."

I roll my eyes. "Shut up. Okay, so what do you think we should do?"

"Do? Nothing, really. It'll probably blow over in a few weeks."

"I'm sorry it ruined your graduation," I say to Skye.

"Oh, it doesn't matter. Graduations are stupid anyway." She sighs. "Ugh, I'm getting so many DMs about them, though. I think I'm going to have to say something, or people are going to keep asking."

"That's shitty," Atticus says. "You don't owe anyone that. If you don't want to talk about it, don't talk about it."

"Yeah, I wish it were that easy. I have like—honestly four months' worth of deliverables I booked for the summer, so I can't just lose a bunch of my audience." She makes a face. "At least their drama is good for engagement. I had almost double my usual views yesterday."

"That's sick," Atticus says. "People are disgusting."

"People are. I wasn't even talking about Mom and Dad—it was just my Motorola campaign. Motorola's going to be like, *Wow, people loved us!*" She laughs. "I should've charged more."

I call an emergency meeting with my two best friends the next morning, before any of us has even had breakfast. We go to Lilith's house and hole up in the den off her kitchen, where there's a huge window with a redwood-framed view of the coast, and Lilith and Eloise sit next to me as I recap last night for them.

"Okay, well, thank God it's just your dad moving," Eloise said. "When I saw the news, I was scared you were going to move to New York too."

Eloise, Lilith, and I have all been best friends since fourth grade, the year our family moved to Stinson Beach. By then I was aware that a lot of what went on in our lives was out of the ordinary, and I was worried I would be too different to make friends. But at lunch the first day Eloise and Lilith asked me if I wanted to join their origami club, and since that first day it's always been easy with them. Lilith had (still has) this huge, amazing dollhouse, a Victorian mansion with an attic and gables and the walls painted a rich, dusky rose, and the three of us were into it long past when everyone else had gotten over dolls. Even well into seventh grade we'd walk to her house at lunchtime and work on making things for it with polymer clay: tiny blueberry pies with lattice crusts that we'd paint with clear nail polish to make them shiny, miniature donuts and cakes. (In seventh grade Atticus had his first girlfriend and also his first hangover, and there I was meticulously rolling out lint-size grapes with Lilith and Eloise, still my favorite hobby.) I get invited to parties because I'm Atticus's twin, but nine times out of ten I'd rather just hang out with my friends. Our family doesn't trust easily—too many people want something from you, want parts of your life to rub off on theirs—and I have always been grateful for the haven of them.

Karissa, Lilith's mom, brings us smoothie bowls while we're curled up on the sectional. It feels surreal to be here as if everything's the same, this place I've watched the sun set probably hundreds of times in my life. Karissa gives me a big hug.

"How awful to have to go through this in the glare of the spotlight," she says sympathetically. She's the kind of parent who hovers, suffocates even, and she's always been a little judgmental of parents with intense careers. "How *are* you, Honor? How's your mom holding up?"

"We're doing okay," I say. "I guess."

"Well, you let us know if you need anything. Anything at all."

"Okay, but *are* you doing okay?" Eloise says when Karissa's gone back into the kitchen. "I wouldn't be."

"Okay, thank you, right? Atticus thinks it's too early to freak out about it, but I'm definitely kind of freaking out. My mom is just devastated. I really don't think she saw it coming."

"No, I'd be freaking out too," Lilith says. "Do you think your dad is cheating on your mom or something?"

"What? No. Zero chance. He's all about loyalty."

"Yeah, he always seems all about your family," Eloise says. "Like how he used to make you guys wear Lo jerseys and go watch whenever someone had a game or a concert or anything."

"Oh God." I roll my eyes, but the memory stabs me. It started with Wrangell, when he used to do track and field. Atticus and I were small then, seven or eight, and mostly our parents were gone, but when they were here, we'd all show up to Wrangell's meets together. Our dad loved traveling around in a pack that way and had matching shirts made for us every year. "Embrace the spectacle!" he'd always say. "People are going to look, so give them something to look at. Let them catch you being there for each other."

"I didn't even realize your parents were having problems," Lilith says. "Were they not actually happy the whole time? Was that just for their brand or whatever?"

"Well . . . ," I say. I'm careful with what I say about our family—I am a Lo first and foremost—but I've always trusted Lilith and Eloise. "The thing people don't know about them is they're actually really, like—codependent." This is contra our mother's persona specifically; so much of what she talks about is self-fulfillment, self-actualization. "I can't imagine either of them without the other. Their whole lives are each other and us, you know? I'm so worried about my mom. I'm worried she's just going to totally crumple."

"Well, you can be strong for her," Eloise says. She gives me a tight hug. "That will be your job. I think your dad will come to his senses and get over this. It's just so out of character. And we're here for you."

"Yes," Lilith says, leaning against me. "Whatever you need, we're supporting you every step of the way."

People magazine

HONOR LO SPILLS ON PARENTS' SHOCKING SPLIT

STINSON BEACH, CALIF.—After Melissa and Nathan Lo shocked fans this week by announcing their separation, a source close to Honor Lo tells us, "Honor says it's just temporary, but she's worried they'll just get further and further apart. Her mom is just devastated. She didn't see it coming."

The source adds that, according to Honor, "some of it is just their public persona, but the thing people don't know about them is they're actually very codependent. Her mom is not that strong of a person. Everyone's worried she's just going to totally crumple."

We meet at Eloise's house this time. I am so upset I can barely speak, and I'm shaking.

"Honor, I swear I didn't say anything," Eloise says. "I wouldn't even know *how* to talk to a magazine. Like, I literally would not know who to call. I don't even like talking on the phone."

"Well, neither did I," Lilith says. "Why would I do that?"

"You two were the only people there."

"Did you have that same conversation with anyone else?" Lilith says. "Maybe someone—"

"*No,*" I snap. "You know I only talk to you!"

They both look at each other. "I didn't," Lilith says to Eloise. "So it had to have been you, then. You must have—"

"*You* must have been the one," Eloise says. "I can't believe you would do that to Honor."

"I can't believe *you*—"

"Oh my God." I feel dizzy. The walls are pressing in closer, my chest tight, and I know if I don't leave this room, I won't be able to breathe. I need to get out. "I'm scared my family is falling apart, and one of you betrayed us and now you won't even confess. I never want to see either of you again."

I make it to the end of Eloise's street before I have to pull over. My heart is beating so hard my vision is squeezing with the pulse, the road wavering through the windshield. I am going to crawl out of my skin.

My family has always tried to tell me people are like this, but I thought it would be different with Lilith and Eloise. I'm sick now thinking about all the things I've ever told them, how much of me they hold.

I'm on the verge of a panic attack. I stay there until I can breathe again, praying no one I know will drive by and see me, and then before I have time to think too hard about it, I text Logan Hesse from school.

Logan's a grade older than us. He's into art—his mom is a famous painter—and he has a way of looking at you like he's visually dissecting you, maybe imagining how he might render your muscles and tendons, that makes him seem like he never hears anything you've said to him. We almost never spoke at school, but he always finds me when he's drunk at parties. I have spent too many nights lying on someone else's bed with him, his hands groping at me, while Eloise and Lilith text me things like are you okay????? do you need to be rescued???? He has a way of turning his face away when he's on top of me and then leaving immediately afterward, barely speaking, that used to make me feel empty inside. Once he called me Skye. He left immediately after, but then, he always does.

I told myself I would stop hooking up with him—it's not something I would miss—but when he picks up now, I say, "What are you doing? Can I come over?"

It's a small enough town that I'm sure he's heard about my parents, and probably about my fight with Eloise and Lilith, too, but he doesn't say anything about either one, the way I knew he wouldn't.

We go into the art studio off the garage. It's a rustic, white-washed wood–planked room on a bluff overlooking the water, and there are canvases everywhere, on walls and easels and leaning against the chairs and cabinets, some partially finished, some with scenes I recognize from Point Reyes and Tomales. There are tubes of oil paint scattered over the tabletop.

"My dad's home," Logan says. "So we can't go inside."

"That's fine. He won't come in here?"

He shakes his head. "He never does."

"Are any of these yours?" I ask, gesturing toward the canvases. Logan laughs. He pulls off his shirt. I'm not sure if that's a yes or a no, or why it's funny, but before I can ask, he circles his hands around my wrists and pulls me down to the floor. I probably wouldn't have asked anyway.

Maybe I shouldn't have come. I find a spot on the ceiling, a knot in the wooden beam, to stare at, and I try to whittle my whole existence down to those few square inches. Nothing else, no one else. I am a body only. For a few moments, anyway, it works.

You're Not Famous: A Snark Site

ynf.com/forums/LoFamily

baconspam420, 11:48:17 pm PST: I find Melissa absolutely insufferable and frankly I don't know what took Nathan so long

calendulateam, 11:49:05 pm PST: the sad thing is she used to seem like a real person with actual interests, but now her only interest is making more money. It's the family animating moral principle. Just try to milk every situation for whatever you can.

knockoffbrene, 11:50:02 pm PST: Honestly my conspiracy theory is that this whole separation is just some PR stunt and they're going to get back together and sell a new conference on rekindling your relationship or some shit.

junco, 11:50:25 pm PST: What's interesting is Nathan is talking about it, posting about it, etc. but Melissa is like . . . pretending it's not happening??? If you were only looking at her social media you would have absolutely no idea. Is she totally in denial? What's happening here?

scampmeetup, 11:51:34 pm PST: right? That's why I think it's fake. If he were leaving her for real she wouldn't be able to shut up about it.

calendulateam, 11:52:26 pm PST: one thing I always think about is how they have to have a million people running their lives, right? as much as they try to hide it obviously we know there are assistants and drivers and cooks and crap. Haven't they been rude enough to at least one disgruntled employee who wants to spill?? be a hero and tell us which one of them is cheating! someone has to be.

CHAPTER THREE

Our dad is scheduled to fly out in three days, and despite Atticus's attempts at reassurance, I feel that countdown threading itself through every hour. Movers come to the house and poach many of his things; he disappears for hours at a time into the gym off the garage. Jamison wants constant updates. Wrangell won't pick up his phone for any of us. Every time I see cars going slower than usual on our street, I'm worried it's someone trying to take pictures, crafting some narrative about the family falling apart.

I'm still getting probably dozens of media requests every day. *Hi, Honor, it's Jessie Yuan from* Vanity Fair. *I'm a child of divorce as well and I'd really love to chat about your thoughts on all this! xoxo.* I ignore them all, but sometimes I wish I could respond. I know Jessie a little—we spent a whole day with her so she could do a profile when all seven of us were still living at home, and she's kept in touch with our mom and written several things about her over the years. I've always thought she was kind, empathetic, almost therapist-like, and I wish I could ask if she thinks our parents are also going to divorce or not. Maybe she saw something I didn't, or maybe she can reassure me.

I feel tender and fragile, repulsed by the thought of being seen in public, so I hole up at home with Atticus and Skye, who are also uncharacteristically lying low. I make tiny clay nigiri and cheung fun and mochi, a tiny bakery box of don tot and a coffee-crunch cake. It's the most productive I've been in ages. "Because all week you've been, like, an emotionally damaged recluse," Atticus tells me. "Like all the great artists."

"Yeah, you can really feel the anguish in this cake, right?" Probably he means I should get out more, feel some sunlight, but instead I make a whole set of banchan and then Spam musubi. I want to have a whole market's worth of miniature food to give Sonnet someday when she's older.

Lilith and Eloise keep calling me. Eloise messages Skye and Atticus, too: Please tell your sister I swear I did not say a word to People or anyone else! Skye thinks it was Eloise, that she's always been a social climber, but Atticus thinks it's Lilith.

"She acts like oh, I'm just so nerdy and unassuming, I just want to do my theater stuff, but secretly she thinks she's better than you," he says. "I always got that vibe from her." He buys me a box of truffles from the chocolatier in Mill Valley I love and plops them unceremoniously on my desk.

"I'm sorry they were so shitty to you," he says. "They were supposed to be your best friends."

Meanwhile, our mother is totally gone. We're not even positive she's sleeping at home. Skye messages her to ask if she went somewhere, but she writes back no, she's just working. I don't know what to make of it.

"I think she'll be back before he's supposed to leave," Skye says. "Right?"

"Maybe this is the new plan," Atticus says. "They're both moving out."

"Oh no! We'll have to call Jamison and Wrangell back in to raise you two," Skye says, laughing. "It'll be like old times."

For all the things our mother unhesitatingly shares with the world, she is not an especially emotionally forthcoming person. She has her practiced anecdotes she tells over and over in public, and to us, and she can spend thirty minutes ranting about lazy workers at a restaurant or car dealership, but she's guarded and inexpressive about so much. She never talks about feeling sad or lonely or rejected, for instance, all things Karissa has talked about with me and Eloise and Lilith anytime she's trying to be relatable or hear what's going on in our lives. Our mother will show irritation or delight or pride, and she likes to ask about our feelings on things, but I can't imagine asking *So how do you feel about Dad?* I can't imagine prying about something that I know makes her feel devastated or betrayed or inadequate.

The night before his flight, our dad comes in at dinnertime. Atticus and Skye and I are all eating at the counter together. We have a pact to eat dinner together as often as possible before Skye leaves (my idea), and tonight we ordered poke bowls, glistening beautifully in a way I want to try to replicate later with my clay. I am expecting our mother to come in at any moment, but I've been expecting that for days now, and I've been consistently wrong.

Our dad is wearing his gym clothes, sweat rings on his shirt. "What are you guys eating?" he says amiably, glancing at our bowls.

"Poke," Skye says. "Do you want any? I think there's extra in the fridge."

"Nah, I'm good. I'll make a protein shake." He stands in front of the fridge for a moment, whistling to himself. The three of us exchange a look. He has always believed that you create your own reality—"No one controls your reaction except you! Your experience of an event dictates what that event is going to mean!"—so it's impossible to know whether he actually feels like everything is fine right now or if it's that he's trying to will that into being. He makes himself a protein shake, the blender explosively loud in the kitchen, then rinses out the blender and leaves it in the sink. He comes and pulls out the chair next to Atticus to drink his shake.

"Look at this," he says, holding out his phone to show us. "Check out these sandwiches. When you guys come see me in Brooklyn, we have to try these. It's this Sephardic family, all these old recipes, that they're fusing with classic deli style, and they look just obscenely good. Never seen anything like it."

None of us says anything. We are staying neutral, for now, and poring over Brooklyn restaurants feels like a bridge too far. Our dad puts his phone away and sighs. "Are you guys all mad at me? You know this isn't about you, right?"

"No one's mad," Skye says.

"Have you even tried to talk about it?" I say impulsively. "She hasn't even been here. I just don't understand why it needs to be right now and you can't work on figuring it out first."

"I can appreciate that that's how it might look from the outside. But the thing is, Honor, if you're holding someone back, that means something's wrong. You need a new paradigm. It's hard to understand when you've never been married, but I'm doing the healthiest and most productive thing I know for myself and for our family, which is I'm taking a step back, because sometimes you need more perspective. This family is my highest priority. You know that. We're Los. That's the most important thing. I am doing this to preserve our family, so I can keep being there for all of you in an authentic way. So I can become the best version of myself."

"I think the best version of yourself is here," I say. "Whoever you are somewhere else—what does that matter if it's not with the people most important to you? There's nowhere else you're needed more than here."

His expression shifts, and before he even answers, I know it wasn't the right thing to say. In the story he's telling himself, this is an important undertaking, one in which he's the main character on a sort of hero's journey, where it's both inconsequential that he's leaving and also vastly important to show his kids the right way to be a person. My feeling this hurt and scared doesn't fit in the version of this everybody else is tacitly accepting.

He sets his protein shake onto the counter just a little too hard, and a wave of the liquid comes glopping out. He swears. I get a bunch of paper towels and try to wipe it up, leaving streaks across the marble.

"I need you guys to understand this," he says, going to the sink for a sponge. "Because this is important. If you're trapped in a negative dynamic, you have to stop it. You have to shift and get out of it. Don't let your past dictate your future. You can't let yourself be trapped that way. No one will get you out of it but you."

"Yeah," I say quietly. "I can see that, I guess."

"Right," Skye says noncommittally. "Totally."

"I just want you to understand. I want you to give yourself permission to make these same choices for yourselves. It's the only way, the *only* way, to show up as your authentic self. And that's everything. That's the work."

He's forgotten the sponge—it's sitting on the counter in front of him. I pick it up and gently wipe away the rest of the protein shake, then rinse out the sponge in the sink. Gritty rivulets of water come out of it, and I wash them away.

In 1851 a boat shipwrecked at Point Lobos, a few hours south of here, near Monterey. It was carrying Chinese fishermen from the Pearl River Delta who decided, seeing the landscape and perhaps no clear path back home, to stay and establish a fishing village. Among them was one of our ancestors, Lum Sang Loy. The village exported fish and abalone and shrimp, sustaining even more Chinese families than San Francisco's Chinatown, until it was suspiciously burned down in 1906, and our ancestors made their way inland through the California Delta, settling in the tiny river towns of Locke and Walnut Grove, and eventually Sam Fow—Stockton, where our paternal grandfather, Joseph Lo, met our grandmother Jane Bauer in high school. Our grandmother was a fifth-generation Californian whose family, once upon a time from Germany, owned significant acreage of almond trees in nearby Gillis. Before they moved to some massive golf-cart-obsessed retirement village in Phoenix, which we never visit, we used to go see them in the Central Valley, and she would lay out sleeping bags for us under the trees on summer nights.

Our dad grew up first in a small apartment in Stockton and eventually on his grandparents' land in Gillis. He was a minor star in the high school sports circuit and was also known around town for his serial dating and his singing ability; when he was in high school, he would make spending money by performing at weddings. He's an only child, and all his life it was assumed that he would someday take over Bauer Almonds, although the aunties and uncles at church thought he should grow up to be a pastor.

When he decided to go to Bible college, his mother never forgave him for abandoning the family orchards. He's always described that time of his life as a turning point. He felt alienated from his parents, exhausted by a lifetime of trying to straddle two worlds and people's expectations of him, bored of Stockton. He thought he would do the thing that would please the church he'd grown up in, and become a pastor. Instead he met our mother.

Our mother grew up in Los Gatos. Unlike our dad, she doesn't like to talk about her childhood, and almost everything we've heard about it has been from him or from Auntie JJ back when she and our mother were still close. They used to be sisters like Skye and I are sisters: on the phone constantly, Auntie JJ forever over at our house. When I was really small, I thought she lived with us. Her first name is Jennifer, and I always assumed JJ was a nickname from that, but actually it came from my mom's mispronunciation of the Cantonese word for "big sister" as a little girl.

Their mother, Mary Chan, our maternal grandmother, was raised in the Ming Quong Home for Chinese girls in Los Gatos after her father was deported and her single mother struggled to provide. The girls attended the public schools, and our grandmother met our grandfather, Roland Lowell, at Los Gatos High School.

Theirs was an unhappy marriage. Our grandfather was demanding and overbearing and resented the almost familial connection our grandmother had to other women who'd grown up in Ming Quong. His family had rescued her from a life of poverty, he insisted, and he found it distasteful the way the women would gather and reminisce. Our grandmother was a strict, hardworking woman who nurtured a secret love of beauty. They lost most of their money in bad investments during the dot-com crash and had to move into a tiny apartment near Campbell, and even there, everything scrubbed clean and severely free of clutter, you'd find our grandmother's vignettes: Lysol and bleach bottles decoupaged with pretty cutouts from a seed catalogue, careful arrangements of branches she'd clipped from neighborhood walks. If you ever complimented her, she would be gruff and irritated. I think it was an inclination in herself she was ashamed of.

Our grandfather used to tell people that our mother was his daughter (a dreamer and a doer, he called her) and JJ (dutiful, overachieving) was our grandmother's daughter. Our mother always longed for her mother's love and approval. But her mother confided in JJ, was proud of JJ, looked more like JJ.

Growing up, JJ was steady and focused, but our mom cycled through different phases: a horseback phase, a Girl Scouts phase, a student government phase. At the end of high school she was deep into her church phase, and when it was time to go to college, Biola felt like a natural choice.

Our parents were aware of each other right away. It was a small campus, and there weren't many half-Chinese students. But it felt too obvious, too expected, and maybe it annoyed them the way everyone assumed they knew each other. The first week there our mother's roommate told her she should marry him. For months they never spoke, until they were set up together for GYRAD, or Get Your Roommate a Date night, and then they went to Disneyland and ate Dole Whip in front of the castle and talked until midnight, when the park closed and they'd both missed curfew. After that they were almost never apart.

Our dad has a gift for believing in people, and so I can picture exactly how it would've felt to have that shining on her. With him, none of her outlandish dreams seemed out of reach. She wanted to travel all over the world? He thought that was brilliant. She wanted to write a book? Sure, she could totally write a book. She wanted to be a singer? Yes, she had an amazing voice, she should do that, too. She wanted kids, a ton of kids? Well, he said, what if we got married? He proposed three weeks after their first date. ("Do not do this," our mom always says whenever our dad tells the story, which is the most her thing ever. "Things are different at Bible college, and I know it worked out for us, but it was still absolutely insane, and you should make sure you know a person very, very well first, and that you have a plan and stability. Two years, minimum. Five is better. And get a prenup.")

They were a kind of royalty on campus. They were beautiful and talented and engaged, and maybe a little mysterious in the ways they defied easy characterization—back then, probably, even more so. (They both understood what it was like to be the half-white kid in an insular, conservative Chinese community, and to be the half-Asian kid in a hugely white evangelical SoCal school, although they had very different ways of dealing with it. Still have—we've done multiple trips to Hong Kong with our dad, trying to feel some sort of ancestral belonging, and our mother has never wanted to go.) They liked to play guitar and sing together in the common areas in the dorms.

They got married their second year and then both dropped out. ("Don't do that either! It's so much harder to go back and do it later.") They got their start writing Christian songs. For a while they made the kind of music together that played only on stations like K-LOVE, but then when Jamison was eleven and Wrangell was ten, they had a hit song, "Between Us." Skye was born; Atticus and I were born; they signed with a bigger label, and then (their big break) they signed on for *Lo and Behold*. Even after that imploded, after our book tour, it had already catapulted them to prominence.

They can be pretentious and obnoxious, especially together. They can be self-centered and insular and annoying in all the ways parents can be, and they weren't there for us when we were small the way they should've been. But the thing is, I have always believed in their love story. Not as a story of two perfect people finding their soul mates. I have believed in it as a story of the ways, somehow, improbably, the generations before you can bring you into existence and you can find someone who brings out the best in you, some-one who believes you and is willing to build something with you. Because that's the whole thing about being a family, how together you can be greater than the sum of your parts.

CHAPTER FOUR

After he's gone, within literally hours, cleaners and professional organizers our mother has hired come in and pack up the rest of his things, then stack the boxes in the garage—all his books in the study, his clothes from his closet—an attempt, I think, at exorcism. The house feels strip-mined. Our mother still hasn't been home.

Skye and Atticus and I go for a long walk in Point Reyes, one of the places Skye says she's really going to miss when she's in Texas, and then we drive the winding, narrow roads up the coast forty-five minutes and buy oysters in Tomales Bay even though it's four in the afternoon, too late for lunch and too early for dinner. It's quiet today, not teeming with the usual San Francisco tech people clogging the roads on their weekend off. We take the oysters to Dillon Beach and sit on the damp sand for a few hours, surrounded by the mossy bluffs, the crash of the surf so loud we have to raise our voices to talk. It's high tide, and cold the way it gets in the summer here, not very crowded. By the time we leave, we're all hungry again, and we drive over to Sausalito to get sushi. We eat on the water, the Golden Gate Bridge peeking up over the hills, and I think about how I don't know how I'm going to make it through the next year without Skye.

By the time we get back home, it's nearly nine and almost fully dark out, and the lights aren't on in the kitchen, so at first we don't see anyone; all we hear is the music.

The three of us recognize the song at the same time—I see it register on Skye's and Atticus's faces, their expressions going wary. It's from *Gathering Days*, an album our parents recorded when Atticus and I were six. They were gone most of that year, first recording and then on tour, the prelude to *Lo and Behold*, which they signed us all to right after the album. The third track on the album, "When," was part of the show's theme song. The chords still bring everything back for me: how quiet it was each day when the crew left the house, how much we hated shooting the same scene over and over, how it felt the first time at a store when a strange adult got angry at me for not wanting to take a picture with her. I was with Wrangell, who screamed at her, and she got the whole thing on a video, which promptly went viral. *"Lo and Behold" Teen Star Out of Control! Does Wrangell Lo Need Rehab for Anger Management?* I always felt safe inside Wrangell's anger, though. It sliced the world into segments that were easier to label and understand, and it gave me something to hold on to. It let me be angry myself. I always wanted to be like him; I love Jamison, but I never especially wanted to be like her.

Our mother starts when I turn on the lights. She's sitting alone at the table in the breakfast nook, and she's crying. My heart turns over.

"Oh," she says when she sees us. She wipes her eyes roughly. "I didn't hear you come in."

I am panicked to see her like this. What are we supposed to say? I don't think I've ever seen her cry in real life before. Skye says gently, "Are you okay, Mom?"

"Oh, yes, I'm fine." She stands up abruptly. "Did you all eat?"

"Yeah, we just ate. Do you want—" Skye glances at me. "Do you want to talk about it?"

"Oh, no, there's nothing to talk about. Everything's fine." She forces a smile. "What did you eat?"

"We got sushi. Do you want us to order you something?"

"No." She hovers next to the table as if she didn't quite think through standing up, tapping her fingers against the tabletop. "Honor, I wanted to talk to you."

"Oh," I say. "Okay, yeah, sure."

She draws a long breath. I try to keep my face carefully neutral. What am I going to say to her? I wonder if she overheard me last night talking to our dad, if something I said made her think I'm siding with him. Or maybe all this time she's been holding on to what Eloise or Lilith told *People* I said about her—maybe she hit some kind of boiling point.

"I've been thinking," our mom says, "and I've been meaning to bring this up with you for a while. I think it's time for you to start thinking about your public profile."

"Um—my public profile?"

"Yes. I was reading some of the coverage of—all this, and it really leapt out to me how much you're a very unknown quantity at this point. At your age Skye was signing campaigns for Lush and Nordstrom, but you've kept to yourself so much that you really don't have very much to build off."

"Oh." In retrospect, I should've expected this. Of course this is what she'd want to talk about; of course the answer to any crisis is to work harder. "Well—I kind of wanted to work on my clay art."

She is extremely not impressed by that. "I think you need a plan, Honor. At least some kind of road map. Maybe while Skye is still here, you should have her show you the ropes. Everyone has to start somewhere. You already have a huge leg up."

"I don't know if that's the kind of thing I want to do," I say, which is an understatement. I am allergic to the idea of livestreaming myself just talking, multiple times a day, or watching my reels reverberate across the internet. I have always told my parents this.

"Well, it would be good to figure out your specific niche, because everyone has a niche, but in the meantime I think it's a good idea to just think about in general your branding, your self-presentation—these are all things you should be thinking about. Should have already thought about, really. You can't do your clay food forever."

"Touché," Atticus says to me, waggling his eyebrows.

"Shut up."

"You know," our mother says, "I always think of our ancestors who came here for the gold rush. They arrived and there wasn't gold just lying around for the picking, so they stayed humble and they pivoted. They built the railroad, and then later on they decided to stay and become businessmen. And that's why you and I exist today. Because they got here and realized they were going to make a life for themselves dangling off the side of a mountain, blasting holes into sheer rock."

I stop myself from rolling my eyes. Atticus doesn't stop himself. "Right," I say.

"This era we're living in right now reminds me so much of that time. Anyone can find fortune if you're willing to work hard and make sacrifices and take risks. It's the new gold rush." She narrows her eyes into the distance. "That is such an interesting analogy, actually. I should talk about this. Or no, maybe that's too niche. Most people aren't Californians. They wouldn't be interested."

"Well, *we're* all Californians," Atticus says dryly, "and yet."

Eloise and Lilith would tease me about exactly this kind of thing—how I do, in spite of myself, have a fondness for these old stories, all their throughlines into our lives. I feel that same small tidal wave I've been feeling dozens of times each day whenever I think of them: sadness that crests into shame and fury. I try to clamp down on the feeling before it pools with all I'm feeling about our dad.

"So!" our mother says, bringing her hand down onto the table with a muffled clap. "I think that's something you should focus on. I don't want you just sitting around this summer, wasting time. I think you need to start seriously thinking about your life."

I don't want to think seriously about my life, though, ew. Who wants that?

As soon as summer is underway, our mother is incredibly busy, traveling almost nonstop for different speaking engagements and meetings—saying, as far as I can tell, absolutely nothing about our father or their separation, which is the opposite of our dad's strategy, which is apparently to ramble at anyone who will listen about boundaries and resets and authenticity and finding yourself. I walk in one day on her and Lauren, her longtime publicist, talking in the kitchen, Lauren telling her she's worried that our mother is losing her chance to shape the narrative. Atticus is doing intensive training for his upcoming season and also coaching at a little kids' volleyball camp, so he's gone most of the day, and at night he goes to parties. Skye drags me out with her most days so I'm not just sitting at home, but she's working constantly too, and there are only so many times I can sit and watch her do photo shoots before I feel like I'm in the way. When I'm at home alone, or when I can't sleep at night, I make a slew of clay Asian bakery items, cakes and fruit tarts and buns and pastries, the exact opposite of what our mom wanted from me.

I had imagined, I guess, that I would spend a lot of the summer with Eloise and Lilith. Eloise lifeguards at the country club and, despite having done this for two years, is always terrified someone will actually start drowning on her watch, and so on school breaks Lilith and I would always go hang out there for moral support. I pictured beach days and hikes and talking each other into going to parties we never wanted to go to and then leaving after five minutes. Sometimes Eloise and Lilith message me, and I ignore them. What's there to say? I wonder if they're hanging out with each other. If they are, it feels like proof they don't care, never took any of this seriously. I unfollow them both.

I wish I had some better version of Logan Hesse, someone I could spend time with and talk to about things we thought were interesting or funny or sad without hating myself afterward. I'm tempted to call Logan anyway, and I do once, out of boredom. I regret it immediately, but, it turns out, not enough to actually stop myself from going.

There's new art leaning against the walls in the studio. I linger for a minute on an abstract painting with dark, bold lines that reminds me of swimming through kelp, that edge of nothingness. "I like this," I say.

He barely glances at it. "Really? I think it's stupid. My mom just slaps random paint on a canvas and it doesn't mean anything. And then someone pays twenty thousand bucks for it."

"How do you know it doesn't mean anything?"

"I mean, look at it. It's just random lines and shit."

"You don't like abstract art?"

"I like abstract art. I've just seen her spend, like, four minutes on stuff she's going to sell."

"Maybe it means something to people looking at it," I say.

"So people get to decide things mean whatever they want? I think that's stupid. That's the whole problem with our culture. Everyone decides everything means whatever they want."

Why does that bother me so much? "I mean, I'm not a nihilist, but why does everything have to have some inherent meaning? You think if someone shares something with the world, they have to decide in advance exactly what it's going to mean?"

He pulls off his shirt. "I think you think you too much."

Fuck you, I immediately think, but don't say, because I am a Lo and I don't lose my poise in public.

"Well, it's been so nice to talk," I say, reaching for my purse, "but actually, I just remembered I need to leave."

He stares at me, shirtlessly, his fingers still working on his fly. "Are you shitting me? We haven't even—"

"So nice to catch up, Logan." I close the door behind me. At least I have the self-respect not to call him again.

We have exactly six weeks left with Skye before she moves in at Baylor, and I try to spend as much time with her as I possibly can. She signed on to do an apparently lucrative campaign with some trendy outdoorsy company, so I go with her to drive around in Mill Valley until she finds a good campground to set up the tent and the other gear they've given her—a sage-green enameled cooking stove and matching water bottle and a sleeping bag and mat—and then she takes pictures in a bunch of different outfits in different areas of the campground so the few hours we're there could pass for a weekend camping. Her contract includes a reel and grid photos, and it takes probably three hours to shoot her thirty seconds of footage for her reel. *Spending time outdoors has always been so important to me*, she writes, and Wrangell comments, *lmao have you ever even seen a tent???* She comments back, *BLOCKING YOUUUUU!*, and then Jamison, who still kind of frets over all of us, even though I'm certain Skye's pulling in more money than she is, messages to tell her she should delete Wrangell's comment in case the brand sees it.

I want her to feel like I'm helpful and useful, so I go through and answer a bunch of Skye's DMs, which are 70 percent product links, 10 percent inane comments like *I love that color on you!* or *omg you look so much like Jamison here!* from strangers who probably think of her as a friend, and the rest criticisms about what she's wearing/saying/whatever or creeps making pornographic comments or people telling her she's a horrible person who deserves to get raped and die. It's shocking, actually. One person sends a Google Maps screenshot of our house.

"Well, work is work," our mom says at dinner when I show her. "The goal isn't *fun*. If it were fun, it wouldn't be work."

"Nah, I think it sounds glamorous," Atticus says. "I think it sounds aspirational. I think everyone should be an influencer for a living. Let's just all stop having real options so we can make money off whatever company is willing to shell out the most to worm their way into our lives."

"You're not the first male to think things like the gym are superior just because they're traditionally masculine," our mom says, and Skye doubles over laughing.

"Get some aloe for that *burn*," she says, poking Atticus.

When I can't bear to read any more of Skye's DMs, I decide

I'm going to throw myself into planning our birthday trip. Our birthday is September 8th, and usually our dad picks a location and then Ava handles the details, but this year I'll do everything. I send a message to our whole-family group chat, which everyone ignores, although Jamison messages just me to say, Let me know if you need help, Honor!!! Probably Atticus is right and she thinks we're still eleven years old, going to botch something like travel specifics.

I choose Kauai, which is close enough that no one can back out because the flight is too long, and which has that same lush, green feel as Hong Kong that our dad loves. I spend the next week researching vacation rentals and restaurants and excursions, until I'm satisfied I've tailor-designed a week to bring everyone back together and heal from what's happening now.

I tell this to Skye. "I see," she says, laughing. "Like a haunted house, if you will, only the kind that . . . makes people married again?"

"Yes, exactly," I say, rolling my eyes. "What do you mean, 'a haunted house'? What does that have to do with anything?"

"I don't know, how you like trap people in rooms for some specific psychological outcome?"

"I *guess*." I give her an impulsive hug. "I'm going to miss you so much when you leave! Maybe I should move in with you. I'll hide in your dorm."

"What are you going to do at school?" she says, tucking her hair behind her ears. "The terrible thing about a school that small is you run out of people to be friends with."

"I honestly don't know what I'm going to do." I try to imagine spending every class period and every lunchtime ignoring Eloise and Lilith—doing a lab report or going over conjunctives while they sit there, watching me for details they can glean to sell somewhere else. "Maybe I'll homeschool."

"Don't do that," she says. "Then it's like they won." She messages our family chat: Everyone needs to help cheer up Honor because her friends suck!!!

I'd been worried everyone would be furious with me after the *People* piece, but they've all had people in their lives sell them out, so actually, everyone was sympathetic. (You're better than them, Honor! You don't need their energy in your life!) After Skye's message, Jamison gets worried, apparently, and flies me out to visit her in San Diego. We go get facials and blowouts at a salon in Bird Rock, where there are glass-jeweled benches lining the streets and the salon opens out onto a back deck with a view of the ocean almost menacing in its blue-skied perfection, and Jamison tells me I should think about the narrative. Am I going to be wounded? Furious? Am I going to be the bigger person? I should decide now so I know how to conduct myself when school starts. When Jamison works, I go with Sonnet and the au pair, Inga, to a children's museum, where Sonnet inspects magnets and splatters purple paint on an old wrecked car outside, and at night Jamison tries to give me some kind of juice cleanse that'll change my life, but Andrew rescues me by bringing home fish tacos with crisp shreds of cabbage and a creamy, spicy sauce. We eat them out in Jamison's courtyard, where her hibiscus and plumeria are blooming and her string lights cast a warm, soft glow. And I think how what Jamison has is all the impossible things I truly want in life: someone who loves me and a baby who will light up every time she sees me, even if I'm only gone for, like, eleven seconds in the next room.

· · ·

Wrangell makes a surprise visit the day I get back from San Diego, swooping in when I'm making a tiny clay guava chiffon cake.

"This is so tragic, Honor, oh my God," he says, laughing, surveying my desk, which is littered with Sculpey wrappers and carving tools. "Just you and your inanimate objects!"

"My only friends now," I say. Maybe that will be, per Jamison, my narrative.

"Stop, you're killing me. Let's get you out of the house. Let's go eat oysters. I've been in the city too long. I feel twitchy."

We drive up to Tomales Bay for lunch. Atticus messages from volleyball camp: I can't believe he emerged from his ghosting to take you to lunch! We eat outside, and Wrangell has an elaborate sunscreen regimen that he narrates in extreme detail as he smears his different creams on his skin. (Which, in fairness, looks great.) Would I be happier if I believed you could solve most of life's problems with exactly the right product? Is that the underlying meaning Logan's after?

"You know," Wrangell says, "you're actually talented with that clay. You should try to sell it somewhere."

"*Sell* it?" I say, amused. "I don't think people are exactly banging down the door for miniature har gow."

"Because they don't know about it. People don't know what they want until you show them. You could start with an online shop, maybe. Just small-batch, limited-edition releases. Very curated. I might know someone, actually—let me get back to you on this. I might have a connection for you."

Later that day, after he's dropped me off, he sends me a message. Someone's going to call you! Make sure you pick up!

The call turns out to be from Hanna Kim, who runs a boutique in Berkeley. She wants to order a set of Asian-foods jewelry for the shop: char siu earrings, pendants of bowls of ramen.

"Wrangell showed me pictures of your work and it is just *adorable*," she gushes. "I've seen clay jewelry before, but yours is so elevated! Like the Alice Waters version! It has such a point of view. I'm so excited to have discovered you!"

"Oh," I say, surprised. The tiny foods make people smile, I think of them as fun and joyful, but I don't know if I would've ever called them *elevated*. But I'm flattered, of course. "That's so kind."

"So we'll do a big launch, because this will be the first time your line has been available anywhere, and we'll stick to a very limited, special-edition release. Have you had much experience with jewelry? Maybe we'll have you do the clay, and we'll find someone who can do the finishings to make sure it's all really high-end."

"That sounds great," I say. It's a little overwhelming, and maybe not what I pictured something I love turning into, but it's also an amazing opportunity—I never expected someone to treat this hobby as worthy and profitable and desirable. You're the best!!!!!!!!!!!!!! I message Wrangell after Hanna and I hang up. Lauren is thrilled. Even our mother, who really would love for me to do bigger things, is grudgingly approving.

"I'll have our lawyers look over the contract," she says. "I don't really know how this kind of thing would scale, but I suppose it's a start."

I spend the next day working on Hanna's order. I start with a plate of soy sauce chow mein, the kind with onions and scallions, and first I look at a hundred pictures of different platefuls to try to pick out the key characteristics of it, which is probably not a very cost-effective way of working (I don't tell our mother), because it takes an hour. I start with the plate, rolling out and then pains-takingly razor-cutting shapes from a dark blue to make a chinalike pattern, and then I make the noodles. I'll lacquer them to make them glisten. At first I mix just a brownish color, but it's too flat and opaque looking, so I try a new mix with translucent clay and it's perfect, and I'm so pleased I almost text a picture to Lilith and Eloise before I remember.

Well, whatever. I have this instead of friends. Maybe I can drop out of school and make clay jewelry for Hanna's boutique full-time.

The next day I'm fashioning speckled little Heath-inspired bowls, to fill with ramen, when our mother calls Skye, Atticus, and me into her office. It's on the third floor, with a wall of windows overlooking the coast. It's my favorite room in the house, but we're almost never in here. It's rare for her to want us to come in. It's late morning, and outside the sun is glinting off the water.

"I have some news about a decision I'd like to share with you." Our mother takes a long breath, and my heart spirals: Are they divorcing? "I've spoken to our real estate agent. We're going to be putting this house on the market next week."

"Wait, what?" Atticus says. "And then what?"

"I think it's important that we go somewhere we have roots. I'm going tomorrow to look at some listings in Los Gatos."

"Los *Gatos*?" Atticus says. "What? No. No way. We have roots *here*."

Los Gatos is two hours south of here in the valley, cut off from the ocean by the Santa Cruz Mountains. We used to spend a lot of time there back when Auntie JJ and our mom still talked, when our grandparents were still alive—even after they lost the house, we'd go with them to visit all their favorite parks and walks—but it's been years since we've been back. But I am overcome, more than anything else, with relief. I will just disappear; I'll never have to see Lilith and Eloise again. They'll hear about me, I'm sure, but I'll be gone, or at least as gone as you can ever be in a world where your face is plastered everywhere, for everyone.

"Wow," Skye says. "That feels drastic, Mom, doesn't it? Maybe instead you could—"

"I'm not moving," Atticus says. "This is a ridiculous plan. You didn't even like growing up in Los Gatos."

"Well, I didn't say it would be easy, but nothing worth having ever is. And there are good volleyball clubs in Los Gatos. Very good, actually. Higher ranked than here. I had Ava look into it."

"But I've been working with Coach Chen for years, and he has so many connections—"

"You're selling yourself short, Atticus," our mom says. "What I'm hearing you say is that you don't believe in your own abilities and your own work ethic, and you need—" Her phone rings. She glances down at it. "Oh, I need to take this call. We'll talk more later. I just wanted to share the news."

Atticus has to leave to coach at the kids' camp, but the minute he gets home, he comes to find me. I'm in my room with Skye, who leaves in less than a month. I still cannot imagine her living in an entirely different state. I'm unpacking from San Diego, which I've still barely started because unpacking always makes me sad, and Skye and I are going through all the serums and oils and drink powders Jamison loaded into my suitcase.

"She's treating us like pawns to use against him," Atticus says.

"*Oh, you'll move out? Cool, I'll sell the house even if it means uprooting the kids.* I couldn't even focus on coaching today thinking about it. They need to, like—work out their own issues without dragging the rest of us into it, I swear."

"Maybe we can talk her out of it," I say. "I'll call Jamison. Or I'll talk to Lauren."

"She's probably just really reactive right now," Skye says. "Trying to just do whatever she can to feel like she's in control."

"I don't know, I think she's going to go through with it." He watches me make an awkward pile out of the drink packets. "You don't hate the idea, though, Honor, do you?"

"I mean, part of me would love to move," I say. "Just get the hell out. But if you don't want to, then I think we should stay. Maybe I can just—I don't know. Graduate early or something. Homeschool myself."

"Do you think you'll try talking to Eloise and Lilith again?" Skye says.

"They're both just going to deny it. And anyway, no, because I don't want to talk to them. This is the worst time of our lives, and they used it to try to, what—make money? Feel important? Make me feel even worse?"

Atticus winces. "Yeah, it really sucks."

"But it's fine. I'll try to campaign to stay." This has always been our unspoken contract, that we'll look out for one another.

"It doesn't matter what you or anyone says. Mom doesn't care. She's just going to do what she wants. In her story she's always the main character. And in her twisted philosophy it's like, yes, the harder the better—if something is a lot of work, then it's what you want. God." He rubs his forehead with his palm. "I can't believe she's doing this. What a nightmare."

"Here." I hold out a small, round jade ball suspended from a magnetic strip. "Jamison says this will make you feel better."

"What the hell is that?"

"I don't know, something about, like, energy ions. It pulls them from the air through osmosis? Or maybe it pulls them from you, I can't remember."

Skye laughs. "Honor, how long was all this going to just sit in your suitcase on your floor?"

"Forever? Unpacking is the worst."

Atticus rolls his eyes. "Yeah, you should've left all these locked up in your luggage. I feel like I could invent some absolutely inane pseudoscience thing and Jamison would totally try to sell it for me online. I should do it. Lo it up. You think she actually believes this stuff? Or it's just a paycheck?"

"I think she's pretty into these. Look at all these things she made me take. I'm supposed to mix these and drink them."

"Maybe she's just convincing herself so she can live with it. Otherwise, you'd just feel gross."

"Maybe these are delicious," Skye says, sliding a few of the drink packages across my desk toward him. "Maybe you'll get hooked. Maybe it'll solve all your problems and make your skin look amazing."

"My skin is fine."

His skin is, annoyingly, fine. Our mom's aesthetician comes to the house twice a week and always has new masks and products for me to try, but my skin never looks as good as his. "I'll try to talk to Mom," I say. "Maybe we can change her mind."

You're Not Famous: A Snark Site

ynf.com/forums/LoFamily

calendulateam, 9:04:36 am PST: it's really weird Melissa has said literally NOTHING about the separation

knockoffbrene, 9:04:59 am PST: (because it's fake and actually there's no separation at all)

hungergamesbell, 9:05:23 am PST: yeah of all the weird times to decide actually you do care about privacy?? or—?? really curious what her endgame is here. is she so delusional she thinks it isn't happening?

gatsby11, 9:06:57 am PST: it's probably a business decision, like everything else in her life. she knows being separated isn't good for her brand. Suddenly she's not the authentic woman who has it all together, she's just a middle-aged divorcee who exploited her kids and family for cash. What's there for her to say?

baconspam420, 9:07:00 am PST: yeah, I don't know if I agree with that. You don't think people would shell out to read her tell-all of their hypocrite marriage? I would pay nineteen ninety-five for that, and I despise all of the Los except for *maybe* Atticus.

We cannot, it turns out, change our mother's mind. Within three weeks, Skye's last at home, the house has sold and our mom has closed on a place in Los Gatos. Movers come to pack everything up. Atticus goes to different farewell parties what feels like every night of the week. I keep expecting Eloise and Lilith to hear we're leaving and try to come see me, but they don't. Which I guess is for the best, because no matter how much I might miss them, no matter how lonely I might feel, I can't get past this. It wasn't just betraying me, it was betraying my family, and I am a Lo first and foremost. It's the most important thing about me, the thing I hold most dear.

We have a joint goodbye party for Skye and the house the night before she flies out to Waco. The house is a moving-box-filled shambles, but Ava finds someone to come transform the yard with string lights and big planters and a single long table, and we have a bunch of the foods Skye's going to miss from the Bay Area: Sonoma goat cheese, Tomales Bay oysters, Acme sourdough, sandwiches from Tartine, black sesame and Ricanelas ice cream from Bi-Rite. It's small, just the three of us plus some people from Skye's class. Wrangell doesn't respond to our messages about it. Our dad would love this, I think. He always loves a good party, a good theme.

Skye's up until three in the morning afterward packing, because she procrastinated, and I camp out in her room, helping her. We both cry on and off. I remind myself we'll have our birthday trip; I can fly out and see her, if I can survive the flight.

"I should stay," she says at one point, around two. "What am I even doing? It seemed like a good idea at the time, but I've literally never wanted to live in Texas! I'm not going to fit in."

"You fit in everywhere," I say. "You're going to do amazing things there. But also, promise you'll come visit like preferably every weekend. Or I'll fly out and stay with you. I truly don't know how I'll survive without you."

"I can't believe you're going to live in a new house and go to a new school I know almost nothing about," she says. "Ew, and I'll be somewhere you guys have never been! We're going to be like strangers to each other."

"Set up a livestream. Literally twenty-four/seven so I feel like I'm there with you."

She laughs. "I will if you will. Atticus will be *thrilled*." She folds a stack of Madewell shirts and says, "I'm actually really sad about the house."

"I am too."

"It's so weird it won't be here for me to come back to. I keep feeling all emo about the dumbest, smallest things! Like sand in my clothes all the time and jogging by the water on weekend mornings. And the fog creeping in at night." She tries to squish her suitcase closed. "Promise me—I don't even know what! That it'll be the same somehow."

"It'll always be the same with us," I say.

"Yeah, maybe that's what I mean." She sighs. "At least they're paying me a boatload, right? God. *Texas.* It better be good."

CHAPTER FIVE

Skye *adores* Texas, she tells the world. It's so sunny and laid-back and the people are so chill! Baylor is so beautiful she feels like she's on the set of some college movie! She decks out her dorm room with fairy lights and planters and new bedding, curtains and a rug from Urban Outfitters. She films herself walking around campus, going to football games, going to parties. She films herself rushing for a sorority whose name I never remember, giddily making friends for life.

A good sister would not secretly hope she'd hate it there, so obviously I don't hope that, but, well—maybe a tiny bit. At the very least I wouldn't mind if sorority people didn't call each other *sister*.

It's astonishing, actually, how quickly things can just unravel, how the parts of your life you took for granted can turn out to stop existing. I wanted an escape, but you don't know the things you're going to miss before they're gone.

Like the house. I miss the stained-glass window in my bedroom and hearing the surf at night. The house our mom bought in Los Gatos is a four-thousand-square-foot new build, a modern split-level with black stone floors and countertops, and a full wall of glass looking over the hills. My room and Atticus's room form a wing that juts out of the house over the downstairs patio, suspended in the air, and we both have balconies made of—glass? Plexiglas? Acrylic? Something clear, at any rate—that are terrifying to stand on. I understand what it is for the whole universe you used to occupy to have vanished.

Our first day of school at the new school, Saint Simeon, our mom comes in, rushed and frazzled, while Atticus and I are eating breakfast. There are two flower arrangements on the counter that our dad sent us: peonies for me, and a round cluster of gardenias that's supposed to look like a volleyball ("Why would I want this?" Atticus demanded. "Why would anyone want this?") with a note card that says, *Good luck today! You'll crush it!* Our mom beelines to the fridge.

"Lauren is on her way over to talk to you both," she says, rifling a little frenetically through the produce drawers. "She'll be here in ten minutes. Don't leave until you talk to her. Did you two eat my smoothies? Where are all my smoothie packs?"

"No, I didn't."

"Did Atticus?"

"I really doubt it." Atticus thinks smoothies are gritty. Ever since we were kids, he's hated anything soft textured like that: applesauce, mashed potatoes.

"Atticus. I asked you a question."

He looks up. "What?"

"Did you eat all my smoothies?"

"No."

"Well, someone must have." She slams the drawer shut and washes an apple instead. "Also, Atticus, I need you back here right after school for the shoot."

"Atticus has a practice," I say.

"He'll have to be late. Atticus." When he doesn't answer, she repeats it, then says, "Look at me." When he ignores her—he can't stand how intense she's been about everything media related—she says, "Are you sexting?"

He doesn't look up. "What's that?"

"Don't give me that. You know what it is."

"Never heard of it."

She reaches out and grabs his phone from him. "It's sending sexually inappropriate pictures and messages over the phone."

"*Oh* my *God*," he says. "What kind of degenerate would *do* that?"

"Atticus, stop it. Did you hear what I said? I need you here after school, before you go to your practice, for the photo shoot. It's important."

He reaches for his phone, but she pockets it. "Why don't you put out an ad and find someone else?"

"I am trying to set you up for a decent life here after our universe imploded, Atticus, and I don't appreciate your attitude. Your ancestors spent their entire lives dreaming of something better—"

And they worked themselves to the bone! Atticus mouths to me, widening his eyes dramatically.

"—and they worked themselves to the bone, and if you'd told them all you needed to do to make a better life for yourself was smile for a camera for a few minutes, they would have laughed in your face. You have no idea how lucky you are. When I was your age, I would have killed for your cushy life. But you know what, luck can run out anytime, and then you have nothing, so you have to take advantage and work hard while the opportunities are available to you. You never know what's going to happen. You have to be prepared."

Those stories have been drilled into us all our lives: a cautionary tale about all the ways the world will give you nothing, about how there's no such thing as working too hard, or being too prepared, or padding yourself against any contingency. They have always been our mom's go-to deflection against any complaints about the ways she pushes us. "Look at my mother," she always says, a catchall explanation. "Look at your ancestors." Our duty has always been to be self-sufficient, to blaze our way through the world with ease. Auntie JJ always told us the same, although her ideas of what that looked like were different: she worked hard in school, got an engineering degree. ("A rule follower," our mother used to call her, not as a compliment.) If anything, our mother's resolve is probably strengthened now: your husband can leave you, and then you're left with only what you've built yourself.

"I really don't think preparation needs to involve some random photo shoot when—"

"Well, if you want to keep your credit card, you'll participate. Three p.m. I don't have time for you to show up late. Okay? Repeat that to me. Three p.m. Three oh one, I call Ava and she cancels your account."

"Touché," he says.

"You'll thank me someday." Our mom gives me a hug and a kiss on the forehead, then Atticus. "Growth is hard and uncomfortable and necessary, and this is a growth opportunity for all of us. If you hate me because I'm pushing you, that means I'm doing my job." She sighs. "Right?" She's less confident without our dad, the one who always affirms her and backs her up. "You're both going to do great today."

"What's his photo shoot for?" I say.

"It's—" Her phone rings. She reaches into her pocket, then swears—it's Atticus's, and she slams it on the counter—and reaches into her other pocket. "Did you hear back from United?" she says. "Are they on board? Okay, great, if that's the case—"

She balances her phone between her shoulder and ear so she can shut the door behind her. I can hear her talking for a little while as she goes down the walkway.

"She needs to dial it down by a factor of, like, a thousand," Atticus says. "She's, like, manic."

"It's probably like a shark, where if you stop swimming, you die."

"Yes, but we aren't sharks." He rescues his phone from the counter where our mom left it.

"Did you hear her last night?"

"What was last night?"

"She was crying again."

He winces. "Did she say anything?"

"I didn't try. I didn't know what to say."

She's been busier than ever since we moved here. She found a new yoga instructor and hair person who can come to the house, she's thrown herself into overseeing the interior decorator. She never brings up our dad; it's clear we aren't supposed to either. I don't know if they're talking. If so, I never hear it. I am trying to stay neutral. I think they can work this out. I love them both. I say, "You think I should've tried to talk to her?"

"I don't know. Maybe." He taps his hands on his knees. "You can come get me next time and I can try to talk to her. It'd be better than fighting over all the pictures she wants me to take. Is that why Lauren's coming? I just wish she wouldn't pimp us out for ads as part of her coping process or whatever."

"I don't think it's her coping process. I think Lauren is worried about her career."

"Why is she worried about her career?"

"I think because Mom won't talk about anything happening, and Lauren's worried she's going to come across as inauthentic now and torpedo her image. I heard them talking about it."

The front door opens, and Lauren calls, "Hello!"

"We're in the kitchen," I call back. Lauren's practically family. She's been our mom's publicist for probably twelve or thirteen years, so she's watched us grow up. Whenever her kids' babysitter is gone or the kids are home sick from school, she brings them with her, and I'm used to her coming in and out of the home all the time whether or not our mom is here. She has her own key. It was Lauren, not our mom, who was home the day I got my first period and explained to me how to use a tampon, calling instructions outside the door and laughing about it in a way that made it a million times less awkward than it could've been.

She hugs both of us and pinches Atticus's biceps and then smushes his cheeks and shakes his face from side to side, which he gamely accepts.

"You both look fantastic," Lauren says. "How *are* you? Fill me in. I've been so busy. But I keep wanting to know how you're really *doing*."

"Gonna have to do the condensed version, actually," Atticus says amiably. "We're going to be late for school."

"Is this a new, responsible Atticus?" she says, laughing. "I like it!" She pulls out the chair next to me, sets her purse on the counter, and takes a sort of dramatic breath.

"Sooooooo," she says, leaning on the vowel, "okay, still unclear to me how this happened, exactly, but it sounds like some of the paparazzi found out where you guys are going to school."

"Excuse me?" Atticus says. "What does that even mean?"

Lauren says lightly, "You're slacking on your *Us Weekly* reading, I see!" She pulls up the site on her phone and shows us. *Lo Family in Shambles!* the top headline blares, with a picture of our parents with scissors marks cut down the middle. Underneath that, a picture of us from a few years ago. *Lo Twins Lose Home, School after Melissa, Nathan Split.* I peer closer, and there's a picture of what I know from looking at Google Maps is the Saint Simeon front hall. *See inside the twins' swanky new school!*

Atticus says, "What in the absolute hell?"

Lauren puts a hand on his sympathetically. "So they did call to let us know they'd be coming this morning, in case you guys wanted to talk to them, which obviously, no, you do not, but it sounds like they're going to show up either way to get some shots, so I wanted to go over some basics with you before—"

"They'll be coming today?" Atticus repeats. "To *school*? What? So, what—we're just like, *Cool, cool, see you there?*"

"This will die down," Lauren says soothingly. "Trust me, your mother isn't interesting enough for paparazzi to be staking out her children at school. To be honest, I'm a bit surprised they're even taking it this far. It's the big story now, everyone is so interested in the separation, but give it a week and I promise they'll forget all about you. And her, too."

"People need to get a fucking life," Atticus says. "Who cares?"

Lauren makes a sympathetic face. "I've called the school to ask about providing you with security, and—"

"Oh God, don't do that," Atticus says, at the same time that I say, "Maybe we can just rush to our classrooms—"

"Well, it's a closed campus, so any visitors have to sign in at the school office, *but* unfortunately there's some weird jurisdiction, where the parking lot is rented from the city, and they can't actually prohibit anyone from being in the parking lot." She sighs. "So, any paparazzi have to stay in the parking lot. They can't actually come onto the school grounds. We can, however, have private security escort you, so I've asked Ava to find someone on short notice."

"Yeah, let's not do that," I say. I imagine being paraded past our new classmates by a man in a mall-cop uniform, everyone gawking. "That would be such a scene."

"Well, it might already be a scene."

"Either way, please no on the security. Should we just stay home?"

"No, eff that," Atticus says.

"It should be very quick," Lauren says. "I'm not worried about you, I know you're going to be fine, I just wanted to make sure you had a heads-up. And I wanted to make sure we had a chance to go over just some important ground rules for you. Don't engage with anyone—don't answer any questions, don't reply, don't listen to what they say. Don't give them any kind of sound bite or information. Don't hide, either—just be mindful that cameras are on you and keep walking. I promise it'll die down soon. Remember you are a brick wall. Don't give them a thing."

"You nervous?" Atticus says on the way to the new school. We're in his car, because another thing about living here is I find driving terrifying. So many winding mountain passes, so many blind curves. We're wearing our stupid, extremely heteronormative plaid wool school uniforms like this is 1950 and we raise sheep.

"Nope. You?"

"Nope."

"That's good," I say. "I might just, like, throw up a tiny bit."

He laughs. "Just some very light fainting?"

"Maybe a tiny bit. Barely noticeable."

"I won't tell anyone."

I get a message from Auntie JJ: good luck today, Honor! Thinking of you! I write back, thanks :), but I wish I could call and talk to her, tell her everything.

"I miss Auntie JJ," I say.

"Aw. You should call her."

"I think it would be weird."

"Maybe. So?"

"Who do you think she talks to now?" I say. Our grandparents died a little after Atticus and I were born, so Auntie JJ and our mom are each other's whole family. "Like, who does she spend all her time with?"

"Her church friends? I don't know."

I watch the sunlight stream between the redwoods. I try to steady my breaths. In, out. In, out. "You think it'll be bad today?"

"Eh, it'll be fine. People are the same everywhere."

I roll my eyes. "You just think that because people like you everywhere."

"You say that like it's a bad thing."

"Some of us just didn't inherit the Lo charisma and have to work very hard, actually, to be liked."

"Nah, you're too hard on yourself," he says. "People will like you."

I wonder what Lilith and Eloise are doing and if they've made up with each other or not and whether they're telling people I'm not speaking to them. And I wonder if people get that, or if they think I'm overreacting and that I shouldn't care so much. Maybe everyone would just tell me that I'm being irrational and unfair, that our parents and siblings tell the world so much anyway. Once Karissa, Lilith's mom, sat me down to ask me somberly whether our mother had my consent to write and speak so much about me so publicly.

Anyway, it doesn't matter anymore. I muted everyone from Rearden, so many people we've gone to school with since we were nine years old. I don't need to watch our old life close over us like a scab.

"I'm sorry we didn't stay," I say quietly. "I wanted to for your sake."

"Yeah, I know." He sighs. "Whatever, I'll be fine."

The school grounds are huge, considering the enrollment is much smaller than at Rearden, and kind of lovely—stone buildings, greenery everywhere. The parking lot looks normal when we get out, clusters of other people talking by their cars, no swarm of photographers, and for a moment I'm flooded with relief: Lauren was wrong! She's always been an overplanner, prepared for every possible contingency, so probably it was just her competence that—

Atticus swears, and then I see him. A white man probably in his thirties with a huge camera strapped around his neck, hurrying toward us. Around us, everyone stops to stare. Atticus takes a step in front of me.

The man picks up the camera and aims it at us. I am probably looking right at the lens. I will look like a spooked animal in the shot, and Atticus murmurs, "Just ignore him."

"Honor, what do you think of your parents' separation?" he

yells across the parking spaces. "Are they divorcing? Atticus, has your father confided in you? Is there another woman?"

"Walk," Atticus says.

I walk next to him, trying to pretend nothing is happening. I imagine us all swimming with turtles in Kauai. Across the parking lot, a white girl with short light brown hair looks aghast and turns and says something to the (also white) guy next to her.

"Pretend we're talking like normal," Atticus says. "Don't look so haunted, Honor. He's not going to do anything. Also, he's a fucking loser. He's chasing kids around a school parking lot. What a creep."

"Was your life totally upended? Are you still on speaking terms with your parents?"

I have seen what it's like to have a crush of paparazzi follow you, the flashes blinding as you try to grope your way into your car—its own force, like a hurricane or an earthquake, choking out the world around you. It's hellish and violating and more than a little scary, but frankly it's also, it turns out, about thirty times less embarrassing than one man with a camera screaming at you from the edge of the publicly owned parking lot on your first day of school.

I have sweated through my cardigan. The walk across the parking lot and through the front gates feels a mile long. By the time we've made it, a bell has rung, and everyone else is streaming through the gates around us. The boy I saw earlier stops in front of us. "Are you Honor?"

I swallow. It's never a good sign when someone knows your name. "Yes."

"Your name is *Honor*?" a second boy, also white, says. "Is that because honor is like super important to your family?"

Does he mean that in a racist way? Before I have to answer, Atticus says, "Yeah, that's why my name is Atticus. White-savior narratives are also super important to our family."

It's a joke that would've gone over well at Rearden, but here only a few girls laugh, probably because they think he's hot.

"I think I'm supposed to be showing you around today," the first boy says to me. "Apparently, we have all the same classes. You guys are twins?"

"Yeah," Atticus says. "Identical, actually." One of the girls laughs for real this time. I hide my irritation.

"Cool," the first boy says. "Well, welcome to Saint Simeon. I'm Caden Lyall."

Caden is tall and athletic looking in a preppy way, with the kind of body designed for leaping after fly balls or lunging with rackets (or lacrosse sticks or golf clubs, given this is Los Gatos), but there's an easiness to his poise, and he has a mild expression that looks maybe on the verge of a smile. I am suddenly very invested in not letting it show that I think he's hot, because Atticus will have a field day and I'm not in the mood. I try to keep my eyes off him as he introduces the other boy standing there as John Gohl, and then the three girls also: Victoria Finebaugh, the one who looked disgusted earlier; Delancey Lum; Blythe Greer. Is this a thing here, that people introduce themselves by their full names? How incredibly pretentious.

There is an immediate, visceral cliquishness to the three of them. I notice they're all wearing matching necklaces—small, abstract gold charms—which should be cringe but feels rarefied somehow here. Victoria has an incredible amount of presence, cult-leader level presence, and I hate her on sight.

"So, wow, what was *that?*" Victoria says, smiling in an unfriendly way. We didn't have an analogous person at Rearden. Maybe Caden being friends with her is a major red flag. "In the parking lot?"

"It's nothing," I say. "Just some creep from *Us Weekly.*"

"Why is he chasing you?"

Because they're vultures, Victoria, what do you think? "They're probably trying to get some picture," I say. "I just ignore it."

"Does this happen to you a lot?"

There are people who would be interested or even impressed, but Victoria is not one of them. I would best describe her as appalled. She looks like she just witnessed something unspeakably gauche. I say, "Almost never."

"Why today?"

I feel my face go hot, a burning in my chest. I despise talking about our family like this, and I debate whether it's worth lying.

"Our parents are having some drama," Atticus says easily. This is the correct move, of course, because if people sense you're hiding something, it always becomes bigger than it is. "People are weirdly interested in their lives."

It feels extremely likely Victoria already knew this and just wanted us to have to say it. She raises her eyebrows. "I see."

"Why are they even allowed here?" Delancey says. "You'd think it would be illegal. Isn't the school private property?"

"You would think," I say. "But there's this weird loophole—"

"Oh yeah." Caden laughs. He has dimples when he laughs, and something slips open in his expression; it's only when I see him do it that I realize how guarded his default expression is. "The parking lot."

"Why do you know that?"

"Believe me, I've heard way more about the parking lot drama than you could possibly imagine."

"His mom's a trustee," Delancey says.

"The parking lot is a long-standing war. Lots of bad blood." He lifts his hand to trace an imaginary line. "Some of the parents want a grove of trees over here to kind of hide the view of the parking lot from the school, but some of the other parents really wanted a fountain and some benches. My mom's kind of the ringleader of Team Grove. Or used to be."

There were wars over parking lot aesthetics? I'm going to hate this school. Clearly, people care about all the wrong things here. Even I care about the wrong things here—inexplicably I want Victoria and Delancey and Blythe to like me. I want them to be impressed by me; I want them to think I'm one of them. I try to tell myself it's just because of Caden that I feel that way, but I don't think it is.

"Well," I say, "it seems like a stupid system."

Victoria and Delancey and Blythe instantly look almost imperceptibly disapproving, and I can tell it was the wrong thing to say, although the why is unclear to me: Because I shouldn't criticize the systems here? Because it's strange to care so much about something they probably don't care about? Because actually the parking lot is sacred?

"I can take you guys to the office," Caden says. Atticus nods goodbye to the three girls. He has persistently, embarrassingly low standards; probably he thinks they're all nice. We follow Caden across a stone-paved courtyard lined with delicate Japanese maples. In the office, Atticus is assigned to shadow a lanky, red-haired junior named Troy, and then Caden says, "All right, first period precalc. It's over in the math wing by the fields."

He is the kind of attractive that makes everything he says feel weighty and meaningful and witty. (First period *precalc*!) Eloise and Lilith always told me I had terrible taste in guys, though, so maybe it's just me.

"So where you guys from?" Caden asks as we walk. The school is noticeably smaller than Rearden, and I can feel everyone staring as we walk by. I'm glad they gave me someone to shadow, though.

"Up north on the coast. Near Muir Beach." The Bay Area is incredibly provincial—no one knows smaller towns more than an hour away.

"So what was your other school like?"

"Well, it was a lot more progressive, for one."

"What makes you think we aren't progressive? Our ascetic namesake? The uniforms? It's the uniforms, isn't it? You should've seen the old versions."

"There was a *worse* version? It already feels like someone's creepy Catholic-schoolgirl fantasy."

He laughs in a way that's somehow both surprised and genuine, and gives me a longer, appraising look, like he's actually noticing me for the first time. People tend to assume I'm going to be meek. Jamison, too, even though she's the opposite. She's always had to tone herself down so much online. Something about him makes me want to tell him things, makes me want to reveal myself to him, probably in the same exhibitionist way people feel about, I don't know—flashing someone, or stripping.

"So what made your old school progressive?" he says.

"It was pretty hippie. Marin, you know."

"Yeah? Were you guys, like, really good at recycling?"

"Yes, actually."

"Yeah?" He watches me, grinning, holding the gaze longer than he has to. Something inside me starts to liquefy. "I can't tell if you're kidding or not."

"I'm not. The class two years above us, their senior project was to make our school waste greener."

"Okay, yeah, the class two years above us here got everyone's parents to donate for better grass on the lacrosse field, so you win. What made you come to this school, then? Are you Catholic?"

"No." I wonder if he is. "My mom picked it. She grew up here."

"Oh yeah? Did she go here? Victoria's mom did."

"No. She went to the public school."

"But she didn't want you to?"

I hesitate. "Public schools are kind of hard for us."

"Yeah, that makes sense." He adds, "Victoria's mom found out you guys were coming here and we looked you up. I think Delancey already knew your sister, though. Or knew of her."

"Skye? Yeah, probably." I feel that twinge of disappointment I always do when I know someone knows us: I'm already formed in their minds. But then simultaneously the relief that I don't have to wonder, the dancing around it.

"I'm kind of out of the loop, though," he says. "So were you pretty bummed about moving? I wouldn't be thrilled."

"Only sort of, actually. My two best friends kind of betrayed me and I never want to see them again, so part of me was sort of thrilled to leave."

"Oh, what?" he says. "How did they betray you?"

"One of them sold something I told them in private to *People*. The magazine."

He winces. "Okay, yeah, that's shitty."

If there's anything I learned from Eloise and Lilith, it's that I can never tell anyone anything, but it was weirdly intoxicating to say that to him. I hope he's not acting interested just because we're famous. I don't get that vibe from him—I feel, actually, weirdly, like there's some spark between us, like we could keep talking for hours. I want him to tell me things about himself, too. We could keep each other's secrets.

But maybe it's just that he's hot and I'm shallow. Who knows? Apparently, I can't read people well at all.

The rest of the day is somehow both uneventful and the worst. After first period I am never alone with Caden again; people cluster around him on the way to every class, including, between several periods, Victoria and various permutations of other people from the morning. Caden is, it turns out, the only good part of the day. He seems to just assume I'll stay with him for recess and lunch, and even though he doesn't talk directly to me, I don't feel vulnerable and adrift the way I might otherwise, even if I still had Atticus. Still, lunch is hell. I can feel Victoria constantly sizing me up, although she ignores me. Atticus, of course, for all his complaining, spends most of the time cheerfully talking with everyone like there's nowhere else he'd rather be. Sometimes I wish he were a pettier person, someone who'd misanthropically just hate everyone with me.

It's a huge relief when the last bell rings. (Just 179 days to go!) After school Atticus caves, like he always does, and does the photo shoot. The photo shoot turns out to be for Crest—Atticus has objectively very good teeth—which even after the first-day-of-school exhaustion is extremely funny to me, enough so that I camp out in the living room to imitate him throwing his head back and pretending to laugh with his mouth open over and over while Kyle, one of our mom's photographers, directs him. When Kyle isn't looking, he flips me off.

"Great work," I say afterward, clapping, when Kyle's finally left. "Some of your finest."

"Shut up."

"No, really, the lighting, the ambiance—just unrivaled. If there were an Oscar for photo shoots to help your mom sell toothpaste, you would absolutely win."

"I hate you."

I mimic his head-back, open-mouthed silent laugh. "Really just such an inspiring performance. The Academy will be thunderstruck. What are you going to get with all your credit card money? Some super-high-end toothbrush?"

"Yeah, nothing for you, that's for sure."

"I'm going to set up a fan account." I send a picture I took of the shoot to our sibling group chat. **Great job Atticus!!!** Jamison says, and Skye says, **lololololol Crest??** Nothing from Wrangell. I say, "Did you check *Us Weekly* yet?"

"What? No." Atticus sends a middle-finger emoji in the group chat, then adds, **that was for everyone except you, Jamie!** "Why would I want to do that?"

"To see if we're on it." I check. We are, but you have to scroll awhile. But there I am, looking like a deer in the headlights, my body and expression contorted in a way that makes me look particularly frumpy and unattractive. Immediately my mind flashes to Caden seeing. (Atticus looks fine.) I say, "Ugh, I shouldn't have looked."

"You're right, you shouldn't have."

"Your teeth look spectacular, though, as always. Has anyone

ever told you you should model for Crest?" I put my phone away and smile when he flips me off. "Have you talked to Wrangell?"

"Not much. He's in another ghosty phase."

"Ugh, I know." He hasn't answered my messages, didn't chime in when Jamison asked how the first day went. "Did you ask if he's still coming to Kauai?" We leave a little over two weeks from now. Everything else sucks, but I can hold on until Kauai. "Apparently, Ava can't get ahold of him to book his tickets."

"No. Why don't you ask him?"

"Because he likes you more."

"Okay, come on, you're just fishing. You know you're his favorite." I smile. "Maybe."

"I honestly kinda think the bigger risk is Dad not coming."

I frown. "Why would Dad not come? He promised. He loves these trips."

"Yeah, but it's going to be kind of awkward, don't you think? If I were him, I'd maybe be thinking about bailing. Do we even—I don't know, should we, like, postpone this year? We could talk to everyone."

"We can't postpone," I say, alarmed. "I think it's really important that all of us be there. That'll be the first time since Skye's graduation night."

"Yeah, but are we even in the mood to go on a trip with everyone? I don't exactly want to be trapped on an island right now with Mom, either. Maybe just you could go, and I can stay home."

"Atticus—you have to go. It's going to be all of us. We can't go without you. It's both of our birthdays."

"But don't you think if we just waited a few months—"

"Please promise me you'll come."

He sighs. "All right, fine, I promise I'll come. But only for you. God." He palms his head in his hand. "Swear all I want in the world is a normal life with normal parents who work as, like, bank tellers."

"No one's family is normal. But thank you. It'll be good for all of us. Also, there's no way in hell Dad doesn't come. He knows it would look so bad if he skipped the family trip." I try to peer at his phone. "Are you texting Wrangell yet?"

"My God, you are insufferable." He's trying to hide a smile, though, so it's okay. "Are you going to be like this in Kauai, too? Perfect way to spend our birthday."

"It'll be good. Think of it as a rebirth."

"Mm. You're really selling it. I'm sold." He grabs his backpack. "Mom was right. You should be an influencer after all."

CHAPTER SIX

Nearly two weeks in and I feel validated in my initial reaction: I hate it here. Saint Simeon is the worst. Rearden was tight-knit and just small enough that you didn't have the numbers to meaningfully divide people into really strict cliques—if you were an artist, you were probably also a jock and into drama, because there was no way you could field an entire soccer team or put on a production of *Our Town* otherwise. At Rearden, Eloise and Lilith and I did Speech and Debate; we were in the Tutoring Club; at lunch we hung out in the art room; we were nerdy, kind of, but I also got along with, say, Atticus's crowd. Everyone went to the same parties.

It's so different here. It's suffocatingly small, and the Byzantine set of social rules is invisible to me. Everything seems to revolve around Victoria, Blythe, and Delancey, who call themselves VBD, which, I'm told, is also an acronym for Very Big Deal. Which, again, in any other context would be truly embarrassing, but somehow there's a kind of irony in everything they do that lets them pull off—anything, apparently. The matching necklaces, the way they link arms sometimes walking across campus. I have never met people more obsessed with one another. Atticus tells me I should meet other friends, but the problem here is all anyone wants to talk about is VBD. Did I know Blythe was on TV before too, because she used to model for Gap Kids? Did I hear they might have a party at Delancey's house next weekend? Does my brother think any of them are hot? They are microinfluencers of the two hundredish people who go here.

And also, they've misclassified me. VBD (correctly) intuited immediately that Atticus was probably one of them, someone who belonged at the social center of things, but they made a category error in assuming he and I were the same that way. Eventually, of course, they'll realize I'm a fraud. And I shouldn't dread this, I should welcome and/or hasten it, but the reason I want to remain in this social circle is Caden.

We haven't really spoken at school, but actually he's quiet in big groups of people, and it turns out here so am I. In two weeks we have had exactly two noteworthy interactions: once in fourth-period chemistry I looked across the room and he was watching me, and when our eyes met, instead of frantically looking away like I would've done, he gave me the tiniest of nods. The other time was a few days ago at lunch, when everyone was complaining about the school uniforms. Caden turned to me, very slightly, and raised his eyebrows in an amused sort of way. It was, I understood, an invitation: Did I have anything to say? Probably no one else saw. But still, the world paused around me for a moment, because it felt like in that whole group of people, suddenly it was just the two of us; he was the only one who cared I was there.

Okay, so maybe those are barely even interactions. But they're exactly the kind of thing that can live rent-free in my head, that I can construct an entire crush around. I can't stop thinking that everything would be different, worth it somehow, with Caden. I think all the time about his forearms, about the way he looks in the school uniform, about the curve of his jaw. He has a muted way of reacting to things, just slightly raised eyebrows or tiny, tiny smiles, that makes every reaction feel private and earned. Maybe Skye's right and he would be terrible for me. I can't help wanting him. I told myself I wouldn't have any more meaningless hookups, but it's hard not to think it would at least distract me from the giant gaping holes in my life. Sometimes distraction is the best you can do.

On the way to school the Monday before Kauai, Atticus's phone rings. I pick it up from the center console to see who it is.

"That Dad?" Atticus says.

"Yeah."

"Don't pick up."

I set his phone back down. "Are you still avoiding him?" I don't think they've spoken. And with volleyball Atticus is legitimately busy during New York waking hours, but it's mind-blowing they haven't talked.

"No. Maybe. Kind of." He sighs. "I just don't really know what to say to him."

"He probably just wants to talk to you. You guys were, like, joined at the hip. And he said you never pick up his calls. Skye says he's calling her just to talk, like, basically every day."

"Yeah, he shouldn't do that. I don't think we super need to be there for every step of his self-actualization or whatever it is that's happening."

It's true that every time I talk to him, he has some tidbit about how Brooklyn is basically the most awesome place ever, but mostly when we talk, he wants to know how I'm doing. Fine, I always lie. "I know you must miss him, though."

"Of course I miss him." Atticus yawns. "Not gonna lie, feels a little early in the morning to be having this conversation."

"Okay then, switching topics. Did you ask Wrangell yet about Kauai? Is he coming?"

"Ah—not yet."

"Can you ask him?"

He sighs. "Why don't you ask?"

"Because when I ask, it's nagging. When you ask, it's fun."

"Well, God forbid anyone think you're nagging."

I pick up his phone again. "Can I send from your phone?"

"Don't you get sick of being this annoying?"

"Shut up. Can I send?"

"Fine, whatever. But be chill."

"Nope. You're sending him a totally unhinged text demanding he call Ava back and get his ticket booked ASAP." I write, yo, you're coming to Kauai, right?

Atticus pulls onto the main highway that'll take us down the mountain. For a long time when you drive up here, you go through old-growth redwoods—it's ten, fifteen minutes before you get to the valley floor. Despite everything, I feel at home in the trees; they ground me. I stare at them, think about how they were here when my ancestors first stepped foot on these shores. I wonder if any saw these trees and this coast and felt the beginnings of some tugging to stay. But probably it didn't go that way; probably they would've given anything to go back home someday. Their lives were hard. I always feel like I'm letting them down.

"Hey," I say, turning back to Atticus, "so what do you think of Caden Lyall?"

"Nothing."

"What do you mean, 'nothing'?"

"I mean I don't think I've ever had a single thought about Caden Lyall. Why?"

"I'm . . . kind of into him. And you're not allowed to tease me. I'm only telling you because I'm starved for friendship. I don't have anyone here I can talk to."

Atticus makes a face. "That guy? Random, but okay."

"Why the face?"

"Just his general vibe. Seems like not that amazing a choice for a boyfriend. Just like—prototypical Saint Simeon boy. You could do a lot better."

"Well, I don't want a boyfriend." Really, I can't imagine anything worse: someone who's there all the time who knows everything about you, someone you tell things to when your guard is down, someone who can leave you or cheat on you or otherwise crush you emotionally. It's too much power to give any one person.

I see Caden as we're pulling into the parking lot, standing with VBD near the west entrance. I always scan the parking lot for his car, and when it's there, or when I see him across campus or when we get to first period at the same time and walk through the door together, so close I can brush against him, I always get that same jolt: of proximity, of possibility. I dislike being at school, but Caden turns each day into potential—a hundred different moments when something could happen between us.

"Stop drooling," Atticus says.

"Shut up. You promised."

He grins. "I did absolutely nothing of the sort."

• • •

At lunch I walk over to where Atticus and I have been eating with Victoria and her crowd; they congregate in a little alcove formed by some of the pillars of the chapel. Caden's not there yet. I also get there before Atticus does, which I hate. I always worry someone will make it clear I don't belong here. Everyone is talking about what job they're going to have someday, a conversation that I would kind of enjoy in any other group of people, but there's only so much you can say about real estate and hedge funds. I should tell people I want to be a miniature-clay-foods artist when I grow up. I bet it would go over great.

I remember too late that Atticus isn't going to be here at lunch because he's making up a test he'll miss on Friday for a tournament, which, ugh. His schedule and really his whole life are dominated by his practice and game schedule—club in the fall, school in the spring, training in the off-season. His team travels aggressively, and this year he has tournaments planned for Hawaii, Boston, and as far as the Philippines and Japan. I'll get into decent colleges if I decide to go, because my grades are excellent, but volleyball is Atticus's whole ticket because he hasn't consistently done homework in years—he'll probably be recruited somewhere, and if he goes to school anywhere worthwhile, which he wants to, it will be because of volleyball alone. The ironic thing is that Atticus is more excited about college than anyone I know, which is saying a lot living in the Silicon Valley. But I think he's always yearned to be somewhere bigger, where fewer people know us and he can disappear into a crowd, only to emerge as himself, separate from whatever baggage he has from the rest of us, from all of it. He has a drawer full of college brochures that he hoards and pulls out sometimes to look at, imagining himself in all those other lives.

Caden's not here yet either. I should've just gone to the library or something. I take out a nectarine to eat for lunch. Half of the girls don't eat here, which makes me feel like I shouldn't eat, and then I'm always hungry.

"If I'm going to work, I want it to be something meaningful," Victoria says. "Like with kids, or maybe a poetry professor. Doesn't that sound fun?"

"Uh, that sounds like my literal nightmare," says John Gohl, the one who asked if honor was important to our family, inching himself a little closer to her. "No, I can see you there, though. Walking around some campus with a bunch of trees. You can get some cute glasses. That librarian look."

"John, you just don't read enough. You should read more. Wouldn't I make a good librarian, too? Maybe I'll volunteer as a librarian."

"Pretty sure you can't volunteer," I say. "I think you need a degree."

"Oh, I'm sure they have volunteers. I could come read stories to kids. All the best stories are the ones for kids, and then they just get depressing."

Blythe says, "You guys, this is so fun, though. We should make one of those time capsules and everyone say their guesses for where we'll all end up, and then in ten years we'll open it and see if we were right. You know what I want to do?"

"Be a trophy wife," John says.

Blythe laughs and swats him. "Okay, that's a given. But also I want to do interiors. Not houses, but maybe hotels or museums. That or a politician."

"A politician?" John says, amused. "Like what kind?"

"Like a lawmaker."

"Can you even name a single law?"

Blythe laughs again. "I get the idea it doesn't actually matter these days."

"Oh, you'd be perfect at either of those," Delancey says. "You have such good taste. You know what I totally want to do? I want to be an influencer."

"Ew, what? No," Victoria says. "Definitely not. That's so tacky. Influencers are such a gross part of modern existence."

John makes an "ohhhhhh!" sound, and Blythe widens her eyes dramatically.

"Yikes, Vic," she says. "Honor's *right* there."

"Oh," Victoria says brightly, "I'm sure Honor agrees with me, don't you? Whoring yourself out for publicity so men with cameras follow you around and humiliate you all the time? It really screams some kind of personality issue. Just because her family does that doesn't mean she can't come up with something else to do. Actually, you know what I think would be perfect for you, Honor? You could be a secretary. You have that whole quiet, invisible thing going. I bet you'd be really great taking notes in some boardroom."

My face goes hot. I hate it here. Suddenly, fiercely, I miss Lilith, who would be not the least bit intimidated by Victoria and would have some perfect cutting remark for her. I want to cry, but I didn't spend my life being pawed at by strangers in supermarkets just to not learn any poise and crack in front of Victoria Finebaugh. Anyway, as much as we endlessly complain about our family, we've never been okay with outsiders insulting us.

"Well, maybe it's not as meaningful as a *poetry professor*," I say. "Clearly, working with kids would be the wrong job for you, since people who work with kids should be role models. Thanks for the feedback, though. It's always so fascinating to see how people respond when they're jealous."

There are still twenty-five minutes left of lunch, because lunch is interminable here, and I escape to the nature preserve behind campus and call Skye. She picks up right away.

"Oh my gosh, I could kill her!" she says when I tell her about lunch and what Victoria said. "Should I kill her? I'll fly out there right now. What a bitch!"

I miss Skye so completely; my body doesn't feel whole. Maybe it will, maybe I will, in Kauai when it's all of us again. "Yeah, do it. I'll livestream. You'll blow up."

"It's a pivot, but you know what, I'll tell my brands what she said, and they'll understand. I'll get amazing engagement."

"I think it's worth it. Ugh, Skye, I seriously don't know why Mom picked this place."

"She's probably trying to weirdly prove something to herself. Like moving back to where she grew up—it's probably her mom issues. I bet when she was young, some Saint Simeon kid was condescending to her or something. So now she can tell herself she made it, except then she miscalculated, because it's the wrong kind of rich. It's all old money there, right?"

"I have no idea."

"I'm sure that's why Victoria said all that to you. In that world if you have money, you buy discretion. They'll always look down on us. Honestly, it's a little like that here, too! My roommate's the same way."

"That sounds terrible."

"Oh, it's not too bad," she says, her voice turning sunny, the way it always does when she talks about Baylor. "I mean, it's just one or two people. Everyone's nice."

I'm skeptical. I have my doubts about the sorority scene in particular, even though she makes it look good. "Are they?"

"Yeah, everyone's just really chill and just nice. It's so easy to meet people."

"Have you met any guys?"

"No, no," she says quickly. "Just having fun. Okay, also, who's Caden? You keep bringing him up."

"He's a guy here." I tell her everything I know about him, which admittedly probably sounds less impressive without the sheen of having a raging crush on him.

"Honor, ew, no. I don't approve! If you're going to date someone, at least pick someone nice. I know Saint Simeon types. No Saint Simeon guy is nice. They always have really predatory vibes. Like, not like they'll date-rape you or anything, more like—they want to consume you. Just, like, use you as fulfilling a specific look or function in their lives or get whatever they want from you, and then, bam, it's on to the next thing. If you have to date a prep school guy, pick someone like Andrew. Andrew is harmless. Andrew . . . would be happy getting a few acres of land somewhere and just, like, driving a tractor around in circles every day. You know?"

"That's probably the only smart way to live. Just abandon society altogether."

"Plus I think he's proud of Jamie and he doesn't, like, hate that she's more successful than he is. And I definitely don't think he would ever leave her. So there's that."

A slice in my heart. "Have you talked much to Dad?"

"He calls me, like, every day. And like—he wants to, like, argue his case and I think for me to be like, *Yeah, Dad, I totally get it, Mom's the worst, good thing you left.* Like he's telling me how he never wanted any of this and it was so much better when she was still just trying to make it happen and it changed who she was, and now she's the one who controls the narrative and no one knows who he really is, his true self, even *he* doesn't know who he is because he let her define his story, blah, blah, blah. It's, like, a midlife crisis or something. But then I have to be like, *Wow, Dad, totally.* Like, every single day."

"Ugh, I'm sorry. I should try to talk to him more so it's not all on you."

"No, it's fine," she says. "I'm just complaining too much. Anyway, most boys aren't like Andrew, especially Saint Simeon boys. It's not even that they're ambitious, they just have to believe they're ambitious. So they would never let themselves be shown up that way. None of them are ever going to respect you for wanting to build something or work hard. That's not in their DNA."

"I kind of think Caden is different, though. You know how you can tell when a guy thinks you're dumb? It's the opposite with him."

"No boy at Saint Simeon is ever going to go out with you because they think you're interesting."

"I don't know, uniforms aside, this isn't 1950."

"Right. So they hide it better."

"Oh my God," I say, laughing. "You are—what's that word? You're such a misandrist." For good reason, I guess. Skye hasn't dated since Preston Campbell stomped all over her heart.

"There's no limit to my misandry when it comes to you! If it were one of my friends from high school, I'd be like, *Sure, whatever, have fun.* I just don't think any of them are good enough for you."

Maybe she's right, and what I'm interpreting as him caring what I say is actually just him imagining me naked. Which, I mean, I'll take it. "I'm just—" Unexpectedly, I feel my eyes prick with tears. "I'm never going to find friends again. Or people to talk to, or who care about me. It's like everyone wants to know everything about us, but no one actually wants to really know me."

"Honor!" Skye says. "Oh my gosh, don't cry. That's all such bullshit! You are amazing! People just have to get to know you. I hate that they're making you feel this way. But seriously, just get through the next week, okay? Then we'll all be in Kauai and everything will be perfect."

The year we went to Barcelona, when Atticus and I turned thirteen, our family was in shambles. Everything had blown up with *Lo and Behold* after what had happened on tour, and everyone was angry at each other still, our parents still adrift. The house felt empty and quiet without the crew there all the time. Skye and Atticus and I wanted to have a goodbye party for the crew, but instead they just never came back, although a few people messaged us to say goodbye. We barely saw Wrangell, and there were always pictures of him at clubs or with random girls, sometimes ones I'd heard of and sometimes not, oftentimes looking completely wasted. And there were stories: He was drinking himself unconscious practically every night. He got into a fight with Preston Campbell's older brother Evan. He was ticketed for going nearly 60 in a 25 mph zone. He was doing cocaine in club bathrooms. I missed him terribly and I worried about him all the time. Jamison, meanwhile, had moved to San Diego, and even though she'd promised it was temporary, I knew in my heart she wasn't coming back.

But then we had Barcelona. Wrangell came, even though we'd all thought there was no way he'd agree to spend a week with us. At night when it was warm still, bustling, we'd all walk together down La Rambla, stopping to buy baguettes or fruit or jamón, or we'd make our way to the beach and walk along the shore, and the city worked at us, dissolved the gaps between us and made us whole again. The city was inspiring to our parents and got them talking about their next act, all the ways they were going to pivot. Wrangell and our parents stopped fighting; before the trip was over, he'd promised to come home more, to answer the phone when I called him, and to take better care of himself. I know people say you can't leave your problems behind, but I don't think that's actually true. Or maybe it's just that you can lay them against a new backdrop and find they shrink or disappear.

These trips are sacred to me; they are our origin stories and the things we build our lives around. So I need this one to be healing, to be redemptive. I want it to bring us back together.

I have seen enough of boys bopping around after a volleyball in an echoing gym to last several lifetimes, but after school I go watch the girls' volleyball game at school because Atticus has practice and our mom is gone and it sounds better than being alone in the house, and also because as we were leaving sixth period, Delancey told everyone they'd better come, and Caden turned to me and said, "You think you'll go?" (I hadn't planned to, but I said yes.) I've been trying to set up my clay to work on the order for Hanna, which I'm supposed to finish five weeks after we get back from Kauai, but nothing is coming out quite right, and in the new house I hate being by myself in a way I never did before. I'll bring homework to do in the stands. At

Rearden we always did that (minus Atticus, because he often didn't do homework)—whatever was going on that day, a game or a play or a band performance, we'd all multitask and study there.

The gym is about half-full, with a lot of moms in school colors on both sides. The cheer team is here, which is new to me. Inside the gym, Caden's in the stands, watching with a couple of other lacrosse-ish guys, and I make my way up to him. I see his eyes travel up and down my length. I'm wearing a short skirt and a midriff top—my skin can breathe again, finally, after all day in the heavy plaid of the uniform—and I don't think I'm imagining it that his gaze lingers on me, long enough to make a point.

"Hey," he says, scooting over to make room next to him on the bleachers. "Have a seat."

"You play any volleyball, Lo?" John says.

"No. But I watch a ton."

He smirks. "You like to watch?" There is some innuendo here I didn't know to avoid. This is how it always is with them—you have to have sharp edges, to be on guard. Sometimes I wonder if making friends would come naturally if I'd been born into a different family, if it felt easier to trust people. Or maybe it's just that people here are the worst. Victoria isn't here, thankfully, even though Delancey's on the team. John teases me for a while about our cat fight, a term I despise, until finally he gets bored and goes back to staring at the volleyball girls. The whole time Caden doesn't say anything, but I am hyperaware of his presence next to me. Am I imagining it that he feels that too? The way he moved over to make room for me— maybe I'm reading too much into it. I try to work on my homework. It's distracting having him right there.

Caden takes a while coming down from the bleachers when the

game is over, and when the other boys have mostly filed down, he says, "You doing anything after?"

"No."

"You feel like going for a drive? I was thinking about driving up to the reservoir."

What do people here go to the reservoir for? I try not to let anything show on my face. "Sure." I message Atticus that I might not be back for dinner.

Where you going?

Hanging out with Caden.

He texts back the queasy-face emoji, and I text back the middle finger, then put my phone away before I tell Skye, too—she won't be excited either. But I am.

He's a more careful driver than I would expect, and he drives just under the speed limit the whole way, slowing on the blind curves. Maybe for him this is routine—maybe he brings girls up here all the time. But I'm nervous, full of adrenaline. I don't quite know how to act. I think this is the first time in my life I've ever had a crush on someone I haven't known since I was nine years old. It occurs to me it could be incredibly naive to have come up here with him. Maybe I've just silenced any alarm bells in my head.

Caden pulls off the road onto the dirt shoulder, and I vaguely recognize where we are. We're overlooking the reservoir, which is low this year. Wrangell dragged us here a couple of times to hike when we were visiting our grandparents. When we were younger, it used to be full—you can see lines where the water used to come. Back then we weren't in a constant state of drought. Where we are now, up in the hills, you can see into the mountains, where the burn marks are from fire season.

"You come up here much?" I say.

"A good amount."

"In a normal, hiking way or a hookup way?"

He smiles, a tiny little smile of amusement. "What is this, an interview?"

"It could be."

"Someday you'll make a really awesome secretary." He says it with a straight face, but when I look at him, he breaks into a grin. I say, "Shut up."

He laughs. "Victoria's a dick."

"You don't like her?"

"We're pretty close, but yeah, she's definitely a dick."

"That apparently doesn't stop people from hanging out with her."

"Yeah, she and Blythe and Delancey kind of rein each other in," he says. "She's not a bad person, she just needs people to prove themselves to her. Heard you held your own, though."

"Yes, well, I've heard so much worse."

"Yeah? At your hippie school?"

"Oh, I didn't mean from school. People just always say crap to my family."

"Ah," he says, and the lightness in his tone makes me think I misread him just now—he wasn't actually asking, he was referencing an inside joke. Or not an inside joke, but I guess as close as we have to one.

"Actually, the school could be kind of vicious, though," I say. "Saint Simeon is nothing in comparison. Easy mode."

He laughs. "Well, sounds like you pretty effectively handled Victoria, so I believe it."

"So what about you?" I say. "Are you Catholic?"

"I don't think so. I don't know if I believe in anything."

"You're agnostic?" I say, and then have a brief moment of fear that he won't know what agnostic means, and then I'll be embarrassed for both of us and all of this will be over; I will have pinned so many desires and hopes on someone who devotes all his extra brain space to video games or sports or making out.

"Kind of, maybe. I read this one article in the *New Yorker* a couple years back—I can still see the cover of the magazine, that's how much it fucked me up—about how some physicists put the odds that this world is the base reality at fifty-fifty at best, and it's way more likely we're just some computer simulation. Our consciousness was the invention of some teenage alien kid living in his twelve-D universe for his homework."

"Well, that's unsettling."

"Sometimes I still find myself—" He points at me, grinning. "Okay, you can't tell anyone this, I'm trusting you here—getting so defensive over shit I care about. Like if I'm pissed or upset about something one day, I'll be arguing in my head with some dispassionate alien being who thinks none of this is real. Or I'll be doing, I don't know, normal human things like brushing my teeth or eating a burrito or, you know, tending to my broken heart or existential angst, and I can't shake the feeling someone's just watching me on some cosmic computer screen, laughing at all these stupid antcolony rituals and civilizations we've created for ourselves. But then maybe that's the wrong approach. Maybe if this is all just some advanced simulation, we don't have to really care about anything." He pauses. "My mom's Mormon."

I don't know why this surprises me. "Really?"

"Yeah. Our ancestors were pioneers."

"Is your dad Mormon too?"

"Nah, my dad's just an asshole. That's all there is to him."

"The aliens didn't put enough effort into programming him?"

He laughs, a surprised kind of laugh. "Yeah, they forgot the part where you're supposed to give a shit about other people. Factory defect."

"That's unfortunate."

"It is unfortunate. Maybe it gives them something to entertain themselves. Watch the miserable human simulations fuck each other up emotionally. I don't see him much, at least. They're divorced." He rolls his window down a few inches. "You think about this kind of thing a lot?"

"Sometimes. Our parents—our dad especially—have always been really into it. When we were little, they were in an evangelical phase, but by the time we were nine or ten, they were big into their deconstruction phase. We'd be at dinner, grumpy from the day or whatever, everyone just trying to eat, and our dad would be like, 'So . . . Derrida.'"

"You miss him?"

"Derrida? Not especially."

I regret the joke immediately. Probably Caden has no idea who that is. But he jabs me in a friendly way, making the car seem smaller somehow. "You know what I mean."

"Honestly, I'm kind of mad at him."

I regret that instantly too—it's not the kind of thing I ever say to people, not like me to open up like that. Caden says, "Those aren't mutually exclusive."

Unexpectedly, my eyes fill. I don't know why Caden is the first person in my life to put it that way for me. "I guess they aren't."

"Yeah, I feel you. It's the same for me. Speaking of factory defects. So much easier if you just hate someone, right?"

"It was a big oversight on the part of our alien overlords."

"I should not have told you about that."

I laugh. "Yeah, probably not."

He gives me a long, appraising look, a look that collapses all the space between us. I am hyperaware of each breath I'm taking, because it seems explosively loud in the quiet. Then Caden says, "I'm into you."

I try not to look as surprised as I feel. "Oh?"

"You can do with that what you will. Just putting it out there because I always think it's most respectful to be honest."

I feel flushed, my heart beating a little faster. "Well, if we're being honest, I think I might also be into you."

He grins. "You think, huh? Jury's still out? Fair enough."

"I don't know why I'm hedging. Yes. I'm into you also."

"Well, that's pretty convenient for both of us."

"I'm not looking for, like, a relationship," I say. "Just to be clear. I've never had a boyfriend. I'm not interested in anything super serious."

"So you're into friends with benefits."

"You make it sound so crass."

He laughs. "What would you call it, then?"

"I would say that—in the history of the universe and the future of the universe there are so many billions of people, and the fact that you encounter any single person in a lifetime feels kind of against all odds, so you might as well make the most of it."

"Yeah, okay, that sounds better."

I can feel the moment tilting away from whatever other things we might've said to one another and into something else altogether, but I think maybe, if I wanted, I could still nudge it back. Some reckless part of me wants that. Maybe he's someone I could show myself to, someone I could know and be known by.

But no, I just told him that's not what I'm here for, and it's not. There are easier, safer ways to have a part of someone.

"Anyway," I say, moving closer to him, "we can stop talking now."

After, both of us back in our own seats, I rake my hands through my hair. Caden turns on the car and looks over his shoulder before pulling back onto the road.

"Are you going to tell people about this?" I say.

He looks amused. "Are you afraid I will? No, I wasn't planning to. Why, were you?"

"Like who, Victoria? When we're hanging out being besties? No, I don't talk to anyone at school anyway."

"You tell your brother stuff like this?"

I hesitate a second too long. Caden says, "No, it's fine. I think it's cool to have a twin. I always wished I had real siblings." He slows down around the curve. "Why don't you talk to anyone at school?"

I feel lighter physically, and thrumming with energy still, and it makes the thought of keeping up my charade exhausting. "I don't fit in with your friends. Atticus does, but not me."

"What's your kind of person?"

"Well, historically I've definitely been more into, like, school than parties."

He shrugs. "Why not both? I mean, people can surprise you. You talk about Derrida to Blythe, for instance? She did a whole research project on semiotics last year. She probably has lots of thoughts about him."

So I was wrong, then, to assume earlier that Caden had no idea who Derrida was. But hearing him say that about Blythe—how is that possible when she didn't even know the kind of laws she'd want to enact someday as a politician? I know the answer as soon as I think it, though—why does any girl play down the things she knows or the ambitions she has, especially in front of boys?—but I can't quite locate now why it feels like something stabbing in my chest. Is it because I was wrong? Is it some weird attachment to the idea of our family being unique and special, when really our dad was just spouting high-school-level philosophical material?

"No, I haven't talked very much to Blythe."

"I can see where maybe people come off intimidating, but they're not that bad once you get to know them. You just can't get all wrapped up in caring what people think." He takes his eyes off the road for a moment to glance at me. "Not like I'm trying to tell you how to live your life in general, I mean specifically at Saint Simeon. Like, Victoria thinks it would make her life for you to be a secretary? Fine, cool, whatever. Don't get invested. Who cares. Everyone gets so wrapped up in all the drama. Who said what about who or who secretly thinks what about who."

"That's definitely the vibe I've gotten. Why is that?"

"Eh, it's a small school. And everyone's probably just too stressed out."

"Stressed out about what?"

He gives me a weird look, like the answer should be obvious to me. "Mostly college, probably."

Something crystallizes for me then. This is what bothered me,

I think: being thoughtful and knowledgeable, caring about things like what someone believes about the world, felt like the thing about me that I could give him that was unique to me, who I am because of my family. Who cares if I'm not beautiful or poised or powerful like everyone else here, because isn't what I am better? Only it turns out those things aren't mutually exclusive after all, that someone like Blythe or Victoria is probably better than I am at those things too, and I was lying to myself to feel better. And I am not selflessly delighted to learn about their good qualities—I'm irritated they're encroaching on what I tried to mark off as mine.

We're mostly quiet the rest of the way home. I keep waiting for him to say more, and I'm both disappointed and relieved when he doesn't, because I feel a greediness about him, some wanting that feels dangerous to me, dangerous because it's not like I plan to let him peek in all the crevices of my life. But I recognize the way he talked to me, saying things that sounded intimate and vulnerable but weren't, actually, at all. My family excels at that art. I know it when I see it. So maybe for him it was done as soon as we were pressed against each other, and that was all he wanted from me. Maybe that's all I'm supposed to want too.

I play around with fillings for my clay dim sum in Atticus's room that night while he ignores his homework, like usual, and instead does his elaborate routines with the weights he keeps on his bookshelf. There's a gym above the garage, but he doesn't like the way our mom has it set up, and anyway, since we moved, he's kind of been holing up in here when he's home at all. I've made a handful of items I could, in theory, send Hanna, two sushi boats and a bamboo steamer of joong, but I keep second-guessing myself: Are these "high end"? Will people think they're worth the price? After I carefully crimp the pale yellow edges on some siu mai, I open my laptop to check the different alerts I have set up and the accounts on my rotation.

"Ew," Atticus says, watching. "Why do you do that to yourself?"

"Just to see what people are saying."

"What's that?" he says, reaching over to click. It's a headline from Jezebel: *Is Nathan Lo a Misogynist? Wrangell Lo Weighs In.*

Wrangell gave an interview to someone there, apparently, who asked what went wrong between our parents. "The thing about my dad," Wrangell told them, "is he's always wanted to be known as a thought leader. You know, someone whose dream was to be asked to give TED Talks or speak at the Aspen festival, that kind of thing. He wanted to be known as an intellectual, and frankly, I think maybe he resented that so much of his audience was made up of women. Personally, I think he wants to strike out on his own and shed all the marriage content."

"Everyone is so exhausting," Atticus says, closing my laptop harder than is strictly necessary. "Christ. I wish everyone would get a normal job and stop trying to one-up each other in the media."

"Do you think that's true about Dad?"

"I mean, do I think it's true that he wanted to talk about stuff that he thought made him sound smart more than he wanted to only ever talk about marriage and relationships? Yes. Does that make him a misogynist? Don't get me wrong, I think he's being a jerk, but I mean, what—is Wrangell saying women aren't interested in those things? But yeah, I mean, I bet he'd love if people just only asked his opinion on things like politics or race or whatever."

That's probably true. Our dad will go through phases where

he'll dive deeply into something and feel like he's an expert on it—global warming, political partisanship. He went through a long phase when he wanted to talk about race all the time, convinced that as a mixed-race person, he had an enhanced perspective on race relations in America. He would go on Instagram Live for long monologues he'd caption *What you don't know about being white in America* or *Race: beyond the black-and-white binary*. Our mother never joined him for those. "No, I despise talking about race," she said when he tried to get her to. "I've always hated it. What's there to say?" He made it a series, I remember, calling different people to come and dialogue with him.

"The five of you are all lucky you're the same as your parents," our mother told me once. "You didn't have to grow up in a sea of people forever trying to categorize you and rank you and dissect you." She pitched her voice an octave higher. "'Melissa has never looked Chinese to me at all!' 'Melissa's not like her sister, I just always think of her as white!'" I have seen the way she looks around a room, though, the mental calculations she does to try to place herself, and I recognize it because I always do the same. I have always wondered what it would be like to claim a space as fully your own. Atticus has never felt the same way, though; he's someone who's always immediately belonged wherever he goes.

"Maybe it wasn't specifically about women," I say, "but I agree he always has to be the smartest and most thoughtful and most philosophical person in the room."

"Yeah, I mean, that's a given. Man, Wrangell can get away with murder. I would get my ass kicked if I said something like this to a magazine."

"I miss Wrangell and Jamie and Skye so much," I say. I miss

Wrangell in particular tonight. The ways he's angry can feel so comforting. "He still won't answer me about Kauai. Do you think it means he isn't coming?"

"I don't know. He was pretty mad at Skye's graduation."

Something twists in my chest. "I just really, really need this week. I need us all to be together."

"Yeah, I know," Atticus says. "I think he'll probably come. You've always been his favorite. I really doubt he'd just bail."

Two a.m., still awake, realizing the true reason I was upset earlier hearing Caden talk about Blythe as if she was so thoughtful and smart: maybe I recognized something of our dad in myself then, in that urge to sabotage whatever might exist around you just to preserve what you want to believe about yourself.

wait to see if things will be different with Caden at school the next day, but they aren't. I don't know how to read that. Maybe he's doing what I wanted and not telling anyone, or maybe he regrets the time with me. I hope it's not that, because I would go back up to the reservoir with him literally right this second if he wanted.

For the next few days, though, there's no sign of anything from him. Skye says, you deserve better!!! he sounds like a garden variety jerk!! Then on Thursday, two days before we fly to Kauai, I'm leaving seventh period at the same time as Delancey, who has been friendlier to me than any other member of VBD and also probably anyone else at school. We are sort of walking together and sort of not—I'm not sure which, and so I don't know whether to start walking faster or fall back or anything—when Victoria and Caden appear. My heart clutches, the way it always does when Caden walks by. Victoria grabs Delancey's arm.

"What?" Delancey says. "What's happening?"

I know familiarity can code in your mind for beauty—it's part, though certainly not all, of why everyone thinks our mom and Skye and Jamison are so iconic—but the longer I'm around Victoria, the more I think she is in fact extremely pretty. She has hazel eyes and a small nose and a ton of freckles, and at first I wouldn't have said she was attractive, but her face is interesting to look at, and the more I see her, the more I can see why people would think she's hot. I spend a lot of time trying to pick apart why people's faces work the way they do, which parts mean what when taken as a whole. I mentioned this once, and Skye said, "Yeah, I think all mixed people do this, right?" and Atticus nearly choked on his water, he was laughing so hard. "No," he said, "no, zero percent, I promise you absolutely not. You think Dad does that? Wrangell? It's definitely just you guys."

"Come on, we're going to Caden's house," Victoria says. She wiggles her fingers at Delancey. "No parents!"

"Oooh, fun!" Delancey says, clapping. Then she adds, to me, "Honor, you should come."

I wait to see if Caden will say anything. He doesn't, although he turns toward me like a kind of silent question.

"Well, if you aren't doing anything," Victoria says, maybe a little flatly, "you can definitely join us."

I don't think she means it as a challenge, but I take it as one anyway. "Great!" I say brightly, matching Delancey's tone. "Sounds fun."

I ride in Delancey's car. She drives a dark teal Tesla, and she's not eighteen yet and thus technically can't legally drive me, but like with Caden the other day, no one here seems to care. (At Rearden we cared; we Ubered everywhere.) I worry we won't have anything to talk about, but then when we get into the car, she wants to spend the whole ride telling me how much she likes Skye and how she's bought, like, six things Skye posted about, and then she describes each one. What people don't know about being famous, or famous adjacent, is it's actually extremely boring. Just an endless loop of the same surface conversations over and over.

Delancey's nicer than I thought she was, though, when she's by herself. Maybe she'd be a better person if not for VBD, if not for Victoria specifically. I don't understand the friendship. Maybe they're just terrified of her. She's been grudgingly tolerant of me, at least, since the one day.

"I bet you could totally do influencing too if you wanted," Delancey says. "You have an in already with your sister."

She's not Team Victoria here, I guess. "It's not really my thing."

"Why not?"

"I'm not as charismatic as Skye is, for one, and I also just feel weird about it all sometimes. It just feels like unnecessary consumerism."

"Well, I'm not necessarily disagreeing," she says, "But companies invented the whole idea of your carbon footprint to distract you from the fact that you can stop using straws for the rest of your life and not make a dent in their fossil fuel consumption." She motions out the window. "Every time we drive up 9 or 17, I'm like, *Oh my God, are the redwoods still here? Have they fried yet?* So, is your brother into anyone? I think he's really cute."

"Atticus?" I say, amused. Maybe it's the whole reason they're letting me orbit around them. I imagine telling her that I made out with Caden—how confounding it would be. "Probably. I'm not sure."

"Oh, who? Do you guys talk about that stuff? It must be so fun to have a twin."

"We talk about most things."

"He's always so busy with volleyball! I'm always like, you should come out, and then it's like, oh, he has a tournament the entire weekend in, like, Fresno."

"Yeah, the schedule sucks."

"Is he good? I bet he's good."

"The tournaments are really fun. You should go watch," I lie, feeling only a tiny bit guilty. "He'd love it."

"Ooh, really? Maybe I will."

My conscience wins out. "No, I'm just kidding. They're so boring. Just a bunch of tall guys yelling in some old converted naval hangar in the middle of nowhere. Never go."

We snake through a thick grove of redwoods, and then there's a clearing with a long driveway. Caden's house is a surprise: an old Victorian mansion, not something I would've expected to see out here in the woods. When we get out of the car, I take a long breath. The air feels so clean up here. I feel most myself in the Bay Area mountains.

The sense of serenity disappears when we go up to the door. There's music playing, loudly, and a car shows up at the same time we do, boys I can still barely tell apart and who feel interchangeable to me—John Gohl, Luke Jensen, Carter Angelino, Atlas Nolan. I start to feel a creeping sense of unease. I shouldn't be here; this is not my scene.

Help, I message Skye as we all walk up the front path. I came to Caden's because his parents aren't here and a bunch of people showed up and I am so not in the mood for basically anything that might happen!!

😬, she writes back. Where's Atticus?

Practice.

Ugh. How'd you get there?

One of the girls drove me. It's like, out in the woods.

Well, be careful!!! she writes back. Don't do anything you'll regret!! get an uber if you need. or make Wrangell come get you. It's not that far.

Victoria opens the door for us. "Party at Caden's!" she says, and I can't tell if it's supposed to be ironic or not. I think about what everyone at Rearden is probably doing right now—how tame and familiar it probably is. Working on homecoming floats, maybe. It's that time of year. I'm tempted to send a group text saying I miss everyone. But I don't, because I doubt they're missing me. It isn't like they're texting me. We follow Victoria through the kitchen and into a living room area. The house is beautiful, with elaborate molding and staircases and built-in hutches. I'm tempted to take pictures to send to Wrangell, who would love this place.

Caden's in the living room, sitting on a slim-profile wood chair, his left ankle resting on his right knee. He has *Out of Our Past* out, the AP US History text, and he lifts a few fingers in a hello. In public he seems like a different person than the one I went to the reservoir with.

"Your house is beautiful," I say. "How old is it?"

"Ah—1850s, I think. Some logging baron built it. That's why all the redwoods here are new growth."

"We're talkin' about wood?" John says, sitting down on an antique velvet couch with carved legs. "Lyall's wood?"

"Honor has lots of questions about it," Victoria says, and then they all laugh, minus Caden. I feel my face go hot.

"Ignore them," he says. "They were all raised by wolves."

"Sensitive topic for him," Carter says, grinning. "Christ, Honor, you come into his house and talk to him like that."

"Oh my God, you guys, leave poor Honor alone," Delancey says, swatting Carter with a throw pillow. I can't decide what her motivation is—if it's to be condescending toward me or flirty with Carter, or if it's supposed to be nice and it's because she likes Atticus. I want to get up and go somewhere else, but it will look like falling apart, so I stay.

What happens next is genuinely unexpected, though: everyone pulls out homework or books, and for the next hour and a half everyone actually studies. Partway through Victoria gets up and rummages around in the pantry, then comes back with a box of crackers and a jar of fig jam, and Blythe and Carter talk for a while about the lab report they're both working on, but otherwise it feels like some kind of planned study session. I keep waiting for something to happen, someone to break out alcohol or cocaine or something, or even pot, but no one does. Then a little before six Victoria says, "Okay, I have to get home for dinner or my mom will lose her mind. Caden, what are you doing for dinner? Do you want to come over?"

"Nah, I'm good."

"My aunts and uncles and cousins are coming, so there will be a million people there already. What are you going to eat? I bet it's something dumb like frozen hot dogs. You should just come."

He laughs it off, then he turns to me. "You need a ride home?" he says more quietly. "I can take you."

"Oh—it's pretty far out of your way."

"Yeah, but it's a pain in the ass to try to get an Uber out here. I'll take you."

When I look up, Blythe is watching us. She gives me a small, clipped smile, one I can't read, and looks away.

. . .

I wonder if offering to drive me instead of me going with Delancey or someone is a veiled way of asking me to stay, but we walk outside to his car instead. Caden opens the passenger door for me and waits for me to get in before closing it behind me. Despite what Caden said earlier, the boys here all in fact do have good manners, in ways that don't count—they'll hold the door for you while leering at you behind your back.

I feel confused about the whole afternoon. There was something unspoken rippling through it all, something I couldn't read. When Caden gets in, after he asks where I live, I say, "Do you guys study together like that a lot?"

"Sometimes."

"And it's just studying?"

He turns the car on and twists around to back out of the driveway. "As opposed to what?"

"I don't know, when Victoria said everyone was coming over because your parents weren't home, I was expecting—something else."

He looks amused. "Like what, an orgy?"

"Definitely not a study session."

"Well, sorry to disappoint you. Everyone's freaking out about the quarter-terms, though."

It still felt like more than that to me. "So where are your parents?"

He pulls onto the road. "My dad's in New Zealand. Where he lives. My mom's in rehab."

He says it so casually I think at first that he's making a joke. When I look at him, he says dryly, "I thought I told you they're divorced."

"You did. But your mom—"

"Yeah, she's addicted to pain meds."

"So you're here by yourself? How long is rehab?"

He shrugs. "Kinda varies. Couple days, couple months. You kind of never know."

"You don't have siblings or anything?"

"No siblings."

He looks a little impatient, like he's waiting for me to get over myself. But I guess this is old news for him. I say, "Is that—I mean, is that awful? It sounds awful."

"Eh, you get used to most things. Day to day it's pretty whatever. Doesn't actually change that much, I guess."

"How long has your mom been gone this time?"

"She just left yesterday."

"She just left yesterday, and already everyone's like, wow, party at Caden's? That was fast."

He's quiet for a moment. We pass through the clearing we came through on our way in. Then he says, "Victoria worries about me. When it's not great with my mom, she always tries to get me to do stuff. Everyone here—you know how it is. We've all known each other a long time."

Something small breaks open for me, and I feel the world around me rearranging itself. I have the sense that I'm looking at the top of a glacier, the rest of it looming, invisible, underground. Maybe I will never find my footing here—maybe it's a world that needs translation because observation won't suffice. "That's kind," I say. Which it is, so I don't know why it also makes me feel a new surge of dislike for Victoria. Maybe it just feels unfair that you can be a hateful person in general but also matter, clearly, to someone like Caden. "I was wrong, then. I thought everyone just wanted to go over to drink or something."

"No, I don't drink or do any drugs. For obvious reasons. I don't like being around people when they are, either. Which everyone knows, so."

We're back on 17 now, heading down the hillside toward our house. "Do you want to come for dinner?" I say, silencing the part of myself warning me back to safer ground, where no one cares too much about anyone. "I usually just eat with Atticus. We'll probably just order something. Or—I don't actually need to go home. We could go do something if you want."

"Nah, I'm all right. Yesterday was kind of a mess, so I have a lot of work to catch up on."

"You're just going to go home to your empty house and do homework?" I say lightly, hiding my disappointment. "I see why Victoria worries about you."

He laughs. "Yeah, you guys are alike, apparently. Maybe you're destined to be friends."

Zero chance. "But seriously, you just want to be by yourself?"

"You probably know how it is," he says. "You have parents who've made their issues everyone's business. Sometimes you just don't want to deal with anyone else. You get tired."

I'm still thinking about that later that night, when Atticus and our mom aren't home yet and it's dark and quiet in the house. That's the fundamental thing about me, I think, that apparently isn't true of everyone: I never want to be alone.

Skye calls that night, when I'm hanging out with Atticus in his room, to see what happened at Caden's house. I can hear someone talking in the background, a guy, and I say, "Where are you? Who's that?"

"Oh, I'm just in the common lounge. My roommate has some-one over." (I wish I could picture it—have some concrete sense of her life there, the people in it. Even the way she says "my room-mate," like the name wouldn't mean anything to me, feels so dis-tant.) "Okay, so what happened at Caden's?"

I tell her. She repeats skeptically, "He said he's into you but then just wanted to be alone?"

"Yes."

"Boooooooooooooooooooooo," Skye says loudly, and Atticus looks up from his weights to say, "Yeah, he's not into you. It's just a thing guys say."

"He probably had a shitty day. Week. Maybe he really did want to be alone."

"Yeah, it means he doesn't view you as someone he wants to, like, talk to," Atticus says. "He's just not that kind of person."

"I just think it's really clear what he wants you for," Skye says. "Either sex or visibility, and I vote no. Find someone better. Or just no one. He really sounds like the kind of guy who just uses you."

Does it matter, though? That all you really want is something physical is not the kind of thing you say to your siblings, obviously, but all the same, I'm surprised they'd think what I want is, what, some kind of fantasy relationship with a boy who wants to see inside me and know me on some deep level? Some kind of deal where you can see and hold each other's worst parts but still love and trust each other anyway? Caden's angry and lonely, probably, and so am I, which is plenty to have in common when there isn't much else. Probably they're right and this isn't anything to him, but it doesn't have to be anything to me, either. And anyway, I don't think it's the worst thing to be used. To be useful, to have a purpose—maybe those things aren't really so distinct.

I'm walking to my car after school the next day, Friday, when Blythe flags me down in the parking lot.

"Hey," she says, raising her voice a little, "I wanted to talk to you."

I put my backpack in the back seat and close the door, and in the time it takes me to do that, she's made her way to the car and is just a few feet away from me. "What's up?"

Blythe studies my car for a moment, her gaze raking over the backpack and jacket and water bottles scattered across the back seat. I feel involuntarily defensive. I drove myself today, uncharacteristically, because Atticus had to go straight to volleyball. Blythe says, "I've heard some rumors about you and Caden."

I raise my eyebrows. "Oh?"

"Are they real?"

"That depends on what the rumors are."

She smiles, surveying me a little more closely. "I'll be honest, I didn't really think you were his type. I was just . . . surprised."

I'm unclear what the purpose of this conversation is. Is she into him? Is this some kind of veiled warning? I say, "All right."

"I'm curious, though," she says. "What you see in him. There are plenty of hot guys around if that's all you need. Because he's like . . . not really a nice person. His life is just kind of fucked up. In case you think underneath it all he's just, like, stable and normal and sensitive and caring. That's just not him."

I keep my expression neutral. "Why are you telling me this?"

Her expression opens up just slightly, something falling away.

"I don't know, actually. I guess because I was into him for a long time and I felt like, you know, I'm going to change him, I'm going to bring out all the good in him, and then eventually I just realized— no, I'm not." She laughs in a humorless way. "I just, like, was pretty messed up for a while over him."

"Did he like—did he do anything to you?"

"No, no, nothing like that. I just think where normal people are, like, able to connect and care about other people, with him it's like this black hole." She looks through my car again—I wish I'd cleaned it—and then leans against it, folding her arms over her chest. "Is this just like a hookup for you, or are you actually into him?"

"Honestly—" I hesitate. "There's something in him that makes sense to me. The things you're saying about him, maybe all that's kind of true of me, too."

"Wow," she says. "Well, that's kind of interesting. I hope it ends up being good for you, then. Maybe I was just the wrong person for him."

"That probably just means you're a good person."

She laughs. "You don't think you're a good person?"

"We can't all be."

"Maybe Caden likes that about you."

"I'm not sure how much he likes about me."

She hoists herself off my car, her hair falling gracefully into place. "Well, don't take that personally. He's just like that. Anyway, who knows. Victoria didn't want me to, but I just thought I should warn you."

CHAPTER EIGHT

Saturday morning, the day we're leaving, Wrangell messages to confirm he's coming after all, and the part of me that was waiting for everything to fall apart finally relaxes. We'll figure things out when we're all together; we always do.

On the ride there, though, as the hills and redwoods give way to overpasses and cities, I have the fleeting, irrational thought that maybe Atticus was right and we should've postponed. Not because it'll be weird to see everyone, but because it still feels bizarre and lucky and fragile that Caden's interested in me at all, and I'm not confident that interest will survive me disappearing from his physical sphere.

Probably Blythe wanted things from him that I don't. I keep thinking about what she said to me. I can see what it is about him that makes you wish you could keep talking forever, just going deeper and deeper until you've told each other things you've never told anyone else. I think it's his mildness: it tricks you into thinking that when you tell him something, he's holding that for you.

I spend most of the ride thinking about messaging him. But I'll be gone a week; it's not like I have anything to offer him right now. You don't invite someone up to the reservoir because you fantasize about asking her how she's doing while she's on a family trip.

Our mom disappears into one of the private rooms while Atticus and I wait in the lounge. I think the book tour was the last time we went through normal terminals to fly, and in a weird way I miss it. Atticus always disliked the private rooms, how hermetically sealed they feel; he'd rather be in the lounges, talking to people, but we never see anyone interesting. The prince of Monaco once, and once an Apple exec. There's sushi and panini and a spread of desserts, but I'm too anxious to eat. I take an Ativan, which never works beyond making my terror feel like a groggier, otherworldlier version of itself. I think about Caden's mother, how I can understand needing a way to soften the edges of the world sometimes. Probably most people just hide it better.

As the driver takes us to the plane to board, I feel my throat constrict. I used to bombard Lilith with messages every time I had to fly anywhere. She'd tell me to breathe and send me a bunch of reassuring information about the sounds I was hearing (that's just the wings coming up, totally normal!) and joke around to try to distract me. Lilith always wanted to be a therapist. For a second I contemplate messaging her now, telling her I'm on a plane. A part of me thinks she would go for it, would just pick up where we left off. But I imagine her taking careful note of everything I'm saying to sell it off later, and I don't message her.

Instead—to his delight—I clutch Atticus the whole flight, panicking at every hint of turbulence, unable to relax enough to read or watch anything. I keep an obsessive eye on the flight attendants, watching hawklike, probably socially inappropriately, for any signs of alarm. The flight stretches on interminably, terrifyingly into the future. Five hours is unforgivingly long.

I'm exhausted and drenched in sweat by the time we descend,

but flooded with relief when the wheels touch down. I sit up straight and release Atticus from my death grip.

"Thanks for coming," I say. "It means a lot to me. I know you weren't thrilled about it. I think when we're there, it'll be good."

"Yeah, no worries. I know you've been working really hard on planning." He glances at me. "I just don't want it to not live up to your expectations and then it ruins everything for you. Like, I feel like maybe it's going to be pretty awkward and—"

"No, I don't think it'll be awkward."

He ignores me. "And I just don't think you need to think of it as, like, the last time we're all going to go on a trip as a family or something. Just—no pressure."

We pick up a rental car—our parents dislike having drivers on vacation—and as we follow the road, it hugs the curve of the island, the shoreline to the east, bright wooden shops and flat pastures giving way to jungly blue-green mountains to the west. Chickens strut across red patches of dirt. The house is in a gated community, and Atticus punches in the code, and then we pull through and drive down a side street lined with palm trees and plumerias. Our house is near the end of a cul-de-sac, a black contemporary hovering near the edge of a cliff.

When we open the front door, we're in a courtyard with a mossy living plant wall and a fountain coursing over a cement planter. The great room, overlooking the ocean, has a wall of glass that pushes open. I spent hours combing through listings to choose this place.

"Oooh, Honor, nice find," our mom says approvingly. "This will be perfect. It's not Bora-Bora, but I don't think I've ever needed a vacation so badly in my life."

I spent a long time agonizing over the number of bedrooms, texting Skye to debate. Should our parents share? Not share? Skye pointed out they'd just make us share instead, which I'd be fine with, so for a while I looked for places with good main suites and cramped, small extra bedrooms, but eventually I gave up when Skye said it could backfire and maybe our dad would just get a hotel.

Everyone will start arriving in an hour or so, and Atticus and I go wander around the grounds while we're waiting. The property is filled with fruit trees: mango and banana and papaya, passion fruit vines climbing the walls, and nestled among all the greenery are small fountains and sculptures. A path in the backyard winds down the cliffside and then ends in a flight of wooden stairs going down to the beach. A green-blue stretch of shoreline opens up in front of us, framed by the mountains, jagged and lush and otherworldly. No one else is around.

"Do you think she'll be different?" I say, poking at the sand with my bare toes. It's soft and almost silky to the touch.

"Who, Skye? Nah."

"No? Jamison and Wrangell are both so different now that they're out of the house."

"You think so?" he says, watching a plane go over us. From the time we were little, Atticus has always loved planes. Before he started playing volleyball, he used to want to be a pilot. Proof of nature over nurture, I suppose. "I don't know if they're actually different. I think we just aren't as close anymore because they're gone."

It's a twinge of pain to hear him say that, in the way it always is to hear someone else put words to one of your fears. Despite every-thing, I miss the *Lo and Behold* days, when all of us were together at home. There's really no joy in going from a family of seven to a family of three. At least we have Sonnet now.

"Do you think it's going to go well this week?" I say.

"I guess that depends. Like, what's your metric for success? Literally Dad moving back in?"

"My metric for success is seeing sea turtles. If I get to show Sonnet a sea turtle, I think I'll die happy." I love turtles; turtles are perfection. "No, I think we just all need to actually talk."

"Ah yes, I got your message."

"Did you? Because everyone ignored it." I'd sent a few messages in our whole-family group chat, which had been silent ever since Skye's graduation, with various trip details, and in one message I'd said that it would be a good time for all of us to talk and try to work through some of our patterns and issues. No one responded. "Like, we have these whole cycles where Wrangell just ghosts when he doesn't want to deal with things, and Jamison just disappears into her own life, and now Dad also—and I mean, you still won't even pick up Dad's calls, and you're always low-key annoyed with Mom, and Mom won't talk to Dad or to any of us about how she's actually feeling. I think it would be good to just get everything out in the open and figure things out. I think if we can, probably Dad will get over himself and just move back. He has to have gotten it out of his system by now."

He raises his eyebrows at the ocean. "Mm."

"You don't agree? Isn't this, like, exactly what your psych books are about? Finding ways to have hard conversations and break old patterns and connect? I thought you'd be all over this."

"Did you?" he says dryly. "Because when you said Kauai, I was thinking, okay, cool, I'll lie on the beach, I'll swim, I'll play with Sonnet—"

118 • KELLY LOY GILBERT

"We don't have to talk about things the whole time, obviously."

"Just, what? Fifty percent? Eighty percent?"

"Yeah, shut up."

"I really don't know if it's that simple. I mean—you think all this can be fixed in a week?"

"How much is there to fix? He can just move back in, and that's most of it right there."

"I don't know," he says, "I mean, we're kind of hurt, right? And you have to imagine it's magnified for Mom. Like, at least he's called us and been like, yeah, this isn't about you, but then with her it's like, yup, this is totally about you."

"I mean, sure, we're hurt, but we can get over it. People get over much worse."

He smiles. "You are really such an optimist. How exactly are you planning on making these talks happen? Do I want to know?"

"Well, you know Dad. He always wants to talk. So then I've just scheduled a couple of times when I think it would be good. Like, not when we're at the beach or whatever, but maybe when we get takeout and we're all at home anyway, or after dinner after Sonnet's asleep. And I've been looking up different prompts and discussion guidelines. Just ways to get people talking and thinking." I pause. "And you saw the house, right? That room upstairs with all the couches—I was thinking that would be the perfect place. We can pile everyone in there and just go for it."

"Do you ever get sick of micromanaging?" he says, grinning.

"Never."

"You know, it's too bad our ancestors got Christianized, because I bet, actually, Buddhism would've been good for you. Just—acceptance. Take what comes."

"My God, you read one book on Buddhism, and suddenly you're an expert on—"

He tosses a handful of sand at me. "I bet Skye's almost here. Let's go see."

Skye is there when we get back up to the house, and so are Jamison and Sonnet and Andrew and Wrangell, and—surprise!—Wrangell's girlfriend.

"This is Julie," Wrangell tells us, all of us congregated outside to greet them, a little (maybe unjustifiably, considering) shell-shocked. "We've been going out awhile now."

"What?" I say, remembering too late to smile.

Julie is full Asian and has a thin, athletic-seeming build and long hair, and natural-looking makeup, the kind of look boys always think means you aren't wearing any at all. She's dressed in a floral halter dress and sandals. I should've realized he'd bring someone. His bar for bringing a girlfriend to family things has always been shockingly low: girls he's been dating for less than a month will be there for Christmas or Chinese New Year, will expect a seat at Mother's Day brunch. I've always wondered about the girls themselves, if they assume they're welcome or if they think it's some way to plant roots in his life. It never works.

"Honor!" she says. "Wow, it's so great to meet you." She steps forward to hug me. I hate nonfamily hugs. Probably everyone who's ever interacted with fans does.

"I had no idea you were coming!" I say, hugging her limply in return. "None of us did!"

"Oh, really?" She looks at Wrangell. "I hope it's not a problem."

I smile. "Of course, it's a little too late to pack you up and ship you back out, so . . ."

"Well, if you do, bill Wrangell. He told me it was fine."

Skye laughs in surprise. "Wrangell, do you finally have a girl-friend who won't put up with you? I like this girl."

"Then don't scare her away," he says. "Be nice." He points at me. "Especially you, Honor. Watch out for this one, Julie. She runs the family."

It's not the way he usually talks, which makes it feel like he's showing off for her, which makes me simultaneously like her less and him more. It's endearing, sort of, that he cares. He always cares about the girls, is always sweet and solicitous and devoted, until suddenly he isn't. Sometimes after he dumps them, they try to talk to us, usually to Skye. *What did I do? Is he going to get back together with me? Can you talk to him for me?*

"It's so great to meet you," Jamison says warmly. "I've heard so many great things about you."

"Thank you!" Julie says. "It's great to meet in person. I feel like I know you all already."

I feel my smile go thin. It's my least favorite thing people always say to us.

"Ugh, we're going to have to be nice to her all week," I say to Skye and Atticus when we've gone back upstairs. "Or not? Maybe? Because we're always nice, and then he always breaks up with her, like, a week later."

Skye laughs. "Touché."

"Except actually we're not always nice," Atticus says.

"Probably part of why Wrangell's like, *Ugh, my family.*" Skye gives me a hug, then Atticus. "Okay, but it's *so* good to see you! I've missed you so much."

"I know! Please never leave again." I am relieved she feels the same, that it feels the same with her. I didn't need to worry—it's Skye. "I just seriously can't believe Wrangell. I have everything all planned out, too, and now there's this extra person." We're going to ride helicopters over the mountains (which will probably be terrifying, but at least beautiful). We'll lie on the beach and swim and build sandcastles with Sonnet. We'll snorkel and go on a yacht tour and eat poke and garlic shrimp. I certainly didn't picture a plus-one at any of those things. "Do you think he brought her to sabotage the week? How much can we really all talk if we're just trying to include her? It's like he needs some kind of buffer just to be around us."

"I don't know," Skye says. "The part that was interesting was it sounds like he's told Jamison about her. I don't think he usually does. Maybe it's different this time?"

"I really doubt that. Wrangell always says that."

"He so does. Well, maybe with her it'll be less weird when Dad gets in."

"You think it'll be weird?" I say.

"Maybe."

"Have you still been talking to him a lot?" Atticus asks.

"Yeah," Skye says. "Like, almost every day."

"Does he sound like he's closer to coming back?"

She's quiet for a moment. "I think the thing about Dad is he's literally *so* sensitive. I think he's probably in his feelings about Mom being so much busier lately. Did you know she has higher speaker fees than he does now?"

"You think he's leaving her because she has higher speaker fees?" I say. "That sounds nuts."

"No, I wonder if it's more like——" Skye hesitates. "I think their dynamic has always been, like, he feels like she needs him, and maybe lately he just feels like she doesn't as much anymore. Which, honestly, maybe she doesn't. She really has been so busy. Her book is doing so well. I think he's super insecure, like he needs all these weird external markers to tell him he's doing okay. He's always been like that. Just so defensive about all the things he's not or all the different paths he could've taken. I think it's his weird mixed-race trauma."

"What does that have to do with anything?" Atticus says. "All of us are mixed."

"Don't you feel that sometimes?" she says. "Just the, like . . . rootlessness. Not having, like, your people. Or just always feeling less than."

"Why would you feel less than?"

"Like how whenever you're with white or Asian people, which is, like, almost everyone we know, by definition you're half of what they are."

Atticus makes a face. "I think metrics have broken your brain."

"Cool," Skye says, "thanks."

"I mean, maybe he just wants to know she still wants to be with him," I say. "That seems like such an easy fix. I think if they would just *talk* instead of him bailing, this could be solved in, like, eight seconds. I swear sometimes they have the emotional maturity of a pair of fruit flies. But they think they're so evolved!"

"I guess compared to their parents they probably are," Atticus says. "They are, like, exponentially better adjusted."

Skye laughs again. "Low bar."

I am so happy to have her back with us. The way we've slipped right into our easy closeness gives me hope it'll still be a good week—all of us together, even with Julie here, even with our parents' situation. When we go downstairs, everyone's in the kitchen, hungry.

"When's Dad supposed to get in?" Jamison asks our mom.

Our mom raises her eyebrows at the window. "I haven't heard from him."

"Not at all?" Jamison says. "You aren't talking? Sonnet, no." She lunges to stop Sonnet from toppling off one of the stools, and our mom watches her, then turns away without answering the question.

There's cut fruit in one of the refrigerators, a platter of mango, lychee, pineapple, passion fruit, and dragon fruit, and we take it into the living room while we wait for our dad to come. Wrangell reenacts his inner monologue before asking Julie for her number, using Sonnet as a prop, and everyone's laughing. Except our mom, who's barely listening, doing something on her phone. But I try to relax. Maybe I'm imagining it that the mood is strange, or maybe it's just Julie. Things are good, right? We're all here; we have all week. The glass wall is pushed open, the trade winds coming in, and there are dramatic clouds hovering over the water with streams of light pouring through. Maybe it's kind of basic to go to Hawaii for a family trip, but really, it's gorgeous here. The lighting inside is perfect. Everyone looks beautiful.

"So you're giving him a chance, huh?" Atticus says to Julie, smiling. "Trial run?"

"Honestly, I was worried! I knew who he was, and I am just so not someone who's into the whole social media scene, like at all. I don't even have a profile."

Our dad pulls into the driveway, gets out of the car. I see him through the floor-to-ceiling glass, checking his phone, checking his watch, patting his pockets, and I wonder if he's procrastinating coming inside. I will be kind, I tell myself; I will be welcoming and gracious and not angry, because that won't solve anything. I can't read our mother's expression, and her face doesn't change when the door opens and he calls cheerfully, "Hel-Los!" his signature greeting.

So all right, he's going to act like everything's the same. I wondered if he would act weird around us, if he'd seem guilty or distant, but in retrospect, I should have figured he wouldn't.

He's holding a giant, wild-looking bouquet of plumerias, which he hands to our mom. She takes them gingerly.

"Ah," she says. "Okay."

He leans over to kiss her on the cheek. She doesn't move, and the bouquet gets squished between them. He says, "You look great."

She considers that for a long moment. I think how easy it would be here, how far it would go, for her to tell him how much she's missed him. How hard it's been without him. That she can't just pretend everything's fine while he's gone, because it's not. I hope he recognizes that. They have always understood each other. Finally she says flatly, "How was the flight?"

"Oh, it was fine. Long. I got a good amount done. What about you?"

"Fine." Then she adds, "Actually, it was a bit rough. Honor was scared."

He turns to me. "Aw, baby, what happened? Was there turbulence?"

"A little."

He scoops Sonnet up, then lifts her into the air, beaming at her.

"Honor, you're so brave, you know that? I don't think most people push themselves to do things that really scare them the way you do every time you get on a plane."

"Let's figure out dinner," Jamison says. "Everyone's hungry. Honor, you said you'd researched some options? What were you thinking?"

We spend the next twenty minutes debating where to eat. I had a list of places we could order from, but our dad is insistent we should go somewhere, probably because he wants to be seen out with his family, like everything's good. Atticus, as always, wants something casual and laid-back and not touristy; our mom wants somewhere nice we can sit down. Julie watches the discussions with an almost anthropologic fascination, while Wrangell looks on with something that could be amusement or embarrassment, I'm not sure which.

"We take food extremely seriously," our dad says, grinning, to Julie. "This is nothing. Wait until it's actually some kind of high-stakes meal."

"Let's look at the menus," Jamison says, scrolling on her phone. "I want to find a place with clean food."

"What's clean food?" Atticus says.

"You know, unprocessed and natural. Not too much sugar. You'd be shocked at how much sugar is hiding in things you wouldn't think about."

"Yikes," he says mildly. "Maybe it's better to just not think about it."

She rolls her eyes. "This poke place looks okay."

"Oh, it's so casual," our mom says. "Aren't we all tired from traveling? Don't we want to sit down and have a nice dinner?

How about this place in Poipu? You can ask for ingredients, Jamison."

"Maybe casual sounds nice," our dad says. "Don't forget Jamison has Sonnet."

"Yes, I know that," our mom says a little sharply. "Sonnet is a person too. She's allowed at restaurants."

"All right, I'm making an executive decision," Jamison says. "Let's do the place you wanted in Poipu, Mom. How many cars will we need? Dad can come with us, Skye and the twins and Mom can go together, and Wrangell and Julie, we'll meet you there."

I have missed Jamison's reassuring bossiness. I think she's been toning it down so far today to let me be in charge, which is sweet—it's probably killing her. We all go in our assigned cars.

I plan to ask our mom if she's okay, if it's weird for her to see our dad like this, but as soon as we get into the car, she says, "Maybe being around the baby will make Wrangell want a baby. What do you guys think of Julie? Is she marriage material? I think she's cute. When you're in a new relationship, you have this frantic energy to you, but I don't see that in her. She's much more comfortable. Or at least comes off that way. But I do worry he's just not mature enough for marriage." She switches off the radio. "Wrangell won't talk to me, have you noticed that?"

"Well, there's a lot of people around," Skye says. "We all just barely got here. And he's probably trying to look out for Julie."

"No, it isn't that. I think he's angry with me about your dad. I think he blames me."

"He seems normal to me," Atticus says. "He's how he always is."

"Mm." She reaches up and smooths her hair. "Well, that's good. My hope has always been that the five of you are close. Someday I'll be gone, so just as long as you have one another, that's all I care about."

SO DRAMATICCCCCCC OMG, Skye messages me and Atticus. Atticus writes back, DANGLING FROM SHEER ROCK!! Aloud, Skye says, "Wrangell's probably just distracted with Julie, Mom. I'm sure it's not personal."

"No, it's definitely personal."

"Oh, you know how he is," Skye says smoothly. "Look, Mom, there's the restaurant up ahead. Wow, it's gorgeous! The sunset views are going to be great. Let's have a great dinner and not think about anything but dinner and the ocean. Really, all you need in life."

I love the feeling of all of us descending onto a restaurant together, of everyone scrambling to find a table big enough to fit us—I think these are the moments I feel the absolute most like myself. Before the show, when things were calmer, we used to go to dim sum most weekends when our parents were home, because there was always a big, round table that would fit us, ready to contain our chaos just temporarily with the promise of food.

While we're waiting, though, Julie is clearly embarrassed, apologizing to the hostess and murmuring to Wrangell that we should've called ahead, sneaking agonized glances at everyone openly watching us. She looks ready to leave. I'm irritated. What did she expect?

We're seated out on a balcony overlooking the water. The waitress sheepishly asks for a picture with our parents. They both lean against her, smiling, and in that posture they look so happy and normal I'm fooled, momentarily, into thinking I just imagined the past months.

When she's gone, though, our mom drops her smile. She pulls out the seat as far away as possible from our dad.

"This kind of reminds me of the time we went to Hong Kong," I tell my dad, mostly to make up for our mom's silence—it was one of his favorite trips. "Something about the island feel."

"Mm," he says distractedly. "Hong Kong. Yeah, I can see that."

We busy ourselves debating the menu, ordering. The food is excellent. "Great pick, Honor," Jamison says, and there's a warm glow around the words. We eat lilikoi-braised short ribs and an omakase platter, thin sheets of fish laced around gleaming orbs of fruit, chicken lollipops in some kind of soy-based sauce, a sort of deconstructed salad dotted with purees and fruits. Sonnet chases grains of garlic rice around her plate with her index finger.

"You know what I can't find in Brooklyn?" our dad says. "Good Cantonese food. I'm sure it exists, but I don't know where. I have the feeling maybe it's something you need to speak Cantonese to find. The rest of the food scene there, though—you guys have to come try it. Just mind-blowing."

Our mother's expression slowly closes off, and for the next ten or fifteen minutes she says nothing at all.

Sonnet decides she's had enough of the rice and tips her plate onto the floor, then pushes her silverware off before anyone can stop her. Jamison looks exhausted, but our mom says, "Oh, she's okay. She's just being a toddler." She pulls Sonnet onto her lap. "Are you ever going to be a big sister?" she asks Sonnet in the lilting voice she uses only with babies. "Are there going to be more of you? You are just so, so cute, I want a dozen more of you!"

She spears a piece of short rib and offers it to Sonnet.

"That's too big," Jamison says.

"Oh, it's soft," our mom says, but she bites off a piece of the mango first, then stands with Sonnet and leads her to the balcony railing. "Sonnet, can you see the ocean from here? Do you want to play at the beach tomorrow?"

Jamison is watching Sonnet and our mother, her eyes scanning back and forth like they're on a ledge. "I don't think—Mom—don't let her get close to the balcony like that."

"What do you mean?"

"She's too close to the rail."

"She's not going to fall off, Jamison, it's three feet high. She can't even see the top of it."

"No, she's—" Jamison lunges for Sonnet, scooping her away from our mom. Our mom makes a surprised sound in the back of her throat.

"She was *fine*, Jamison," she says. "I did raise five children, you know."

Wrangell mutters something I can't quite hear, but I see the expression on Atticus's face.

"What was that?" our mom says a little sharply. Jamison pretends not to hear and busies herself brushing rice from Sonnet's hair.

Let's talk about this, I want to say, *it's weird, we all feel how it's weird, let's figure it out,* but every youngest child knows you can't throw something like that out and expect to be taken seriously. Besides that, Julie's here, and she's not someone with the level of separation (crew, audience) that our family would talk like that in front of. Wrangell has already moved on to saying something quietly to her, her eyes darting between the rest of us like she's taking notes.

Our dad could make something of this, though. One of the

best things about him is how he knows how to extend a moment, always has a feel for how to reach further into a conversation and get somewhere deeper with it. How he's willing to push conversations no one else is. I look at him, hopeful, trying to signal him with my eyes. *Talk to Mom. Tell her something honest and real.*

"So, Julie," our dad says brightly, turning to her, "you travel much?"

It's unlike him; it's a cop-out. I am miserable the rest of the meal. As we're leaving, I hang back and ask Atticus what Wrangell said.

"'No you didn't,'" he repeats. "'We raised ourselves.'"

I had imagined us staying up late talking, playing card games or something in the loft, but everyone's quiet on the way back, and at home Jamison and Andrew take Sonnet to bed, and Wrangell and Julie disappear upstairs. Our parents go into their separate bedrooms, Atticus goes for a run, and Skye has work to do. There are so many reasons to avoid each other, I guess, when we want to.

I want to message Caden, but I can't think of anything to say. (*Have you missed me? Have you thought of me? It's been a day and a half!*) I have pictures in my Camera Roll of me and Skye in bikinis, and we're at Muir Beach, but the close-cropped shots could probably pass for Kauai. I wonder if he'd like the pictures. I stop myself from sending any. Maybe I'll treat this week as a test to see whether I'm anything to him after all, if he's still into me when I'm not physically there. *Prove Blythe wrong*, I tell him silently. *Make it different with us.*

I wait up at night to see if he'll message me, but he doesn't. I'm awakened the next morning by Wrangell poking my cheek repeatedly, possibly the most irritating sensation neurons can register early in the morning. I bat him with a pillow, but he just pulls it away.

"Come on," he says, "aren't you on California time still? Let's go jogging."

"Jogging?"

He grins. "Multitasking. I wanted to talk to you."

I go with him, partly just so he'll get out before he wakes up Skye, too. We make our way out of the gated community and cross the main highway to a dirt trail that disappears into a thicket, almost electric green. The dirt here is reddish and clings to your shoes.

"Okay," I say, out of breath, coming to a halt, "this is the part where I walk. What did you want to talk about?"

"You're soft!" he says. "You guys live in the hills now. Perfect for trail running. I'll tell you some good training shoes to buy. Okay, so I know you've been playing travel guide this week. You have plans for every day?"

I do, in fact, have plans for every day. I booked a helicopter tour and a tour of the Na Pali Coast, a snorkeling excursion and a river float. There's a day we're going on an intense hike, for Atticus and Wrangell, and I will probably die, so they'd better appreciate it. I found a league that does drop-in beach volleyball, so we can all go cheer for Atticus, and a vintage Hawaiian furniture shop for Wrangell. I found a luau that's particularly kid-friendly for Sonnet.

"Nice," he says when I tell him that. "Okay, well, I have a favor to ask. I wanted to see if you'd let me take over tomorrow."

"You wanted to take over tomorrow? Why? What did you want to do?"

"I wanted to plan a Julie day."

It's a Herculean effort to keep my expression neutral. "What's a Julie day?"

"I wanted to plan a day for her that's all the things she likes. I want her to feel, you know, special. Not just like she's getting dragged on a family trip."

"I see," I say. "Well."

"You want to know a secret?"

"Yes. I love secrets."

He laughs. "I know you love secrets. I bought a ring."

I stop walking. Wrangell bumps into me, and the jungle is so thick on either side of us he nearly stumbles into a cluster of deep green, sculptural-looking ferns.

"You bought a *ring*?" I say. "Did you bring it with you?"

"Did I bring it with me? Am I proposing to my girlfriend on a trip with her hopefully future in-laws, the absolute height of romance?" He pokes me, grinning. "No, it's at home. But Wednesday is our two-month anniversary, so—"

"Two months?" I say, laughing. "Wow, *Wrangell*, congrats. Are you going to go to prom together? Are her parents letting you take her to the mall?"

"Yeah, shut up."

"I can't believe you're talking about proposing to someone you've known for two months."

"Yeah, actually, me neither. But here we are. And I want to do something special for her. I want her to feel comfortable with everyone all together like this. So tomorrow? That okay?"

I wonder how you get people to care about you for all you are like that, not just the shinier surface parts. "If it means that much to you."

He reaches out and punches me lightly on the shoulder. "You're the best."

"Just make sure it's some kind of activity that can work for Sonnet."

"Yeah. Jamison said maybe she'll just take Sonnet somewhere instead."

"They're not going to come with us?"

We pass under a huge mango tree, the ground littered with rotting fruit. Wrangell leans over and inspects a few, then picks up one that's mostly just ripe. He rips off a patch of skin and takes a bite. "She and Andrew are having some problems."

"Wait, what? They are?" I'm shocked. They look so happy in everything she ever posts, and she's said nothing about it.

"Maybe I wasn't supposed to say anything."

"What kind of problems?"

"Eh, she works too much, I think. And he thinks she doesn't know how to connect with him. Don't tell her I told you."

When we get back home, Skye's just getting back too, and she tells me she went to get coffee with our dad.

"What'd he say?"

Skye hesitates. "Just—a lot of things. He's kind of having a hard time."

"He is? What does that mean? What did he say?"

"I think he's just kind of all over the place right now. Not sure what he wants, all that."

Definitely not what I wanted to hear. "Do you think Mom thinks everyone is on Dad's side? I wonder if she wanted us to not invite him."

"I think—" Skye hesitates again. "That's possible. I think maybe she senses that he's—I don't know. I'm not sure. Maybe."

"Senses that he's what?"

"Well, you know how things are," she says. "You always worry someone else isn't as invested or committed as you are, you know. Maybe she just feels like that."

"Is that what Dad said?"

"Honestly, I think he's more just thinking about himself right now."

"I wish they would just *talk*. But it really doesn't seem like either of them is willing to make the first move. Why did they even come?"

"They came for you guys, I'm sure."

"I think that's pessimistic. I think they also came because they know they *can* work things out."

"Maybe," Skye says. "I hope you're right. Anyway!" She claps her hands together. "I'm so excited to ride a helicopter. You've done such an amazing job planning everything."

The helicopter ride, our first planned activity, surprisingly does not trigger my airplane terror, but it also doesn't trigger any kind of familial reconciliation because (I should have thought this through better) we're divvied up into so many small groups. I ride with Jamison, Andrew, and Sonnet. Andrew and Jamison both dote on Sonnet but mostly ignore each other, and I remember what Wrangell said. I lose my resolve and send Caden a message from the helicopter, a picture of the ocean from above, and tell him it reminds me a little of the reservoir. Which it does, but only because I'm thinking about him. I wait all throughout the ride for him to answer, but he doesn't.

After the ride Jamison and Andrew take Sonnet back to the house to nap, and the rest of us eat garlic shrimp from a food truck. It comes on paper plates, which always feel weirdly comforting to me because we always used paper plates when we were filming so the mics wouldn't pick up clanging cutlery. I take pictures of the food—maybe I'll try to make a tiny garlic shrimp plate to add to Sonnet's future collection, a souvenir of her first time here, even though I've never gotten shrimp right. We sit at picnic tables outside the truck, and our parents sit at opposite tables with their backs to each other. Wrangell and Julie wander off to go look at the water and are gone most of the time we're eating, which means our mother is sitting at the table alone. I get up and go sit with her, which seems like a bigger statement than I intend it to be, but she's doing something on her phone anyway and mostly ignores me. I give up and go back to sit with everyone else. Caden still hasn't messaged me.

Back at the house, the person Ava found comes to do pedicures, and then most of us, everyone but our parents, go lie on the beach; we swim and build Sonnet an elaborate sandcastle, and Andrew and Wrangell dig her an enormous hole. All day there's nothing from Caden. I shouldn't care.

When we get back, we all congregate outside on the lanai, where the caterers are setting up dinner. I text our mom to say we're almost ready to eat, and she writes back, on a call, start without me. Sonnet inexplicably becomes obsessed with a particular section of the railing, inspecting it and caressing it and dragging Jamison and Andrew over to show them, and then we eat. The food is beautiful: cut fruits, mounds of poke with avocado, fish steamed in some kind of leaf, garlicky rice, lilikoi panna cotta, and mango mousse with candied orchids. Jamison avoids the rice and desserts. I make a plate for our mom.

Nearly everyone's on their phones while we eat, except for Wrangell and Julie, talking quietly to each other, and I scroll for a while too, trying not to wait for Caden. And then I see it. The world fades out around me, my pulse throbbing in my forehead, and next to me, Atticus murmurs, "You okay? You're kind of pale."

I hold out my phone. My hand is shaking. "Read it."

"You gotta stop reading this shit online," Atticus says.

"No, Atticus, read it."

He takes my phone to look and his expression changes. "Oh shit."

You're Not Famous: A Snark Site
ynf.com/forums/LoFamily

junco, 3:08:36 pm PST: honestly in their Kauai posts they all look kind of miserable. can you imagine being a fly on the wall for that?

knockoffbrene, 3:09:00 pm PST: ok has anyone else noticed that literally every time Skye posts about them they're all just sitting there not talking to each other unless they see she's videoing them helppppppppp what a messed up family I can't stand it

baconspam420, 3:09:59 pm PST: yes well cut them some slack, they probably literally don't know how to talk to each other unless there's a camera around

calendulateam, 3:11:31 pm PST: omg not Skye posting their castle-sized rental and caterers cooking for them. in this economy!

redwoodfog, 3:12:36 pm PST: Okay soooooo . . . I've been lurking here for a while but this trip to flaunt their wealth is pushing me over the edge. I actually know this family. Honor has spent like half her life hanging out at my house. And I just have to say that you would not *believe* the rampant materialism in that family. Melissa and Nathan feel guilty about not being, you know, actual parents and try to buy their way into it instead. If you talk to Honor she'll admit Wrangell and Jamison raised her. Her mother's freaking *assistant* taught her what to do when she got her period.

"It has to be either Eloise or Lilith, don't you think? Whoever talked to *People*." I'm trembling. "I never did anything to them. I tried so hard to be a good friend. Unless—do you think before it was Lilith, and Eloise was hurt I didn't believe her? Or vice versa?"

"No, I bet it was the same one. It doesn't matter. I think you're right."

"What's wrong, Honor?" Jamison says, and our dad goes on alert. Everyone crowds around me, and Atticus says, "One of Honor's best friends—former best friends—is talking shit about her online. The same one who went to *People*."

"That girl again? Just snake behavior. Just absolutely despicable," our dad says. "What kind of child goes to *People* magazine to sell out their best friend? Honor, sweetheart, forget them. We're Los first. You are a Lo. We are your people. Forget them. You're better than them. I think I might call their parents and get to the bottom of this. No one treats Los this way."

"Don't do that," Skye says. "That will just make everything worse."

"We should sue."

"We're not going to win a lawsuit," Jamison says.

"We're not going to win a lawsuit, but while it's going, we're going to make them wish they'd never met us. No way they have a decent lawyer on retainer."

"I don't understand how someone like Victoria Finebaugh can have actual friends," I say to Atticus, "and people who love her, and meanwhile, the people I open up to the absolute most will sell me out without a second thought. Like, they know how hurt I was, and they're still doing it again."

"I'm sorry," he says. He pats me on the back. "You deserve better."

"Who's Victoria Finebaugh?" our dad says.

"A girl at school," Atticus says. "She's, like, socially powerful. She and Honor had a run-in."

"Well, then Victoria has something people want," our dad says. "People are drawn to others by what they want in themselves. That's the bedrock of social relationships. The people who try to get close to you see something in you that they want for themselves. It's not about you, baby. You've done nothing wrong. It's just the nature of humanity."

I wipe my eyes. "I think that sucks."

He wraps his arms around me. "The best thing you can do is focus on yourself and your achievements. That's the part that's within your control."

Jamison says, to Atticus, "What did they say?" He hands her my phone and she reads it.

"Well," she says, "if the worst thing someone can say about you is that your family is materialistic, Honor, I think that means you're doing pretty great. I can't even tell you how many mean things people have said about me."

"The meanest thing anyone ever said about me online," Skye said, "is there was this whoooole bit about when I die, who would sponsor my funeral."

"That's cold," Wrangell says. "Okay, but what were the answers? Who's going to be the lucky sponsor?"

Skye rolls her eyes. "People were like, *Ooh, some sunglass line, so all of you can wear matching dark glasses.* Or, like, Dior or someone can make me some really good dress to wear in a casket. Or skin care, like, can they make me look not dead?"

"Okay, that's nothing," Wrangell says, grinning. "Wait, I think I saved it." He scrolls through his phone. "I had to screenshot it." He sits up straighter and reads aloud: "'Wrangell Lo is like if the great Gatsby discovered MLMs.'"

"Oh my God, that's so accurate." Skye laughs so hard she doubles over. "I'm dying. I'm actually going to die laughing. You'll all have to pick your sunglasses sponsor."

"People say I look like a platypus," Jamison says a little mournfully.

"Wait, what?" Atticus says, laughing. "A platypus?"

"Maybe it's because I have the Asian nose."

"You all got my father's nose," our dad says.

"Okay, but don't platypuses—platypi? What is it? Don't they have long noses? Like that beak thing?" Atticus pantomimes one. "It's the literal exact opposite."

"Yes, well, maybe to white people that's how it looks. Who knows?" Jamison says. "White moms can be seriously so mean."

"Well," our dad says, "you're the most beautiful and competent platypus the world has ever known."

"People are trash," Wrangell says to me, slinging his arm around me. "That's the problem with literally most people. But you're better than that."

"You'll always have us, Honor," Jamison says.

"I honestly don't know how you all handle this constantly," Julie says. "I've read some of the comments you all get, and they're so cruel! Like Jamison is an exploitative mother whose husband doesn't actually love her? Skye is the perfect symbol of everything wrong with late capitalism? Melissa is only successful because she's a knockoff Asian Brené Brown? I would crumple. You all must have the thickest skin in the world."

I stare at her in horror. Those are things I would never say aloud. And we were having a good moment, too, despite what precipitated it. Things were feeling normal between us. We were Los again, us against the world.

"Yes, well," Skye says lightly, "I do get free sunglasses! So it all evens out, right? It's worth it in the end."

The next morning is Wrangell's day, and I wake up feeling hung over even though I didn't drink anything. Probably it's more emotional. Obviously, Caden doesn't actually care about me, but that's fine. I didn't want anything serious anyway, like I told him. So I'm not going to think about that, and I'm not going to think about Eloise and Lilith or all the things they might be telling people about me. I am going to live in the moment. It'll be a good day.

Wrangell's planning starts with all of us eating acai bowls down on the beach, where a circle of yoga mats is waiting ominously.

"These are just decoration, right?" I say, to make a joke, because despite all of us except Andrew and Sonnet being here, it's unusually quiet. "A little ambiance to make you and Julie feel at home?"

He laughs. "Still not a fitness person, I see."

"Does worrying burn calories? I think I'm good."

"Yeah, so today's actually going to be just a series of different workouts," he says. "Happy birthday. First we'll do some mega-intense yoga on the beach for a few hours, then we'll drive around until we find some CrossFit, rack up some PRs, and then—"

I kick some sand at him. "Is this a glimpse into your and Julie's relationship? This is what you do for fun? Am I going to be this boring when I'm old like you?"

He smiles. "Shut up. I think you're going to like what I have planned, actually."

"Not inspiring confidence here."

"Okay, give the yoga a chance, it'll be good for you, and then after that I got us a tour guide to take us through some of the grottos and the canyons."

"Oh, actually," our mom says, "Wrangell, that sounds so fun, and so thoughtful, but we've had a slight change of plans for the day, so let's call and have them change our time slot. Do you all remember Jessie Yuan, from *Vanity Fair*? Really sweet woman. Anyway, huge stroke of luck here—she called me up to say, oh, Melissa, I would just love to talk to your whole family together while you're all here in one place, people would love to catch up with your family."

"No," Wrangell says. "Absolutely not."

Our mom ignores him. "So she's actually flying out, she'll be here in a few hours, and she'll just tag along today. Really small and casual, just her and a photographer and then a stylist just at the beginning. She'll talk with us in our natural habitat."

"I was not made aware of this," our dad says. "Did Lauren call Jeff?" Jeff is his publicist. "Because this is the first I'm hearing of it."

"Oh, did she not mention it? She might not have had time."

"Well, I don't know that I'm prepared for this right now."

"What's to prepare? You're here, your schedule is open."

I swallow. My face feels hot.

"Yeah, that is not happening," Wrangell says. "Everything's all planned for today. It's the twins' birthday trip. We're not doing any media anything right now. This is just family."

"Oh, it'll still be just family. No one even has to talk to Jessie if you don't want. She's just going to be around to get a better sense of her story, and then if anyone *wants* to talk to her, even just to say hi, you're absolutely free. Lauren thinks—oh, that's her right now." She picks up her phone. "Lauren, hello." She holds up a finger to us, then gets up and goes inside, closing the sliding door behind her.

"I'm sorry," Wrangell says to Julie. "She gets these stupid ideas—we'll talk her down."

"Well—how flexible are your plans?" Jamison says. "I'd kind of like to hear a little more about this interview."

He stares at her. "You're shitting me, right?"

"Wrangell, I could push a shopping cart naked across a parking lot and *Vanity Fair* would never call me."

"But you know it's not going to be about you, right? It's going to be about Mom and Dad."

"Sure, but I can probably get some good quotes in, and people actually love hearing about the behind-the-scenes of interviews like that. And anyway, there will be pictures—and Sonnet—"

"He actually spent a long time researching how to make the tour work for your baby," Julie says, her voice a little icy.

Wrangell puts his hand over hers and starts to say something. Before he can, Atticus stands up. "Yeah, well, count me out. I don't think we need to be talking to anyone right now."

"Well, hold on, hold on," our dad says. "I think this is a decision we'll make as a family, so if we all decide—"

"You said you didn't want to do it either," Wrangell says to him. I think it's the first time Wrangell's spoken directly to either of our parents the whole trip.

"Well, no, I said I wasn't aware of it. But if it's happening, I don't know that it's the right thing to just bow out."

Wrangell snorts. "Don't put on a front here. Obviously, you're going to do it. When have you ever turned down the chance to talk at people?"

"I think I might have to," Jamison says to Wrangell. "Don't judge me. We could just do the girls, maybe. Three generations of Lo women. But my numbers have been terrible lately, and I've been trying everything—"

"I think it would be good for us all to have a voice," our dad says.

Jamison ignores him. "But you don't have to," she says to Wrangell. "You guys should go and do a hike or something. Just don't judge me. I know how you feel about it. I just—financially I need to be in a good position if—"

"No, it's fine, James," he says, defeated. "Do what you have to do."

In the end our dad decides that if our mom is going to do the interview, he will also, which is what I predicted. Jamison and Skye and I will come; Wrangell and Atticus will not.

The crew will be here in less than forty-five minutes, so Skye and I both go upstairs to shower. I'm anxious in a skin-crawly way, and in the shower I close my eyes and try to relax. I don't think I've done a real interview since the tour. When I come downstairs, Wrangell and Julie are talking in the stairwell. Quietly, but not enough so that I can't hear.

"I'm just saying, as an observation, that I think it's really a selfish thing for Jamison to do," Julie is saying. "After the way you've talked about her—I don't know, I was expecting something different."

"Jamison is doing what she has to do. She wants to support her kid, she wants to do things on her own terms, and ironically, sometimes you just have to play the game to do those things."

"Do you? Because she could get a normal job like every other person in the world. No one's making her do this weird influencer shtick."

"Yeah, that's true, babe, but to be honest with you, people don't understand what it was like for us. Actually, randomly, every now and then I meet someone who grew up fundamentalist or something, like homeschooled with eleven little siblings, and they know what it was like."

I will have to tell Skye and Atticus that Wrangell calls Julie *babe*. I'm near the bottom of the stairs now, and they look up and see me. Julie gives me a very neutral smile.

"All ready for the big interview?" she says.

"I guess, yeah. Are you guys going to do the tour still?"

"We'll go with Andrew and Atticus," Wrangell says. I can't tell whether or not he's mad at me. I want to ask him, but not in front of Julie. I also want to tell him I hope it's good, that they have a great time, but it feels too fraught, so I just nod.

"Hey," Wrangell says to Julie, "be right back. Let me talk to my little sister a minute." He pulls me over to one of the couch-and-coffee-table configurations, the one closest to the windows.

"You don't have to do the interview," he says. "You could come with us instead. This is supposed to be your birthday trip. You don't have to do what Mom wants just because she's sad. It's not your job."

My guilt is a black hole in my chest, swallowing everything he's saying. "I mean, it's not that bad. You talk to someone a few hours, and hopefully they make you sound good."

"Yes, Honor, thank you, I'm aware of the process." He glances back at Julie. "I just worry about you getting shoehorned into something the way Skye and Jamison have. But you don't have to make this your life. You can walk away."

As far as I know, our parents' money still mostly supports him. Has he walked away? Is that what he thinks he's doing by ghosting us any given 30 percent of the time? "I don't think this one interview is going to have that much bearing on the rest of my life one way or the other."

"But you're almost eighteen," he says. "One more year and then you're free. You know what they say—begin as you mean to go on."

It's worse, actually, than if he were just mad. I would rather he yell at me. I feel sick to my stomach. "I'm sorry," I say. "I really am. She should've come a different day. But I do—I think it'll be good for them to talk. And you know they're always better at that when someone else is around, or there's an audience—"

"Okay, but that's their problem. That's not your problem." When I don't answer that, he sighs. "So you're doing the interview, then? You're spending your birthday trip running PR for your parents."

"Mom said it'll only be a few hours."

"To talk. But the makeup and the styling and the pictures—you know it's going to be the entire day."

Tears spring into my eyes. "I'm sorry about messing up your day."

"It's fine, Honor. Don't worry about me. I just hope you think

146 • KELLY LOY GILBERT

about what I'm saying. You're almost seventeen years old, and you can do literally anything with your life. Don't waste it on people who don't appreciate you or see you. You deserve better. You want to spend your life shilling for Clorox or whatever like Jamie? You can do better than that."

The stylists show up and take over the ground floor, a small troop ready to do our hair and makeup and styling. The makeup is muted, natural colors with dramatic eyebrows. I watch a new self emerge in the mirror. Skye looks like a sharper version of herself, elegant and beautiful. When she smiles, though, it doesn't reach her eyes.

"What's wrong?" I say.

"Oh, I'm just tired." She sighs. "And not totally thrilled about this right now, to be honest. I would've rather done Wrangell's grotto tour."

Again with the cavernous, yawning guilt. I debate telling her, but maybe there's nothing to be gained from it. "How mad do you think Wrangell is?"

"Oh, he'll get over it."

"Do you think so?"

"He always does."

They dress us all in austere-looking gray neutrals—a pantsuit for Skye, a jumpsuit for me, our mom in a sheath dress. We traipse down to the beach for a photo shoot, where Jessie and the photographers are waiting.

"Jessie Yuan!" our dad says. He's always had a way of smiling at you that makes you feel like his life is complete now that he sees you, that he's been waiting for this. "Can't believe you made it all the way out here. Welcome to the island."

"Well, my goodness, so much has happened in your life since I last saw all of you!" Jessie says, giving everyone a hug. "How have you been *doing*? I can't wait to catch up. Honor, it was so nice to hear from you."

My heart stops, but I don't think anyone notices her say that.

"It's just so nice to see you again too," our mom says warmly to Jessie. "What a delight! The girls were absolutely thrilled. We can't wait to talk."

The photo shoot takes three hours. For forty minutes we walk back and forth across a ten-yard stretch of beach, pretending to laugh and talk while the photographers shout out directions and occasionally come to pose us or fuss with their light filters and have us retake shots. Our dad makes Jessie and the photographers laugh. I wonder what Caden (who still has not messaged me) would think right now, if he'd think this was exciting and glamorous or just incredibly shallow and odd. Sonnet is a mess by the end, flopping face-first, screaming, into the sand. Jessie mostly watches, occasionally writing something down. I've always hated that—the observations journalists make while you're doing something else, like anyone should glean any information from watching Jamison frantically try to wrangle Sonnet, or Skye gamely following directions.

"Let's go back up to the house and have some lunch while we chat," our mom says, linking her arm through Jessie's. "Oh my goodness, these shoes! I'm going to break my leg." She takes them off and loops her hand through them.

The caterers have set up inside: cut fruits, mounds of poke with chips and flatbread, a charcuterie and crudité board, braised pork belly on toothpicks, and small cupcakes and chocolate truffles painted with vibrant colors and gold leaf. We settle into seats in the living room. I'm nervous in a way I almost never am in situations like these. Our dad sits down next to our mother and rests his hand on her knee. I see Jessie notice. Our mother doesn't move.

"So this separation kind of rocked all of us!" Jessie says. "But okay, so now you're a few months out, you've had some time to process. What's happening now? What's the status?"

"Yeah," our dad says, nodding. "Right, right. Melissa . . . God, how do you talk about Melissa? She's incredible, first of all. Just an amazing woman. Just absolutely zero regrets about our lives together and what we've built. She is an endless source of awe and inspiration to me. Ah, but in terms of where we're at right now— you know, I've spent my life feeling like I don't fit in anywhere. Anywhere I've ever gone, I've had to fight to carve out space for myself there. And I'm proud of that, but I think I'm tired, too. And Melissa—it's been different for her, you know? She hasn't done that same carving out. Melissa is able to—to mold herself. So I think we've shaped the world around ourselves differently."

"So where does that leave you?" Jessie says. "What's next?"

"I don't know," our mom says. She turns to our dad, her eyes searching. "I've been having the same question."

Her voice is quiet and unadorned, not her usual public voice. I thought this would be good for exactly this reason: they are more forthcoming, more civil and articulate, with an audience. I knew they would be. An audience is perhaps the force in their lives they've most worried about being accountable to. If they can make strides together here, then probably it's worth how upset Wrangell is. Right? I hope.

"I think where it leaves us is in this period of learning and growth," our dad says. "You know, deconstructing the things we thought we knew, and the things we've built our lives around. Sometimes you have to go back to those foundations. The human condition is to seek stability, and we crave sameness, but it's an inherently destructive tendency because it doesn't allow us to meet an unstable world."

I can see right away how our mother's expression closes off. My heart sinks. I don't know how he can miss her signals this way. Because she was being honest, she was trying to talk to him, and he's talking right past her with one of his TED Talk–type answers.

"So when I heard about you two separating, I have to say, my thoughts immediately went right to the kids," Jessie says. "Skye, how are you processing all this when you have such an especially public life?"

I hope Jamison doesn't take *especially public* as an insult. My chest feels tight.

"I'm so lucky in that I have such an amazing community. Literally every person is so supportive," Skye says brightly, a clear lie. "I think people can really relate. You know, everyone's been in a situation where you aren't sure if a relationship is working, where you're trying to balance your own needs against your family's—I've gotten a lot of encouragement from people who have walked that same path."

"So you're sympathetic to your dad here, then, it sounds like?" Jessie says. Our mother makes a quiet, involuntary strangled noise.

"Oh—" Skye looks panicked. I know enough by now to know how these things will stay with us, how something you say to someone like Jessie in a single moment will be churned out onto hundreds of thousands of copies, will be internalized by people who'll repeat it your whole life as gospel truth, and will maybe be thrown back in your face some other time like this, down the road, maybe by her again or someone else. When so many people know you, there are all these dozens of versions of you—only none of them is quite you—that will haunt you, people you're expected to constantly be. "I don't know if—I think—I think we all believe in possibility. We believe in a story that's still unfolding. You know, that we'll look back on this time and see the ways it was going to eventually draw us all closer. That we'll learn a lot and grow as people, and even with our dad and Heather—"

She stops, stricken, and our dad closes his eyes.

"Christ," he mutters, and we're all stunned into silence. "Skye, I trusted you."

Our mom and Jessie both start talking over each other.

"Who is Heather?" Jessie says, and our mom says, "Oh my *God*, Skye, *what?*" The look on her face—I think it will haunt me forever. And I have a weird feeling of connection to her in that moment, because even though I've never thought we looked alike, that I always looked like a more smudged version, I think if you held up a mirror to me right at this moment, I'd look exactly the same.

Our mother ends the interview immediately. Heather, our dad tells us reluctantly, is Heather Young, the HGTV star who can't be much older than thirty, if that. Skye won't meet his eyes.

"Obviously, Jessie, anything to do with this part was off the record," our mom says.

Jessie pauses. "I'm not sure if—we hadn't actually gone off the record, so ethically speaking, I'm not bound—"

"Oh, I know," our mom says, "Of course not, but I'm asking you as a favor. We've spoken so often over the years, and I would hate to have to cut ties! I hope I can trust you on this. I'll have Lauren call you to chat."

Jessie gives her a tight smile but doesn't promise anything. I feel sick. The fallout of this getting out would be apocalyptic.

"Leave," our mother says to our father while the photographers are still packing up, still murmuring with Jessie. "I can't believe you would come here pretending we're a family while you're hiding this—just go. Leave. You shouldn't have come."

"I think we should talk about—"

"There is absolutely nothing for you to talk about with me right now. Go."

"It's not going to look good if I leave early."

"It's not going to look good if someone sees you with a child girlfriend," she snaps. "I mean it. Leave."

He says something quietly to Skye I can't hear. I see one of the photographers hold up his camera for a shot of our dad walking away.

Immediately our mother calls Lauren to try to figure out a way to contain the story. Jamison joins the call too, which leaves me and Skye, but when I turn around, she's gone already. She must have gone back up to the house.

By the time I make my way back, still shell-shocked, everyone's heard. Atticus calls me from their tour.

"You think Skye said something on purpose?" Atticus says. "Maybe she never intended to keep the secret. For that matter, maybe Dad didn't either but he was too much of a coward to tell Mom himself."

"Yeah, I don't think so. He was really angry with Skye." There's a humming in my ears that won't stop. "Do you think people are going to find out? Jessie wouldn't say if she'd keep it off the record."

"That should be, like, the least of our concerns."

It's not, of course. An hour later we're all congregated in the living room, minus our father, who, according to three random people on social media, has been spotted at Lihue Airport. Skye's eyes are red.

"Ava has booked us for flights back home this afternoon," our mother says. "You'll need to hurry and get packed. Unfortunately, there's going to have to be a big effort now to do whatever we can. It's going to be all hands on deck. We're going to need to work to clean up this mess and make sure this story doesn't get out."

No one says anything, and she looks around at us. "Is anyone going to acknowledge this? Did you all hear me?"

"Yes," Skye says. "Definitely. It'll be quick to pack."

Our mom pauses. Then she says, "That's the part you want to acknowledge?"

That heavy, cold feeling around my lungs settles in, like Icy Hot dousing my organs. We all sit quietly, unmoving, no one wanting to speak first. Finally Skye says, "Yes, all hands on deck. I think it'll be okay, Mom."

"You think it'll be okay? Surely, you must be able to imagine what a big deal a scoop like this would be for Jessie. It's just—it's so corrosive," our mom says. "It's such a toxic thing to do. For you to know that about your father and withhold it, and then blindside me with that information during an active interview—I don't know what you thought I was—" She turns and looks out the window and blinks fast, her face crumpling. "The five of you are everything to me. You are my entire life and the reason I do everything I do."

"You know," Wrangell says, "maybe instead of turning yourself into the big victim here, you could actually acknowledge that Skye was in a shitty position because Dad was telling her crap he—"

"No," our mom says sharply, "No, Wrangell, I am not going to let you gaslight me here. You do not get to determine emotional boundaries of what I am allowed to feel."

"Okay, but what you're feeling is—"

"No," she says. "This is a boundary I'm setting right now. This is not up for debate."

"But whatever anyone else is feeling is up for debate?" he says, smiling in a hostile way. Next to him, Julie is watching him intently, her expression unreadable. "Or no, I guess there was no debate there, either. You just do what you want. Who cares if you gave Honor literal panic attacks, right? Your daughter's psychological health is a cheap price to pay. You know what," he says, standing, "I'm done. I'm just done. I don't want to keep dealing with this kind of shit in my life over and over. I'm done."

The drive to the airport is beautiful, lush, unable to penetrate the haze around me. The Kauai airport is tiny, and I find myself wishing it were bigger—the kind of place you could walk into a different terminal to get a coffee or buy a purse or nice soaps or something. Skye's flight is first, and then Jamison's, and saying goodbye feels a little like a funeral. I ask to hug Sonnet, and I hold her as long as I can and try to smile at her, and then she wriggles away from me and back to Jamison.

Ten or fifteen minutes before we're supposed to board, I slip away to the bathroom and sit in the stall so I can cry. There's someone in the next stall, so I try to be quiet. Then I'm irritated with myself. It does nothing to cry and feel sorry for yourself, and anyway, things are never as bad as they seem; you just have to change your attitude about them. I am bigger than this. I don't want to be someone who sobs in airport bathrooms because I wasn't able to manifest whatever I wanted to in my life. You get up, you try harder.

I'm washing my hands at the sink when the stall door that was next to me opens, and Julie emerges.

"Oh hey!" she says, and then she looks at me more closely. "Oh—are you crying? Oh no, Honor." She gathers me up in a hug. I pull away from her. I do not need hugs from random girls my brother brings home.

"I'm fine," I say a little sharply.

"I am so sorry your birthday trip turned out this way."

I try to wipe my eyes without making it look like a big deal. I clear my throat, steel myself to make my voice sound steady. "It's just a birthday. We'll have more."

"Wrangell didn't want to come at all, but the only reason he did was because it was your and your brother's birthday."

I don't know what to say to that. "Well. It's unfortunate it turned out like this."

"He said with your parents it's always something."

That's not something I would ever say to an outsider. "It's not anything you would understand."

"The way you guys have grown up—it's just all so fucked up. Sometimes Wrangell's like this black box, and seeing this glimpse of what it must have been like to—"

"You know, Julie," I say, "I'm sure you feel that way, and that's great, but I have to tell you, it always goes like this. It's always some sweet girl who thinks she's going to understand him like no one else has ever understood him and she's going to fix him, and then by the next time we see him again, it's all over. Maybe you know he's had a million girlfriends and maybe you think, *Oh, no, for us it's different, I'm the one who's going to get through to him*, but—well, all I can say is every single one feels that way."

She blinks at me, stunned. "Okay, well—"

"So it's been nice meeting you," I say. "I doubt I'll see you again."

CHAPTER NINE

After our fifth season of *Lo and Behold* the network wanted to send us on tour to interact with fans, so they signed us a book deal. They hired someone to compile a bunch of pictures of us, and we wrote (had ghostwritten) the story of our family. The book starts with our parents' chapters on how they met, and all five of us each wrote (also had ghostwritten) a chapter giving a behind-the-scenes look from our perspective.

Wrangell was sullen and uncooperative about the book, the tour, everything. And Auntie JJ didn't think Skye and Atticus and I should be included in the book, and for a long time she and our mom went back and forth about it. Auntie JJ had stopped letting herself be filmed for the show, a constant tension point with our mother because it required a lot of retakes to make it seem like she wasn't there, and also because it meant Auntie JJ didn't approve. They argued about Wrangell—and Auntie JJ thought he should be allowed to quit all of it.

"You don't understand how this works. It's a job," our mom said. "People do things for their jobs they don't like. Maybe Wrangell needs some consequences to help him learn that."

"The kids are kids. They shouldn't have a job."

Our mom snorted. "Wrangell is twenty-one years old, and

we pay for his apartment and all his bills, so yes, it is his job."

That was when Skye was dating Preston Campbell. It was a whole story line on the show. (First love! The two of them planning surprise dates! Our parents having heart-to-hearts with her about love!) At the time Preston was mostly doing modeling and YouTube, and in retrospect, probably his manager thought the show would be good visibility, a way for him to capture some different segment of the market, although that's not something that would've occurred to me at the time. He was sixteen and Skye was fourteen, so it's not like they were going to get married, but she loved him. His fans were vicious to her on her accounts, saying she wasn't good enough for him and he was only with her because of her last name. She was ugly. She was full of herself. Her voice was super annoying. She wasn't talented at all. She was a privileged white bitch exploiting her faux Asianness. She made Asians look bad. She was too needy. She wasn't affectionate enough. She should kill herself. I know she was insecure about it all, always trying to show how much she cared about him, always looking for signs he still cared about her. She was making him a little album of Polaroids from every stop on the tour, writing on the back of each one something she missed about him or something she wished they were doing together in that city.

We had a two-week, fifteen-city tour for the book, and it wasn't until then that I realized that filming the show had been, in a weird way, a kind of cocoon. The core people on the crew had been there for literally four years; they had watched us grow up. And when our parents were gone, which was often, Jamison and Wrangell (I understand this now) shielded us. They kept us home a lot, or they took us to familiar places where strangers wouldn't come up and talk to us. Skye was different, with Skye it was too late, but they didn't let me and Atticus log in to our public accounts ever; they changed all the passwords so we couldn't. So when we did the book tour, people lining up outside bookstores with their hardcover copies of *Lo and Behold: The Tell-All* to be signed, it was the first time we'd ever experienced anything like that. Before I had always been one of my parents' many kids, but now people knew my name, recounted stories about me like they'd been there for them, wanted to hug me or take pictures with me, or wanted me to be friends with their daughter who was the same age, or wanted me to help their kid start a YouTube channel, or wanted me to give them my number so we could talk. I found it terrifying. Atticus was nice to everyone, but he hated it. I just froze. Auntie JJ had come on the tour too, and she and Wrangell and Jamison wanted our parents to end the tour early, or at least send me and Atticus and Skye home.

We were at O'Hare, about to board a flight to Minneapolis, when Preston cheated on Skye with Chanel Knight, who at the time was staying in a collab house in LA. Skye found out with the rest of the world because Chanel livestreamed.

"I'm heeere with Preeeeestooooon!" she said in a singsong voice that still lives rent-free in my head. "So I guess he and Skye are over now? Because he's here, sooooooooooooo . . ." She panned over to him on her bed, and he flashed a peace sign. He wasn't wearing a shirt. She made a peace sign of her own, her mouth open in a silent laugh, and then perched herself on his lap, wrapping her legs around him, the camera jostling all over the place before she turned it off.

That night during the Q-and-A part of our event, the moderator, who I think was the owner of the bookstore, turned to Skye.

"So, wow, you were very publicly broken up with today!" she said. "I think a lot of us were shocked to see that rather crass video, my goodness. Did you know it was coming? What did you think?"

A normal-looking woman in a cardigan and glasses, probably someone with kids and a cat and a favorite tea mug, casually referencing my fourteen-year-old sister's heartbreak in front of hundreds of people like she was discussing a movie plot—this was what Wrangell and Jamison had tried to keep us away from. It was like I felt the exact moment we shifted from being real people to being a spectacle, free to ogle and dissect, and I understood that it was never going to be like it used to be. There was going to be no normal to return to.

That night in the hotel I had what felt like a heart attack. We missed the Tulsa stop because I had to go to the hospital. I left with a prescription for Ativan and a printout on panic attacks. When our dad and I got back from the hospital, Wrangell blew up at our parents, saying all of this was their fault, and the three of them had a shouting match so loud security came and knocked on our door, which they didn't care about, and also JJ came, which they did.

Auntie JJ sided with Wrangell. "You need to stop," she told our mother. "You need to call all this off. Look what this is doing to your children. This is indefensible. This is a wake-up call. You can't keep doing this."

Our mom brushed it off. "It's been a long day. We're all tired, but tomorrow—"

"No," Wrangell said. "Stop talking about tomorrow. We're done. We reached our limit. That was it. If you don't call all this off, I swear to God I'll sabotage it and make you wish you had."

"Don't you dare threaten us," our dad said, his voice low. "You're a Lo. Act like it. We don't throw in the towel as soon as things get hard. Remember where you come from and get it together."

"What else is he supposed to do if you won't listen to him?"

Auntie JJ said. "I've held my tongue as much as I could, but what you're doing to them isn't right."

"What we're doing to them?" our mom said. "We pay for their apartments. We can give all of them a down payment for a house. Skye can't even drive yet, and she can charge six thousand dollars for an Instagram post. You're just like Mom. You just want me to know that nothing I do, no matter what I achieve, is ever going to be good enough for you."

Auntie JJ looked stung in a way that made me wonder if she felt guilty that she had always been their mother's favorite. "That has nothing to do with anything."

"You know, every single day I wonder what Mom would think if she could see me now. I wish she were still here so I could buy her house back, and I could take her on trips—"

"Okay, well, she can't see you," Wrangell snapped, "so maybe you should take a look at the actual people who exist in your life instead of trying to prove yourself to your dead mom."

Jamison went pale. I thought our dad might hit him. But Auntie JJ said quietly, "You need to listen to what Wrangell is telling you and stop exploiting the children, otherwise all this is going to come out publicly. I love the kids, Melissa. I can't stand by and watch this happen to them. I won't."

It wasn't technically blackmail, but it was close. Our parents' whole brand was built on them being wholesome and simultaneously relatable and aspirational, and if they looked like they were exploiting their children, there would be no coming back from that.

We canceled the rest of tour "due to a family medical emergency," our parents both posting a picture of me in the hospital room with captions that made it sound like something much worse had happened to me, and then they withdrew from the next season of the show.

Skye was fine, though, the whole time. She turned to social media as a kind of catharsis post-breakup, videoing herself crying and debating whether or not to call him, videoing herself after a disastrous call with him. She dramatically burned all the Polaroids in the hotel bathtub. The sprinklers turned on and the whole hotel had to be evacuated. (Our parents made the producers pay the bill.) Skye livestreamed from the parking lot. Even at her saddest, maybe especially at her saddest, Skye is so funny and likable and self-deprecating, and that video—her wide-eyed in the parking lot, pointing the camera back over her shoulder to show all the angry hotel guests streaming out of the emergency exits, her shouting out somewhere in the building that her doomed Polaroid ashes had clogged a bathtub drain—blew up. She came out of the breakup with something like a million and a half new followers.

But those days after the tour were awful. Everyone was either gone or fighting or both. Atticus and I would escape to the beach as much as possible, and I hid in the shower to cry a lot. Auntie JJ stopped coming over, and she and our mother mostly stopped talking unless it was absolutely necessary, and that was the part that terrified me. Our mom and Auntie JJ had been like me and Skye. I had genuinely not thought that closeness between family could dissolve that way. Until Barcelona, I was terrified Wrangell would never talk to our parents again.

And then we had Barcelona. We were together, and we remembered who we were. In our family there's a center you hold on to, and you drift away sometimes, but then you come back, and back again.

CHAPTER TEN

take a Xanax before boarding, which as always doesn't help. But then we get on the plane, so the trip is officially over now, which means my test is too: Caden never answered my message. I feel stupid for trying to invent more between us when he was just giving me the kind of lines guys give you when they want to sleep with you. If anything, he was honest with me—he told me early on that he was into me and didn't want anything serious. Why would I have interpreted that any other way? There's no reason to be disappointed about it.

I try to distract myself with my phone. The news hasn't broken, so I wonder if Lauren has gotten through to Jessie yet.

You're Not Famous: A Snark Site

ynf.com/forums/LoFamily

knockoffbrene, 5:02:16 pm PST: Wait, they're leaving already?? Weren't they supposed to be gone a week? Something's up.

gatsby11, 5:02:22 pm PST: Maybe vacations don't go well when you stick together a bunch of vapid people who probably hate each other.

calendulateam, 5:03:08 pm PST: Their lives are a fucking vacation already

dollypardon, 5:04:14 pm PST: maybe they canceled the trip because they looked at their pictures and realized they all look like crap. I've never seen uglier bathing suits than the ones Honor and Skye were wearing. Just monumentally unflattering. I'd flee the state too

"On YNF," I tell Atticus, "people are talking about us coming home early. I'm nervous people are going to figure it out soon."

"Stop talking about it," he says immediately. "Stop reading it. It's random people who have nothing better to do than to talk shit on the internet. Why do you care?"

"Well, it's at least one nonrandom person, so——"

"Okay, but she's talking to randos. And if she has something to say about you, she should say it to your face."

"It's exactly that facelessness that gets me, though." It could be Eloise or Lilith, but also it could be anyone, everyone. Those same ugly, fleeting encounters our mother had in the grocery store, the same shadowy lawmakers writing bills to ban our ancestors from the country, from buying homes, from marrying whom they wished. All those ways we're measured and sized up: by colleges and advertisers and pollsters, by the algorithms that herd us to our shopping carts, by shareholders who don't care what it takes to pad their profits. Sometimes at school I look around and wonder how everyone can be so blissfully unaware of the way things work; they think it happens organically, that everyone is into Moncler at the same time or goes on vacation to the Virgin Islands, as if these things are just currents in the air. Our lives are controlled by a series of machinations made by people we'll never see. You don't have to know someone well or even identify them for them to wield power over you—it could be anyone, and that's the point. It could be anyone. People in the same forums used to say they bet our dad was cheating on our mom, that he was miserable, and I always thought it was stupid, but they were right, weren't they?

"Well, either way, you should stop," Atticus says. "They're never going to say what you want."

I already miss Skye; she's so much easier to talk to when Atticus gets like this. He's right, though, that no one is going to say what I want, which is *They seemed happy, it looked like an incredible trip, they all love each other very much and everything is fine.*

Our mother sits two rows in front of us, frantically typing on her laptop the whole flight. The second the wheels touch down, she's on her phone, although we're too far away for me to hear whom she's talking to. When I turn mine back on, there's a message from her: *I'm going straight home. Please make sure they get my bags too.*

While we're waiting in the lounge for the driver, Atticus turns to me.

"I can't believe it," he says. "I thought about it the whole flight. It's just so out of character for him. There has to be some kind of—I don't know, explanation or something—it just doesn't feel right. I really don't believe he'd do that. And then he just left and we never heard his side of the story. We should call him and get some answers."

We call when we get home. "No, yeah, I'm glad you're reaching out," our dad says. "That was a lot to process, and obviously, the way everything unfolded was not ideal. Your mother wasn't willing to let us all have a conversation. From my end, you know, it's not what it sounds like. Look, why don't you guys come out? We can talk. I can explain."

"Come out to New York?" I say.

"Just come for a few days. It would be nice to have you here. I can show you around a little."

"Why don't we just talk now?" I say.

"I think it would be good to connect in person. You were going to be in Kauai right now anyway. You already planned to miss school, right? Fly out. We'll talk. It'll be good for us."

"You want to do *what*?" our mother says. She's in her office still with Lauren and her manicurist, Becca, and she swivels around to stare at us. Becca adjusts herself smoothly to keep up with the swiveling. "No. Absolutely not. Is this a joke? No."

"I think it would be a good idea," Atticus says evenly. "I want to hear it from him what the deal is."

"You want to hear it from him? We've heard from him. What else is there to hear? You're not flying to New York." She turns to Lauren. "I mean, am I wrong? This is nuts, right? Do I have to let them see him?"

"You could certainly do a custody battle," Lauren says carefully. "It would be a gamble, but—well, when Grady and I split, what we had to do—"

Our mother throws up her hands. Becca bites back a choking sound and rushes to repair the damage.

"You know what?" our mother says. "Fine. Go. I don't have time to go to court over this. I don't have time to fight with you. Go to New York. Let him tell you himself. Call Ava. She'll book your flights."

Ava gets us on a red-eye that night. I'm skeptical still, but if Atticus wants to go, we'll go; I won't make him go alone. We get through security quickly, the airport almost empty, and the flight's only maybe a third full when we board. I hope no one sees us.

"Did you tell Jamie we're going?" Atticus says.

"No, did you?"

"No. I'm hoping we can just keep it on the DL. I keep thinking, like—I don't know, how hard is it to just say yeah, I'm not seeing anyone? It doesn't necessitate some big in-person conversation. So, like, in that sense, I'm nervous about what he's going to say. But then I also can't see him dragging us out there just to look us in the eye and be like yep, I'm having an affair. So I guess we'll see." It takes me a minute to place it, because it never happens, but from the way he's drumming his fingers on the armrest, I think he's nervous.

Our dad picks us up at the airport. He parked so he could come in and wait at baggage claim, and he beams when he sees us. I feel weirdly conspicuous walking over to meet him, like everyone's watching us, everyone wondering why we're here. I am not noteworthy or interesting enough, most of the time, to have my movements tracked or plastered over tabloids, but it doesn't take a publicity genius to know it's different right now. For a moment, though, when he wraps his arms around me in a hug and I feel safe and enclosed in that familiar childhood way, I think everything's going to be fine.

"You guys sleep?" he says, slinging my bag over his shoulder and running his hand over Atticus's hair. "That coast-to-coast flight's always such a killer. Two hours longer and you could actually sleep, or a few hours shorter and you just stay up, but there's no real solution."

"I slept," Atticus says. "Honor didn't."

"You need to sleep before we go anywhere?"

"Honor probably does."

"Yeah, that's fine," our dad says. "We can go back to my place for a little while. Maybe Atticus and I can hit the gym while Honor rests. Then we can all go get lunch. I want to take you to get what's very likely the world's best pastrami."

"You want to go for a run instead?" Atticus says. "I'd rather be outdoors right now."

"Perfect idea. I'm right by the park."

This better be good, I think, watching them fall into their easy companionship together. Somehow when I imagined coming, I had only imagined us talking—I hadn't pictured all the other trappings of a visit. I'm exhausted, though, so I guess whatever answers we came for can wait.

He's staying in a brownstone in Brooklyn Heights, on a pretty tree-lined street with an old brick church at the corner. Inside, the apartment is light and bright, with bay windows looking down onto the street, and a carved marble fireplace. It reminds me a little of Caden's house with its intricate old millwork and gleaming patterned wood floors. It's not the kind of place I would've imagined my dad selecting—usually he likes a sleeker modern feel. It's beautiful, though. I look for signs of someone else staying there, but I see only his things—the coffee pods he likes in the kitchen, some self-help-type books lying on the coffee table.

"Nice place," Atticus says very neutrally.

"It's gorgeous, isn't it? The first night here I just sat here and tried to imagine all the different lives of people who would've been here. It's prewar. You guys have to come up and see the rooftop deck, too. Maybe we'll have dinner up there. Atticus, you bring good running shoes?"

168 • KELLY LOY GILBERT

"Not if we're going more than a mile or so," Atticus says. "You have an extra pair?"

"Yeah, let me grab you some. Honor, I'll show you your room first."

The guest room opens to a balcony with a view of Manhattan across the river. I fall into a deep, immediate (maybe vestigially Ambien-fueled) sleep, and I don't stir until Atticus taps me awake and I bolt upright, completely disoriented.

"Did you forget we were here?" he says, grinning, seeing my face. "Come on, we're hungry. Let's go grab lunch."

"It's kind of a hike to the places I want to take you," our dad says, squinting in the sunlight as we walk down the street. "But it's worth it. These are going to blow your mind. It's funny, you think you can get everything in the Bay Area, and then you come to New York and realize—actually no, you can't."

"You can get enough," Atticus says.

"Well, you'll see." Our dad pats his pocket, then his other one. "Rats, I left my phone."

"Do you want to go back?" I say.

"Nah, I think I can navigate. It'll be good to be unplugged a little bit. Test how good my navigation's gotten here." He grins. "I try to walk and take the subway as much as I can. I don't have a driver here. I've never even called a car service."

We descend behind him into a labyrinthine subway station. It's warmer than it was aboveground, claustrophobic feeling, and I'm very conscious of cars driving over us. I'm ready to get back in the open air again. When we're inside one of the train cars, I say, "So what's the deal, then? With Heather Young?"

"Let's talk when we're eating," our dad says. "You know, I was thinking—have you guys ever been on the subway before? I don't think you have. We always had a town car before when we were here. And we've never taken you here just for fun. There was always some purpose. No time to just explore. Get lost a little."

This was one of our tour stops. I haven't been back since.

"You guys are almost done with high school," he says. "It's good you've gotten to see so much of the world. Figure out where you want to land next. It's good to challenge yourselves. Leave your comfort zone. People don't do that enough, and it's why there's just so much stagnancy right now. So much of polarization is just the fact that we're trapped in these stagnant bubbles."

The two women behind us, right in the target audience to be into our parents, are watching us with interest. Atticus notices at the same time I do; I sense him stiffen. Our dad says, "If people would just—"

"Please don't be so loud," Atticus murmurs.

Our dad looks amused. "The one constant in the universe is kids will never stop being embarrassed by their parents just existing, huh? Life goes on. So it goes."

We emerge back into the sunlight on a busy, bustling street, low-slung storefronts with faded colored lettering lining either side. I could be wrong, but I think our dad's good mood is genuine. I had expected something else—contrition, maybe, or some quiet mal-aise. I wasn't prepared for him to be happy here.

"You guys had doubles before?" he says. "Trinidadian food. So good. The flavors are going to blow your mind. Wait out here. I'll go order."

Atticus raises his eyebrows at me when our dad goes inside. "What do you think?" he says.

"I don't know what to think. What did he say when you guys went running?"

"Nothing. We just talked about running."

"How do you talk about *running*? No, don't answer that."

Our dad comes back out and hands us each a wrapped package, still warm. "All right, this is just an appetizer. We can eat and walk. There's a pastrami place I want to take you to after this. Try it, though. So good, right?" he says, watching us eat. It's soft, pillowy bread stuffed with curried chickpeas. "The way they combine flavors. All right, onward."

I ball the paper up, scrunching it smaller and smaller in my fist. I wish we were inside somewhere, away from people.

"It's great here," our dad says. "Don't you love it? The East Coast energy is so different from California energy. I'm just soaking it all up."

"Okay, but like—we're all at home still."

"It's so great having you here," he says. "You know, every time I go anywhere, it's never the same without you guys."

At the deli, the man behind the counter picks up what looks like a segment of petrified wood, gleaming and black, then cuts into it, and glistening pink slices fall away from his knife. It's easily the best pastrami I've ever had, possibly the best sandwich I've ever had, but none of that matters.

"Where to next?" our dad says. "We've got the whole day ahead of us."

"I think it would be good if we went back to your apartment for a while," I say. "I think we should talk."

"Maybe we could find a quiet park, or—"

"I think Honor's right," Atticus says. "We can walk around later. We came here to talk. Let's go talk."

His mood shifts on the subway ride back, less exuberant. A few times I see him reaching for his phone, and he looks irritated every time he realizes it's not there. We ride mostly quietly. My stomach is vaguely unsettled. When we get back into his apartment, he spends a few minutes making an espresso, then making a phone call to someone who doesn't pick up, while Atticus and I sit waiting in the living room.

"All right," he says finally, coming to sit down with us. He puts his coffee on the side table next to him and crosses one leg over the other. "I'm really glad you guys could come out. Kauai was—well, none of that was ideal, and I imagine you probably have a lot of thoughts and questions. And I don't know what you've heard from your mom about any of this."

"Nothing," Atticus says.

"Ah. I see." Our dad drinks some of his coffee. "Your mother and I—nothing is ever going to change what we have between us. Just off the bat, I have to tell you I truly believe that. But the past few years we've maybe had some—some divergences in what we want to do, what we want to explore. Your mother loves stability. Sometimes the prospect of adventure is exhausting to her, which I get, because she works hard, and she's raised the five of you, so I get that. I get it. But—"

The door opens. Our dad looks alarmed. A female voice calls out, "Hello?"

"Heather," he says. He stands up. She comes into the living room. I've seen her on TV a few times, and she looks the same in person: pretty, angular. She's taller than she seems on-screen.

"Did you not have your phone?" she says. "I wasn't sure where I was supposed to meet you guys for dinner, so I thought I'd just pop by. I figured you'd forgotten it."

"I didn't have my phone. I just called you," he says. "You didn't pick up."

"Oh, I didn't hear it." She takes her phone from her pocket. "Oh, there's your missed call." She turns to us. "It's really nice to meet you guys. I've heard so much about you. What did you get for lunch? Did he take you to A&A and David's? Those are the first two places I took him."

"She's lived here almost a decade," our dad says. I understand the quiet plea in his voice, the look he gives us: *Please don't make a scene.*

It's so tempting to imagine. All the things we could say. But we're Los, which means we've been raised to never show a crack in public, and Heather is absolutely public—she's not someone I care about or ever plan to speak to again. She's not someone who will ever know me.

"How nice," I say, giving her my brightest, most plastic smile. "What an amazing place to live."

She stays for probably fifteen minutes, each one exponentially multiplying my anger, asking us a barrage of getting-to-know-you questions. What are our favorite things to study? Do we know what we want to do after high school? What do we think of New York? I can go forever, I can answer every one of her stupid questions without revealing a single thing—I love studying everything, I'm excited to see what the future brings, I think New York is just magical—but I sense Atticus's fury starting to dissolve his poise, and my dad feels it too.

"Heather," he finally says, "I need some time to talk with the kids still. Can we say six? We'll order from Francie."

"That's perfect," she says. "It was *so* good to finally see you guys in person. You'll love Francie. I'll see you at six."

The three of us wait, in a tacit silence, until we hear the door close. As soon as it does, Atticus says, "You have got to be fucking kidding me."

Our dad closes his eyes and massages his temples. "Okay," he says, "that was not ideal timing, but I think we all need to just keep an open mind here so we can talk. I acknowledge that we're all going to have a different lens, but I think we can hold that tension and hold those differences here while we talk."

"Sure, perfect," Atticus says. "Let's do it. Let's talk. Tell us about *Heather*. I would love, just really *love*, to hear how you think this isn't what it looks like."

"Well, people come into our lives—sometimes for a season, sometimes for many seasons—and we can all learn from each other and experience moments of grace and beauty in connections, and—"

"You're shitting us, right?" Atticus says, laughing incredulously. "That's what you're going to try to say this is?"

"Heather is—she's helping me work through some things. This is not something final, this is not even about your mom, this is just about me and the work I'm doing in myself. I think when you get to know her, you'll understand how—"

"You made us fly out here so we could get to *know* her?" Atticus says. "She's practically young enough to be our *sister*. What are you doing? Are you telling her you'll leave your family and marry her?"

"Heather doesn't believe in marriage."

I snort. "Of course she doesn't."

"Honor, are we talking, or are we not? We don't have to if you're not ready."

"Don't condescend to Honor like that," Atticus snaps. I have never seen him so incandescently angry. "I stuck up for you when everyone else said this was sketchy. I was like, no way would you fuck over our family this way. I told everyone no way, Dad loves us, he wants to do the right thing, he'll do the right thing."

He yanks his phone from his pocket. Our dad says, alarmed, "What are you doing? Are you posting something?"

"I'm getting an Uber. Obviously, we aren't going to stay another night here."

"You're getting—okay, no, we're Los, we don't run away from hard conversations. You're not getting an Uber. Sit back down. If you have questions, I'm happy to answer them."

"How long have you been cheating on Mom?"

Our dad sighs again. "Maybe when we can all take a step back—"

"You said you'd answer questions. How long?"

"Well, Atticus, I don't agree with your framing there. So there's your answer."

Atticus looks at me. "You done with this conversation, Honor?"

The pathetic thing about me is that I never want to end a conversation, that I would rather have a terrible time together than none at all. This has always been true of me. "Well—"

"Listen, sweetheart, this doesn't change anything about our family. We all have people who come in and out of our lives. Heather is—you know, she's helping me work through some questions. She's a fresh perspective."

"We've been missing you so much," I say. My voice shakes. "So yeah, it doesn't exactly feel great to come here and see this person you're replacing us with, and—"

"Honor, sweetheart, no one's getting replaced."

"No one's getting replaced?" Atticus says, smiling violently. "No one's getting *replaced*? You've spent all day parading us around this stupid city to show us how you're so *cool* now, you ride the *subway*, you eat all these great *foods*, you have this great new *soul mate* showing you how to *live* again—what did you think was going to happen? We were going to come out here and meet your child girlfriend and think yeah, cool, good upgrade, Dad? You traded Mom and you traded us for a fucking pastrami sandwich." He jams his phone back into his pocket. "The driver will be here in three minutes, Honor. Let's go."

He's silent in the Uber there, through security, while we're waiting in the terminal. A little before we board, Jamison messages us: **You went to see Dad??** Which is how I find out that our dad posted about it, an artsy shot he took of Atticus at the park. *Great visit with @atticuslo @honorlo.*

You know that looks like you're taking his side, right? Jamison says. I write back, **I know, it was a huge mistake, we thought he wanted to talk!!** Atticus stares blankly at the customer service desk and doesn't look at his phone. I don't tell him to.

Finally, when we start to taxi down the runway for takeoff, as I'm trying to breathe through my panic, cursing the failed Ativan, he says, "You okay?"

"I'll live." The engines roar like they're tearing some curtain of the universe, and my heart lurches, my pulse screaming in my ears. "Or *will I.*"

He allows himself a small smile. I say, "What about you?"

"Yeah. I just can't believe I thought he would actually have anything to say. I don't know why I always do that with him. Like after he left this summer, I should've been like, all right, peace out, we're done. But then in Kauai I was like okay, maybe he's trying—God. How fucking naive can you get?"

"I'm sorry," I say.

"I can't believe we're all just covering for him too. Why are we even doing that? I should call a reporter when we get back and be like yo, my dad is having an affair with Heather Young."

"You can't do that," I say immediately. "Promise you won't."

"I would love to see the look on his face."

"You can't do that to everyone else."

He sighs, resigned. "He's such a joke."

We lift off the runway, hovering in nothingness. I grab his hand.

"Maybe the default is just things falling apart," Atticus says. "Maybe it's more shocking when things work out."

I should just ignore it, it'll just make me feel worse, but I do a quick search when we land to see if there's any reaction to his post, and there is, of course: *Lo Twins Show Support for Father!*

I'm sure Lauren's seen, which means our mother has too, and I'm braced for the worst when we get home. But then we go inside, and our mother is in the kitchen, frantically chopping bell peppers and radishes. There's a platter next to her on the counter half-filled with charcuterie and crudités. There are fresh flowers on the dining table and the kitchen island and the entry table in the foyer. I say, "Is someone coming to do an interview or something?"

Our mother doesn't look up from her knife. "Your aunt is coming."

"Auntie JJ?" I'm shocked. "She's coming here?"

"Yes. She just called. She's on her way."

"Why is she coming here?"

"To gloat, I'm sure. Everything's falling apart, and I'm sure she feels just so pleased with herself for being right. I'm sure she wants to come and tell me if I'd just listened to her earlier, none of this would be happening."

"Does she know about Heather?"

"Does she know about Heather? That's a great question. Apparently, everyone's spreading the word."

The doorbell rings. Our mom closes her eyes. "Just exactly what I needed right now," she mutters, then opens her eyes and pastes on a smile to go answer the door.

I sweep up the rest of our mom's crudités scraps with my hand and put the plates on the counter, and then our mom and Auntie JJ come back into the kitchen. It's a slight shock to see how much older she looks. She has her hair cut short, a pixie cut, and she's wearing jeans and a black zip-up from Apple, where she works, and the same jade cross necklace she's always worn. She's carrying a pink pastry box.

"Honor!" she says. "Look at you. You're so grown-up. I was crossing my fingers I'd get to see you, too. Here, this is a burnt-almond cake. Maybe it's not your favorite anymore, but I'm too Chinese to show up empty-handed."

It did use to be my favorite. She hands me the pink box, then gives me a huge hug, the box getting semicrushed between us. I'm not sure what to say back. This would be easier if our mother weren't here watching. Up close I can tell Auntie JJ is sweating.

"Melissa," she adds, and embraces our mother. Our mom gives her a tepid hug in return.

It occurs to me that I don't think I've ever seen them hug, probably for the same reason I never hug, say, Atticus: I think you can be close to someone in a way that makes it feel like you're never actually gone from each other, like even physical distance doesn't interrupt your togetherness, and a hug would be weirdly formal. Or no, maybe it's just that neither one of them is especially affectionate. I think they're more alike than not.

"Wow, so this is your new place," Auntie JJ says, looking around. "It's beautiful."

Our mom brushes it off. "Oh, it's all right. It still needs work."

"Back in Los Gatos! Who would've thought? That must be weird."

"It's not."

Auntie JJ raises her eyebrows. "Well, that's good, then."

"Yes." Our mom crosses her arms, then uncrosses them and slides the charcuterie platter across the counter to Auntie JJ. "Are you hungry?"

"Oh, you didn't have to do anything." She doesn't touch the food. "I hope you didn't clean."

Our mom smiles tightly. I take a slice of salami, since no one else is. Maybe I should cut into the cake. Our mom says, "It was such a surprise to hear you were coming."

"I saw you and Nathan were having some problems, and then I

saw you ended the twins' birthday trip early, and I just—are you all okay? I was worried."

"We had some work to do at home."

"All of you?" Auntie JJ says skeptically.

"Oh, you know how it is."

"Well, I don't, because we don't talk."

Our mom starts to say something, then changes her mind. "Well, of course you're always welcome here," she says. "The kids would love to see you more. Wouldn't you, Honor?"

I am a prop, I'm aware of that, but whatever, I'm a willing one. "Yes, definitely." I would love if things were all right between them again, if we could see her without it feeling fraught or traitorous.

"Why don't we all do the holidays together this year?" Auntie JJ says.

Our mom smiles, a fake smile I'm sure Auntie JJ recognizes as such. "If we're in town, that would be lovely."

Auntie JJ reaches for a piece of fennel but doesn't eat it. "We're all the family each other has. Our parents would be heartbroken to know we barely talk."

"Well, that would be the first time you disappointed them, wouldn't it?"

Auntie JJ's jaw tightens. "My guest room looks exactly the same," she says. "Did you know that? All this time I kept thinking, gee, I really should just move into a one-bedroom place, rent is so high right now, but I kept—" She shakes her head, her eyes glittering. "I kept dreaming about the kids coming to stay in my guest room like they used to. Every holiday I spent with whatever family at church didn't want me to be alone. I would pretend to myself all of you were coming by later to see me. Every birthday I thought well, maybe as a surprise they'll show up. Maybe they've missed me."

I would've gone to see her. *I would've come see you,* I want to tell her. My chest hurts.

"I think it's time to stop being angry at each other, Melissa. It's not worth it. I shouldn't have to read about the twins starting a new school in *People.*"

Our mother plucks a misshapen radish half off the platter and intently rearranges the ramekins of hummus. "Well," she says finally, "I know you've always wanted what's best for the children."

"The holidays would be great," I blurt out, unable to stop myself. "Or before, maybe."

Auntie JJ gives me a grateful smile. "That would be so wonderful."

"Yes," our mom says. "We can try to get something on the calendar. You have Ava's number, don't you? She handles all my scheduling."

"I guess that's better than nothing." Auntie JJ picks up her purse. "Well, Melissa, if and when you're ready to talk, you know how to find me. It doesn't have to be heavy. We can just get dinner. You can tell me about everything happening with Nathan. And the kids are always welcome."

"Did you mean it?" I say after Auntie JJ's gone and our mom and I are in the kitchen still.

She looks at me. "Did I mean what?"

"That you want Auntie JJ to be in our lives again."

She dumps the contents of the charcuterie platter into the trash. "People want to watch you fail so they feel better about their own lives. I'm sure she wants a front-row seat."

"You think that?"

"I know my sister." Does she? "It's just like before. She doesn't approve of what I'm doing, and so she uses the five of you to try to manipulate me. It's the same way she used to guilt me about how our parents wouldn't like whatever I was doing. It's sad, really. She doesn't know how to not live for the approval of others."

There's just a glimmer of something in her tone, though, some kind of wistfulness she can't quite hide. "Why didn't you tell her that, then, instead of saying we'll do Christmas?"

"Sometimes it's just easier to go along with things," she says. I guess even though she's built herself a platform on speaking your truth, it's not something she can bring herself to do with her sister. She washes and then dries her hands. "So. How was New York?"

I have whiplash. I had, for a moment, completely forgotten about New York. "It wasn't great."

Her face falls before she adjusts her expression. "Yes, well, who's surprised?" Then she says, "I saw the pictures he posted."

I wince. "Yeah, that was his idea. Atticus specifically told him not to take pictures."

"It's fine. It's probably better that way. It looks suspicious if people think there's a rift between you."

I replay that moment, though, the rest of the day—that flicker of bare grief in her expression. I think she was hoping to be wrong. Maybe it's why she let us go, because some small part of her hoped we'd come back saying, *It was all a mistake, it was just a misunderstanding, he still loves you and everything's fine.*

CHAPTER ELEVEN

There's a heat wave back at home: the air dry and harsh, the news blaring red-flag warnings, and driving through the hills by the house, I think how flammable all the trees feel, all those parched redwoods and all those crackling oak leaves. It looks different after Kauai—I used to think it was so green here. But we've been in a drought for years, and it's hard not to feel the planet slowly immolating.

My jewelry order is due in five weeks and I've barely done any of it. I make a few half-hearted attempts at home, but I can't focus.

Caden finally calls me on Saturday, the day we were supposed to come back.

"You doing anything?" he says. "You feel like coming over?"

Maybe self-respect should dictate that I don't go, but whatever, I do feel like coming over. I don't think I can handle the drive, so he comes and picks me up. His house is quiet and empty-feeling, and there are dishes in the sink. His mom must still be gone. Nothing in his face is an invitation, though, so I don't ask about it, and I don't tell him about New York, even though I wish I could. I wish we could talk. I wish we were friends, I think, and not just whatever this is. But his hands move roughly across me in a way that feels electric, and I try to forget everything else.

Is this what every relationship is like behind all the public posts? Just you and another person in a room, the feeling of being hunted and being invisible all at once, rifling through the moment for the parts that feel good or true or real.

In advance of Jessie's *Vanity Fair* article coming out, our mother and Lauren set up what they call a war room, which means Lauren's kids stay with their dad for three days while she sleeps in the guest room and basically lives out of our mom's office, making calls practically all day long. It's still unclear whether Jessie is going to write about our dad and Heather, and everyone's panicked. Probably three separate times I walk in on our mom venting about how stupid it was for him to do something so totally poisonous to our image. On Monday our mom and Lauren call me in after school to tell me they've made me a public profile, bought me a few hundred thousand followers, and booked me for a bunch of publicity spots.

"It'll be just a really good way to share what you're passionate about," Lauren says. "I'm *excited* for this, Honor. I've always been so eager to see the ways you're going to use your voice in the world."

"Yes, Honor is such a beautiful and wise soul," our mom says. "And really, this is a long time coming. You're going to be great, Honor."

"In the next day or two it would be good for you to post something about your mom, just something casual, to balance out the pictures from New York," Lauren says. "And other than that, just be yourself! Should we talk messaging? You're so smart, Honor, I know you already know all this, but just, you know, keep things super positive. I can write up some posts for you if you're too busy, no problem at all. And we'll get all your interview questions in advance, so you should be fine. It's going to be *great*."

My face feels cold. "I don't know if I want to do that. I don't really like being so online that way." People picking apart everything you say, using it as proof you fit some idea they have of you—people thinking they know you, thinking they own some part of you.

"I get it, sweetheart," our mom says. "I know you're a more private and thoughtful person. But we're really in an all-hands-on-deck situation right now."

"I just—it's not me. I don't belong in all that."

She watches me for a long moment. Her eyes are sad.

"We only belong where we make ourselves belong," she says. "I don't know why your father always thinks he's the only person in the world who doesn't fit in. Nothing is ever guaranteed, and so much can be taken from you. You have to build what you need yourself and protect it, and not let up. It's always been that way for us. Look at this country—there's no safety net. No one looks out for each other. No one is ever going to take care of you except you. This is just how it is here."

"That's sad," I say.

"It's less sad than if you aren't honest with yourself. But that's how it is. What else are we supposed to do? Where else are we supposed to go? China? And anyway, you never know what's going to last. That's why you have to take whatever opportunities come and always work hard. Someday you're going to have kids and you're going to realize you would give anything in the world to make sure they have a good life."

"Don't you think there are other ways to build something for yourself?" I say. "You could do anything. You could start a business or—"

"This is what we do," she says. "Your ancestors sold their

bodies. They came here and risked their lives every day, blasting the mountains with dynamite while dangling off sheer rock. If your grandmother hadn't gone to the home, she probably would have been sold into sex slavery. You just have to decide which parts of you are going to be just for you, that you aren't going to share with anyone ever, and the rest is how you'll survive."

The next day, with no warning, Wrangell sends us an email.

At this time I have decided to go no contact with the family for the sake of my mental health. I will not be reaching out and ask you to do the same.

Immediately the day implodes. Our mom calls Wrangell, who ignores her, then sets up a family conference call with our other siblings, but it ends up being just me, Jamison, and our mom, because Skye is in class and Atticus is at volleyball. Jamison hasn't heard from Wrangell either; no one knows what's going on. He doesn't answer any of our calls or messages. You'd think by now I would recognize the quickness and the randomness of things coming apart, but it's caught me totally off guard again. There's a hollow ache in my stomach.

"Do you think this is Julie?" our mom says. "I liked her, I didn't think of her as the jealous type, but do you think she's trying to drive a wedge between him and his family? Is that what this is about?"

"Oh, I *forgot* about the new girlfriend," Lauren says. "Maybe. Very possible. Okay, but the real question, and maybe this is a question for Jamison, because you probably talk with him the most, is whether he's going to try to put this out in the public sphere."

"Wrangell would never do that," our mom says.

"Are you sure?" Lauren says. "I love Wrangell, you know I love him like he's my own child, but he can certainly be a little—volatile.

Maybe, you know, he wants to lash out, he posts something like this—and the timing, on top of Nathan, would look like things are really crumbling. I wonder if we want to try to get ahead of this."

"Try to get ahead of it how?"

"Maybe we want to put out a statement. We don't want this to get away from us. If it looks like first the husband leaves, then the son—I don't like how that's going to translate if we sit it out. I'm thinking maybe we should frame this as fallout from Nathan's affair. Wrangell's searching for himself. You can talk about how it's impacting all your kids."

"I really don't think so," Jamison says. "It creates a big story. I don't think Wrangell's going to go public in any way. I think we should just give him space."

"People are going to read *so* much into a statement like that," I say. "There's no real way for it not to turn into a huge thing."

"Well, I think there's a way to do this where it's still relatable and it's not turning people off," Lauren says. "If we can communicate, you know, you all love each other, you're still very committed, and because of that love and that commitment to sincerity and truth you're giving each other space to—"

"I can't," our mom says quietly. "No. I know you're worried, but I just—no."

Lauren looks a little alarmed. "The thing is, Melissa, at some point, if there are multiple things you just aren't going to address—the thing about you that's so wonderful that people really respond to is your authenticity, and they're so invested in you and what's happening in your life, and so I think if you're boxing people out, it starts to look like you're hiding something, or you're just contemptuous, or that maybe this is all about *you* or something you—"

"I know, Lauren, I know that, I know you keep saying that. But I just—" She cups her hands around her mouth and draws a shaky breath. "Nothing about Nathan."

"I can write up a statement for you. Just *something*, you know, just to let people know—"

"She doesn't want to," I say impulsively. "She shouldn't have to." I am angry, suddenly, at all the faceless people who feel owed these parts of us. I'm angry at all of it. Why are we talking through these digitized public channels, as if anyone eavesdropping matters here?

Lauren sighs. She runs her hands over my shoulders. "You're a good daughter to her," she says resignedly. "Always looking out."

In the end Lauren and our mother and Jamison, probably in conjunction with our dad, agree the best solution with Wrangell is to wait and see. I wish they'd try harder to talk to him, but waiting is probably better than anything they could say publicly. I am sick with worry and sadness, haunted by what I said to Julie in the airport, unable to sit still or think about anything else.

Atticus tells me he thinks it'll be fine, that Wrangell's just being Wrangell and needs space. Skye is weirdly, uncharacteristically hard to reach. (So many posts about the amazingness of Baylor, though!) I have nightmares all night that she's on his side somehow, also trying to distance herself. I wake up at three so distressed I debate calling Caden. Maybe I could spend the rest of the night there; it might even be worth the awful drive. I could lie next to someone and maybe he'd put his arm around me, maybe I'd nestle against him, and I would be able to turn off my thoughts. Then I fall asleep again anyway and descend into more nightmares.

The next morning I wake up on edge that Wrangell's going to say something more public, and I'm distracted with worry all through class. By third period I can't take it anymore, and at recess I find Atticus to tell him I'm going to go talk to Wrangell.

"Right now?" he says. "Does he know you're coming?"

"I've texted him, like, four times since last night, but he hasn't answered."

"So, what, you're just going to show up at his house?"

"That's the plan."

"How do you even know he's there? What if he's at Julie's?"

"They said she has roommates. I doubt they're ever at her house."

"I don't know if it's worth your time," he says. "What are you going to say? You know how Wrangell gets. He's probably still mad about his day in Kauai and pissed how everything turned out."

"I know he probably is. That's why I think someone has to talk to him, so it doesn't just get worse. Everything's just—falling apart. And I don't think it's fair for him to blame Mom and everyone else like this. Dad, sure, yes, but Mom's not the one having some bizarre fling with Heather Young. She's a victim too. If Wrangell's so angry, he should just have it out with Dad."

"Yeah, well, if you try to tell him that, I see that going exactly nowhere."

"Also—I haven't told anyone this, but I'm worried he might be mad at me specifically."

"Why you specifically?"

I debate telling him everything but lose my nerve. I tell him about what I said to Julie at the airport instead.

"Oh fuck," he says. "Does Wrangell know?"

"I don't know. I don't know if Julie told him or not. Don't tell him."

"Yeah, obviously I'm not going to tell him, because I would like for my twin not to die at seventeen. Maybe you shouldn't go see him. He's really into Julie. He's probably going to kill you if he knows."

"Well, if he does, then I'll apologize. I can talk to Julie."

He sighs. "Honestly, I'd probably just give him space."

"You can't give people space forever, though, Atticus! That's not a plan! That's what everyone did with Dad, and look at him now! You can't just wait around for things to get better. Everyone should've tried to work things out before it ever got to this point."

I lower my voice because I feel people turning to look. Caden isn't one of them; I have been hyperaware all day of where he is, if he's close by. So far we haven't spoken.

"Okay," Atticus says skeptically. "How are you going to get there? Have you ever driven to the city by yourself before?"

"You want to come? You could drive us."

"I can't. I have volleyball after school. Also, I would like to not be murdered by Wrangell." He makes a face. "I'll come if you need me to, though. I can miss volleyball."

"No, it'll be okay. No one's going to be murdered by Wrangell. It's going to be fine."

I debate taking an Uber all the way up to the city, because Atticus is right that I've never driven that far alone, but the thought of getting stuck with someone who recognizes me or someone who wants to talk changes my mind, and I take one home instead to get my car. I feel ill and shaky the whole drive up, going fifty-five in the right lane with a death grip on the steering wheel. I hate driving. I hate all of this.

Wrangell lives in Cole Valley. I haven't been to his place in years. It's a beautiful apartment, an old Victorian subdivided into four units with crown molding and built-in nooks and a window seat I'm obsessed with. It takes me the better part of half an hour to successfully find parking, and by then I'm so flustered I walk around the block twice before knocking so I can steady myself. A tiny part of me hopes he's not home, that I can at least say I tried.

He answers the door when I knock, though, wearing sweat-pants and a T-shirt. He looks surprised to see me. "I thought you were my ChowFast."

"Ew, no, don't do ChowFast. They're the ones who spent all that money to screw over their employees and not let them unionize."

"What are you doing here?" He glances at his watch. "Shouldn't you be in school? Is it some kind of holiday?"

"I really needed to talk to you."

"Ah—" He rubs his forehead. "All right, okay. You want to come in?"

The times I've seen his house, I've always felt like it should've been a clue to the girls who fell for him, who built their whole futures together in their minds. There's nothing sentimental or soft here—it's all clean lines and minimalism, all unwelcoming bare surfaces that look wrong if you leave anything on them, a sweater or a purse or a hair tie.

"You eat lunch yet?" he says as we go down the long hallway into his living room. The walls are adorned with lots of bright, clean-looking modern art, like a gallery. "I have noodles coming. I can order more for you."

I was too nervous to think about eating before I came. I'm still a little nervous, but it's better being here—things are always worse the way you build them up in your mind first. At heart I am my mother's daughter, who believes you can fix things if you try hard enough, and here I am trying. "Sure, I could eat."

"All right. We can do shifts." He scrolls through a menu on his phone for a little while, then puts it in his pocket. "I got you kuro ramen."

That was always my favorite; I'm touched he remembered. "Sounds amazing. Thanks."

"You want coffee?"

"Sure."

He has a gleaming, elaborate espresso maker on the kitchen counter, and I pull out one of the stools to sit while he makes it. He tamps down the grounds deftly, practiced. I like these little glimpses into his dailiness.

"I see you have a public profile now," he says.

"Yeah, Lauren's handiwork."

He snorts. "I figured."

"So where's Julie? Is she working?"

"We broke up."

"You what?" In spite of myself, I'm relieved, and a little amused. Of course they broke up; how could it have gone any other way? "Wrangell! You had a ring! I thought this one would last at least another few weeks."

He sets a ceramic mug down in front of me, extremely gently, like he wanted to slam it. "Well, I thought it would last forever, so. I still have the fucking ring."

He says it very quietly, a little flatly, and I know him well enough to understand that he is devastated. Immediately I realize my mistake. I wish I could take back my flippant comment. "So did—she's the one who ended things, then?"

"Yes."

"Oh no, Wrangell, I'm sorry. I had no idea." To my knowledge, this is the first time anyone's ever broken up with him. "What happened?"

The doorbell rings. "Ah—excuse me," he says. I resist the urge to follow him down the hallway. While he's gone, I message Atticus and Skye: Julie broke up with Wrangell!! He's heartbroken.

He comes back with a bag of Styrofoam containers—broth, noodles, toppings. He separates them into two bowls without speaking.

"You can have it," I say. "I can wait for the next one coming."

He waves it off. He eats his efficiently, still without saying anything. The broth is rich and salty, laced with tender kakuni and springy noodles and dots of scallion, but there's a lump in my throat that's making it hard to eat. After a few attempted bites I say, "So are you doing okay?"

"Not really."

"Oh, Wrangell." I twirl some more noodles around my chopsticks. I don't know exactly what I'd planned to say to him—I was going to play it by ear—but obviously whatever I would've come up with before wouldn't have worked.

Wrangell gets up and rinses out his bowl, then slides it into the dishwasher. "Everything with Julie just put a lot of things into really sharp focus for me," he says. "She didn't want to be a part of all the toxicity and codependence and all the general bullshit that's our family. She said that trip was like looking into the future. And a lot of stuff, you know, I kind of knew but hadn't really put the effort into thinking about, or maybe I just wasn't defining it to myself the right way—but it made me realize I just need to get out. I'm done." He sits back down next to me. "I was thinking about you guys, though. You and Atticus. Soon enough you'll be eighteen. I think you have the chance to be in such a different place than I was when I was eighteen. Honestly, I should've gone no contact then. You should start thinking about it."

"You wish you'd stopped talking to us seven years ago?" I say. I think about all the things we've done together since then—all the holidays, all the trips. All the group chats. He would throw all those away? "I know you didn't mean it this way, but Mom is honestly devastated. After Dad, and then this—she really is not doing well."

He taps his fingers on the table a few times, a very Atticus-like gesture, without looking at me. Then he says, "Honor, that's—kind of the point."

Something goes cold inside me. "What do you mean it's the point? You mean you're trying to hurt her?"

"No. I'm not after any specific emotional response. The point is that it's completely toxic to expect me to base my life around what she feels, or what all of you feel, and to constantly be running from one thing to the next to try to fix every fucked-up thing in this family so we can have some shiny, perfect image all the time."

"I think you're being unfair to Mom here. Who wouldn't be devastated if their husband was cheating on them and then their child was like, *Both sides are at fault here*? Dad's the one cheating."

"Yes, that's on him, obviously, but the way she handles every-thing—like torpedoing the whole week and expecting everyone to just rally around her and try to fix her public image—I can't keep doing that. I'm just done."

"I hate that kind of thing too, but I think in her way she's trying to look out for all of us."

"The thing is," he says, looking past me, "is that for you, okay, whatever, maybe everything feels normal. That's fine. I'm glad. I mean that. I'm glad it doesn't feel like this traumatic thing for you. But frankly, Honor, you're seventeen years old and you don't know shit yet. When I was seventeen, I didn't have anything figured out yet either. But it's just—it's an insane amount of gaslighting about things that are going to fuck you up for the rest of your life."

"You think we're all just totally emotionally damaged? I don't think that. Everyone else is fine," I say. "Look at Jamison. She's even—"

"You think Jamison is fine? Jamison is not fucking fine. Jamison is the most miserable person I know. Come on, Honor, you're not stupid. Stop lying to yourself. Jamison is trapped in needing to look good the way everyone in this family is trapped. Look at you. Here you are cutting class today to try to guilt me into just forgetting everything because you're worried maybe things aren't the public fantasy of a big, happy family. You don't think Mom has ruined you? Think harder. She's a toxic person."

"I think you're being too hard on her. Wrangell, I have to tell you something." I swallow. "I was the one who called Jessie about an interview."

He narrows his eyes. "What do you mean you were the one who called Jessie?"

"I didn't know it was going to be on your day. But when we got there, Mom and Dad weren't talking at all, and I read something that made me think—if they had a reason to actually sit down and talk to each other, they would do it. And I thought if there was a neutral party—so I called Jessie and told her we were all in Kauai that week but we had time to talk if she wanted to set it up with Mom."

Wrangell is staring at me. There's no hint of softness in his expression. I say, "Please don't be mad at me."

"I really thought you were better than that."

"I never meant for anything to go the way it did."

"In retrospect, I don't know why I expected better from you. You care about image more than anyone in the family. You just know how to wrap it up better in pretending it's because you care about people."

Wrangell has never spoken to me this way. I'm shocked at how painful it is. My heart feels like it's going to slam its way out of my chest. I have always believed in our family first and foremost, have always believed in our family compact—that under everything, what matters is one another, that we are here for each other no matter what. That's been our promise, and I have moved through the world believing that. I have survived the world on the basis of that promise.

It occurs to me for the first time how tenuous that's always been. Maybe everything is entropy, everything is made to fall apart, and you can keep things together only by sheer force of will, and that's not sustainable. Do people make up after saying this kind of thing to each other? How? I came here with good intentions—I came here because I believed the best of him, because I thought I knew who he was. But maybe that was wrong, and now I don't understand how we'll ever not be in this moment, how I'll ever look at him the same way again.

"How can you say that?" I say, my voice shaking. "I care about our family. That's the only thing I've ever cared about."

"You care about our family? I just lost the love of my life because our family messed that up, and now you're here telling me who cares, it was just a fling, I need to be nicer to our mom? This family is completely toxic. Ask yourself why you don't have any real friends. It's because our parents set up this life for you where if you want to keep it, you have to play by all their stupid rules. That's fucking abusive, Honor. If you're smart, you'll get out now." He peers at me. "But no, maybe you'll keep doing the exact same thing because that's what matters to you most. That's just who you are."

I am on the verge of sobbing. What is happening? How did we get here? I came here to try to fix things. "I don't think wanting you not to abandon us is some ridiculous request, Wrangell. You're our brother. And I've been having a terrible time these last months too and you've just been gone, and—"

"You know what?" he says. "I spent my entire adolescence taking care of you, which, fine, whatever, it is what it is, but you're practically an adult now, and it's incredibly fucking selfish to keep trying to drag me back into this, Honor. I think I've been clear about my boundaries, and this whole family is just obsessed with trying to erode them, my God. I think I'm just done."

Everything he said loops again and again in my mind for the rest of the day, cloistering me away from whatever else is going on. My vision is blurred and I can't focus on anything else. Wrangell reposts a set of pastel-colored slides about narcissism from some mental health influencer account. Lauren flips out. I'm too afraid to tell them I went to go see him.

I tell Atticus I don't want to talk about it. Which isn't true: I also spend hours and hours in imaginary conversations with him and the rest of the family, workshopping how I'd frame it to them, the tone I would use to be believed, to have everyone side with me. *Of course he's wrong about you, Honor! You're not shallow or image obsessed or selfish; you aren't toxic; our family is fine.*

You're Not Famous: A Snark Site
ynf.com/forums/LoFamily

snarkandchill, 11:02:43 pm PST: lol ok so who's Wrangell's mystery narcissist???

baconspam420, 11:02:53 pm PST: you think it's just one? because . . . lol.

knockoffbrene, 11:02:59 pm PST: he's probably talking about Nathan. We still haven't figured out why they left Kauai early and Nathan left before the rest of them. I am still convinced something went down.

ambergris, 11:03:03 pm PST: yeah it literally could be any/all of them

cookiemonstera, 11:03:43 pm PST: Nathan leaving his family to find himself screams narcissism to me

strawberryguava, 11:04:12 pm PST: yeah I left my husband and he's an actual narcissist and convinced everyone I was the actual narcissist so if that's what's happening here I fully support Nathan getting out of a toxic situation

edwardfickett, 11:04:50 pm PST: lowkey my money is on Honor. She's always had NPD vibes to me, like when they had to cancel their book tour because of her mystery illness that no one ever explained. That feels like such a classic narcissistic move

calendulateam, 11:05:26 pm PST: I would truly pay thirty (30) US dollars right now for Wrangell's tell-all!

baconspam420, 11:05:59 pm PST: omggg, I have been hate-following them for literal *years*, I deserve that

I wake up that night around four because I'm suffocating. My chest is so tight I can't let in air. I grope my way to Atticus's room.

"Atticus," I gasp. "Atticus. I can't breathe."

He bolts upright in bed. "What time is it? You okay?"

"I don't think so." I haven't had a panic attack in so long. Even when our dad moved out, when we started at Saint Simeon—I thought I was over this. It's different this time, the symptoms worse. Maybe this is something else.

"Try to take slow breaths," Atticus says. He wipes his eyes with the heel of his palm and squints at me in the dark. "Count with me. One, two."

I don't tell people about the panic attacks. I find them pathetic. There is nothing worse than having your own body betray you; I think it's weak, and I don't want to give it daylight in my life. But in the moment, in the moment—it's all-consuming. I will never exist outside of this moment ever again.

"I'm not getting enough air," I tell Atticus. It comes out as a whimper. My throat is collapsing itself. I can feel the oxygen dying out halfway down my airway.

"You are," he says. "You wouldn't be able to talk if you weren't. You'd have passed out by now."

The minutes creep by as I try not to suffocate. I think about all the things that could be going wrong inside my body. I pull my sleeve up over my fist to make a pocket I can breathe into. I'm light-headed.

"What happened?" Atticus says. "Is this about Wrangell?"

I shake my head no, a lie. It's the first time in my life I've ever not been able to tell Atticus something. But I can't, because the possibility that he might agree with Wrangell is too much; that would wreck me. You don't talk about the things that you can't bear to be true. This is what people never realize about anyone famous, that any vulnerability is almost never real; you're always picking out the parts you're fine offering other people. No one actually knows us at all.

I wonder if Wrangell is talking to Jamison or Skye or Atticus—I'm afraid to ask all of them. Anytime a message goes unanswered for more than a few minutes, by anyone, I start to panic. Even Skye, whom I've never had any kind of conflict with in my entire life, is harder to reach, and I worry about it endlessly. Every time she streams, I watch obsessively, looking for any kind of hint. She seems tired—once or twice she doesn't answer for a long time and then tells me afterward that she was sleeping, even though it was, like, three in the afternoon her time—and it makes me worry a little about how she's doing. I send her a care package of foods she's always loved from home. I send Sonnet little baby activity kits, a set of carved wooden blocks in a beautiful array of rainbow colors, a personalized stuffed sea turtle. I send Jamison a basket with different all-natural, low-sugar crackers and nut mixes.

Eloise and Lilith both follow my new profile. I try to check the time against the time stamps of posts on YNF, reading obsessively to see if either of them will say anything revealing, but it doesn't get me anywhere. Lauren schedules me with a photographer to take a million headshots and candid-looking pictures I can post with, and the photographer insists on going downtown for it, where I'm constantly afraid I'll be spotted by someone I know from school. I hate how every picture looks. I'm worried I'm just proving Wrangell's point.

Lauren writes suggested posts for me. Her version of me is a bland and placid approximation, unplagued by any of the things I try not to think about. A picture of me surrounded by redwoods downtown: I love nature; I never worry about the planet immolating! Pictures of me in a Swedish bakery, a Taiwanese boba shop, a Mexican seafood place: I love other countries and cultures; I never worry about how soulless men are controlling the global levers of power and causing untold suffering! Lauren thinks it would be good if I could ignite small, meaningless controversies, things that have a chance to go viral enough to even temporarily bump down results about our parents, so she writes those, too: I think everyone in the family should share one toothbrush to cut down on the use of disposable plastics; I don't believe in dating before age sixteen; I think TikTok is a worse drug than cocaine.

"Of course you can put your own spin on them, or better yet, rewrite them altogether," she says. "And let more of your personality shine through. People are going to love you."

I tell her she can just use the posts she wrote for me. I hate thinking about people I know seeing me splashed all over this way like I think I have fascinating, valuable things to say that the world absolutely needs to hear. I don't tell Atticus very much; he refused to make accounts of his own, and I know what he thinks about them using me to change the narrative. But I, too, desperately want to change the narrative. I want to stop having long imaginary conversations with Wrangell in my head every night instead of sleeping; I want to stop imagining future Christmases when Wrangell has kids our parents have never met. I want to stop spending all day not thinking about our dad and Heather Young. I want everyone to be plotting how to come back together instead of new terrible ways to fracture apart.

It's funny the things you miss, looking back: The sound of the garage door opening for your last sibling when you're lying awake late at night waiting for everyone to come home. The way you used to fight over the bathrooms, how chaotic it was in the mornings with everyone trying to get ready. Maybe this will be like that someday too, I tell myself, and I cling to that. Maybe later somehow this whole time will transform in my memory into something precious and beloved, and all that'll be left will be the parts we posted about: all of us standing together near the ocean in Kauai, the carefully plated food, Sonnet sprawled out on the lanai.

CHAPTER TWELVE

A week after my fight with Wrangell, and it hasn't faded from my mind. If anything, it's worse now; I have memorized the same snippets, and they play on loop all day long. On Friday after school that week I linger at my locker, watching VBD leave together, their arms linked, all laughing about something. I watch the way they talk to each other, no gaps in the conversation, just a long, endless flow of things they want to say. I rummage distractedly in my locker, unseeing, imagining their afternoon: the three of them sprawled across a bed or a living room floor, laughing and talking and rifling through their catalogue of secrets and inside jokes, not caring what they look like, telling each another everything. I would kill to have that right now.

"You going to the parking lot?"

I jump. It's Caden. He reaches for my books. "I'll walk you."

· The campus has mostly emptied out, and the fall late-afternoon sun is streaming through the redwoods. Technically, I wasn't going to the parking lot. I didn't ride with Atticus today because he has volleyball, so the driver is idling somewhere nearby, waiting, because I still hate driving here.

"What are you doing after this?" he says. "You want to come over?"

A little flare of panic, both because I don't want to and because I do. "Maybe."

He smiles. "Maybe? Did Blythe successfully warn you off?"

"I see you heard about our conversation."

"I did."

"From who?"

"Victoria."

I don't know exactly what to make of that. Probably no good can come of trying. "I see. Anyway, no, I don't really care what Blythe thinks. Why?"

"Just wondering."

"Why were you wondering?"

"Why was I wondering?" He looks amused. "I don't know, because all of a sudden you pretty much vanished? We were talking and then all of a sudden—we weren't?"

I can't read this here, if he's trying to tease me or if he actually means it's how he sees things and I've offended him.

"Well, nothing ends well, right? Eventually everything falls apart." I say it lightly; I'll humiliate myself if I sound like I mean it while he's just trying to have fun. "Maybe I'm just sparing us the trouble, since I doubt that's what you want."

"Actually," he says dryly, reaching for his keys, "you'd be surprised how little self-preservation I feel."

As soon as we're tangled up together on his bed, it turns out I did want to be here after all. Maybe someone else's body is another story you can lose yourself in. My mind is blank, greedy, reckless. Pressed against him, my heart thudding, his body warm against mine, I haven't felt this unencumbered in ages.

We kiss, his tongue thrust inside my lips, our hands roaming around each other's bodies. I feel like a sparkler wherever he touches me, flashing and flashing. He pulls back, out of breath. "Do you want—?"

Yes, I want that; yes, I want it to subsume and obliterate any other part of me. I want to exist solely in the visceral, animal world, nothing else. He takes out a condom from his drawer, and I wait, hot and impatient, while he puts it on. I am having something of an out-of-body experience. The world has funneled away. It is only me and Caden, this person I maybe barely know, who maybe for right now can be all I need. I want that to be true. I need that to be true.

I close my eyes as we move against each other. I try to lose track of time. I try to let myself uncoil. He shudders against me and then goes still. This is the problem with sex, I guess, that sooner or later it's over, and then do you feel better afterward? I don't think I do. I'm still the same person, the same world still bearing down on me.

Caden stays lying down while I sit up, hook my bra, and slip it back over my head. He rests his hand lightly on my back, which strikes me as unusual: he's not an affectionate person. I suppose neither am I.

"Are you okay?" he says, peering at me, and when he says it, I realize I'm crying.

"I'm fine." I wipe my eyes carefully, with one finger, trying not to mess up my makeup. "God." Crying after hooking up with Caden Lyall is potentially the most embarrassing thing that's happened to me in my entire life. Which, frankly, is saying a lot.

He looks worried. "Did I hurt you?"

"No, no. I'm fine."

"You look fine."

I roll my eyes. "Shut up."

He watches me for a moment. I put my shirt back on. Then he says, "You want gyros?"

"Do I want *gyros*?" I wipe my eyes again, more roughly this time. What the hell? Why did I think he was going to mean anything in my life? I am, suddenly, exhausted.

"I don't know, it sounds good," he says. "I think I'm going to order some. You want to stay and eat?"

We wait downstairs. It occurs to me after we order that it probably takes forever to get food up here. Caden's house is a disaster. The kitchen sink and counters are overflowing with dishes, and there are empty pizza boxes and some takeout cartons strewn across the island. The last time I was at his house it was immaculate in a way that made me associate it with him: he was someone who was neat and in control. But today's version of the house is a different story.

"I should get a dog," he says, apropos of nothing. "You like dogs?"

"I'm allergic."

"Oh. Sucks." He looks around the house. "Maybe it would get lonely while I'm at school all day, though. Maybe it wouldn't be fair."

"I'm going to do your dishes," I say, getting up.

"Oh—don't do that."

"It'll give me something to do." I turn on the tap and wait for the water to run hot. "Do you have people come clean or anything?"

"We did, but they haven't come in a while. Maybe my mom hasn't paid them. I don't know."

"Do you know how to cook?"

"Nope."

"How is your mom?"

"No idea." His voice is sharp. Something must show on my face, because he says, a little clipped, "Sorry. I'm just—I'm done with it all."

I'm not in the mood to push for more details. I focus on washing the dishes. There are a ton of them, mostly bowls and silverware— the kind of dishes you eat off, not that you use to make anything. I turn the water as hot as I can stand. I clear a space on the counter to put the dishes to dry. When I look up, he's just sitting at the counter, his forehead propped up in his hands.

"You don't have to do that," he mumbles.

"I know. I don't feel like sitting still."

"I know other ways we could not sit still," he says, but not like his heart is in it. I ignore it.

There's a knock on the door, and he gets up. He comes back with the food and puts it on the counter. I don't eat lamb—baby animals bleating in terror for their mothers is a bridge too far for me—so I got a hummus plate instead. I have no appetite. Actually, now that I'm sitting down, flushed from the hot water, I feel sick. I'm not sure I still want to be here. I also, simultaneously, cannot fathom leaving and going back to the actual world.

I think eating cheers him up, which is weirdly endearing, or would be if I were feeling better. Atticus is the same way. It must be amazing to be a simpler person. I pick at my pita bread.

"You don't like it?" he says.

"It's fine. I'm not that hungry."

He looks more closely at me. "Are you going to tell me what's wrong?"

"No."

"Or why you were crying earlier?" He crumples the wrapper from his gyro and tosses it onto the counter, a little addition to the trash landscape. "You can tell me if you want. I know something about keeping secrets."

You should never trust people who want secrets from you, for obvious reasons, but something about the way he says it gives me pause. "Do you not tell people about your mom?"

"Some people, but not for the reasons you think. I don't care who knows, but teachers are technically supposed to report it if they hear."

"What do you mean, 'report it'?"

"Because I'm not supposed to be here. When my mom's gone like this, I'm supposed to go live with my dad or in a group home or something. Because I'm a minor. So, you know. Can't be left unsupervised." He waggles his eyebrows at me. "Might get into trouble."

"Do you ever think about going to stay with your dad?"

"Going to stay with my *dad*?" He snorts. "No, I do not think about going to stay with my dad. I'd rather live on the streets. He could die tomorrow, whatever. Him, my stepsiblings, his new wife. I don't give a shit."

His expression is mild, as always, but in his voice there's a barely suppressed fury that catches me off guard. I say, "Wait, I thought you told me you didn't have siblings."

"I don't. They're not real siblings."

"Are they younger?"

"Yep."

"How old?"

"I don't know. Three and six or something. My dad sends me

pictures of them to brag about everything they're doing. They're *so* good at sports. They're *so* smart. Just perfect, perfect kids." He pauses. "He called me yesterday because he heard about my mom somehow. I don't even know how."

"What did he say?"

"Just wanted to bitch about my mom. Nothing like *his* perfect family."

I wince. "I'm sorry. He sounds like a dick."

"Well, not to his other kids. They'll probably turn out better. I'm sure it's different when someone gives a shit about you."

"You don't think anyone gives a shit about you?"

"Nope."

"Really?"

He gestures around the room. "Does it look like anyone cares about me?"

Coming over when everyone else was here, him telling me about things like existential crises or his mom being in rehab—I understand suddenly that in both those times he was still fundamentally very much in control of the story and the image of himself he was projecting, that there was nothing actually vulnerable in that. Maybe he's more like me than I realized in that he's always conscious of how things play with people. He was telling me something everyone else already knew. And this is different; this is something else entirely.

He takes an abrupt, choking breath. "Sorry. I'm not handling it well this time."

This is what he was doing when I felt like he was ignoring/forgetting/getting over me. Maybe in reality he was just wrapped up in all this. Probably it took a lot of effort just to get up and go through the motions every day. My heart twists thinking about it. I put my hand on his. "I won't tell anyone."

He wrestles with his expression for a moment, and then he's back to his implacable, unreadable self. "So what about you?" he says.

And then, impulsively, I'm telling him about fighting with Wrangell. It's a sanitized version, because obviously I can't tell him about our dad and Heather Young, but I tell him how I wanted to help when Wrangell was angry at our parents, and I tell him all the things Wrangell thinks about me.

"That sucks," he says. "You go there trying to play peacemaker and he says all that to you? I think that's unfair."

"Really? I can't stop thinking about it. Because I *was* trying to push him into something he didn't want. I could've listened when he said he didn't want to talk to anyone."

"I mean, sure, whatever, sounds like that was the wrong call, but then he wants to twist that into you categorically being incapable of genuinely caring about people? You don't love your family, you just want to look good? I think that's a shitty thing to say to you. Way out of bounds."

"You're not just saying that?"

"I have no skin in the game here. Why would I say that?"

It's shockingly validating to hear. I understand all at once why people go to confessional or why they tell each other things. Maybe I haven't ruined everything, and maybe I'm not a horrible person, Wrangell will come around, and things will be okay. I'm hungry again. I eat my hummus.

CHAPTER THIRTEEN

Almost immediately, like clockwork, Caden vanishes again. All weekend and then the next week, too, he doesn't call, doesn't ask me over, and I feel sick with how stupid I was. Why did I give him so much of myself? Now he carries that with him, part of me parceled away and out of my own control. The fight I had with Wrangell plays in the background of my mind at all times, spliced with the world before me, and I measure everything against it. Is this why Caden isn't talking to me? I feel aware of all the ugly contours of myself all the time.

After school on Wednesday I have an interview with Skye for *Variety*. I've had knots in my stomach all day, the same sick feeling I get when I log into the accounts that were made for me, which I've been doing as little as possible since I noticed Delancey followed me. I wonder if Caden's seen any of it. It seems like the exact kind of thing Victoria would be appalled by, and I imagine her withering reaction. I wish I were self-actualized enough not to care what people think.

Today will be fine, though. None of us are strangers to this kind of thing, and Skye will be there.

Only then Skye doesn't show up on the call. I put Wendy, the interviewer, on hold while I message Skye, and then call her, but she doesn't answer. I am terrified Wrangell somehow turned her against me. We do the interview without her, and it's easy soft-ball questions—why do I think girls' education is important, how does our family cultivate a culture of giving?—but I can barely get through them because I'm spiraling. It's so unlike Skye to miss something like this.

She calls me a few hours later.

"I'm so sorry!" she says, and I can tell right away from her voice she isn't mad at me. The relief is overwhelming. "I totally forgot. I was at the doctor and it went long."

"You were at the doctor? What happened? Are you okay?"

"Oh, I'm fine. I just had to do some tests."

I am instantly on alert. "What kind of tests? Should I be worried?"

"No, no, of course not. Just routine stuff."

"Did everything look okay?"

"I didn't get the results yet, but I'm sure it will."

"Can I come see you?" I say. "I can come this weekend. If you're sick, I can make you jook and we can just lie around all weekend."

I want her to say, *Yes, oh my gosh, come tomorrow.* Instead she says, "That sounds so fun, Honor, but we should wait. I'll let you know when I'm better. It'll be more fun then."

"I don't care about fun. What are they testing for? You're kind of worrying me."

"No, no, don't be worried! It'll just be boring for you to come all this way. Soon, though, okay? I'm sure I'll be back to normal soon."

You're Not Famous: A Snark Site
ynf.com/forums/LoFamily

knockoffbrene, 3:02:21 pm PST: So what do we think is going on with Skye? Since her last vaguepost a week and a half ago, we now have:

> A vague doctors appointment and test
>
> A vague post about waiting for test results
>
> A vague post about doing hard things
>
> A selfie of her without makeup looking gaunt and weird (Skye, honey, wash your hair)
>
> Some stories saying she's done a bunch of tests and they still haven't pinpointed what's wrong but her symptoms are getting worse (also, maybe I missed it, but did she talk about what her symptoms are anywhere? are we talking like she's shitting herself or bleeding randomly or ???)
>
> A video about how she feels like her doctor is just brushing her off and not taking her seriously
>
> . . . And a bunch of normal-seeming posts where everything is fine again

So what are our theories?

cookiemonstera, 3:02:59 pm PST: honestly? I bet she's pregnant.

junco, 3:03:19 pm PST: I doubt anything's wrong with her. I think that her life at home was extremely sheltered. She lived in an extremely specific bubble. Just a constant echo chamber of all of them thinking they were just so special, so smart and beautiful, so perfect, and now she's outside that bubble for the first time in her life and realizing there's nothing that special about her after all. That's a huge adjustment and I doubt they grew up learning healthy coping mechanisms. She's probably depressed.

disneymom, 3:03:44 pm PST: I don't know. I think something could be really wrong. Just looking at her skin—it's really sallow, like she has some kind of liver issue or something. And she seemed pretty happy before this. She doesn't strike me as someone who would get depressed because she's so whatever about everything.

calendulateam, 3:04:12 pm PST: Maybe she has an STD.

fossilmulch, 3:05:06 pm PST: Skye, we've never met, but just wanted to tell you that I'm sending all my positive thoughts your way, and also, this is how things started for me when I was diagnosed with cancer when I was nineteen. I urge you to press your doctors to take you seriously and to find a different doctor if necessary. Many doctors aren't willing to take women seriously. Especially young women, and I wasted months trying to get my doctor to listen.

CHAPTER FOURTEEN

am frozen in my seat. I can't move. If I get up from this chair and let the rest of life swirl around me, this will be real. I can't let this be real.

You're Not Famous: A Snark Site
ynf.com/forums/LoFamily

calendulateam, 4:56:34 pm PST: holy fuck she's really sick. I . . . feel awful now. Fuck. She's so young to have to go through that.

hungergamesbell, 4:57:11 pm PST: I would not wish cancer on my worst enemy

schildpad, 4:57:34 pm PST: I honestly thought she was just making this up for attention or that she was depressed or something. I feel awful now. And she's already starting chemo? what an absolute nightmare. I truly wish her the best.

gatsby11, 4:58:12 pm PST: even though I can't stand her, I don't think she deserves this. I bet her family is absolutely flipping out. Is this why they've all been so quiet lately?

marnie, 4:59:43 pm PST: I wonder sometimes if people like that who live in such a bubble of wealth and privilege and being able to control the narrative are just totally incapable of weathering something like this.

Like . . . can you imagine the Los actually handling this? What are they even going to do? I am going to hell but frankly y'all are being way too nice and deferential just because someone we all hate got sick and all I can say is, I am absolutely here for this shitshow

Atticus finds me what could be a minute or fifteen later, still staring at the screen, my mind cratering in on itself.

"Are you okay?" he says. He's pale.

"No."

"Take some deep breaths. Who have you talked to so far?"

"No one yet."

"Not Skye? I called, but she didn't pick up."

"No."

"She's going to be okay," he says. "She's young and healthy. Also maybe they misdiagnosed it, right? You never know."

"You don't know any of that."

"Yeah, but we don't not know it."

The room is still tilting around me, going blurry in my peripheral vision. This house still does not feel real to me. I miss my real room, our real house, our real lives.

"Where's Mom?" he says.

"I don't know. Working somewhere."

Jamison calls, our dad calls. Our mom comes rushing in, Lauren and Ava with her, Lauren with tears in her eyes. No one can get ahold of Skye. A million phone calls, a million arguments, and finally she picks up Atticus's call three hours later. I don't know why we thought talking to her would fix anything; she still needs more scans and blood draws, more tests, and so she barely has more information than what we already know, which is that she was just diagnosed today with cancer of the thymus. They don't know how much it's spread, but they think maybe a lot. We all beg her to come back home, but her doctors want her to start treatment immediately, and once she does she won't be able to leave—she'll be immuno-compromised from the chemo and flying will be out of the question; even something like catching a cold at a gas station could be catastrophic.

"Then we should come to you," I say, but Skye tells us no, not yet, she wants to get oriented first and she just wants to rest. I imagine her in the dorms, germs flying up and down the hallway, viruses clinging to her roommate's clothes and skin. The call is a blur, everything filtering to me late, fragments that I'm sure will float back to haunt me when I can function again.

"Are you *okay*?" our mother says at one point, leaning over Atticus's shoulder, and Skye says, exhausted, "I'm fine. I just need to get some rest." Our dad, who's listening in because he called my phone, which I'm holding up next to Atticus's, snaps, "Obviously, she's not okay. Melissa, do you hear what she's saying?"

"I need to rest," Skye says. "I'll call you when I know more, okay? Right now there's nothing else to tell. Don't worry too much. I'm sure it will be fine."

CHAPTER FIFTEEN

At school the next morning everyone's waiting for us in the parking lot, everyone clustered in a quieter-than-usual mass, and they descend on us as soon as we get out of Atticus's car.

"We saw Skye's post," Delancey says. "I'm so, so sorry, you guys! I can't believe it. I would never have imagined Skye getting sick. She's so vibrant."

"What are the odds with someone that young?" Blythe says. "They have to be, like, one in a million."

"Yeah, it's pretty shitty," Atticus says. "You really just never know."

"How is she feeling?" Delancey says. "I know she's never met me, but I've been checking all morning to see if she's updated! I just feel so awful for her."

"It's really awful," Victoria says quietly. Something in her tone feels more human to me. "You guys must be reeling. What kind of cancer? Do you know the staging yet?"

The boys hang back, subdued. Michael Stratton pats me on the back. I'm on the edge of a strange precipice, waiting to see what Caden will say. I don't know why it feels like whatever he says will have special power somehow—will define for me what I feel, or will be prophetic, if not about Skye, then about me, or at least me and him. Why do I still care? I should be done here.

He's standing next to Michael, his hands in his pockets and his sleeves rolled back, his expression quiet and watchful. When I turn to him, he says, "Really sorry to hear that."

Is that it? That's all he can muster? When the first bell rings, all the girls give me hugs. Michael pats me on the back again. Atlas says something I can't hear to Caden, and Caden laughs in his muted way. I linger for a moment, waiting to see if Caden will come up to me, but he leaves with Victoria, and then the final bell is about to ring, so I leave too.

As I walk between classes all day, it beats out a constant, staccato pattern in my head: *My sister is sick. My sister is sick.* I fail a Spanish quiz in third period. When I check at lunch, she's posted a selfie: her in the hospital with an IV in the crook of her elbow, and she doesn't answer when I message to ask if she's okay. I think about everything I've heard about how ill chemo makes you. I imagine her dying. I thought I was a more optimistic person than this. I make Atticus eat with me; I don't want to be with anyone else, suffering through their inane conversations while my sister is reckoning with this diagnosis in another state. We drive a mile down the road so we can eat without anyone else seeing us, because I don't want pictures of me crying showing up anywhere, or pictures of us eating with some kind of caption about us faffing around enjoying ourselves while she's sick. Jamison calls while we're eating. It feels very much like her to know exactly when our lunch break is.

"Okay," she says, "okay, here's what we're doing. Ava is finding us a rental in Waco near Skye. The way the medical-industrial complex treats women especially is just not something she should be trying to deal with on her own, so we're going to want someone going with her to all her doctor visits. And obviously, she's going to need a lot of support. I need you both to figure out what you guys need to do for independent study."

"She said we shouldn't come yet," I say. "I don't think she wants us there."

"Okay, well, what's her plan? Cancer *alone*? She probably just didn't want to disrupt everyone's lives, but that's obviously not how this works. I'm going to aim for—what's today, Tuesday? I'm going to aim for all of us there by Friday."

Yes, I think, flooded with a sudden relief. We aren't going to just helplessly stay here like there's nothing anyone can do—we're going to go there and save her.

"Wow, okay," Atticus says. "Is Wrangell going?"

Hearing his name is piercing. I have been thinking about him so frequently, replaying our fight over and over in my head, that his name spoken aloud when I'm not expecting it feels like someone broadcasting my shameful secret. I still haven't told Atticus anything about our fight. I thought maybe after telling Caden I'd be able to, but back in the circle of our family, I realize that was wrong. I'm too afraid they'll side with him. I could tell Caden only because he shouldn't matter to me, because the stakes were never high.

I have the ugly thought that if he doesn't show up, if he doesn't reach out to her and put all this aside when she's been diagnosed with *cancer*, it will be enormously vindicating to me. It'll mean he's the crappy person here, not me.

But no, what a shitty thing to think. No, of course I hope he's there for her, I hope he's doing as much as he can.

"Yes, I talked to him," Jamison says, and immediately I feel sick when I think about the various possibilities that could mean. That he told her what happened and she's taken his side—that my fears are true and this is a permanent rift. "So I need you both to figure out your schedules for school and volleyball."

"I love you, Jamie," I say. "You are the best sister."

She makes an irritated grumbling noise, which means I embarrassed her—I can picture exactly how she's blushing. When we hang up, I say, "That means we're going to have to see Dad."

"What? She said we'd come up with a schedule. We'll just be in a different time slot."

"No, she said she wanted everyone there Friday."

"I thought she just meant she wanted as many people as possible Friday. We can just wait until he's gone."

Can we? Does that mean I can wait until Wrangell's gone too? At least with our dad I didn't do anything wrong, I have nothing to feel guilty or uncertain about, but I can't fathom facing Wrangell right now. Or ever, actually. "Yeah, I don't think we can wait until he's gone."

"Maybe I'll wait."

"I mean—forever? That's your big plan here?" I say, "Do you know the difference between you and me?"

"I'm on the edge of my seat."

"Shut up. I think the main difference is what we're willing to do for relationships. I think sometimes you're happy to just, like—let people drift away from you and it doesn't keep you up at night. Whereas for me, that kills me and I'll do whatever I can."

"Yeah, that's called enmeshment."

He must have been reading more pop psychology. "You can call it whatever you want. I think it's true, though."

"I don't think I disagreed with you." He finishes his burrito and crushes the wrapper into a ball. "Does that mean you're going to try to talk to Wrangell?"

My heart flips over. "What's that supposed to mean?"

"It means obviously it didn't go well when you went to see him in SF, but you didn't want to talk about it." He glances at me. "You're still not going to tell me? Was it really that bad? I know how Wrangell can be, but that's just how he is."

"When I went to go see him, we had a fight, and the things he said—it was a lot of awful stuff I didn't know he thought about me. I don't think he plans to ever speak to me again."

"What does he think about you?"

"Um—" I swallow. "He thinks I'm selfish, I guess, for trying to force him into relationships that are toxic to him, like how I keep trying to get him to talk to our parents still. And he thinks I'm shallow. Obsessed with us having a perfect public image versus actually genuinely caring about anyone."

I regret saying it right away. Because won't Atticus think he's right? Is that exactly what I'm doing right now with Atticus and our dad? I can't look at him. But Atticus says, "What? What the hell? That's such an overreaction. I can't believe he said that to you. I don't blame you for being mad."

"It's not that I'm mad, it's that—" My voice catches. "I play that conversation on loop in my mind every night for, like, hours, and I had to unfollow him because every time I would see him post anything, it would just bring it all back. I've been viscerally dreading seeing him in person, and I don't know how to act around him at all. And I can't even talk about it to anyone else because maybe they'll be like, oh yeah, he was totally right, and I just—I can't." I swallow again. "Is that what it's like for you with Dad?"

"No, I'm just furious. Every time I think about his smug mouth trying to talk like he's still the greatest person around, I honestly want to punch him in the face. You don't think it was just Wrangell saying stupid shit? You know how he can be."

"I am telling you that it was not that. I don't know how I can possibly make this clearer for you."

"Okay, okay—I'm sorry. I believe you." He pats my arm. "I believe you, okay? But that's just how Wrangell is. He's so hot-headed. I think it'll blow over. I think everything will be fine."

I genuinely don't see a way how. I can't imagine, just on a physical level, my body ever not reacting with this same fear and dread. The thing about family is that you're twined so tightly that any wound can never be only skin deep; it will always go all the way through you, to pierce you to the bone.

There's a strange way in which he and Skye are tied up together for me—like I'm transferring them onto each other, and it's as if he died and Skye's the one who feels betrayed by me. Sometimes I understand our dad's impulse to turn everything into a podcast, or Skye's and Jamison's ways of culling bits from their days to share online; all the things you never tell someone have a way of curdling inside you. Everything is possible now; nothing is safe.

An immediate wrinkle in the plan is that Saint Simeon, it turns out, doesn't offer an independent study option for longer than a week at a time. The front admin, Mrs. Hall, explains to me that unfortunately it's not possible because our program is so rigorous, and so focused on doing what's best for each student—I walk out before she gets another sentence in. I text Ava to tell her, and then right after I hit send, I have to grip the phone and take deep breaths. Outside everything feels too loud, a crush of noise crowding my eardrums. Victoria finds me there leaning against the wall, staring at nothing, and puts two fingers on my wrist to monitor my pulse.

"You look like you're about to lose it," she says.

The revulsion I feel for her in that moment is so strong I think it blazes from me. "I am absolutely not in the mood for your condescension," I say, my voice shaking, but Victoria just laughs.

"No," she says, "I wouldn't be either. What's wrong?"

"I don't remember saying I wanted to talk."

"Yes, I'm aware of that, but you look like you're going to implode."

"I was trying to go on independent study, but apparently you guys have *such* important things happening in the classrooms here it's just impossible to miss. Everyone here is just so incredibly full of themselves." I am too furious at everyone, at everything, to care about the venom in my tone or the look on her face as I turn to walk away. "I absolutely hate it here."

Jamison messages us in the group chat to ask how it went with the school, but I'm too scared to answer, knowing Wrangell will see it. I type and delete probably thirty versions of a message, worried that literally everything I could say might be twisted into further proof of my selfishness and toxicity. Ava must have one of the lawyers call the school, though, because later that afternoon Mrs. Hall leaves a message saying of course they'll accommodate us however we need, it would be their pleasure, just let them know. Ava calls low<malle

.

also to tell us that she's booked our flights for Friday and that our mom decided it makes the most sense for us to do a week-on/week-off schedule, and then Atticus calls to argue with our mom over the logistics, because he can't miss a week of volleyball at a time.

"You can't fly back and forth from Texas to California three times a *week*," she says. "That's absolutely absurd. Skye wouldn't want you to run yourself ragged like that either."

"I'll sleep on the plane. It's not that big a deal."

"Not to mention all the pathogens you'd be exposed to in that human soup—no thank you. Once a week, Atticus. That's the plan."

He wants to call Jamison to complain, but I don't let him because she has enough on her plate, and in my opinion this is not something that rises to the level of needing her attention. Instead he calls his coach, and his coach calls a coach friend in Austin, who calls someone he knows in Waco, who says Atticus can practice with his team during the week to stay sharp, and then he can spend weekends at home to play tournaments. I don't know why that's the thing that touches me, but it does—I blink back tears when he tells me. I imagine scores of faceless people around the world holding Skye in their hearts, sending light her way. I imagine her lifted up in their prayers. Focus and attention have always felt talismanic to me, the light shined on you by thousands of people's thoughts, all the force of their collective desire. Skye is beloved, Skye is admired, Skye will be fine.

You're Not Famous: A Snark Site
ynf.com/forums/LoFamily

wetweightedblanket, 9:45:51 pm PST: okay I am dead inside but Wrangell's post about how much he loves Skye got me 🫠

baconspam420, 9:46:03 pm PST: Yeah I can't snark on any of this. What an absolute nightmare for all of them. I would not wish cancer on my worst enemy.

knockoffbrene, 9:47:25 pm PST: Yeah I don't know, feel free to tell me I'm a bitch, but I just don't trust anything they say! I would not put it past Skye to do this for attention or engagement.

I'm at my locker the next day after school, robotically gathering my things, when I feel someone's hand touch lightly on the small of my back. I turn, and Caden's there, alone.

"How are you doing?" he says. "You feel like going to get something to eat?"

The offer catches me off guard, and it takes me a moment to pinpoint why: I have never been anywhere alone with him in public. There has always been something clandestine feeling, something covert, about my time with him: us in his car, us in his house. We never talk alone at school. "Right now?"

He shrugs. "Whenever."

"I'm not hungry. But I'd get coffee."

"Yeah, that's fine," he says. "Whatever you want."

We go to a place downtown, a few blocks away from school, which has a dark, sleek interior and some elaborate method of making the coffee. We mostly don't talk until we're sitting down, and then he says, "So are you doing okay?"

"No. I'm constantly on the verge of throwing up."

He stirs his coffee and then drinks half of it in two big sips. "Yeah. It'll feel like that for a while. It gets easier, though."

"What the hell is that supposed to mean? Do you even know what it's like to have someone you care about get sick?"

"Well, my grandma died of cancer when I was little. She was a lot older than your sister, though. But look up addiction sometime. People think they know what it means, but they don't."

"I don't see what that has to do with anything."

"I'm just saying I know what it's like to wait to see if someone's going to die or not."

His expression is always so unplaceable. It's so hard to read him. Is this a pity thing? Or does he feel guilty, and sleeping with a girl and then not checking how she's doing when her sister gets cancer is a bridge too far for him? I have no gauge of his moral code. Probably I never did.

"It seems early to be worrying about whether she'll die," I say. "Like, obviously she's getting treatment and everything." *Right now,* I think, and have to chase the thought away before I drown in it. "She's healthy and young."

"Sure, of course. But that's the first thing you always think about, right? It never really goes away."

"The stupid part," I say, "is I know the world doesn't work this way, but there are so many people who deserve to get cancer, frankly, and my sister isn't one of them. Not exactly high-level philosophy, but yeah, it really sucks how unfair life is."

He finishes his coffee. I pour an extra pack of sugar into mine, and then another, but the bitterness still turns my stomach. He watches me for a moment, and I pretend not to notice. I wonder if he's thinking about sex with me.

"The other stupid part is that I have to keep getting up and taking precalc tests and writing essays," I say. "Like, what the hell."

"You'd be surprised how fast you'll think of it as normal."

"I hope that isn't true."

"Everything feels normal if you do it long enough. And eventually you put things aside and live your own life. You'd be surprised how little it actually changes for you, too."

"That's such a fucked-up way to look at things."

"Is it," he says, not like a question.

"There is no way in hell it's ever going to feel normal or like it doesn't change anything for me."

"Yeah, well. To each their own, I guess." He crushes his coffee cup between his hands. "Maybe that's how you're supposed to do it. I hope it feels better for you that way somehow. Or however it goes. You want to come over?"

I have gotten used to the drive now—the curves feel familiar to me, the particular trees and groves stepping out to greet me, each one distinct. I came with him not because it seems right or wise or like a good idea, but mostly because it feels like the path of least resistance, because otherwise I would have to talk myself out of it and pretend it isn't what I want and then spend all afternoon convincing myself I made the right choice.

For obvious reasons I have been wishing that we didn't have bodies, that we could just be orbs of thought and feeling floating safely around risk-free, but today I am grateful for my body, for at least the few minutes of escape it gives me. I wonder if Skye feels totally betrayed by hers. To have your home in the universe no longer be safe.

We lie on his bed for a while afterward, both out of breath. He says, "So I hear you're going to Texas for a while."

"Yeah, our whole family's going out."

"Did you and your brother make up?"

"Wrangell?" I'm kind of surprised he remembered. "No. We didn't."

"You'll see him there, though?"

"Yes, I guess so."

"How will that go?"

"Fine," I lie. "Nothing else really matters with Skye being sick." The expression on his face—I say, "What?"

"I don't think it works that way."

"You don't think it works what way?"

"People always think if they change the backdrop, they can change their problems. Move to some new place and bam, you've made up a new world with new rules and everything's fine."

My voice comes out icy. "My sister has cancer and you think I think everything's *fine*?"

"No, I didn't—that came out wrong. Just—I used to try to do everything to help my mom out. Like I'd skip school, or I'd come right home instead of seeing anyone. I quit lacrosse. Because I thought, oh, you know, I can help if I'm around. I can at least watch and see how she's doing. Then when I went to visit her at rehab—you ever seen one of those places? You go and it's, like, this ultraluxurious-hotel vibe, where they spend all day getting facials and lighting candles and doing these long therapy sessions. The first time I went and visited, I had this epiphany that I was what she was trying to get away from. Obviously, me trying to help did jack shit. I'm real life. The point was to get away."

"You don't think she's doing it at least partly so she can be better for you?"

"Oh, I think she definitely tells herself that. It's what she always says to me. Otherwise, how do you justify it to yourself?"

I sit up, reaching for my shirt. "I don't know how to take all this," I say. "If this is like—pity, or guilt, or what."

He rolls over, propping himself up on his elbow. "What's that supposed to mean?"

"I don't know, Caden, it means why the fuck am I here after you completely ignored me most of the time? It means are you the kind of person who feels guilty about hooking up and then ghosting me, because now you know my sister is sick, so you're trying to relate somehow? Is that what this is about?"

"That's what you think?"

"I don't know what to think. I just said that."

"If you don't want to be here, you really don't have to be. I wasn't trying to pressure you. I hope I didn't."

"No. That's not—forget it." Why did I come? But immediately I know the answer—because the hot anger I'm feeling right now is better than marinating in worry the way I would be otherwise. Say what you will about the method, but distraction helps.

I get up off the bed and pull my pants back on. I dislike being naked around him when I'm standing up, when he can see me from a distance. "I can't believe you think I shouldn't go see her."

He watches me a moment. "Yeah," he says after a little while, "maybe you're right. Maybe I'm just being selfish."

"What does selfishness have to do with it?"

I understand what he means a second later, and it surprises me—I see him take in my surprise, and something small closes off in his expression, in a way that makes me think that hurt him some-how. It throws me off. Maybe I was wrong about him—maybe he does actually care about me. I feel something give way inside me, cracking open.

"The thing is—" Caden stares up at the ceiling, and I could be wrong, because I haven't seen it in him before, but I think he might be nervous. "Okay, I'm sorry about ignoring you. It just freaks me out to say the kinds of things I somehow always wind up telling you. But the thing is, I can't advocate trying to lose yourself in any kind of substance, but, I mean, I get needing to not feel things, and this is the best I've got there."

An odd, off-kilter glow inside me, because I think in a way he understands me, because I understand what he's trying, maybe imperfectly, to offer me. I say, "Oh."

I drive the winding roads home, my heart stopping at each flash of headlights around the bend until I'm finally inured to the barrage of them and don't react physically every time. Then the lights hover suspended in my vision, blurry through my tears.

The doorbell rings that night a little after dinner, and when I check the security camera, a big surprise: it's Eloise and Lilith. I hurry downstairs. The animal part of me, the part that's all instinct before I think, is craving their physical presence. It feels that way for a full three or four seconds before I remember. I open the door.

"Honor," Lilith says. "Are you okay? We saw about Skye."

"Can I give you a hug?" Eloise says. "We found out and we both were like, oh my God, she must be falling apart. We need to go see her *immediately*."

"Also—I need to tell you something," Lilith says. "Can we come in?"

Lilith looks nervous. I feel a little sick. Is she going to tell me she's the one who talked to *People*, who's been posting about me? I wasn't ready for it to be her. I wasn't ready for it to be either of them—in a way, when it was both, it was also neither, both possibilities alive and also not alive.

"I was on our computer at home," Lilith says, "and my mom had left a page open, and I saw it was a page of like—gossip about your family."

My hands go cold. "Your mom?"

"So I asked her about it, and I guess it's, like, this stupid hobby she has, and then I asked her if the *People* source was her, and it was. I was so angry, like I know how you have a hard time trusting people and how a lot of people have been fake with your family and I was really, really upset with her."

Karissa, who fed us grain bowls and homemade vegetable soup, who always remembered a little gift on our birthdays. Who came in when we were sleeping over to check if we were still awake and needed anything, who always asked how I was doing. "Your mom did that," I say numbly.

"But now that's Skye's sick, she feels really awful."

She feels awful now? My numbness gives way to fury. "Doesn't she have better things to do with her time than hurt my family? She goes online to post anonymous gossip about us? That's disgusting. She's an adult. That's absolutely pathetic."

"I mean," Lilith says a little stiffly, "you guys put so much out there anyway already."

"Meaning what? This is *our* fault?"

"I mean," she says again, "it's not like she's gossiping about one of our random classmates, it's like, so many people are already talking about you anyway, and it's just a drop in the bucket."

"She sold my private conversation to *People*."

"She said she didn't get any money for it."

"Okay, so then what did she get? She got to feel important? She got to try to take down my family? That's actually worse than if she was just doing it for money. I can't believe you're siding with her." I turn to Eloise. "Is this what you think too?"

"I'm not on anyone's side," Eloise says brightly. "I'm on everyone's side."

"Your sister's sick," Lilith says. "I didn't come here to fight with you. Honestly, it's just some dumb hobby she has. I don't think it needs to be such a big deal. We just wanted to come because we want to support you."

My closest friends, and this is what I'm worth to them.

"I'm glad I know this about you now," I say. I'm a Lo, and we are nothing if not poised, so my voice doesn't shake and maybe I don't sound like I'm falling apart. "Skye having cancer is the worst thing that's ever happened to us, and I absolutely don't have time to waste on people who were never worth it."

I wait in the parking lot the next morning until I see Caden pull up. When he gets out, I say, "Can we talk?"

"Everyone's three favorite words to hear," he says lightly. "Yeah, what's up?"

I glance at the front gate. There are just seven minutes until the first bell. "What happens here if people cut class? Do you get, like, super killed?"

"They call your parents. Which—yeah. You want to go somewhere? You want to go to my house?"

"I meant it that I want to actually talk. What's near here? Can we get a juice or something?"

We go in his car. I can feel everyone in the parking lot watch us go. My heart is pounding—I am searingly nervous. There's still time to back out, I tell myself. I could say, *Actually, never mind, let's just go to your house instead.* It would be easy and familiar.

We drive to a juice bar downtown near the public high school, a huge neoclassical building that looks like a private college. I recognize the neighborhood as close to where Ming Quong was, where our grandmother grew up. It's some kind of health facility now, but our mother drove us there once to see the grounds and the arch. We'd walked around awkwardly for a little while, and on the drive back our mother had cried. We didn't tell our grandmother we'd gone. In the juice bar I am too nervous to read the menu and end up with some truly grim turmeric-celery concoction Jamison would probably love.

"You okay?" he says, glancing at me, as we sit down.

"Yes. Kind of. I don't know." I mean, no, obviously.

"What did you want to talk about?"

Even now I could still back down. I could make something up, I could just say I changed my mind, and I doubt he'd press it. I take a long sip of my sad drink and say, before I can talk myself out of it, "I don't want us to just hook up anymore."

"Oh," he says, blinking at me. "Okay. Meaning, ah—what, exactly?"

"Meaning Skye's sick and I don't know what's going to happen and I'm scared, and all of a sudden basically nothing else matters and it's just made me realize that I want something more than that. I feel like I can talk to you in a way I can't really talk to anyone else. And I want to be able to tell you things and go to you when the rest of the world is awful, and I want to feel like I can be that space for you, too. I want to not have to worry about what you think about me or how much you care about me. I want it just to be, like, a given that yeah, we care about each other. I know we both said we didn't want anything serious, but it turns out that, um, actually I do."

I have never said a more terrifying thing in my life. My heart is pounding. I cannot imagine what it's going to feel like if he laughs at me, says no, this is just about hooking up to him. It's so much easier lying on a bed together, your face buried in someone's chest, when you don't have to look at each other or say anything.

"Ah." He clears his throat. "Look, it sounds really great, but the thing is—"

Oh God. I feel the beginnings of a panic attack. I will perish right here at this table next to the napkin and lid dispensers at the Daily Juice.

"—I don't know how to, like . . . do that. Like, I don't know how to tell people anything about myself and then like, face them the next time in the daylight? It's like, cool you know all this personal stuff about me, and I guess it kind of worked when it was just us away from everyone else, but now it's, like, here we are in chem lab with John Gohl right there? I think I'm not built for that like normal people are. Victoria told me Blythe tried to warn you off. She's right, probably. I think I hurt her. So then it's like, okay, obviously it's better to just make sure no one ever gets especially invested."

"Well," I say, "it's a little too late for that."

"I think you're really great," he says. "Um, which sounds like the prelude to a breakup, now that I hear myself saying it aloud, but I'm actually trying for the opposite here. Like, I think you're a smart and interesting person, and you make me laugh, and I think you're, like, really caring. And pretty." He makes a face. "Should I write

Hallmark cards? I think I have a career writing Hallmark cards. I just don't know how to like——be that person who can just be there all the time like that."

"I mean, neither do I. I don't think it'll be *easy*, but I think it's worth working for." I am our mother's daughter after all.

"What's that look like for you?"

"Like not trying to hide behind being physical, or like us telling each other things and maybe just trusting that we won't judge each other or think each other's stupid or selfish or whatever. Like you not going radio silent on me when I'm not around to hook up with, or——"

He winces. "Wait, Honor, is that what you thought? You mean like when you were in Hawaii? It wasn't like that. When you were gone, I wished you were around to talk to, but then obviously I'm not going to try to drag you down while you're on this big family trip. It sounded like you were excited about it. Things got really bad with my mom. I had to go see her because she was completely freaking out there."

"I'm sorry," I say, stricken. "I didn't know that."

"Yeah, I don't tell people that kind of thing." He exhales. "This one time last summer," he says, "I was a camp counselor, and for the training they locked us all in a room overnight and made us go around and share all these personal things so we'd feel like we were all this super-tight team."

"How was that?"

"Oh, it was a nightmare. Straight-up psychological warfare. The first question was, like, share about a time someone's let you down, and the first girl talked about how her dad has never told her he loves her, and everyone's crying five minutes in, and then they get to me and I'm like . . . fuck. I almost quit on the spot."

"Is that what this feels like now? Is that what you're telling me?"

He laughs. "Mm. Only a tiny bit."

"We don't have to—"

"I'm kidding, I'm kidding. Don't kill me. No, actually I meant, should we try that? We'll both tell each other something we've never told anyone. Um, I'll go first." He pokes his straw into his empty cup, then crushes the whole thing in his fist. "I google my dad, like, every night."

"You google him? Why?"

"I don't know. It's stupid. I don't even pick up his calls most of the time, but every night when I'm trying to sleep I like, go on Google Maps and look at the house he's living in. Sometimes I go around the city to try to image the places he's going. Just pathetic stalker shit."

"I don't think that's pathetic."

"I do." He raises his crushed cup in a sort of cheers. "Your turn."

"I think what's harder for me," I say, "is anything I tell you, it's so easy for you to sell me out. You could go to *People* or just post it on social, and then it's, like, thousands of people who know."

"No, I get that," he says. "I mean, it's true. Most people don't have to worry about that like you do. I don't have to."

"I've been burned a lot."

"Well, for what it's worth, maybe for you it always feels like this weird power imbalance with basically everyone, where anyone you talk to suddenly has that over you, but for me—I don't care what strangers think of me, but I do actually care a lot, like, a lot, what people I know think. So from my end it doesn't feel that imbalanced. If that helps."

"I'm, like, pathologically jealous of people who are fully Asian," I say.

"What? What do you mean?"

"It's something I've never told anyone, even my family. Like, it always feels like this part of me that got taken away from me. I don't speak Chinese, even my parents don't speak Chinese, and whenever I'm around a lot of Asians, I just feel completely inadequate. I like—hoard little bits of knowledge I pick up along the way, like the few words my family actually uses or things other people say to me, assuming I'll know, and then I look them up later, but then I only ever feel like I can use them around white people because real Asians would be like yeah, you're a fraud."

"That's rough."

"I mean, it's kind of dumb. Almost everyone's family immigrated from somewhere. We all lose and gain things over generations. I don't know why it affects me so much."

"I don't think it's dumb at all. Probably it would be different for you if this country were different. I'm sure your ancestors didn't have an easy time here."

"Yeah, they didn't. My mom talks about it all the time, and I always feel like, wow, all these people responsible for my existence would be just totally ashamed of me."

"Speaking of ashamed," he says, "here's another one for you. When my mom went to rehab this time, I told her I wish she'd just stay there. Probably the shittiest thing I've ever said to another person ever. I still replay it every single night in my head."

"Oh, Caden, it's understandable. She probably feels safer there."

"She does, but it wasn't about that. I just couldn't take it anymore and I snapped. I called her to apologize, and it definitely really, really hurt her."

"I'm sorry."

"So this is fun," he says. "You sure this is better than sex? I don't think I'm convinced, to be honest with you."

"I mean—"

He grins at me. "I'm just messing with you. I think this will be good. We'll figure it out."

"We'll screw up along the way. We'll try again."

"Our alien overlords will be so baffled."

"No, they won't," I say. "They'll be like wow, look at these humans outperforming their programming."

He laughs, a genuine laugh. He says, "So are we doing this? We're no longer just two specks in the universe carnally encountering each other against all odds? We're, like, together?"

I take a deep breath. "I'm in if you're in."

"Then it looks like we're both in."

On the way back to school he reaches out and takes my hand and holds it for the rest of the drive, tracing his thumb gently over my knuckles. I allow myself a moment of genuine happiness, of hope. Just a moment, though, because that seems about as long as you should allow yourself when, seventeen hundred miles away, your sister is hooked up to needles in the hospital alone and you're too scared of what that means to even call and ask her how she is.

By the time I've packed for Waco and we're on our way to the airport, some kind of muscle memory has taken over and I feel ready, alert. Our mom does interviews the whole way there.

Skye's news has, for the moment, bumped out any other

possible stories about us, and it's all anyone's talking about online. Yesterday #prayforskye was trending most of the day, which kind of choked me up, actually, even though Atticus rolled his eyes when I told him. Flowers have been showing up at the house practically by the truckload—from Oprah's and Seth Meyers's and Jimmy Kimmel's people, from Shelley Lu and Lila Lee Turner, who were the producer and the story editor for *Lo and Behold*. Even from a few of the crew we haven't heard from in years.

I email Hanna, from the boutique, on our way to the airport to explain that my sister is sick and ask if I can have an extension on the jewelry contract. She writes back almost right away: *Honor, I read about your sister yesterday and have been trying to find words to reach out—I'm so sorry to hear of her illness! Of course, please take all the time you need. xo*

"Do you think the doctors there are actually any good?" Atticus says as we get out of the car. "Isn't it a pretty small town?"

"Yes, that's something we're going to have to figure out," our mom says. "There's so much. We don't even know who her doctors are, what their plan is, what the prognosis even is yet. Aren't you proud of me for not harassing Skye over the phone?"

"Yes, actually," Atticus says, grinning.

"Well, it's taking all my willpower."

While we're waiting in the lounge, my phone rings. Every time it rings, I hope it's Caden, but once again it's a number I don't recognize, so I ignore it. Media outlets have been calling and emailing nonstop, which is disgusting, so I've ignored them. Lauren came up with some anodyne statement for our mom and sent me a five-hundred-word email on what to say (basically: nothing) if anyone got ahold of me. She also checked to see what I was posting about Skye too, wanting to edit everything first, which normally I wouldn't have cared about but this time quietly infuriated me. I will say whatever I want about our sister.

"Are you nervous?" I say. "I'm super nervous. My hands are all cold."

"What part are you most nervous about? The flight? Seeing Wrangell and Dad?"

"Yes, all of that, but also I'm nervous to see her. I'm worried it'll be weird, or I'll be weird, or just—all of it. I don't know." I've barely heard from her since she first posted about her diagnosis, a strange feeling because in that time my life has also mostly revolved around her. It's made it easier, I think; I've been able to hide away from the fear and pain she's probably feeling, and anyway, dropping everything to go be with her is more than I could think to say aloud to her anyway.

"It's still Skye. She's the same person."

Why does she already feel so unknowable to me, then? Like she's crossed a bridge into some mythical land, and we can't follow her, can barely make her out if we squint. "Maybe we should've researched more."

"Nah, all we have to do is be there for her. And you're great at that. Relax. Seriously. It's Skye. She'll be happy to see you."

"I'm just so worried I'm going to fuck it up somehow."

"How could you possibly? There's zero chance that will happen."

"I don't know. I'm afraid I'll say the wrong thing or do the wrong thing or like—I don't know. Have the wrong vibe."

"It's not possible," Atticus says. "The important thing is that you're there. That's it. Everything else will fall into place."

My phone buzzes again, another number I don't recognize, and then a voice mail from someone from *Us Weekly*. A few moments later a text from Jessie Yuan: Thinking of your family, Honor—always here if there's anything you'd like to talk about! Keeping Skye in my thoughts. I should get a new phone number.

"I think we need to be civil to Dad, by the way," I say. "Everything that's happening—we can just put it aside for right now. It's not the right time."

"Mm," Atticus says, "yeah, no. Fuck that."

The flight is terrible. When we cross over Colorado, the ground flat and distant and unforgiving below us, we lurch probably thousands of feet through the sky, and I think how awful it would be if we all crashed right now while Skye needs us most.

We don't crash, though. I remind myself that sometimes you get a happy ending.

There's a driver waiting for us at the airport, and as we drive away, I take in our first views of Waco. It's a lot more rural here than I was expecting, wide expanses of fields hemmed in by power lines, flat swaths of dark in the night. It feels empty on the roads, both because there aren't many other cars and because, I realize after a few miles, there aren't sidewalks or medians here. As we get more into town, we pass dirt roads, a water tower, an HEB.

The house Ava found for us is in northwest Waco. She told us tourism is huge here now because people want to come see the *Fixer Upper* houses and shop at the Magnolia Silos, a fact Atticus finds extremely depressing, he tells me about eleven times. The rental is a sprawling farmhouse-style home on an acre or so of land with oak trees that remind me a little of Los Gatos. Except that it's so flat here, the city stretching out and out around you, so each house set back on its huge lot feels like a small fortress surrounded by nothingness. I feel unmoored when I'm not by mountains or water.

There's a small fleet of rental cars waiting for us in the driveway. My heart starts to pound as we pull in, and I wonder if I'll have to talk to Wrangell now. It's nearly one in the morning Texas time, though, so maybe he's not up. Our dad is usually a night person, always reading and working late, and Skye, too, although maybe that's different now.

"You're going to be nice, right?" I murmur to Atticus as we get out of the car. "For Skye's sake, if no other reason."

He rolls his eyes. "You're lucky I care about you."

Before we're halfway up the driveway, a light goes on and then the door opens. It's our dad and a woman, backlit, and for a horrible second I think he brought Heather with him. Our dad comes bounding up to see us right away, which feels so much like him it makes me ache, and the part of me that's furious is subsumed by the part that wants to fall into his arms and cry. I stop myself from the crying part, but when he hugs me, I let him. I wish I were small enough to let him hold me and tell me everything will be fine.

"You look great, princess," he says, and kisses me on the forehead, then turns to Atticus for a hug. Atticus steps away, stone faced, but our dad just says, "You look great too, bud. It's so good to see you guys."

I still can't see the face of the woman making her way to us. Then our mom holds out her arms and says, "Oh, baby," and finally it hits me that it's Skye. "You shouldn't have waited up for us. You should be sleeping."

She looks thin but not emaciated, and the lack of her hair is a shock. I didn't realize how much someone's hair changes the shape of them, the way your mind categorizes them visually. I've seen her in pictures and videos, obviously, but in person the whole shape of her is different, and my mind doesn't know how to reconcile it at first. She looks pale and washed out. I'm frozen in place.

I feel something shift in Atticus when he sees her, too—some way all this becomes real to him. He goes to Skye first and wraps her in a bear hug, almost defiantly. She doesn't hug back so much as let herself be hugged.

"I can't believe you're here," she says. "I can't believe you guys all came like this."

"I would not be literally anywhere else in the world." My eyes fill with tears, and I fight them back. "I can't believe this is happening to us, Skye! But it's going to be okay." I sound like Atticus. "It's going to be fine."

The five of us go in together. (A picture-perfect family!) Wrangell and Jamison must be sleeping. The house is open-concept in a sort of awkward way—a big space with furniture clustered together in a few different seating areas, all around the kitchen, and then the dining room awkwardly closed off next to the kitchen. The house is blindingly white, shiplap everywhere and industrial-looking black pendants hanging over the white quartz island. The entry has a hutch-turned-coffee station with a collection of white ceramic mugs with tall, thin black lettering that says things like SWEATER WEATHER, EARLY BIRD, and ¡HOLA, BONITA! The bedrooms are all in a wing, arranged around a long hallway. Mine overlooks a trio of oak trees in the backyard, with string lights hung between them.

There's a clean, soft pajama set waiting on my pillow, and I put it on and slip into the sheets, and then I lie there for probably an hour. I'm frayed and exhausted, but I'm also wired, and I can't sleep. Finally I give up. I can hear sporadic thuds coming from the direction of Atticus's room—he had weights shipped here—and when I go in, he's lifting them, grunting like he thinks he's in the Olympics.

"Can't sleep?" he says.

"Maybe it's all the gymlike noise."

"Sorry. Was I too loud?"

"No, you were fine. It's just everything else." I lie down on his bed. His windows look out toward the street, which is quiet and dark. "People think she's faking."

"They think she's *faking cancer*? Why the hell would people think that?"

"Because she's not, like, super educated about it yet, I guess."

"Why should she be educated about it? She just found out."

"I know. Maybe we should talk about it differently. Or something. I don't know."

"What do you mean talk about it differently?"

"Like, more technically or something. So it seems more serious. Do you think we should try—"

"No. I don't think we should try anything. I don't think I can convey how much I absolutely do not give a fuck what anyone on the internet thinks, about this or anything. They can go to hell." He lets the weights fall with a thud. "I hope she's not reading any of that."

"She probably is. You know she reads almost everything."

"I don't know why you guys do that to yourselves." He lifts the bottom of his shirt to mop off his face. "She looks like shit. Didn't you think?"

"Cool. You should tell her that."

"I'm just saying. I was like, totally unprepared somehow. She looks bad, right? I've never seen her look this bad. Even the way she moved."

I feel oddly untouchable here, in this strange place where no one knows me, where we're a flight apart from our real lives. It makes the situation seem at the same time more dangerous and less real, like whatever happens here doesn't count. "She looks bad."

My room is next to hers, and later that night, around three, I hear her throwing up, an awful gagging and then retching like she's being turned inside out. I freeze. Should I offer to go help her? Pretend I didn't hear? I wait, and the toilet flushes and then she goes back into her room, and I don't follow her, mostly because I'm too scared it would be the wrong thing. I hate myself a little bit for it.

I used to be so body-close to Skye when we were smaller, and even when we weren't but she still lived at home: us piled together in bed, her legs sprawled across mine on the couch, the way we would shower or undress in front of each other; she would inspect herself in the mirror in front of me, turning back and forth, complain about the curve of her hips or the mole on her back. I can't stop feeling like I should've known somehow that something was off; I should've been able to feel it. Or maybe that's all just one feeling, and the one feeling is that it should've been me instead. There's no reason I should've been spared.

When I wake up in the morning, I'm the opposite of disoriented: I remember immediately where I am, why I'm here, as if I was still thinking about it somehow overnight. I am overcome with the desire to be literally anywhere else, even to be back in class at Saint

Simeon, but obviously I can't avoid our dad and Wrangell forever, and so I force myself to get up and out of bed. I take an extremely hot shower and wish briefly I were the kind of person who felt centered and transcendent doing something like yoga.

Our parents are both up already, working in the living room. Our mom introduces the new Waco assistant, Elissa, a pretty and energetic twentysomething, who's setting up breakfast: cut fruit along with some takeout boxes with ingredients for grain bowls. Atticus comes into the kitchen, takes in the scene, and goes to rummage through the cabinets for cereal without saying anything to anyone except for a friendly hello to Elissa.

"Actually, I thought we could all eat together," our dad says. "This is supposed to be one of the best breakfasts in Waco."

"Pass."

Our dad notes his tone, debates saying something, then changes his mind. "So," he says heartily, "we'll get something to eat, and then I've called a family meeting to figure out our next steps with—"

"I thought Jamison called the meeting," Atticus says.

Our dad slams his phone on the coffee table. "You know, Atticus, I understand you have a lot of feelings right now, but ultimately we're all going to have to work together to—"

Atticus leaves. Our dad closes his eyes and takes a long, pinched breath through his nose. Elissa discreetly ignores all of us, but still I feel the pull to say something cheerful to smooth things over in front of her. I don't, only because there's nothing I feel like saying to our dad.

I make a grain bowl with chia seeds, coconut flakes, fruit, and maple syrup. Every time there's a sound in the house, I expect to look up and see Wrangell, and each time my heart skips. Our dad makes a bowl with sautéed kale, eggs, and chili sauce, then sits down next to me at the table. I am saved from any attempts at conversation when Skye comes into the room. Immediately we all stand up.

"How are you feeling?" I say, and at the same time our dad says, "Good morning, princess, there's breakfast here."

"Oh—I have to go into the hospital, actually." Skye's wearing soft green joggers and a matching pullover and her glasses still, no makeup. There are dark circles under her eyes. I am overly attuned to her every gesture. Is she frail? Did Wrangell tell her what happened? Am I supposed to pretend away the possibility of either one?

Our mother wraps her arms around Skye and rests her cheek against Skye's head, then cups her hands over Skye's face.

"My beautiful girl," she says quietly. There are tears in her eyes. "You shouldn't have to go through this."

"It's fine," Skye says. "I'll be fine."

"It has killed me not to be with you or know anything about how you're doing. When do you need to be at the hospital? We'll pack up and we'll all go with you."

"They don't allow visitors in the cancer unit."

"*What?*" our mom exclaims, leaning forward. "You aren't allowed to bring an advocate with you to appointments?"

"They don't allow *visitors?*" our dad says at the same time. "What the hell kind of policy is that? We can get tested, we can wear masks—"

"That's a truly toxic policy," our mom says. "I just find that absolutely unconscionable in this day and age, knowing what we know about mental health—"

"They're worried about infection," Skye says. "It's so sad because sometimes you see these old people who, like, they can still get around on their own, so they don't have to have a caregiver, but they just look so lonely."

I had imagined being there with her for all of it—bringing her water and soft blankets, holding her hand or rubbing her back. Maybe they'll make an exception.

"Okay, well," I say, "we're here as your personal valets. We'll take you to your appointments, we'll wait outside if we have to, we'll research things, we'll memorize your schedule, we'll do literally everything. All you have to do is get better."

"You guys are too much," Skye says. "Seriously, it's everything that you're here. Don't do a single thing more."

"We'll give the hospital a call," our dad says. "There must be a way around it."

Our mother nods. "I know you don't want to make waves, Skye, but you know, they're there to support you, not the other way around, so we need to just do whatever is best for *you*, not the hospital."

I am caught in the moment, in how familiar this feels—the small ways our parents unite over something, ready to bend the world to their shared will. Being here like this, it's hard to imagine everything that happened in New York was real.

"Let's still all go together," our dad says. "Your mother and I would like to go in and meet your doctors. We won't visit, we'll just meet with them and then go."

"No one can go in at all."

"Well, maybe they can come outside and discuss with us, then."

"They're with patients all day, so I don't think they can just come outside."

"That's just not going to work," our dad says. "I'm sure they're taking good care of you, baby, but for our own peace of mind we would like to have some discussions with them."

"Maybe I can have them call you," Skye says. "I can ask."

Our parents look at each other, then our mom sighs. "All right, we can start with a virtual meeting."

"Please tell them we'd like that to happen before we have to fly out," our dad says. "Today would be best."

"I don't know if they'll be able to do that."

"Skye, sweetheart, they're going to have to make it work for you," our mother says. "In the grand scheme of things it really isn't asking for very much. And I know your personality is to go along with whatever they tell you, but really it's so important right now that you advocate for yourself and you have advocates in us. And we absolutely will not hesitate to—"

"I'll ask them today, then," Skye says. She looks exhausted. "Whatever you want."

Since there won't be the meetings with the doctors we'd wanted until later, I take Skye to the hospital. While she's getting ready, I busy myself packing her a little bag with things I brought her: a blanket and slippers and a lavender eye mask; magazines I read first to make sure there were no ads of Preston, who's doing a Chanel campaign; a bar of chocolate; and a water bottle. I keep expecting Wrangell to burst in, or to run into him as we're leaving, but he must still be asleep.

I'm nervous to be in the car alone with her, nervous about saying the wrong thing, nervous to be driving on unfamiliar roads. I grip the steering wheel and check my blind spot a thousand times.

"So how are you doing?" I say. "With everything?"

"Oh, I don't know. I guess fine. You know."

I want to ask her if she's scared of dying, if she thinks she's going to get better. I need her to reassure me, but I stop myself from demanding it. "I love you so much, Skye."

"Aw, Honor! Don't get all emotional on me."

"Sorry. I can't help it."

"I'm going to be fine," she says. "Seriously. Everyone's so great to come here, but really it's all kind of an overreaction. Everything is fine."

The hospital is fifteen minutes away, a blocky, impersonal beige building on a flat stretch of land dominated mostly by asphalt roads. I'd thought that seeing her in person had made everything feel real, seeing her official diagnosis, but I was wrong—it's seeing the hospital that does it. The sight of it explodes across my stomach and I can hardly breathe.

"This is such a depressing place," I say, and then immediately regret it. I didn't mean to make her feel worse. When she doesn't answer right away, I feel the words curdling on my tongue. Finally I say, "Where do I park?"

"Oh, just drop me off in front."

"I was going to park and just hang out."

"No, don't wait around. It'll be hours."

"Then at least I'll be close by if you need anything or you end early."

"No, you should go back! You should hang out with everyone before everyone flies out. I'll text you when I'm almost done and you can come back then. Seriously. There's no point in waiting here."

"Okay, if that's what you want." I reach over and give her a tight hug. "I wish I could go sit with you."

"I know, me too. But the bag you packed is so nice. That'll help."

I stay idling in front of the entrance as long as I can, until another car pulls up behind me, and then I drive unseeingly forward into a corner of the parking lot and pull over. My stomach and throat are clenching, my forehead clammy with sweat, and I open the door and lean out, hunched over, waiting to see if I'll throw up. A line of ants plodding across the asphalt kaleidoscopes in and out of my vision until I blink away my tears, and wipe my forehead, and get back inside the car.

CHAPTER SIXTEEN

When I get back to the house, still shaky from the drive, Jamison greets me at the door, wearing yoga clothes and no makeup, her hair in a ponytail. She has new eyelashes, which have looked great in pictures but are a little jarring in person. She looks tired.

"We're going to have our meeting now," she says, which means Wrangell is up. I wonder what, if anything, he's told Jamison. "Also, hi, Honor." She gives me a hug. "I'm glad you're here."

Atticus and Wrangell are sitting at the dining table, both wearing sweats, and for a brief moment they look alike to me. Wrangell doesn't so much as glance in my direction, and I don't know whether to say hi to him or acknowledge him or not. My mouth is dry.

"Well," our dad says, clearing his throat, "obviously can't say much for the circumstances here, but it's good to see everyone, and I'm proud of us for coming together as Los here. This is us. This is what we do. This is the Lo way. Whatever else is kind of swirling around us, anything else we have going on, for the big things we still—"

"Okay," Jamison says, leaning forward, "so I sent out a spreadsheet for scheduling, and I also emailed everyone some more information on Skye's type of cancer, I don't know if you all saw, just because I think it would be good to educate ourselves. It's thymic carcinoma, a cancer of the thymus. Usually, surgery is the first-line treatment, but in Skye's case the cancer has spread already to her heart, so they wanted to get going right away with chemo, and they're going to see if it responds to the chemo before they try surgery. Her schedule is going to be erratic. They test her blood every day to get a sense of what the chemo is doing and whether they want her to go in and do more."

"It's spread to her *heart?*" our mom says, her face draining of color. "What does that mean? What stage cancer is that?"

"It's stage four," Wrangell says flatly.

"Stage *four?* What's the survival rate of—"

"There's no reason to be pessimistic here," our dad says sharply. "Percentages don't matter. We have a hundred percent of Skye. We don't care what the numbers say about anyone else."

"Who are her doctors?" our mom says. "Are they competent? Do we even know if they've seen this kind of cancer before?"

"I would definitely like to talk to the doctors," Jamison says. "And to Skye. I'm sure they're just expecting her to go along with whatever they say, and I'm sure they're overmedicalizing everything, and I want to make sure she knows what her options are and that she's also focused on giving her body tools to heal."

"What does that mean?" Wrangell says. He has a neutral expression on his face, his eyes narrowed, and I can't read what he's thinking. Does he regret being here? Is he angry at how we're handling things, disgusted to see me here?

"I just think they're probably following some protocol or algorithm, and I doubt they're in touch with her body at all. There are a lot of people who've reversed cancer through diet and supplements, and I bet Skye hasn't even looked at that. And the doctors, obviously, they're not telling her any of that. I'm going to work on finding her a good naturopath and some holistic practitioners to get some second opinions."

"I just cannot believe they don't allow visitors," our mom says. She's still pale. "Hopefully, it's not indicative of the overall quality of care here. We're going to have to be prepared to push back and advocate for her."

"Yeah, I think we should probably trust the doctors," Atticus says. "Can anyone in this room even point to where the thymus is? Why are we even weighing in on that part?"

"The doctors have their very specific paradigm of what to do, and that's what they're trained to do, and that's kind of the limit of their—their imagination," Jamison says. "When I had Sonnet, they were very insistent that I had to have a C-section, but I trusted my body, because our bodies know so much more than we give them credit for. The medical-industrial complex is like anything else under capitalism. It's about profit first."

"Okay, yes, health care under capitalism is a special hell, but I just don't think you can use food to cure—"

"Well, we can do more research together," Jamison says. "Let's talk about how we're all going to post about all of this."

How we're going to post about it? I brace myself for what Wrangell might say.

"Yes. Very, very important to stay positive," our dad says. "Both publicly and privately. This is not the time for us to be complaining or making any negative predictions or focusing on the bad. We're not talking about how this is hard, we're not entertaining any dire possibilities or outcomes, or—"

"No, I don't think that's right at all," our mom says.

"What do you mean you don't think it's right?"

"I think it's important right now to tell this authentically."

"Our daughter has cancer in her *heart*, and you think we need to tell that authentically?"

The world goes dim around me. I want to stop him and ask him about that, if it's a real number or if he's just throwing it out, what it means, but I'm too afraid to say anything in front of Wrangell. I think I might throw up.

"There's nothing in life worse than your child suffering. Nothing," our mother says. "And it's important for me right now not to hide the anger and grief and messiness of that. Our daughter deserves those from us. We don't honor her experience by pretending it's not that bad. It is bad. Everyone wants to know how she's doing, and I'll be honest, this is the first time in so long that I've felt—I've felt true humanity radiating back to me. People around the world from all walks of life are holding her and lifting her up."

Atticus snorts. "I mean, Honor said people are already saying crap like she's doing this just to get attention, so—"

Wrangell turns to me, making my heartbeat percussive. "Really?"

"Um—I don't—I—" I swallow.

"It's because she always reads the dregs of the internet," Atticus says. It's true; while our mother is getting flowers from the staff of *The View*, I'm reading conspiracy theories from baconspam420. Of course she feels better about humanity.

"Well, that's garbage," our dad says. "I'll have the lawyers look into it." Atticus starts to say something, but our dad silences him with a look. "I feel very strongly that Skye needs to be surrounded by positivity right now. That's what we can do to support her. That's how we're going to see her through."

Jamison comes to find me in my room a little while later. I am down a deep rabbit hole on thymic carcinoma, even though most of what I'm reading is going over my head and I'm not finding what I actually want, which is reassurance that Skye will be fine. I messaged Caden to tell him the news, and he tells me he's sorry. I want to actually talk to him, tell him everything that's happened here, but it feels like so much to dump on someone half a country away.

"We're going to go shopping for some things for Skye before Wrangell and I have to fly out," Jamison says. "We'll all go. It'll give us a chance to spend some time together. Come on."

"Oh—" I can't think of a plausible excuse not to go. Obviously, I'm not doing anything. I wonder if this means Wrangell hasn't told her anything at all. "Okay."

I follow her out to her car, my stomach churning. While we're waiting for the boys, I look at the spreadsheet she sent us, little color-coded squares for us to indicate when we can be here. "Do you think you'll bring Sonnet next time?" I say.

"Maybe. I'm not sure. Andrew said she's having night terrors with me gone, and I feel so awful. I always promised myself I'd never be flying in and out her whole life. I know what that feels like."

"Aw, Sonnet. That's heartbreaking."

"It's absolutely crushing. I sobbed on the flight here."

"You should bring her back with you. I can stay longer and babysit." I picture them setting up camp here, the house brimming with Sonnet's shrieks and footsteps—all of us just staying the whole time, not the in-and-out trading off. "Skye would love it."

"Maybe. I'll see what Andrew thinks."

I hesitate. "How are you and Andrew?"

"We're fine. The same."

"The same good or the same bad?"

"You know. You just keep moving forward. Now we're here." She takes a long breath. "Everything happens for a reason."

"Do you think so?"

"Yes. Don't you? How do you even get up in the morning otherwise?"

"Yeah, good question." I reach up and mop my face with my shirt. It's so hot here—I don't know how you ever get used to it. Since we arrived, my heart rate has never fully settled down. "How indeed."

Jamison wants to go see the Magnolia Silos, so we drive across town as Atticus teases her the whole way for turning into a middle-aged white mom. The sun beats down on the windows, the asphalt, the low, grassy fields spanning between buildings. It's a little less claustrophobic here than in the rental, talking about Skye's diagnosis, but only a little. I sit in the back seat next to Wrangell, trying not to take up space or touch him, or let our eyes meet, and he and Jamison spend a long time talking about logistics. As Jamison's pulling into the parking lot, Atticus sends me a text: I'm pretending to be cool w him for the sake of family unity but actually I'm pissed! Just so you know!

Really, how do people go through life without a twin.

The Silos are in the middle of an industrial-feeling neighborhood, a tiny village of gleaming white shops and food trucks and a huge indoor marketplace selling farmhousy decor—metal watering cans and woven baskets and rustic white ceramic vases—the kind of home decor that makes it look like an Instagrammable coffee shop. Which, now that I think about it, is in fact kind of Jamison's vibe. Beigey house walls, beigey clothes. Jamison has always craved the safe and comfortable—stability, maybe. I make a mental reminder to discuss this insight with Atticus later. Wrangell buys a sandwich from one of the food trucks.

"How rich do you think this is making them?" he says, crumpling the wrapper and looking around for a trash can. "Pretty mind-blowing what an empire they've got going here."

"I feel kind of dead inside," Atticus says. "This place is sucking my life force away."

"My God, be more dramatic," Jamison says.

"I mean it. It's pure nihilism here. A case study on how to reduce every individual in a square-mile radius into just a mash of capitalistic urges."

I stiffen; that feels too close to what Wrangell told me. But he doesn't respond, so maybe I'm overreacting. Or not. Does he think the same things about Jamison as about me? We find a corner with rustic, tasteful, Texas-themed everything: waffle makers, cutting boards, bath mats, wall art.

"So what are you into?" Atticus says. "Yeah, for me—just Texas. That's my main thing."

"Such a good state for cutting boards," Wrangell agrees.

"Yeah, state-shaped cutting boards are my passion."

Jamison rolls her eyes. "You guys better shut up or this is what you're getting for Christmas for the rest of your lives."

Wrangell takes a picture of himself in front of the cutting boards, making a peace sign. *Texas!!!* he posts. *Here to cheer up @skyelo!* Jamison posts a bunch to her stories too. We wander in and out of shops, sweating. Jamison buys some wooden toys and floral clothes for Sonnet.

Skye would like it here. She would love having the five of us all together like this. I am flooded with guilt to be here without her.

"I've always felt like Joanna Gaines and I would get along," Jamison says. "Or maybe not even that. I've always felt this one-sided affinity with her. Like, I understand her. I have this theory that mixed-race people are natural influencers. Everyone projects whatever they want to onto you. Don't you already feel like you're good at shape-shifting? Just being whoever is required at any given moment in time."

"No," Atticus says. "I don't feel that way at all."

Jamison laughs. "Well, good for you. Maybe you have a stronger sense of self."

Wrangell turns to look directly at me. "What about you, Honor?"

A trapdoor swings open in my chest. "What about me what?"

"How's your sense of self?"

Is this a trap? Is he trying to prove something about me? I fumble over an answer, trying two or three different sentences before giving up and going quiet. Atticus tries to laugh it off, a gift to me, but Jamison gives me a strange look. When she goes into the next little alcove, a place selling white linen flags with black line art on them, Wrangell says, "Can I talk with you for a second, Honor?"

I follow him a few steps away to where he stakes out a spot for the crowds to stream around him. My mouth is dry.

"Listen," he says, glancing around, "I know we had some words last time we saw each other. And it's been weird between us."

Has it been *weird*, or has it been psychological torment? "Mm," I say.

"But I think it's best if we just put that behind us. Obviously, the important thing now is Skye. I regret losing my temper like that with you, given everything. I hope you can forgive me."

"Oh—of course." I blink. Of all the possible outcomes, this was not one I internalized. "I hate fighting with you. I don't want it to be awful between us. I'll try to be better. I'm sorry too."

"Nah, you don't have to apologize. I was going to call you, but then I just came here and I figured I'd see you in person soon anyway. At the end of the day, we're family, and tomorrow isn't guaranteed. As soon as she told me she was sick, I was like—damn it, nothing else matters, you know? I wish it could've been me instead. Skye doesn't deserve this."

"She really doesn't."

He wraps his arms around me in a hug. "We okay?"

I hug him back. I should be able to breathe again now, but my body hasn't caught up yet. My heart is still pounding, and I step back from the hug so he can't feel it. "Yes, of course."

When Atticus and Jamison come back, I feel obligated to signal somehow that things are better, that Wrangell's taken this step. "Wrangell bought you both Texas cutting boards," I say. "That's going to be his next collab."

Wrangell laughs. "Honor's trying to negotiate a finder's fee."

Atticus raises his eyebrows at me slightly—*Are things okay?* I raise mine back—*I guess?* He bumps his fist against mine surreptitiously.

"You know what we should make Skye?" Wrangell says. "One of those Build-A-Bear things. Those bear dolls."

"What's a *bear doll*?" Atticus says, laughing, while Jamison says, "What? No."

"She'd think it was funny. Can't you make them with voices? We can record all of us saying something to her."

"Why do you know that?"

"Lina was weirdly into them."

"Oh God." All of us hated his Lina Chung era—the constant fights they had, the eternal phone conversations, and how she'd show up on our doorstep crying when he didn't answer her calls.

"Skye used to give me so much shit for it."

"Very deserved," Atticus says.

"She never liked Lina. And she thought the bears were bullshit."

"Skye hates animatronic anything," Jamison says. "One year we tried to take you guys to this Christmas light show, and we had to leave early because Skye *flipped* out at this moving Santa."

"And Disneyland," Wrangell says, laughing. "You remember that Mr. Potato Head by the Toy Story ride? Skye was *terrified* of that thing. Okay, we've gotta find one of those bear factories. I think it's going to be the thing that cures her."

"Should we video chat her or something?" Atticus says. "It feels shitty that we're all here together and she's stuck in the hospital alone probably feeling like crap."

"Whoa, whoa, whoa," Wrangell says, "I think you're violating our cult of toxic positivity."

Atticus snorts. "Right," he says. "I forgot if you label something good, then it's good."

"The family ministry," Wrangell says. "James, how have Mom and Dad been with Skye? I know they were so pissed at her in Kauai. Have they been giving her a hard time?"

"No, not for a while," Jamison says. "Definitely not since she got sick."

"I was thinking we shouldn't leave them alone with her," Wrangell says. "At least one of us should always be around so she has a buffer zone."

"I plan to be around a lot," I say, even though I don't necessarily agree with him. "Right now we're doing a week on and a week off, but I bet I could come more if I need."

"I knew you would," he tells me. It was worth the anxiety of coming here, it was worth seeing him, to hear that.

That evening, with Skye back and everyone but me and Atticus packing to leave, I fall asleep on the couch after dinner without meaning to, and then Jamison is shaking me awake.

"We're meeting with one of Skye's doctors," Jamison said. "He's calling now."

I sit up, my heart thudding, and stumble into the living room, where Jamison's set up her laptop on the coffee table. All of us try to cram onto the sectional to see.

"Okay," Skye says, "I'll tell him we're ready now." She messages someone on her phone and then logs on to Zoom. A few moments later a man sitting at a messy desk, filled with papers, comes on the screen. He's young, white, extremely attractive. I wonder if he's too professional to be into Skye.

"Hello," he says. "Hi, Skye, nice to see you. You all must be Skye's family. I'm Dr. Bandley."

"Dr. Bandley, I'm Skye's father, Nathan Lo," our dad says. "Thanks for making time for us. We all have a lot of questions."

"Well, wonderful to see all of you," Dr. Bandley says. "Cancer is a terrifying diagnosis. It's hard on the patient, it's hard on the family. So let me walk you through whatever questions you have, and hopefully that can allay some of your fears."

"Well," our dad says, "we're looking at this conversation as an opportunity to get on the same page here. We're eager to hear the plan to make sure Skye beats this thing."

"One thing I'd like to know," our mother says, "is what the underlying logic is here. Granted, I'm not an oncologist, but it seems unorthodox to be deciding last minute every day whether or not she's getting treated—"

Our dad tightens his jaw, but Dr. Bandley says, "Right, yeah, totally." He has a very Coachella vibe. I can imagine him with a wristband drinking a beer. In another world maybe he and Wrangell would've been friends. "Well, here's the thing. In advanced staging, when you have cancers that have entered the bloodstream, like Skye's has, you want to be very agile and nimble in your treatment, and you want it to be very personalized to the patient as much as possible. Could I give Skye, you know, a very rigid treatment schedule and not deviate from it? Sure, we could do that. Is that in her best interest? No. Is the uncertainty difficult, in an already difficult situation? Yes. absolutely."

"Well, for our own understanding, what exactly is the goal of treatment here?" our mom says.

He pauses a moment. "Well, the goal is always going to be complete remission. We want to see the cancer responding completely to the treatment. We want her to be healthy."

"Of course," our dad says. "It's the twenty-first century. We have every tool at our disposal. So you're doing chemo, radiation, and surgery? Is that right?"

"That's right. Hopefully the chemotherapy can shrink the thymic tumor so we can go in and surgically remove it, and then the chemo and radiation can also work on the metastases, and meanwhile we'll address any organ problems as they arise. And to be clear, we're being aggressive here. If we find that we're not seeing the success we'd hoped for, at that point our options become a bit more limited."

Wrangell looks ill. He shifts himself closer to Skye, as if he can shield her somehow. I feel like I'm falling through endless trapdoors, the room disintegrating over and over around me. I wanted him to reassure us—I wanted him to say it was fine, they weren't that worried, everything was under control.

"Have you explored any naturopathy?" Jamison says. "Any homeopathics?"

"We encourage our patients to supplement our treatment here if they like."

"So," our dad says, leaning forward, "what kind of timeline are we talking about here?"

"That's very difficult to say."

"If you had to say."

Dr. Bandley pauses. "It's really more about—you know, is the primary tumor responding to the chemotherapy, are we seeing the radiation reducing the metastases—"

"Well, if you had to pick a date," our dad says. "At some point you have to say, all right, great, we've maxed out the benefits here and it's time to move on to the next stage. When's that point?"

Dr. Bandley hesitates again, longer this time. Finally he says, "I guess I would say in five or six weeks we should have a clear sense. She would still need to complete more courses of treatment at that point, so it's going to be more of a marathon than a sprint, but I would expect by then to have some clarity."

"All right," our dad says, "so by Thanksgiving, then."

"I see," our mother says, and then her face crumples. Skye looks down at her hands, pushing at her cuticles with her thumbnail, her expression empty.

"Well, that's good news, baby," our dad says to Skye. "You just have to get through six weeks. You're doing great. You get through this stage, and then you'll be well on your way."

But that means she'll be sick on Halloween, I think, inanely. Skye loves Halloween.

"It's a lot to take in," Dr. Bandley says, "but you know what, we all care about Skye here, we think she's really great, and we're doing our best. She's in good hands. I'm sure you all might have more questions, so what I'm going to do is I'm going to just give you my cell phone number. I don't have much time to take calls in between seeing patients, but shoot me a text anytime you need, and I'll get back to you as I can, all right? We want you to feel like you're being cared for as a family, too, because that in turn is going to help Skye. So you just hang tight and support her in whatever she needs. That's the best thing you can do."

CHAPTER SEVENTEEN

J amison, Wrangell, and our parents fly out that evening. Atticus and I stay behind for the first shift, with our mom planning to come back to join us in a few days. It isn't easier dropping Skye off the next time, even though Atticus comes too. We offer to stick around and wait for her, but she tells us it might take all day. Atticus is uncharacteristically quiet and moody afterward, and then he goes to spend basically the whole day at the gym. I wish I'd brought some of my clay with me. I have some delivered, but it's the wrong brand, and I don't have the right tools, and something about the idea of people unknowingly buying some necklace I made while Skye was actively having chemo pumped through her feels cursed to me. Anyway, my hands are shaking too much.

Nothing helps. I feel like I'm losing it. It isn't easier dropping her off the next time either, or the next.

That first week feels a decade long, but we develop a kind of routine. I am alone a lot at the rental house because Atticus goes to the gym or to practice with the other team. Once or twice I go with him to the gym, just to not be by myself in the house, but immediately regret it. It's weird being out in public, though—I feel increasingly disconnected from the rest of the world. At night I lie awake trying to imagine all the ways that things could turn out okay, actually.

Maybe in the morning she'll tell us her counts are looking good, the treatment's working. And then every morning we go out into the kitchen to wait for her, picking at the breakfast Elissa has set up, and eventually she'll come out of her room, her phone in her hand—every morning that same catch in my heart in that split second of possibility—and then she tells us no, her numbers look bad, she has to go in. I start to have an immediate physical reaction whenever I see her look at her phone. Sometimes it's in the morning, sometimes in the afternoon, and once, even, close to dinnertime. Then we drive her to the hospital, trying to joke around in the car so it doesn't seem as funerary as it feels, and then we go back to the house, and sometimes Atticus goes to the gym or practice, but I just wait, my phone on loud, for her to call and say she's ready to be picked up.

Every morning when I wake up, there are aches deep in all my muscles, and my jaw hurts; I think I'm grinding my teeth all night. One tooth is so sore I wonder if I've cracked it. My allergies are bad here too. I always notice it in the late afternoon or early evening after we get Skye—driving into the sunset, sneezing uncontrollably. Once as we're driving home, going by a massive high school football field, I mention they've been much worse here.

"It's probably all the grass and trees," Skye says. She plucks a short hair off her sweater, then takes the sweater off and balls it up in her lap, and the tinge of defensiveness in her voice makes me wish I hadn't brought it up. Maybe it makes her feel guilty I'm here. "So much grows here."

"It's pretty, at least."

"Is it?" she says. "I guess."

At the end of the first week, a little more than a month until we know if her treatment worked, I push past my nervousness and make myself call Caden. I don't have a reason per se, so I make myself ready to abort mission and attempt, like, phone sex or something if he thinks it's weird I'm calling just to talk.

He picks up after a few rings. "Hi, Texas."

"I fly out here and that's who I am now?"

I can hear a smile in his voice. "Seems like it kind of swallowed you up, so yeah, it fits."

"Swallowed me up?"

"I assume that's why I haven't heard from you."

"Oh." I don't tell him I was waiting for him to reach out. "We've just been busy with Skye."

"I figured, yeah. I haven't wanted to bug you."

"Oh, no, it wouldn't have been. There's a lot of downtime, actually. And anyway—I called to tell you that I think you're wrong about running from your actual life."

"Oh?"

"I've been thinking about you saying that. And I think the truth is that wherever you are just becomes your real life."

"Hm." There's a pause. "I don't think it's as easy as that."

"No?"

"You're still whoever you were before."

"Yeah, thanks for the reminder."

He laughs. "Eh, you're not so bad."

"This conversation is really going to go to my head if you're not careful."

He laughs again, and then there's a silence. I want him to say more, to keep me on the line, but I don't want to fill the silence with something that will trap him either. I want him to want me to stay, those parts of me he can't touch or use right now.

"Well," he says, and I think he's going to hang up, "so how's your sister?"

"She's really sick. It's awful." I hesitate. "My family's all, like, yes, she's going to beat this, she just has to get through this part, but I'm scared. I don't know. I wish we knew."

"It sounds like literal hell to have to go through treatment like that, just crossing your fingers hoping it'll be worth it."

My eyes fill with tears. "Yes, exactly. Like, I keep picturing her making herself sit there and get this treatment that's, like, practically killing her, and then I think about how she's going to feel if it doesn't help—I know you can't think like that, but I just can't get it out of my head."

"Is she glad you're there?"

"What do you think?"

"I don't know. That's why I'm asking. My mom never wanted me around."

Something squeezes in my chest. "I'm not certain she wants us around either," I say. "She said she does, so Atticus thinks it's in my head, but—I think he's wrong. She's just in her room most of the time when she's home."

"Yeah, you're probably not just imagining it. It's not you, though, you know? I mean, who knows. That never meant shit to me."

"You don't think your mom wants you around?"

"No. I make her feel like she's failing. Even if I try to tell her, you know, you're trying, that's all I care about, the real problem is that I exist."

"I'm sorry, Caden."

"It's what it is. It doesn't matter."

"It does matter."

"Nah," he says. "We're such small specks in the universe. A hundred years from now it'll be like we never existed."

"I knew I could count on you to cheer me up."

He laughs. "Yeah, anytime."

Halloween has always been Skye's favorite holiday. She threw a legendary costume party every year, and practically the whole school and all her influencer friends in the Bay Area would come. Her rule was that you had to be fully costumed, masked and all, and could reveal yourself only after midnight. Halloween is Skye's Super Bowl. One year she had food poisoning, but she just took a bunch of Zofran so she wouldn't miss it.

I want it to be special for her still, to at least mark the holiday. The day before Halloween I put a note in every mailbox on the street: *Hello, we are living on this street while my sister is undergoing cancer treatment at Hillcrest. She would love to see some trick-or-treaters! Please feel free to stop by 757 with your costume—we'll have lots of candy!* I buy tons of king-size candy bars in all the varieties I think kids would like, and I go to a Michaels to buy out basically their entire stock of decorations. With the clay I have at home I make little jewellike pumpkin pins to pass out to trick-or-treaters, because I love imagining at least one or two kids thinking it's special, something to treasure. While she's at the hospital that day, Atticus and I spend hours hanging lights and decking out the yard.

"This looks so tacky," he says, laughing, surveying the mix of harvest pumpkins and cute ghosts and hideous bloodied-zombie blowups. "I feel like Skye likes classy Halloween. This is . . . not that."

"Shut up. I tried."

"Eh, it's probably a good thing you suck at aesthetics."

"Should we have costumes too?" I say. "I bet I could go find something. I thought my bad costumes would just be kind of sad, but maybe it's better than nothing? We could find some kind of funny ones to make her laugh."

We find a Spirit. The pickings are slim. We get a slightly too small Spider-Man costume for Atticus, a slightly too large dirndl for me, a black-cat onesie for Skye. We put them on when we go to get her from the hospital, as a surprise. Atticus says, almost contemplatively, "It's actually impressive. I think these might be the worst three costumes I've ever seen."

She's finally done a little after six. I almost don't recognize her when I see her waiting outside. I haven't gotten used to her hair, and also there's something about her whole posture that's different: exhausted, defeated looking. Immediately the costumes feel insensitive and garish. When she gets in, she says colorlessly, "You guys are funny."

I wish we hadn't worn them. I say, "How was your appointment?" hating myself for how cheery my voice comes out.

"It was okay."

"I mean—obviously it sucked. How are you feeling?"

She leans her head back against the headrest and closes her eyes. "I'm okay. I'm just tired."

"Are you nauseous or anything?" Atticus says, reaching up to take off his mask.

"Yeah."

My stomach clenches. "That's terrible. How long does it usually last?"

"I don't know."

We pass a strip mall, a car dealership. She keeps her eyes closed and stays very still, and I wonder if she's trying not to throw up.

"I think we might get a lot of trick-or-treaters tonight," I say hopefully. "We can have our own little party if you're up for it. I mean—I know you probably aren't feeling well. I don't mean you have to try to feel well. We can just lie there."

We go by a cluster of gas stations, a cluster of trees. She takes a long time to answer, and when she does, her voice comes out strained and tired. "I might just go to bed."

"Oh. Right. Of course." I blink back tears. A mile later I say, "We should've asked you first. I'm sorry."

"No, not at all."

The sun is setting as we drive back, the colors blanketing the whole flat expanse of roads and fields around us. We pass the mostly picked-over pumpkin patch set up next to a gas station, and the waning light falls ghostlike on the pumpkins still there. It's beautiful in a stark way, in a useless way. Skye holds up her phone to take a picture, out of habit probably, then leaves her phone lying on her lap, and the image jostles and blurs every time we go over a bump.

The next few days are, somehow, worse. Our mom posts long musings about everything Skye's going through: the nausea and constant exhaustion, the anger and fear. Her new-followers rate, which has been roughly steady for a long time, skyrockets. So has Skye's, actually. Our dad posts pictures of Skye with captions like *You got this, baby!* Auntie JJ sends Skye a case of Schweppes grapefruit soda, Skye's favorite drink, which we've only ever seen in Hong Kong, and soft socks she knit, with a note saying hopefully they'll help when she's cold getting chemo. Her sorority sends flowers and then nothing else (so much for sisters for life). One morning someone we don't know drops off flowers and homemade cookies at the house, which is a little terrifying because no one's supposed to know the address, so Elissa hires a security guard. I sort through all the gifts people send her, I do interviews so they'll stop bugging Skye as much, and I try to stay on top of everything people are saying, even though Atticus tells me I have no sense of proportion and most of these aren't worth bothering with. There's the truther contingent trying to pick apart everything Skye posts for the smallest inconsistency to prove she's faking, the people furious she's not using her platform to raise cancer awareness better, the people who think it's morally repugnant to care about the relatively mild suffering of someone as privileged as Skye, the people convinced our parents orchestrated this to distract from their separation. If something gets enough traction, I send it to Jamison. Jamison sparks a small fire telling our dad about that last one and how catastrophic it would be right now if news of Heather got out, which our dad, somehow, is extremely offended by. While the messages are flurrying in, Atticus comes into my room, holding out his phone to me.

"Take this away before I lose my shit in the group chat," he says. "I'm about to bring shame on every ancestor we've ever had. God, I am so fucking sick of him."

Skye's too sick and exhausted from the chemo to work very much, and I email all her contacts to explain the situation, and deal with all the replies. And I get an email from Hanna: *Honor, just checking on the status of our order. We'd love to get moving on the launch! I hope Skye is doing well!* I don't know to respond. I've been tinkering, making little things for Sonnet or just little versions of things I see throughout the day—the knobby potted cactus on the front porch, the wedge of corn bread that was all I could eat from the barbecue Elissa brought for dinner the other day—but I haven't had it in me to work on the jewelry. While Skye's getting the infusions, I send her messages to say I'm thinking about her and hope it's going well, and when she doesn't answer, I imagine her hunched over a trash can or shaking with pain. Sometimes at night when she gets back, we try to watch movies together, but mostly she wants to be alone in her room. She barely eats, and maybe it's my imagination, but I think her skin looks grayer. I hope beyond hope our dad is right. I'm worried he's not. I don't say it to anyone aloud, not even Atticus.

When Atticus flies back home at the end of that week, I'm supposed to go with him, but I don't want to leave Skye yet, so I stay. I miss Atticus intensely as soon as he's gone. Wrangell flies back into town again. We have movie marathons with Skye and do a take-out tour of all the different burger options in the city, then all the different breakfast places. He makes it easier with her, less fraught. When she's at the hospital, he and I hang out together—we get cupcakes, we go see a movie, we browse some antique shops, we go to FedEx to figure out how to ship a chair he bought. I am grateful for the time with him, for the ways he makes us laugh, but underlying everything is still the same fear I thought I'd let go of. I still worry what he thinks about me, still worry that something I say will unintentionally end things forever. He leaves after a few days, and our mom comes back.

Skye's numbers, meanwhile, don't budge. The tumor markers stay high. She has a scan to see if the cancer has shrunk, and while we're eating dinner that night, she gets the results: it hasn't started working yet. None of us sleeps well that night, and then the next day, right before the one-month mark, Skye wakes up with chest pain.

It's just me and our mother there with her at the house, and our mother wants to call an ambulance to take her to the ER. But Skye's doctors want to see her themselves, so we drive her there, going twenty above the speed limit.

"Call us as soon as you can," our mother says as Skye unbuckles. "Tell us any news, no matter how small."

She's shaking. We watch Skye walk in, and then from the parking lot we google "cancer patient chest pain" while we're waiting. It's probably a mistake. *Ischemic chest pain presents as tight, squeezing pressure. Aortic dissection presents as a tearing, ripping pain. Cancer patients are at higher risk for venous thromboembolism.*

Our mother calls someone she used to know years ago, a daughter of one of the Ming Quong women, who's an oncologist, to ask advice. "The cancer's in her heart already, and now she has chest pain," she says, and then listens intently for a long time. When she hangs up, she tells me, "Grace doesn't think her doctors are handling this well. She thinks they should've tried surgery first. And more rounds of chemotherapy, plus radiation. These small-town doctors! I just don't know."

I am, suddenly, exhausted on a cellular level; I have a split-second understanding of my existence being composed of mitochondria and nuclei and cytoplasm. How fragile and random it all is, how obscenely incomprehensible. I miss all my siblings so much in that moment I could cry.

We spend an excruciating day waiting at home for her to update us on the battery of tests she's subjected to. Finally Skye messages: everything looks stable. I'm feeling better now.

The next morning our mom comes into my room to see if I'm awake. The room is stark and empty except for the explosion of

276 • KELLY LOY GILBERT

clothes spilling out of my suitcase in the corner, which I haven't had it in me to tidy up, even though I have endless amounts of time.

"Feel my pulse," she says, ignoring the mess, which is how I know she's not herself. She presses two fingers to her wrist, then holds out her wrist to me. "Do I need to call 911? Why can I not calm down?"

Her heart is racing. She's pale. I have the same momentary freak-out I have now at any slight twinge of any symptom—*It's cancer!!*—but I say, "It's probably anxiety, Mom. Do you want a Xanax? See if it gets better."

"No. I'll go do some yoga." She sinks onto the foot of my bed and covers her face with her hands. "I feel so useless as a mother right now."

"You're not useless. Are you okay? Do you want some tea?"

"You're such a good daughter, Honor. I hate that you have to go through this." She drops her hands. "I can't even work. Isn't that pathetic? My hands keep shaking and I can't type. I think yesterday with the chest pain—it was too much."

When we go out to eat breakfast, I message our siblings to ask what I should say to her.

Nothing!!! Wrangell messages back. **She's an adult. That's not your job.** But she's clearly not okay. She doesn't work the rest of the morning, wandering aimlessly around the house and periodically checking her pulse instead. Finally I slip outside and call Auntie JJ.

"Auntie?" I say. "It's Honor. Um—what are you doing this week? Do you think you could come to Waco? I think my mom needs you."

• • •

I'd hoped maybe she would have time sometime during the month, ideally maybe later this week, but she gets on a plane literally within hours. She must have left for the airport as soon as she hung up. I don't tell our mom she's coming until the doorbell rings, and I brace myself for her to be furious. She isn't, though. She just looks exhausted. She gets up to get the door, but I wait in the hallway because I think, somehow, they'll connect differently if I'm not there, if it's just the two of them. For once I don't think our mom wants an audience. I can still see them from where I'm sitting, although I don't think they notice.

"Oh, Melissa," Auntie JJ says. She gathers our mom in a hug and holds her for a long time. When she lets go, they both have tears in their eyes. "How is she? How are you? What's happening?"

"I can't believe you came all the way here," our mom says.

"Of course I came. I would've sooner, I just didn't want to be in the way. You should've called me. I can stay as long as you want. I can work remotely. What do you need? What can I do? I've been having nightmares about Skye. It's just so awful, I can't believe it. What's the latest from her doctors?"

Our mother fills her in on the meeting with Dr. Bandley, Auntie JJ shaking her head slowly the whole time.

"And I don't know about the caliber of doctors here," our mom says. "He's extremely young. He can't be much older than Wrangell—he must be right out of med school. I'm just so worried we're wasting time here in this second-rate institution, and we really don't have time to waste. And I'm not convinced that Nathan grasps the seriousness of the situation. Everything he says is just magical thinking. Like if Skye can get through the treatment, she'll be fine, which is obviously not how anything works."

"Right," Auntie JJ says quietly.

"And to some degree it's just how he functions, it's his survival mechanism, but right now I just—I can't. I just feel completely betrayed. He's leaving me alone to worry about this—" Her voice breaks.

Auntie JJ draws in a long breath. "I'm not supposed to tell you this," she says. "He called me last week."

"He *called* you? What about?"

"He wanted me to pray with him. He wanted to pray for Skye. And he wanted me to connect him with Pastor Ken so they could talk. He thinks maybe God is punishing him for Heather and that's why Skye's sick."

Does that mean he'll end things with Heather, then? Does he feel guilty? He should. But knowing him, maybe he's already found some way to talk himself out of it. Auntie JJ says, "You know I'm always skeptical when it comes to Nathan, but this time I thought he sounded very sincere."

"Well, that's fine, he's still Skye's father, but I don't want him crawling back because he thinks I'm penance." Our mom carefully wipes her eyes. "What did you say to him?"

"I told him God doesn't work that way."

Our mom sighs. "You should've told him that's exactly what's happening."

Auntie JJ laughs, surprising me. "You're right. I should have. Maybe it's not too late."

"I feel so incredibly guilty for things I've said to Skye," our mom says. "Especially in Kauai when I found out about Nathan and Heather. I keep replaying them over and over in my mind. Did I ever tell you my internal voice sounds exactly like Mom? That's why my therapist told me the work of my life was going to be replacing her voice in my head with a kinder, gentler voice. Which, apparently, I have not yet done."

"Well," Auntie JJ says. "You could apologize to Skye. Maybe that would help."

"Ugh, I'm afraid if I do, I won't be able to stop. She's so miserable already—she doesn't want me dumping all my guilt on her. I am so useless to her right now. There's literally nothing I can do to make this better for her."

"You're here for her," Auntie JJ says. "You're where you need to be."

"She's just so ill, JJ. I am so scared."

"Let's go eat something," Auntie JJ says. "It'll help. Look, we're still just here standing in the entryway, and you're wearing mismatched sweats. You look awful. Are you sleeping at all? Let's clean up and go find some food."

We find a pho place that's open late. It's probably been a long time since our mom has been somewhere like this: dingy tables, a check for less than twenty dollars a person. The food is delicious. I wish Skye had felt well enough to come. Maybe we should have stayed home with her.

"I'm just so *angry*," our mom tells JJ. "All the time! Nathan's parents called to say oh, they saw Skye was sick, what's happening, and I wanted to hang up on them. Like, don't pretend you care about my kids. You think everything we do is immoral."

"Do they still send you all the awful email forwards?"

"Ugh, yes!"

"They're punishing you," Auntie JJ says, laughing. "He already abandoned the orchards, and then he met *you*, and now he's not even a pastor, and your punishment is forwards about CRT and the Pledge of Allegiance from now until eternity."

It feels like old times, them gossiping together.

Later that night I tell Atticus what Auntie JJ said about our dad, but he says he doesn't care. Which, maybe I don't either, I guess.

"He can say whatever he wants," Atticus says. "So what? It doesn't mean anything."

Our dad does, however, finally successfully badger Skye into securing a virtual meeting for all of us with her doctors to discuss results of the treatment. The appointment is set for the Wednesday before Thanksgiving, just over two weeks from now. Everyone will come, of course. Jamison sends us all calendar invites, and Ava messages to say she'll book flights.

"It doesn't need to be a big deal," Skye says sharply. "I honestly didn't even want everyone to come. But okay, whatever, if it makes you all feel better."

We're all stung. Because she's sick, we pretend we aren't.

When Skye's at the hospital for treatment the next day, my phone rings, a number I don't recognize. There's a risk it's someone calling for a quote, but I pick up in case it's Skye.

"Honor, it's Victoria. I hear things aren't going well there."

"Victoria?" I think I would have been less surprised to hear from the pope. "Aren't you supposed to be at school?"

"I am at school. I just ducked out of class. Caden says you sound depressed."

"Caden told you that?" Literally not a single sentence she's spoken on this call has failed to catch me off guard. I've been talking with Caden most days, but I try to keep things at least somewhat light, "Well—yeah, my sister has a life-threatening illness, so things are not exactly great."

"I hoped getting them off your case about independent study would help."

I pause. "What do you mean you hoped that?"

"I had my mom call Mrs. Hall for you. My parents donate a lot, so . . ."

Literally not one single thing in this conversation. "Oh," I say blankly. "That's—well, that was really nice of you. Um, that was unexpected."

She laughs. "Yeah, fair."

"Why did you do that?"

"Oh, the school can be so annoying about things." She pitches her voice higher. "That's just not how things are *done*!" Back to her normal voice, she says, "My grandfather died a little over a year and a half ago of pancreatic cancer. And everyone was like oh, you know, he's old, grandparents die, but he basically raised me and he was, like, my person. You know? Probably how like you have Atticus."

"I'm really sorry to hear that."

"It was hell. I talked about it sometimes, but no one understood and it just pissed me off, so I stopped talking about it."

"Yeah, I get that."

"Yes, it's all terrible. But I think you'll be surprised how much you just keep going because you have to."

"What did you do with yourself during the day? The days are so long."

"Well, I got really into vaulting, so that's kind of specific and probably doesn't help you."

"Vaulting? Like with a pole?"

"With a horse."

"Oh." Do I even know what that is? "Yeah, you're right, that doesn't help."

"I do it now, too. You think it's hard when they're in treatment, and it is, but when they're just gone, that's . . . a lot of hours to fill."

I don't want to hear that part. "How did you not absolutely lose your mind?"

"Do you have friends, Honor?" she says. "From your old school? I think you need people to party with or to kidnap you and take you to the beach for the weekend or something to get your mind off everything."

Do I have friends? People have messaged, commented on my posts. "I can't think of a single thing that would get my mind off all this."

"Not a *single* thing? Give Caden another call."

I feel my face go hot. I'm saved from having to answer when she says, "Honestly, no one understands. Everyone just keeps living life like nothing is wrong. That part truly enraged me. There you are, falling apart, and your friends are like, ooh, who's hooking up with who? What'd you get on the bio test? Truly enraging."

Is that why I have an almost physical resistance to working on the order for Hanna? Maybe. I tell Victoria how I hear Skye throwing up at night, how just sitting here waiting makes me want to crawl out of my skin.

"Yeah, it was the powerlessness for me," she says. "I would get all in my head imagining the cells just, like, multiplying inside him—my mom made us go to this therapist who had us do these visualizations of his body fighting it off, and I'm still so furious at her. Like, fuck you. Sometimes people die."

"Oh God, that sounds like something my dad would do too."

"Ew."

Something about the way she says it—it makes me laugh. "I know."

"How long are you going to stay there with your sister?"

"I guess as long as she needs." I hesitate. "Caden told me he didn't think I should come, and I—"

"Caden said that? What did he say exactly?"

"He thought it was constructing an alternate reality. And I think he meant well, but the longer I'm here, the more I wonder if that's exactly what I'm doing. I thought I'd get here and do a lot to help, but I'm just sitting around while Skye's at the hospital. I keep wondering if he was right."

"Don't overthink it. He probably just didn't want to admit he'd miss you."

The words send a flare up inside me, warm and bright. "That's what you think?"

"Probably. Okay, back to class for me! When are you coming home? I'll come kidnap you myself. In the meantime, just take it minute by minute. Tell yourself you can survive sixty seconds of anything, and then do it again."

CHAPTER EIGHTEEN

I fly back to California alone the next day. I'm so busy feeling guilty for leaving, and wondering if another infection complication or something else will happen while I'm gone, that I forget to take my Xanax in time, and I spend the whole flight clutching the armrest at every bout of turbulence and craning my neck to see the flight attendants to make sure they aren't freaking out. As we start to descend, I let myself pretend for a little while that it's still our old life, the one where everyone is home and no one is sick and everyone loves each other still, and it's so painful that I have tears in my eyes when we touch down.

Will things get better? I am both desperate and terrified to hear what her doctors will say at the appointment. Jamison told me once the thing that's interesting about getting older is that nothing changes about your past, but you have more context for it all. (She told me this when we were talking about our parents being gone so much, how she looks at Sonnet now and can't imagine doing that to her.) Maybe this is just the rest of our lives. Maybe it's like climate change—each day is probably better than any subsequent day is going to be in our lifetime. At least we have Auntie JJ back, and Wrangell and I are speaking again. The only good things to come of all this.

It's a relief to get up in the morning and go to school, to at least have something to do. I see Caden's car in the parking lot, and as I scan for him, my heart is beating so hard it's practically vibrating. I cross the parking lot and make it as far as the redwoods at the north end, by the gates to campus, when someone comes up behind me and puts their hands over my eyes. I scream.

"Oh my God, get a grip," Victoria says, laughing. "I told you we were going to kidnap you. I even brought you a change of clothes! Let's go."

I feel so entirely unmoored in all ways from my actual life that I think anything from here on out would've been equal parts surprising and unsurprising to me, but what happens is we take Victoria's car— her and me, plus Delancey and Blythe—and drive the twenty-five minutes over the hill to Santa Cruz and then another ten minutes south to Capitola, where Victoria's family has what she describes as a little beach-town place, which turns out to be an enormous Mediterranean-style villa right on the water. The shoreline is flatter here, wider—none of the bluffs I'm used to, the houses more ostentatious. But still, it's soothing to be next to the Pacific. The smell is the same. As promised, Victoria brought a bathing suit for me. It's cold out, foggy and gray here on the coast the same way it probably is back home, and we go up to one of the decks to the hot tub.

"This is really nice," I say. Maybe I don't hate them. "You guys didn't have to do this."

"It's really a huge sacrifice to miss precalc so I could come lounge by the beach all day," Blythe says airily, "but somehow I'll live."

I close my eyes and rest my head back against the rim of the hot tub, let the heat calm me. The whir of the jets and the crash of the surf make us feel cordoned off from the rest of the world. "Do you guys come here a lot?"

"No, actually," Victoria says. "I'm always so lazy about the drive. But it seemed like a good time."

"Have people been rallying around Skye?" Blythe asks me. "I seriously can't imagine being so sick at our age."

"Yeah, a lot of people are." The hot water and the mist, the weirdness of the day, the white noise—it all makes me feel languorous and loose. "I don't totally get the motivation there. It's all such a nightmare I'm truly not sure what they're drawn to. Maybe when they haven't lived it, people think it's weirdly glamorous or romantic? I genuinely don't know."

"What do you mean, 'what they're drawn to'?" Victoria says.

"People are drawn to others who have something they want, right? Or something they want to be. I'm sure everyone has some reason for wanting to rally around her right now."

"Wait, Honor, that's so fucked up! I'm an enormous bitch, and even I don't think that about people. Probably people genuinely want to try to support her."

I tilt my head back up and open my eyes. "Do you think so?"

"What do you think we're doing right now?"

"I don't know, actually." I pause. "I thought you hated me."

Delancey jabs Victoria with her elbow. "I *told* you." To me, she says, laughing, "Victoria's just mean. We're working on it."

"I'll admit that when you guys first showed up, I thought you'd be really full of yourselves, but you're not," Victoria says. "Delancey told me I had to try to be nicer. Plus Caden always liked you, and Caden doesn't like most people."

"Have you hooked up?" Delancey says.

I go red. Even with Lilith and Eloise I never really talked about this kind of thing. "Um—"

"Does that mean yes?" Victoria says, amused. "Caden wouldn't tell me, which I thought meant no, but *you* not telling me makes me think the opposite."

"Oh, leave her alone," Delancey says. "Her sister's sick! Cut her some slack."

Blythe doesn't say anything, and I wonder if she still has feelings for him. I change the subject so it doesn't make her feel bad if she does.

We sit in the hot tub for probably two hours. They tell me stories about people at school, and then Blythe and Delancey take the car to pick up some lunch, and Victoria and I stay behind. One thing leads to another, and before I know it, I'm telling her about everything Wrangell said to me, about the fight we had.

"I don't know why I can't let go of it," I say. "Obviously, the only thing that matters right now is Skye, and it seems so petty to care about anything else. Like, our mom was basically estranged from her sister for years, and now because of Skye they're really close again, so shouldn't it be like that for everyone? But then here I am still going over it again and again in my mind and panicking about what I'm supposed to say when I'm around him."

"Yeah the thing is, like—you'd hope someone getting sick would bring out the best in everyone, but it can really be the exact opposite. It just lays bare all the shit you were dealing with or pretending to not deal with earlier."

"Did your family have things like this happen?"

"My God, the stories I could tell. The worst was that for a long time my mom was convinced I gave my grandfather cancer because I caused him so much stress."

"Victoria! That's so sad."

"It was. I was doing fine in school and everything, but I was fighting a lot with my mom, and it always upset him. And she was reading how stress can cause inflammation and be really toxic to your body, and she was like, 'Oh my God, Victoria, *you* did this to him.'"

"That's absolutely awful. And not true, of course."

"You think?" She's quiet for a moment. "I've actually never told anyone that. It would really kill me if everyone was like, oh yeah, your mom was totally right."

"No, literally not the slightest chance."

"Okay." She smiles at me. "That makes me feel better, actually. Thanks."

It's oddly exhilarating to feel like I helped. I feel better after talking to her, sort of enormously so. The ways everything's so fractured now—maybe I can just think of it as part of the disease, as side effects. Maybe Wrangell is wrong and what I wanted wasn't so horrible; maybe he's just struggling in his own way. Maybe things will get better. I want to believe in the possibility that this isn't forever. I want to cling to hope.

Caden comes by my house late that afternoon when we're back from the beach. He has flowers for me, which is probably the actual sweetest thing anyone has ever done for me. I am not someone people unironically give flowers to. I tear up, which is embarrassing. "It's been an emotional time!" I say, and he laughs.

"Sure," he says. "Right."

"It has!"

"I know. I'm just messing with you."

We go up to my room. It's the first time he's been here, and he glances around, his gaze landing on my desk, where I was halfway through making some ramen bowls what feels like a lifetime ago. "What are these?" he says, amused.

"Oh—just this hobby I have."

He picks up a tiny Oreo to inspect. "You made all these?"

"Um, yeah."

He puts down the Oreo and picks up my little basket of tiny har gow. I make them with translucent clay, so you can see the pink of the shrimp inside. "Dim sum," he says. "Nice." He replaces them carefully on my desk and looks back at me, grinning an enormous game-day grin. "Man, you've really been stringing me along."

"What's that supposed to mean?"

"I mean I distinctly remember you told me that at your old school you were more into books than parties, whereas *this*"—he gently pokes a clay char siu bao—"is clearly the work of someone who goes all out at ragers."

I laugh in spite of myself. "Shut up."

"I know we had our big talk about wanting to be in each other's lives, but I have to say, now I'm not sure I can keep up with you. Socially speaking."

"Yeah, you're probably right. It was a good talk, though."

"Eh, it could've gone better. Not the most enthusiastic."

"Shut up," I say.

He smiles. "These are actually pretty cool. You're talented."

"I'm kind of freaking out about it right now because I got my first commission and I just haven't been able to make it happen." I tell him about Hanna's order. "I'm afraid she's going to cancel it."

"Do you want to make those for her?"

"I mean, yes. It's just this hobby, and to have a chance to, like, turn it into something I can sell is an opportunity I didn't expect to have."

"Do you want to sell these, though?"

"What do you mean do I want to? I can always make more."

"Sure. I just mean if it's not doing anything for you and the idea stresses you out and you're avoiding it, maybe it's fine if it's not, like, this successful thing. Maybe it's fine if it's just for you." He glances at his watch. "You want to go to the reservoir? We still have a little daylight."

So we drive up there again. And it's good, actually—it feels natural and easy. I could stay with him like this forever. The sun starts to come down while we're there, and we get out and walk around the water, and there's this one perfect flat rock, and he pulls me down onto it and traces his thumb gently down my jawbone in a way that makes my whole body feel electric. I start to kiss him, and then he gets completely distracted by this one squirrel with a stub tail, and we spend probably twenty minutes trying to follow him because Caden's convinced if we go slowly enough, we can pet him.

"No, no," Caden keeps insisting every time I tell him it's a lost cause, "we're bonding. He can tell we're friendly. Come here, buddy. You look so soft. We just want to pet you once. Just one time!"

Driving back, the sky soft with light, I can't stop thinking how it should have been me instead. I have never done anything to deserve a day like today, this kind of happiness, while my sister is chained to an IV and waking up at night to vomit just so she can maybe live. If I were sick, there would be no hashtags for me, no throngs of strangers devastated by the news. It should have been me.

. . .

I stay one more day in Los Gatos, and then I fly back to Waco. There are ten days left until the meeting with Skye's doctors. It's strange, because I still think of Stinson Beach as home, and I still technically hate Saint Simeon, but (despite the fact that I have to fly back in four days) I think I actually miss it. I miss—the people, of all things. I am here in Waco and I should be thinking about Skye, how I can help her more, but instead, selfishly, I'm wishing I could go back to my life in Los Gatos. Caden and VBD all message me—Victoria, in fact, messages me the same thing every morning. You're going to make it through today!! It's a kind of lifeline, something dependable that keeps me anchored.

Atticus is going to fly in on Tuesday, but then our dad comes instead, and Atticus decides he'll skip it. I'm annoyed he skips, but then maybe it's for the best, because our dad is chipper and positive, no hint of the conversation he had with Auntie JJ, and it feels so wildly out of place in the house. Skye tells us her numbers are creeping in the wrong direction, and our dad tells her she just has to hang on, that she's almost there. I'm relieved when he leaves. I think Atticus would've exploded.

The next morning when we wake up, Skye's bloodwork comes back looking good, enough so that she doesn't have to go in for chemo, and as soon as she comes into my room, I know today is going to be different. She's dressed, for one thing, and she's done her eyes and some contouring, and immediately the day feels awash in a sense of hope: if it's good today, why not tomorrow, too, and the next day? Maybe our dad was right after all.

"There's this swimming hole I wanted to go to," she says as I'm washing my face. "You want to go? It's two hours away."

"You're up for it? That doesn't sound like too much?"

"No, I think it would be good."

"You're sure? If you start not feeling good—or you get tired—"

"Yes, I'm sure," she says, a little exasperated. "I'm fine. It's mostly just driving and then lying on a rock. It's a good day for it. I don't have to go into the hospital. If we wait—who knows?"

"Right, of course," I say quickly. "Yeah. Let's do it! It sounds great."

I didn't bring a bathing suit with me, but she has an extra—I'm surprised she thought to pack them—and we spend an hour or so gathering things, towels and sunscreen and some snacks. I am happy for all the small tasks, for a future even if it it's only as far out as later today. We stop and get burgers on the way at a rustic-feeling drive-up place, and Skye gets a milkshake, too. It's warm but not oppressively so yet, and we drive with the windows down. Skye lets her arm rest out the window so the breeze rushes up her arm, and she tilts her head back against the headrest, and it's bright enough outside that I can see through her sunglasses the way her eyes are closed, the soft look of peace on her face.

Eventually the road goes from freeways to winding two-lane roads, hills rising around us, dotted in oaks and scrub brush, under a cloud-flecked sky that goes on and on.

"So," Skye says, taking off her sunglasses, "who were you talking to late last night?"

"Oh, was I too loud? Sorry, I thought I was being quiet."

"No, you're fine. The walls are just thin. Was it Caden?"

"Yes."

"Okay, tell me more about him. What's your deal?"

"I think we're—together, kind of? We used to just hook up a

lot, but then when you got sick—I guess it made me realize I wanted something real. So we're trying that." Immediately I'm horrified at how it sounds aloud, that I've turned her illness into my own personal gain. "I didn't mean it the way it sounds. I would give up him or anyone or literally anything for you to not be going through this."

"Oh, I know, don't worry. I didn't take it like that. Is he nice to you?"

"Yes, in his own way. I think he's not really a *nice* person, per se."

"That's fine, I guess. It's not like we were raised to be nice."

"What went wrong with you, then?"

She laughs. "Genetic mutation, I guess. Well—if you guys have something together, then I can be excited for you," Skye says more quietly. "I trust your instincts. If you like him, I can like him. You deserve someone great."

There's a wistfulness in her tone, and suddenly I am stabbed with guilt. Why should I be happy, with someone I like, when Skye is suffering this way? I'm sure she would love to have nothing more to worry about than whether her feelings are mutual with some guy she's into. I bet she'd love to be obsessing over conversations with him, imagining her body close to his instead of being pumped full of poison.

"What about you?" I say. "Anyone at Baylor?"

She's quiet for a moment too long. I say, grinning, "What! You never told me."

"No, no, no one at Baylor. Honestly, I don't know if I believe in relationships."

"Not at all?"

"I mean, maybe I'm just an unlovable loser—"

I roll my eyes. "Right."

"—but I don't know, like just the idea that you should let yourself trust that someone's going to like, I don't know, love you at your worst or still love you when they know everything about you. Or what if you change? And then they're there when you take off your makeup and you're all grungy? Or when I'm throwing up and my hair is gone? Like, ew."

We drive out on some country roads, big farmhouse-style homes set back from the road, and into a thicket of trees. The swimming hole is down a dirt road deep in the thicket, a property with a house on it and a limestone pool and fountain and a series of limestone steps leading down, improbably, to a lush, shaded grotto with glossy green water and a rocky outcropping where there are several people sunbathing. A man in the house takes our cash and says sternly, "Y'all have fun now."

"This place is amazing," I say as we make our way across the rocks. "It's someone's house? That's wild."

"Yeah, there's nothing like this in California, right? Like, we have creeks and parks, but nowhere where you drive through a neighborhood and then it's, like, a swimming hole. The weird thing is that almost all of it is private. Maybe it's all going to be like this in the future, and you'll have to pay anytime you want to go see nature. I took for granted how much of California is just, like, public land." Skye looks around and then sets her towel and bag down on a flat stretch of rock. It's hot, the waves of heat pulling off the surface. "So—apparently they have turtles here."

"No!"

"I thought you'd like that."

"You are too much."

"Not sea turtles, but still."

"You're supposed to be, like, selfish and angry right now, not thoughtful and sweet. Ugh." I reach up and wipe my eyes. "I can't believe you thought of that."

"It's the least I could do."

"No, don't even say that. That's not how I think of it at all."

It looks like a college crowd here today; different clusters of tanned, glistening white people, a few holding cans of beer. There's one family with three small kids—the kids are fighting over a rope swing that goes out over the water.

It's so beautiful here, so otherworldly. A girl in a coed group a few yards away from us on the rocks keeps looking over at us like she recognizes us, and I see Skye register it, and she makes that tiny shift we're all familiar with—her smile a little more practiced, her posture better. I try and fail not to be annoyed. I don't want to deal with anyone trying to talk to us in the middle of nowhere. I take some pictures, and then Skye sticks her head next to mine for a selfie.

I want this moment as proof, as a talisman. You feel safest around other people instead of inside your own head. The world feels bright and ordinary here, and all these people—it's hard to imagine all of them would let something terrible happen. Maybe I would feel better if I could see Skye's doctors, if I could feel the same thing about them: all of them determined not to let anything bad happen to her.

"I'm going to swim," Skye says. "Are you?"

"Oh—maybe in a little bit. It looks freezing."

I watch her wade in, trying at first to keep her hips above the water, shivering a little, and then plunging all the way in. My phone buzzes—our mom asking how it's going here. I send her pictures of the spring—it's something she'll like and approve of; for all the things she's always made us feel guilty or stifled about, she does forever love to see us experiencing anything different or unique or beautiful. She was so proud when Jamison studied abroad.

Wish I were there!!! she writes back. So proud of you, sweetheart. What an incredible sister you're being. These will be memories to hold on to all our lives. xo.

When I look up again, I don't see Skye anywhere. Immediately my heart rockets against my chest. I leap up, light-headed, and scan the water. She's wearing a bright orange bikini, and she should be easy to spot, but I can't see her. I can't breathe. She's always been a good swimmer. But can chemo weaken you? Or her cancer?

I run my gaze methodically from one end of the water to the other, and she's nowhere. It occurs to me only now that I never saw her resurface.

"Skye!" I scream. *"Skye!"* If she's under the water, I want her to come up. I look around frantically. People are staring at me, but I don't see her anywhere. *"Skye!"*

"Honor, what's wrong?"

My lungs flood, my heart, my skin, all at once. I turn around, and she's on the rocks behind me, talking to the girl who was looking at us before. Both of them are staring at me.

"Oh God," I say. "I thought you were—I thought—"

Then I can't go any further, and my voice breaks. I hunch over, sobbing, trying to pull air into my lungs. The part of me that exists outside myself is horrified at the sight, watching the way everyone steps back, gawking.

"It's fine!" Skye says brightly, but I hear the tinge of irritation in her voice. This is, of course, her nightmare: a public scene that makes us both look bad. "Thanks, everyone. Everything's fine."

I am gasping for air. The sun's glare off the water is coming at me like shards, the trees wavering and hazy around me. My heart is pounding so hard I can't catch my breath. I can't even imagine how long it would take to get to a hospital, but I think I might be having a heart attack. I've had panic attacks before, but this is different. I'm drowning in this. I'm so scared.

"Well, it was nice to meet you," Skye says to the girl. "Honor— it's fine. Seriously. Come on, get your stuff. Let's go."

Skye has to drive home, since I'm not in any condition to do anything but struggle for air, and we're halfway back to Waco before I no longer feel like I need to go to the ER. In the wake of the panic attack I feel a deep disgust with myself. Skye is the one who's sick, and here I am making her drive me home and reassure me, tell me I'm fine. I apologize profusely, which she brushes off, but I've killed the mood.

Later that afternoon, I call Caden to ask if he ever freaked out at nothing that way and saw disaster where really everything was fine.

"No," he says, "I didn't, but—you know. Don't beat yourself up over it."

"I've never had a panic attack that bad before."

"Makes sense."

"I've never told anyone I get them."

"Yeah, well, you don't owe anyone that."

He's being kind, I think; there's a certain gentleness in his voice that I don't think I'm imagining. But that's not what I want from him. I've just told him something about me, and I want him to tell me something in return—to offer something, something that feels like it's just mine.

I'm silent. I will wait him out. Then he says, his tone impossible to parse, "My mom's back home."

"Wait, what?" I sit up straighter. "I didn't know she was coming back already. That's good, right?"

"I guess."

"You guess? I thought you'd be happier."

"It's just—you know. It's the same shit over and over. She's like, I'm a new person, I'm totally different, I'm better now and this will never happen again, and then it's like—yeah, okay, I've heard that before. I wish I could believe it."

"I'm sorry, Caden."

"Yeah, whatever. It is what it is."

"So are you going to spend time with her?"

"We'll probably get dinner or something. But she always has a lot to do. You know. Worried if she doesn't do all her therapy and yoga or whatever, she'll undo all her progress, blah, blah, blah."

"I hope—I hope it's better this time somehow. I hope it's different."

"Well, you're braver than me, then," he says. "Or dumber. I've definitely sworn off hope." He's quiet for a moment, then says, "Honestly, I think it's worse than cancer."

I go hot. "Excuse me?"

"At least with cancer—"

"Fuck you."

I hang up, my hands shaking. I'm so angry I can feel a migraine starting to throb at my temple. I lie down on my bed, my eyes closed, and take long, slow breaths and try to remember the fear I felt today at the swimming hole, to bleed away some of the anger. I doubt it's healthy just rearranging negative emotions that way.

Eventually, though, it works, and I get up and take a shower and then go out into the living room, where Skye is watching TV. I am not thinking about Caden. I will not think about Caden. We order tacos for dinner—they're good—and watch reruns of *The Office* all night, and I'm so happy to be here with her, and that happiness feels heavy and determined in a way that feels like a cousin to that strange way time fractures when you're afraid of something. When we were little and had to get a shot, I would dread it days in advance, and it would feel so close, and then the day of I would tell myself no, I still had five more hours, then a whole hour, then ten minutes, then still all the time for the nurse to swab my skin and reach back down for the needle.

While we're sitting around, me trying to hold myself there in the moment, not thinking about Caden, Skye posts some pictures from Krause Springs. *A magical day with my sister <3*, she writes, and maybe it's for the algorithm, maybe it's part of a narrative, but it also feels, when I see it, like forgiveness, and like love.

Someone at the swimming hole took a video of me screaming for Skye when I couldn't find her, and it's doing the rounds. There I am standing on the rock, looking wildly around, leaning forward to scream.

I wait to see if Lauren will see it and call me; she'll be displeased—it'll incite a flurry of activity as she schemes for something else I can do to bump it out of people's sight. But I guess it never gets enough traction to rise to the level of something she would see. ("Your audience is not a few jealous bitches online!" she's told me before. "Ignore them!") So I do what I always do when something feels incredibly violating, which is I watch it over and over until it doesn't seem real anymore, until I feel numb.

You're Not Famous: A Snark Site
ynf.com/forums/LoFamily

disneymom, 2:11:32 pm PST: I genuinely feel for Honor. I think she really loves Skye. I have a sister who's the same distance in age as she and Skye are and if she got sick I genuinely don't know what I'd do.

kindredhearts, 2:12:02 pm PST: yeah, Honor always strikes me as extremely fake but this felt genuine

junco, 2:13:14 pm PST: can you imagine growing up like that? At least with Jamison and Wrangell they probably remember what it's like to have a normal life, but I definitely think Melissa had Atticus and Honor for the purpose of posting about them. I give her something of a pass for that

baconspam420, 2:13:46 pm PST: eh, maybe when you're like eight, but she's, what, seventeen now? Like yeah, she has no privacy, but she also has literally every privilege in the world so I don't exactly feel bad for her

knockoffbrene, 2:15:22 pm PST: Okay but if she's on chemo should she really be out around that many people? Wouldn't she be neutropenic? Is that even on her radar? Did she just get lucky? Because the stuff she's doing—eating sushi, cavorting in literal standing water with dozens of people—are exactly what we didn't do with my mom when she was neutropenic. Everyone had to gown up and she wasn't allowed to eat raw vegetables or undercooked eggs. No one was allowed to bring her flowers. Maybe Skye just doesn't have it, which, lucky her, but she's been doing chemo for *so* long that to me this seems extremely unlikely.

baconspam420, 2:16:07 pm PST: THANK YOU, I am shuddering thinking about what pathogens are lurking in that water!! Extremely selfish of Honor to want to bring her somewhere like that

kindredhearts, 2:17:19 pm PST: honestly—that's so unfair. My mom had cancer and I still cherish the memory of every single day she felt good enough to go out in the sunshine somewhere or even a little bit good at all.

schildpad, 2:18:32 pm PST: I don't mean that about your mom at all. I'm so sorry for your loss and I hope you have a lot of precious memories of her. But I also lost a relative to cancer and if Honor cares about her sister, she should be responsible for once in her life and not gallivant off to some scenic Instagram bait right now. Like, what the hell? Can you imagine going through chemo and you're baking on some rock in the sun? I'm so angry just looking at these pictures. This family sucks

knockoffbrene, 2:18:58 pm PST: Yeah, I just have to say that Skye doesn't talk or act like any cancer patient I've ever known. Like if your platelet counts are too low for chemo that's actually bad?? But she's definitely said oh my numbers are good today and I don't have to go in. Maybe she's just too stupid or privilege-afflicted to comprehend what the doctors are telling her but honestly the more I see the more I'm convinced this is all some incredibly sick act.

kindredhearts, 2:19:28 pm PST: Yeahhh I think I'm done with this board. Not everything is a conspiracy. Sometimes shitty things happen to people and I think it's disgusting to question someone's tragedy just because you don't like them personally.

wetweightedblanket, 2:20:04 pm PST: Where's @redwoodfog to confirm??

• • •

I hear Skye throwing up again late that night, and my heart stops. I don't know whether to go see if she needs help or not, and I stand in my doorway a long time, waiting. After a little while the toilet flushes, and I get up and knock quietly on her door. She doesn't answer, and I knock harder.

"What," she says, her voice the opposite of an invitation.

"It's me. Can I come in?"

Her eyes are red and her face is drawn when she opens the door, and I try to stop myself from crumpling—she would feel obligated to comfort me.

"Hey," I say. "Are you feeling okay?"

"No." She closes her eyes, the muscles in her face twitching. "I just threw up blood. There's a tear in my esophagus from throwing up so hard."

"Oh my God. Should we go to the ER? Can you call your doctor about—"

"No," she snaps. "It's not dangerous. I'm not going to the hospital in the middle of the night."

Tears fill my eyes. "Skye, I'm so sorry. Can I get you anything?"

"I just need to sleep."

"Okay. Do you want me to sit with you or anything? Or I could turn on a—"

"No. I just need to sleep."

For once in my life I am almost too distracted to be afraid on the flight home, which is to say I spend probably only 90 percent of the time in sheer mortal panic and the rest of the time not thinking about Caden. I am not thinking about him when we hit a patch of turbulence and I wish I had someone's hand to hold. I am not thinking about him every time the adorable eighty-year-old couple in front of me sweetly fusses over each other, unfolding each other's napkins or sharing the last of the pretzels. I am not thinking about him when we land and it means I made it safely to the ground and will have to see him tomorrow at school. I'm a Lo. I was born to let go of people easily.

Except that driving home, sitting in the back seat of the car driven by a man who studiously ignores me, I start to cry. It turns out, actually, this did mean something to me, does mean something to me, and I don't want to let it go. Is it too late? It's probably too late. I should try, though, right? That was our deal. Maybe I owe that to myself. Maybe some things are fixable.

When I get home, I go for a walk on the trail behind the house with Atticus. Jamison, who got to Waco right after I left, FaceTimes him while we're on the walk to tell him that Skye seems sicker compared with just two weeks ago, when Jamison saw her last: she's grayish, she's lost weight.

"I'm making her a lot of smoothies," Jamison says. "I think it's helping her get her energy up so she can heal. Dad thinks we should ask the doctors if we can move the tests up a few days. I think he's worried."

"What does Skye think?"

"Skye's very resistant. She trusts her doctors. But I will say I got kind of a bad feeling from the one we talked to. I thought he was sleazy."

"You thought he was sleazy?" Atticus says. "He seemed fine to me."

"I really did not get a good feeling."

"What's Dad going to do?" Atticus says. "Is he going to try to make some big scene? I think we should just trust Skye and let her do what she wants and thinks is best. It's her body."

I am struck with my selfishness. How right now, as they're actively discussing threats to our sister's life, I am preoccupied with Caden.

After he hangs up, Atticus says, "Well, of course Jamison didn't get a good feeling, because she hates doctors."

The redwood needles are spongy under my feet, a carpet on the forest floor. It's colder in here than out in the sunshine. I would like to just lie down on the carpet and close my eyes and wake up a year later and learn that everything is all right again. "Yeah, I guess so."

"I think I'm going to quit volleyball."

I stare at him. "Wait, what? You think what?"

"I think someone needs to be there to stand up for Skye and stop trying to push her into all this homeopathic stuff, or make her think if she has the right attitude, that's all she needs to do. It could literally kill her."

"You're going to just live there full-time? Wait, Atticus, I don't know if you should do that. You've always said this is one of your most important seasons."

"Who cares?" he snaps. He gives me an apologetic wince, for his tone, and then says, more evenly, "My season's already fucked because I've missed so much. But I mean, what's going to happen with Skye? Either they say yeah, it's working, she just has to stay the course, and then I'm never going to forgive myself if the freaking quacks in our family somehow talk her out of it. Or they tell us it didn't work and then we just—don't have much time."

"Don't say that."

"I just think we have to consider it as a real possibility."

"What happened? You were the one telling me she was going to be fine. I was just with her. She had a good day. I told you we went to that swimming hole."

He pushes at some of the redwood needles with his sneaker. "I just—I don't want to turn into Dad and, like, bail on my family exactly at the worst time."

"I guess if you're positive that's what you want. I mean, I can make sure they don't try to convince Skye of anything weird too. It doesn't just have to be you."

"I know. I just feel like I should be there." He sighs. "On the plus side, you can stay here more and hang out with Caden if that's what you want. I guess depending on how the appointment goes."

"I think that might be over."

"You think it might be over? Why?"

I tell him about our call yesterday. Atticus raises his eyebrows.

"Honestly, I don't think what he said is even that bad," he says. "I mean, yeah, maybe kind of insensitive, but addiction sounds like no picnic either. I'm not saying you have to rush back to him or anything, but honestly, you seem kind of happy with him. It's weird."

"I am, I think. Was?"

"Do you think—" He hesitates.

"Do I think what?"

"I don't know, do you think you're, like, sabotaging it because deep down you didn't expect things to work out? You're not used to being happy?"

"I seriously need you to stop with the psych books."

He laughs. "People pay good money for this kind of advice."

"You have your teeth commercials. You don't need to try to monetize every thought that pops into your head."

306 • KELLY LOY GILBERT

"What can I say," he says, "it's the Lo way."

I'll call Caden, I decide. But when we get back inside and I pick up my phone to fret over it for, like, an hour before finally taking the leap, I see Skye's live, and I watch.

"So people have been asking how I'm doing, which, thank you so much, you guys are the sweetest. I'm having a lot of side effects from the chemo, and my doctors are just waiting to see how well it's working, so right now it's just a lot of waiting and hoping that all of this is going to be worth it. I think the hardest thing right now, honestly—it's just the mental and emotional side of things. Um . . ." She reaches up and wipes her eyes, pausing a moment to compose herself. Suddenly everything I thought was anything in my own life, anything sad or happy or beautiful or hard, seems petty and selfish and small. "The thing about this is just you're so alone, and no one really understands what it's like in any real way. You spend all day with people prodding you and watching you and studying you, but none of that's—real. If that makes sense. And it's just so much pressure, you know, to get better, and to make everyone happy, and sometimes all you want to do is just disappear. So I guess that's how things are going." She forces a smile. "I hate complaining like this. I'm probably going to delete this in a couple of minutes. No one likes complainers!"

Before school the next morning Caden finds me at my locker.

"Hey," he says, "listen, I was out of line the last time we spoke. I owe you an apology. That was a dick thing to say."

"Oh," I say, whatever's left of my anger deflating, leaving a deep exhaustion in its wake. "It's all right. I don't know why I reacted that way. It's not like there's only one kind of tragedy in the world."

"Yeah, I don't know why I had to turn it into some kind of competition either. Sometimes I just think—I don't know, if my mom were sick with something else, it wouldn't feel like she was doing it to me, she'd just be sick. But I shouldn't have said it like that. I don't blame you for being mad."

I start to tell him I get it, that maybe the worst parts of Skye being sick are the parts she chooses—like how distant she seems, how unreachable—but every time I think about her now, I think about her crying in her last post, and I go quiet. It has been running through my mind on and off ever since, every time I imagined how it would go when I was here with him. I think about Atticus giving up the one thing he loves in life. I say, "Caden, I think I need this to be over between us."

His expression doesn't change. "I see," he says. "Well, okay then."

Really, I want to say, *it's that easy for you? No argument at all?* "My sister's sick, and that's kind of it for me right now. That's all there is."

"Right," he says. "All right. Well—be well, then."

The bell rings. I want him to ask me more, to point out why I'm mistaken here and that actually it's not morally wrong to be worried about falling in love while my sister is this sick, that really it's fine for me to be happy while Skye isn't, but he's said all he's going to, apparently, because he leaves without a backward glance.

I'm supposed to stay so I can fulfill my requirements from the school, but I last less than half of the rest of the day. It is excruciating having Caden in every single one of my classes. It takes nearly all my concentration not to look at him. A few times I sense him looking at me, but when I check, I'm wrong and he's ignoring me.

At lunchtime I leave, and I ask Ava to arrange for me to do a full independent study with the school. She tells me I can be gone most of the time as long as I can meet with my advisor in person once a month; everything else I can do virtually or on my own. Which, fine, whatever. Ava rebooks my flights.

As much as I want to be there with Skye, as much as I know I need to be, I have something like PTSD on the way back to the airport with Atticus. I don't think I realized until coming back how small and suffocating our world is there, the days dominated by the constant fear. But whatever, it's a small sacrifice to make, considering. How incredibly selfish to complain.

We arrive four days before the meeting with the doctors to find Skye colder, weaker, distant. You can't take a person's depression personally, I know that, but then at the same time this is also true: you absolutely can. The next day her numbers are dismal, and she's at the hospital most of the day. Atticus and I go pick her up, and she rides with her eyes closed the whole way, Atticus trying his best to drive slowly and avoid any bumps, and when we get home, she goes right to her room. Jamison sends a barrage of links about supplements and alternative treatments, and our parents start to make noise about taking her from the hospital and finding a new care team in some wild eleventh-hour bid. Atticus spends the whole night on the phone arguing with them.

Which is to say, I guess, that none of us are handling this well. Definitely not me, combing through all Caden's accounts obsessively, even though he hasn't posted anything in over a year.

Maybe she's getting better, I tell myself. Her sickness is a sign the treatment is finally working. I try to visualize the cancer cells shrinking and dying off, Skye getting stronger and stronger. Her hair growing back. Right now, before we know better, the possibility can live.

Someday, I know, I'll look back on these days and I'll feel them in fragments—in the heat pouring through the car as soon as you open the door and the cold feel of the house's bathroom tiles on my bare feet, in the sight of my life packed messily into suitcases I never got around to unpacking and the particular hollow, fluorescent feel of the hospital parking lot lights and the crackle of Topo Chico in my throat. I hope beyond hope that I'll look back at this as one of the worst periods in our lives, not as the time I'd give anything to have back.

Our mom flies in the next morning, and then a few hours later Wrangell does, with—surprise again!—Julie. Atticus, Skye, our mother, and I are all in the living room when he comes in, our mom on her laptop and the rest of us watching TV, and we're all momentarily stunned into silence.

Atticus recovers first.

"Good to see you," he says, standing up to give Julie a friendly hug. "Welcome to Waco. It's a trip."

"I know, right? I love it here," Julie says. "It's so cute. I can't wait to see all the *Fixer Upper* houses. Skye, when you're feeling up to it, you'll have to show me around the city. Can I give you a hug?" She leans down to gingerly embrace her. "I'm so sorry to hear you've been so sick. I want to do whatever I can to help. It's so nice to see you."

"Such a nice surprise," our mother says, getting up to hug Julie herself. "Are you hungry? Did you eat on the way?"

"We had a weirdly huge breakfast at the airport. I'm going to go freshen up," Julie says. "Wrangell, which room are we in?"

"*Well,*" our mom says when the two of them have left the room, "*that's* a surprise, isn't it?"

"Wrangell looks happy," Skye says.

When he comes back in, he's sans Julie, and immediately our mom says, "Wrangell, we're dying to hear what happened. You're back together? How? Is this serious?"

I expect him to bristle at the questioning, but he just sits down next to our mom.

"Yep," he says. "She was willing to give it another go. We stayed up until five in the morning talking last week, and we've been together almost every minute she's not at work since."

"The dream," Atticus says wryly. Atticus has always been happier single.

Wrangell laughs. "Yeah, you'd love that, wouldn't you? Maybe someday." He's visibly happy. Aggressively happy, happy at us. Happy enough to bring his apparently on-again girlfriend to the week we find out whether Skye has a chance. I think about giving up Caden, Atticus giving up volleyball. I guess we're not all prioritizing Skye, then. Wrangell says, "I've learned a lot the past few months—a lot of it thanks to you, Skye. Not that I wouldn't trade it all to have you better. But it's made me realize what's important and who I want to be in life. And Julie's part of that. Julie's—most of that."

"Well," our mom says, "relationships are so, so hard. We're here for you whenever you need support or advice."

I doubt I can avoid Julie the whole time she's here, and also the thought is so completely exhausting I don't want to try. I'll go make peace now. I catch up to her in the hallway while Wrangell's out getting their bags from the car.

"Honor," she says more warmly than I'm expecting. "It's nice to see you."

"I'll be honest," I say, "I didn't expect to see you again."

"Yes, I believe you made that point clear."

"Oh—" I feel my skin go hot. "Right. No, I meant after you broke up with Wrangell."

"Yeah." She reaches up and fingers her necklace, a round gold pendant. "We had a lot to talk through."

"I imagine."

"Seeing your family like this, though—and seeing him, too—just the way everyone's rallied around Skye—it's nice. I mean, it's awful, it's all so incredibly awful, but I have a small family, and if I got sick, I doubt my brother would upend his life like this just to be there for me."

That's sad, honestly. "Ah. Wow."

"And just seeing everyone in a different light—I don't know, I think I was just freaked out by the dynamic at first because it's so different than what I'm used to, and I mean, obviously it's really unique anyway, everything you guys do, but Skye getting sick was just kind of a weird light bulb to me. Like, you know, we all have awful things happen to us, and life is too short to get hung up on our differences. I wanted to be here for Wrangell."

"Well, I'm sure he's really happy you're back in the picture."

"That's nice to hear. I hope it's at least some small comfort to him right now. He's been such a wreck. I know he tries to put on a brave face when he's around Skye, but he isn't sleeping well, and when we go to the gym, he's just totally possessed. He feels so guilty it's not him. Hopefully, you know, this will all be over soon and she'll go into remission and then everyone can just work on healing. I bet you're all just in survival mode right now."

It turns out I still don't especially like her, or at least I'm not wild about her coming to psychoanalyze us from the outside. Still, though.

"Julie, I obviously owe you an apology for what I said in the airport. I understand if you hate me. It's fine, I can fake being nice for Wrangell's sake."

"Oh, Honor, of course I don't hate you. You're young and in a very toxic situation. I think we can be friends."

The morning dawns cloudless and bright, the last day before Skye's results, bringing Jamison and Sonnet and Andrew and our dad. Sonnet is so much bigger than she was in Kauai. She roves around the house like a tiny wolf, tackling our legs and pointing to anything remotely circle-shaped (the coffee table, the clock) and declaring it a ball. It's immediately better with her here, and besides that, Skye wakes up to the first good news in a long time: her numbers are excellent today. Tears spring into my eyes when she tells us. I have been viscerally craving good news.

"I just have to go in for some quick scans this afternoon," she says as most of us are sitting in the kitchen, hunting for objects to hold up for Sonnet to inspect for ballishness. "But no chemo! So I get to come back early."

"You look good, too," Jamison says. "There's more color in your face. Have you been taking the spirulina I gave you?"

"Yeah, I have, actually."

"That's great," Jamison says, beaming. "I'm so glad. You look great. I brought some new supplements with me I've been reading up on."

"Maybe you should check with the doctor first," Atticus says.

"This is so outside their paradigm."

"Okay, but compared to, like, Katie from Instagram with essential oils, doctors actually study—"

"Atticus," our dad says from the dining room, where he and our mother are working, "I want to speak with you a moment."

Atticus waffles, and I don't think he'll comply, but he goes over. I follow a few steps behind; I don't like the sound of "I want to speak with you." When we reach the dining room, our dad closes the door behind us.

"Your sister's just trying to help Skye," he says. "You need to check your attitude. The meeting's tomorrow. We don't need this kind of negativity."

"Oh, we don't need negativity?" Atticus says. "So sorry, I didn't realize *that* was our big problem here."

"You know what, Atticus, your sarcasm is not as witty as you think it is. It's a low-value person who sits on the sidelines making snide comments. Don't make that your personality. If you don't want to be the kind of man who can contribute something intelligent or helpful to a discussion, you can always keep your mouth shut."

"Yes sir. I'll get right on that."

"Why don't you watch your tone with me."

"Totally. Whatever you say, boss."

Our dad shoves his chair back and stands up. "You're making it really tempting to pop you across the face."

"Yeah?" Atticus says. They square off. "Do it. You want to hurt me, that's a much more efficient way than moving out and shacking up with someone half your age. Way faster, too."

"Is this the best time for this?" our mom snaps. "Is this what we want to be doing right now when the meeting is tomorrow?"

"Okay, so what, then, we just all pretend things are great?" Atticus says. "No *negativity*? We're supposed to be here acting like oh, we're such a great happy family, everything's fine? He's such a fucking hero for flying back to be here for his daughter? Come on, Mom, you deserve better than this."

"Obviously, everything is not fine," our mom says. "No one is asking you to pretend that, Atticus. Just try to have some respect for the situation at hand."

"You don't think *I* have respect for the situation at hand? I sacrificed the rest of my season, possibly my college prospects, so I can be here for Skye. I'm not the one who spent years saying crap about Lo men and real manhood and then, boom, I'm out the door with some girl basically Jamison's age."

"You'd better watch how you're talking," our dad says, his voice low.

"I better watch how I'm *talking*? Because, what, you want to find some perfect, smart words to make all this sound better than it is? You're so fucking obsessed with your image you forget some things are actually real."

"You know what, I don't need——" Our dad stops himself. He stares at the wall for a long time, then says, his voice measured, "You think I feel good about it? You think there's not a day that goes by I don't picture myself bumbling around Brooklyn like a joke while my daughter was getting a cancer diagnosis? Pretty asshole move, don't you think? You think that ever stops playing in my head every time I have two seconds of quiet to think? Because it doesn't. That's all over now, I ended things, but I was selfish and stupid. I fucked up. Okay? We all know it."

There's a moment of silence, and I can feel the various ways this can go. Our mother's face is unreadable. I wish I knew what to say. I wish our sisters were in here, or even Wrangell, because they would know.

But Atticus surprises me—he loops his arm around our dad in a side hug.

"Wait," he says, "am I hearing this right? Did Dad actually admit he was *wrong* about something?"

Our dad glares at him. But Atticus says, "Check his pulse, Honor. Is he still breathing? Do we need to call Skye's doctors? Maybe they should look you over just to make sure you're going to survive."

"You're grounded," our dad says. "Six years."

"Should we mark this in our calendars as some kind of historic first? I'm going to go tell the others. They'll never believe it."

"Ten years."

"I didn't believe in miracles before, but I do now, actually. Skye's going to be fine."

"Grounded for life," our dad says, but he's smiling now. He leans over and kisses Atticus on his forehead. "You're going to be a better man than I am."

"Going to be?"

"Yeah, don't push your luck."

"So are you moving back home, then?" Atticus says, looking between our parents.

"That's—up to your mother, to be honest with you."

Our mom watches. It's impossible to say what she's thinking. Does she want us on her side against him? Sometimes I wonder whether if I met her as an adult, if we'd never known each other, we'd become friends.

"Well," she says, "good. I'm glad we can all come together and focus on what matters. We're all here for Skye."

I go with Andrew to take Sonnet for a walk. She wraps her small fist around my pinky finger, and we wander up and down the street, pausing every time Sonnet wants to squat and pick up a leaf or a stick. We go probably fifty feet in an hour.

"You want kids someday?" Andrew asks me.

"Oh, for sure."

He smiles. "Yeah, it's a lot of fun. Lotta work, but fun. Hey, can I ask you something?"

"Sure," I say, surprised. This is probably the most I've ever talked to Andrew in my life.

He pushes his cap backward and motions toward Sonnet. "You think she's going to be screwed up when she's older? Would it be better if Jamison got a regular job?"

"Jamison's such a good mom. I'm sure Sonnet's going to be just fine."

"Yeah, sometimes I wonder. It's like nothing's ever enough for her."

"For Jamison? I mean, she's ambitious, sure."

"No, it's not that. She can never turn anything down. Has to work constantly, like she's afraid it's all going to dry up. Maybe if she'd been compensated better for working all those years on your parents' show. But they controlled all the money."

I hadn't thought of it in those terms. "Well, tons of parents work. You work. I don't know why Jamison working would be some unique threat."

"Just having Sonnet in all her pictures and posts all the time," he says. "The other day I took her to the store, and someone recognized her. Not gonna lie, it freaked me out. I was just wondering, if you could go back and change it, if you would."

"Of course not," I say, a little more sharply than I mean to—he's just trying to be a good dad. "I wouldn't change a thing."

When we get back, Andrew takes Sonnet in for her nap. Skye, Atticus, and Jamison are all sitting on one of the couches in the living room staring at Atticus's phone, and when I come in, they all look up almost guiltily. Atticus shoves the phone into his pocket.

"What's going on?" I say.

They exchange a look. "What's wrong?" I say, my heart starting to thud. "Is something wrong, Skye? Did you get bad—"

"No, everything's fine," Skye says. "Um, Honor, maybe you should come sit down a minute."

I lower myself in the leather armchair across from the couch. Jamison says, "Honor, we're here for you and it's going to be okay. So—I don't know if you remember Preston, who Skye used to—"

Where could this possibly be going? "Of course I remember Preston."

"I think we have another Preston situation," Jamison says. "It's going to be okay. I'm going to get the lawyers on standby to see what our options are, and meanwhile—"

"What do you mean, another Preston situation?"

"Show her your phone, Atticus," Skye says.

He looks at me. "I don't know if it's actually—I mean, we weren't there, so we don't know what—"

"Atticus," Jamison says, and he pulls out his phone. It's on Delancey's account, a string of pictures from last night, and I'm tagged in one of them: *wish you were here @honorlo!* Caden and Blythe and Victoria with their faces pressed together, their eyes squinting against a flash. Blythe kissing Victoria on the cheek while Caden watches, laughing. A blurry shot of someone's arm trying to grab the camera. *I'm heeere with Preeeeestooooon!* My vision wavers, goes fuzzy at the edges.

"So you said he and Blythe used to be together, right?" Jamison says gently. "This is a message being sent, Honor. There's a narrative happening here."

I stare at the pictures. "I didn't think he was like this," I say weakly. "I thought he was different."

"I'm going to get the lawyers on this. We'll make sure they don't mention you in any way. And—"

She rattles off more of her battle plan, but the world shifts around me and I stop hearing. I close my eyes. Skye grabs my hand. I'm not sure which betrayal feels worse: Caden's or Victoria's. When we went to her beach house, I honestly thought we connected. I believed that all those messages she sent, asking how I was doing, were genuine. But no, she was gleaning information about me for her own purposes, the same way everyone does, the same way everyone always will. Of course she would've been looking out for Blythe first.

Maybe the worst part is that I thought it would be different this time. Different somehow for me.

My phone is buzzing in my pocket. I take it out to look, and it's Caden. Something fluctuates in the edge of my vision, like a rubber band snapping. "It's him."

"He's *calling* you? I'll talk to him. Let me have that." Jamison grabs my phone and puts it on speaker. "Listen, you worthless prick, you would not believe how prepared I am to make your life a living hell if you—"

"Oh," he says. "Uh, hello? Is Honor there?"

"Okay, wow, you've got to be kidding me. You think I'm going to let you talk to Honor?"

"Um," he says. "Okay, well—"

I motion for the phone. Jamison frowns, but I say, "No, it's okay, I'm okay." She purses her lips, but she hands it to me.

"I saw your pictures," I say. My heart is thudding so hard I can feel the blood rush to my face.

"Honor? Hi. You saw what? Oh, Delancey's pictures? Yeah, they kidnapped me. Apparently, it's their new hobby. They decided I needed an intervention so Victoria could be like, all right, loser, stop moping around and try harder, basically."

"What do you mean, 'an intervention'?"

"Ah—I told them about how you ended things, and Victoria said that you're going through so much right now with your sister that whatever you're feeling is probably really complicated and maybe not what things seem like on the surface and I have to try harder to make sure you're okay."

"Why did they tag me in the pictures?"

"Did they tag you? I don't know. Probably because they were talking about how it was too bad you weren't there to hang out. Victoria said you need more time to hang out with friends."

"Oh," I say.

"And after talking to them, I thought, all right, maybe this is part of that trying harder you wanted me to do," Caden says. "So here I am seeing if you want to talk about it."

That's the behind-the-scenes of those pictures? My eyes fill. So

Victoria went out of her way to try to do something nice for me, to see that I was taken care of. I blink at my siblings. Jamison crosses her arms, but Atticus raises his eyebrows: *I told you!*

There's a pause. Caden says, "Am I on speaker?"

"Um. Maybe."

"Was that your sister?"

"And my brother."

"Oh," he says. "Uh—hi, Atticus."

Atticus clears his throat. "What's up, man."

I close my eyes again, this time in mortification. "Um, I'm taking you off speaker now." And going into a different room, maybe a different planet. Atticus mouths *You got this!* to me and gives me a thumbs-up that really does not do much heavy lifting here. I go into my room and close the door behind me.

"Caden, I'm sorry," I say. "They thought—we all thought—I don't know if you ever saw, but Skye was with Preston Campbell for a while, and then he dumped her by going over to this other girl's house, and they taunted her for, like, weeks posting about it."

"So that's what you thought I was doing?" He sounds genuinely confused. "Why would I do that? And you already broke up with me."

"We just thought—" I sigh. "It probably sounds totally paranoid to you. But that's the kind of the world we live in." I guess when I think about the pictures objectively, if we hadn't all been through Preston, they would have looked like pictures of people just hanging out. Everyone was clothed. Caden wasn't making out with anyone. He wasn't alone with anyone. No one was drinking or doing drugs.

But why would he want to deal with this kind of drama? Even if he thought he wanted to try again, probably this killed it. I feel so frayed. It's all been such a roller coaster. I mumble, "I think maybe we overreacted."

He laughs. "You think perhaps?"

"Just a tiny smidge."

"Well, we can let that slide."

"No, you don't have to. My sister's husband and my brother's girlfriend are apparently miserable being part of our family. I think we just come with so much extra baggage. It's always complicated with us."

"Nah, you're fine. It was a misunderstanding. It happens." He pauses. "I guess I just wanted to ask you—I was thinking more about what you said and how your sister being sick is all there is for you right now. Which I get, because when my mom's gone, I always feel guilty doing anything. I'm kind of just there. So I was just wondering if that was why. Like you feel guilty."

"That's exactly why." Was I not clear? "How can you be off living your life when they're not?"

"Right," he says. "I mean, when I hear you say it, I'm like no, that's not how it works at all, but then, yeah, that's exactly how it feels."

"I think it's incredibly selfish to be off doing whatever you want. No one's going to come right out and say yes, please be miserable with me, please hate your life, but like, people can't help but notice the imbalance, right?"

"Yeah, I don't know," he says, "maybe that's true, but also maybe not. But yeah, I get that you're working through that"—am I working through that?—"so I just also wanted to say if you want to just, like, try being good friends right now, I'm cool with that too."

There is a deep kindness in that offer, in this conversation, because I recognize it for what it is: he is doing the best he knows to do. I am suddenly shy. "Okay, maybe."

He's laughing. "*Okay, maybe?* Don't get too enthusiastic, though. It'll go to my head."

I feel myself go red. "I mean, what am I supposed to say? I want you in my life. In some form. Any form. How do you sound enthusiastic in a nonridiculous way?"

"No, you're definitely nailing it. You did it. That was perfect."

"Yeah, never mind on the friendship."

"Well, we had a good run."

"Shut up," I say, smiling. It's a weird, unfamiliar feeling, but I realize what it is: He makes me happy. I feel safe with him.

The feeling stays with me as I drive Skye to the hospital, and as we pull onto the main road, I let myself imagine this being one of the last drives. Maybe everything is working. Maybe her tumor markers will get lower and lower, will vanish, after tomorrow will become part of the past.

It's the golden hour right now, the sun spilling across the fields, so they glow, and the light hits Skye's face in a way that makes her look otherworldly. I'm overcome with love for her, with grief for her.

"I think he actually really cares about you," Skye says, turning to face me, as we pass the HEB. "I mean, he was willing to face Scary Jamison and all."

"Do you—" I hesitate. "It must be weird to see people doing normal-life things while you're sick. If it were me, maybe I'd hate everyone."

"Yeah, what is everyone *thinking* not dying miserable and alone?" she jokes. "What the heck?"

"I'm never going to be happy as long as you're sick. For what it's worth."

"No, Honor, that's so sad. You have this guy who's into you. You deserve to be happy. You should enjoy it while—"

Skye's voice breaks. She forces a smile, swiping roughly at her eyes. I grab her hand, squeezing as tightly as I can, my chest collapsing on itself.

"You're going to get better," I say. I say it with all the conviction it deserves; I will it into existence. All of us together, all of us holding on to this one hope, surely wanting something enough to make it real, to force it into being. "The doctors are going to call tomorrow and say, *You know what, it worked, we're going to operate and that'll be it. This is over.* Then you'll go back to Baylor, and you'll still have most of the year left, and—"

"No, I don't think so."

"Wait, Skye, why? Is there more the doctors have told you? I thought your markers looked good today!"

"No, no one said anything yet. Don't worry, Honor, it's fine. Don't freak out." She wipes her eyes again, then plucks a hair off her cardigan. "I'm just not going back to Baylor. Honestly, I was so miserable there."

"Wait, what? You looked so happy."

"Well, I wasn't."

"Why not?"

"I just didn't fit in. The same as everywhere. It doesn't matter. It's not important."

There's a bitterness in her voice I've never heard before, and it slices me. I, too, would be bitter if I had tumors seeding throughout my body, if I had been through weeks of physical torment with no promise it would help me live. I, too, would see everything through a retconned lens of misery. How do you even remember what happiness feels like when you aren't guaranteed it'll ever belong to you again? I have tears in my eyes.

We're at the parking lot, and I pull in, but I don't want her to get out of the car. I don't know how to tell her what I want to. How much I love her, how much I would do to stop this from happening to her.

"I'll wait here," I say. "You said it won't be long, right? Maybe after we can drive around and find some good coffee or a cupcake or something."

"It'll still be about three hours. Go back home. Go play with Sonnet. I'll message when I'm ready. There's no point in you being here."

I can't go back to the rental house today. Even though it's useless, and I know that, I need to sit here and be close by. I park so I can face the hospital building, so I can turn myself toward her and pretend I'm in there with her. I am still so lost in the ghost of our conversation, trying to keep from crying, that my brain doesn't register it at first when I see her.

She's coming out the doors at the main entrance into the loop, walking toward a small black car. She opens the passenger door and gets in. I sit for a moment, blinking at her. Why would she be getting into a car?

The car pulls out of the loop, and almost before I know what I'm doing, I turn my engine back on and pull onto the road behind the car. It's a black Acura, and the driver is a man, I think—tall, blondish—although I can't see anything else because there's a dog in the back seat, bopping up and down and obscuring the sight line, some kind of big husky.

What am I doing? I guess I'm following him. He pulls onto the main road, and I go behind him for a mile, then two. I turn onto a side road when he does, and when he pulls into an apartment complex, I follow, my heart thudding. The complex is older, a dark wood, the parking lot studded with speed bumps.

Why is Skye in this person's car? Nothing makes sense. He parks in a spot near a bank of mailboxes, and I realize I don't have any kind of game plan here, and I'm not sure what to do now, so I drive past slowly.

My phone rings, and I nearly jump out of my skin. It's a reporter I recognize from *New York* magazine. I pull over to the curb, my heart still hammering, and send the call to voice mail. I wait, watching the Acura, and then the door opens and the man gets out.

It's Dr. Bandley. I recognize him right away. He's wearing a fleece pullover and jeans, not like someone who was just at a hospital. Why is Skye in Dr. Bandley's car? I watch as he gets the dog out of the back seat. It leaps up on him, and he rubs its head affectionately, and then Skye gets out too.

I am losing my peripheral vision. My head is spinning. I watch as Dr. Bandley unlocks the main glass door of the apartment building and goes inside, the dog following him, Skye by his side. I idle there for what could be five minutes or an hour, and then, still dazed, I leave the parking lot and pull back onto the road.

I have no idea where to go next, or what to do, so I go back to the hospital parking lot to wait for her to come back. I feel ill. I'm too afraid to tell anyone what I just saw, even Atticus, because somehow it feels like that will place it in the realm of reality.

I check my phone a million times to see if she sent me some kind of message I missed, something that will explain this. Finally, when I've been sitting there for an hour that feels like a year, she messages me, almost done with the scans! I should be out in about 30 min if you want to come back now!

Fifteen minutes later I see the Acura pull into the loop, and Skye gets out and goes into the hospital. After fifteen more minutes she comes out the main entrance and sits on the bench in front of the sliding doors. I drive into the loop to get her.

I have a pounding headache and my palms are sweating. She gets up when she sees me.

"Hi," she says, smiling, slipping into the passenger seat and buckling her seat belt.

"Hi."

"It's nice to get out so early today," she says. "Do you want to stop and get coffee or a cupcake or something on the way back?"

"Um—sure. Okay."

"Which one?"

"Whatever. Anything."

"Should we be bad and do cupcakes, then? We won't tell Jamison."

"Okay."

She glances at me. "Is something wrong?"

"Maybe you should tell me."

"What? What's that supposed to mean?"

I take a deep breath, hold it until my lungs feel like they're going to burst. "Why were you in Dr. Bandley's car?"

She reacts like I've struck her. "Why was I *what?*"

"I followed him," I say. "I saw you get into his car, and I followed him to—I think where he lives."

"You did *what?* You followed him? Why would you do that? He was probably just going home from work."

"But why were you with him? What were you doing? Why weren't you at the hospital?" My chest is heaving. "Are you lying to us, Skye?"

She starts crying. *She's dying,* I think, and the world bottoms out around me again. She grabs my hand.

"I'm sorry," she says. "I'm so sorry, Honor. I don't even know what to say."

The roof of my mouth aches, and I sneeze twice. My eyes are watering. We're on the road, and it's busy, but I pull over. "You have to tell me, Skye."

Skye closes her eyes. "Okay, but you have to know I would never want to hurt you, and this was all—this just—"

My voice is rising, frantic. "Skye, just tell me."

"Okay." She keeps her eyes closed. "I'm not sick."

"Oh my God." I let go of her hand. "You're not sick? Not at all?"

"I don't know, Honor, I still feel awful all the time, so I really think maybe there's something—they did run a bunch of tests and they never found anything, but—"

I can't breathe. "You were making it all up?"

She opens her eyes to look at me, and her eyes are red. "I'm so sorry. I don't know what to say."

I don't either. "So all this time—when we were here—all the time you were at the hospital—"

"I'm sorry."

"Why were you in his car?" Flashes of the past weeks are barraging me, rapid-fire, like artillery. "When he met with us—he was lying too? How—I can't believe a doctor would—"

"He's not a doctor. His wife is a doctor."

She could be a stranger in the car with me. "My God, Skye."

"His name is Paul."

"Are you having some kind of affair with him? He's *married?*"

"It's—it's complicated."

"Did he force you into this?"

"No, no, of course not," she says quickly. "He wasn't going to be involved at all, but then you guys were, like, insisting we have a meeting with the doctors, and I just thought, to reassure everyone—he's getting his MFA in acting, and he's a really talented actor, and he knows a lot of medical stuff because of Amy, so—but no, it wasn't his idea at all. He's a really good person."

"Oh my God, Skye, words have actual meanings. He's, like, the definition of not a good person. When were you going to tell everyone? Everyone's here for the meeting—were you going to just sit through that and let everyone feel awful while he lied for you? And then what?"

She twists around in her seat so she's facing me. "Honor, please don't tell everyone. I know you probably think it seems like the right thing, but it's just about assuaging your own guilt. It's not about what's best for everyone. Trust me, I've been down that road a billion times myself."

"Don't *tell* everyone? What do you mean don't *tell* everyone? Your plan is, what—to just keep lying about it? You don't know how terrified we've been. I've been having panic attacks. We keep imagining you *dying*. Jamie has been leaving Sonnet behind—and Atticus gave up volleyball—" I was willing to give up Caden. I tried to give up Caden. "You can't let everyone keep doing this."

"I know. I know. But it's better to give everyone a happy ending. We'll do the meeting with Paul, and he'll say the treatment worked and I'm in remission, and Jamison can think her powders she's been giving me worked—everyone will be so happy. You would've been so happy too, Honor, I hate that instead it's this—God." Her eyes fill. "I hate myself so much. Everything is such a mess."

"I feel like I have no idea who you are."

"I know. You can hate me for the rest of my life. I deserve that."

"Of course I don't hate you. I could never hate you." I can hardly breathe. I can't believe any of this is real. "But I just don't understand how you could do this to us."

"I didn't know it would be like this. I didn't know everyone would come out here like this and Atticus would quit volleyball, and—but in some ways it's been good, right? Dad wants to work things out with Mom, and he and Atticus are good, and Wrangell's back with Julie. So really it's kind of all for the best, right?"

"How could you *possibly* think that? God, Skye. I don't think you understand what you've put us through."

She's not dying, I remind myself. She's okay. Except obviously she's not.

"Don't cry, Honor," she says. "I'm so sorry. I'll do whatever I can to make this up to you. I swear." She reaches out and tries to take my hand, but I pull it away. "I just hate that you're part of it now too. You're not going to tell them, right? This is the only way we can make it better for them."

• • •

Back at the house, Jamison is setting the table for dinner. She looks up when we come in. We've both been crying, and I must look shell-shocked, because Jamison puts down the handful of forks she's holding and rushes over.

"What happened?" she says. "I thought it was just a short appointment today. Did you talk to the doctors already? Was it bad?"

"We're just emotional," Skye says. "Nothing happened."

Jamison puts her hand on her heart. "Okay. You scared me."

"No, everything's fine. Do you need help with dinner, Jamie?"

"Yeah, I've been working so hard on it all day," Jamison says. "Kidding. Elissa picked it up. Just rest, Skye. Sit down. I was going to make you a smoothie."

"That would be great," Skye says. "I think they've really been helping."

"Honor, can you go round everyone up?" Jamison says. "I think we're about ready to eat."

I'm in a trance as I walk down the hallway. I find Atticus in his room, our parents in each of theirs, and Sonnet and Andrew outside in the backyard with Wrangell and Julie. Julie and Wrangell are holding hands, Wrangell radiating happiness again. I can't look anyone in the eye.

Everyone comes in to eat. Skye sits next to me. The salad has pansies in it, and Sonnet is entranced. "Flower," she tells Andrew. "Eat it flower!" Everyone is happy, laughing at Sonnet. Isn't this everything I wanted? All of us together, everyone here. I pick at my food. Skye drinks the smoothie Jamison made her, telling her how much better it's making her feel.

"Well, baby," our dad says, "I'm so proud of you. You've made it so far. I have a good feeling about the meeting tomorrow. You've done everything right. You've fought. I think you're beating this."

Skye takes a long breath. She won't meet my eye.

"So," she says, "about that. I actually have some news on that front."

Jamison drops her fork. Wrangell inhales sharply, and Julie leans against him.

"I spoke with my oncology team after the scans today. Um, and they actually were really, really happy with what they saw on the scans. My numbers are down and everything looked really good. They actually might not even need to do the surgery. So—they think actually the best course of action is to just continue for a little bit longer. You guys don't need to stay if you don't want. It's just going to be more of the same."

It's quiet for a moment while everyone tries to absorb this. Jamison says, "So it's working? Everything's working?"

"Yeah, everything's working."

"Wow," our dad says. He blinks a few times at the wall. "Skye, that's absolutely huge. You won't even need surgery, baby? That's huge."

"I know," Skye says. "Fingers crossed on that part. It would be really great."

"So is this a definite?" our mom says. "They know for a fact you'll go into remission?"

"I'm not going to announce anything publicly just yet, but it sounds like in time that's where things are headed."

"Well, what exactly are they telling you? Because I would love to know clear benchmarks so we know what specifically we're dealing with. I would still like to meet with them tomorrow to discuss."

A flicker of exhaustion passes across Skye's face. "I can ask. I think they might have—I told them they could reschedule, because I was so happy it didn't seem like there was that much to talk about, but I can ask."

"I think we should also fly you to Sloan Kettering or Cedars-Sinai to get a second opinion," our mother says. "When I spoke to Grace Cheung, she had some concerns about your doctors' decision-making. So now that you're feeling a little bit stronger, maybe that's a good time—"

"No, I don't think that's going to work." Skye doesn't look at me. "I trust my doctors. Grace has never met me. And anyway, I'm not up for flying across the country right now."

"We'll make it as easy as possible," our mom says. "I think we could even try for tomorrow, or maybe the day after."

"I might need to go in for treatment," Skye says, her voice sharper.

"I think we can arrange something with your doctors. Or, you know, you can just tell them, all right, this is how it's going to be, and they'll just have to deal with it. Maybe they call in whatever treatment you need to LA or New York, and we can have you do that while you're there. Let's loop in Ava—"

"I'm saying no. This is really unnecessary. Like, yes, I could fly to any doctor in the country if we wanted to really be careful, but my doctors have everything under control."

"I think this is a good step," our dad says. "Making sure we're not leaving any stones unturned here. Giving this our all."

"No." Her voice is stronger. "This is my body and my life. I am the one who gets to make the decision here. I don't need other opinions."

Our dad says, "The thing is, Skye—"

"She's telling you what she wants to do." Wrangell's tone has shifted. "She's right that it's her life. She's a legal adult. This is up to her."

"This is true, but we're a team first and foremost, we're Los, and I think—"

"But we aren't the ones with cancer. She's old enough to decide," Wrangell says. "You can't know what it's like to be in another person's body. I think she's right that a multistate trip sounds like a lot right now, and if she says it's too much, then we shouldn't push it. If she's getting better, that's good news. That's what we want. It really is up to her."

Skye says pointedly, "Thank you."

"I have nightmares that the doctors missed something," our mom says quietly. "That talking to Grace was a sign to me that we needed to push more and yet we just accepted whatever the doctors here were saying because it was easy, because we weren't willing to put in the effort to push for more answers, and that down the road we realize oh, now it's too late, they weren't actually as thorough as they thought, or they were too optimistic or just not knowledgeable enough—"

"But this isn't *we*," Wrangell says. "Ultimately it's up to Skye."

Our mom shakes her head. "You don't understand, Wrangell. You're not a parent."

Wrangell makes a choking sound. I know immediately it was the wrong thing for our mom to say. Jamison says to him, "We don't have to—"

"No, fuck that," he says, turning to our parents. "Are you kidding me? You two completely bailed for basically years' worth of when you were supposed to be taking care of Skye and the twins—and me and Jamison, too, for that matter—and you're going to try to play the parent card? Who got them ready for school and picked them up every day while you were off with all your concerts and tours and crap? Who had to drop everything when they got hurt and figure out dinner and—"

"All right," our mom says. She crumples her napkin and tosses it onto the table. There is naked pain on her face. "Fine, Wrangell. I was a flawed mother and this is my punishment. I'm not allowed to protect my daughter and fight for her life. Fine."

"Yeah, I gotta be honest, I think everyone's missing the point here," Atticus says. "I mean, holy shit, Skye went through hell and she's beating cancer! She's going to be okay! The vibes, as they say, are off. We should be celebrating." He lifts his bottle of Topo Chico. "Skye. You're a badass. You're a freaking beast. Seriously, hats off to you for all you've been through."

I don't think it's going to work. Literally everyone at the table looks like they still have about thirty things more to say. But Julie, of all people, smiles at Atticus.

"Skye," she says, and raises her own glass. "You are truly an inspiration. If I'm being really honest, you're the reason Wrangell and I got back together. You have handled all this with such courage and grace."

Wrangell's expression slowly relaxes. He takes Julie's hand and says something to her I can't hear. "It's true," he says. "Skye, you're the best of us."

"You guys are too much," Skye says without a hint of the discomfort or agony I am stewing in. "I really could not have done it without all of you."

Our dad exhales. "This is part of our story now," he says. "This time in all our lives. Skye's most of all, of course, but I think this has been a growing and stretching time for all of us. I'm proud of the way we've come together. We're Los."

Atticus is looking at me a little strangely. I must not be pulling this off. I force a smile and raise my cup of water.

"To Skye," I say. "To the Los."

When Atticus comes into my room after dinner, I'm in the middle of messaging Ava. I need to not be here. I ask her to get me a ticket home as fast as possible, tonight if she can, first thing tomorrow at the absolute latest.

"I can't stop smiling," he says. "God, it's like nothing else even matters. In life, you know? Like, was there ever anything else I cared about? I don't think so."

"I know," I say. I put my phone in my pocket before he can see it. "It's amazing."

"I don't think I even completely realized how much the stress has been eating at me. Like, anytime these last few months I thought I was happy—no, I wasn't."

"I know, right?"

My phone buzzes, Ava telling me she can get me on a flight tonight if I can be ready to go in fifteen minutes. Which, yes, I can walk out the door literally right now if necessary. I say, "Hey, I think I'm going to fly back home for the night."

"You're going to what?"

"I have some things to do at home?"

He gives a short, surprised laugh. "Like what? Is this about Caden?"

"No." I should've said yes. "Kind of. Maybe."

He peers more closely at me. "Are you okay?"

Atticus is the hardest person in the world for me to lie to. "It's just all been a lot, and I think—I don't know, I think my anxiety is just getting out of control and I need to just not be here."

"Ah," he says. "Yeah, I kind of feel like—right now I'm, like, euphoric, but maybe there's a lot of shit from all this I haven't emotionally dealt with yet that's going to hit me tomorrow. And maybe you're already there."

"Maybe that's it."

"You want me to go with you?"

I know he's excited to be here, in the center of everything. "No, no. I'll be fine."

At the doorway he turns around. "Are you sure you're okay?"

I panic that I'm going to reveal more than I mean to. I can't tell him, obviously. I can't drag him into this with me. We'll live in different worlds from now on, and that's fine. I won't ruin this for him.

I force a smile. "Yeah, definitely," I say. "Stay and have fun. Make sure Mom remembers to actually be happy about this."

CHAPTER NINETEEN

When I wake up the next day, momentarily disoriented, it's eleven a.m. in Waco. It's only nine here, still second period, but the thought of sitting in class and trying to focus makes my head hurt, and so instead I drive to Stinson Beach.

It's about two hours to get up there, a little longer because I hit commute traffic in the city, but once I cross to the Marin side of the bridge, I get such deep pangs in my heart I have to pull over and wait. I drive by our old house, I drive by Rearden, I drive down to the beach. I don't know why I'm here, exactly, but I think I just wanted to feel in touch with my old self. I used to know who I was, I guess, and maybe when I lived here, it was the last time that was true.

Or no, maybe that's overdramatic. I know who I am. I have always been, first and foremost, a Lo.

I turn off my phone and sit on the beach for a long time, watching the surf pound against the sand. I'm high up from the water because even though it's medium tide, the surf can be rough this time of year, riptides and sneaker waves. When Wrangell and Jamison used to take us here, Jamison would freak out every time we turned our backs to the ocean. It's freezing, but I knew it would be.

I miss the days when it was the seven of us here. Even if they weren't good for Wrangell, and maybe not for Jamison—maybe not entirely for our parents, either. Maybe it was mostly just me, but I was happy.

Nothing was ever solved by just sitting on a frigid beach, though (*There's never a good excuse not to be productive!* our mother's voice rings through my head), so while I'm here, I try to rehearse what I'll tell people about Skye. I turn on the front-facing camera on my phone and practice saying "The treatment worked and she's doing so well, we're all so happy" until my expression doesn't look like that of a teeth-baring hyena. A small mercy that no one is here watching me babble repeatedly into my phone like an absolute clown.

The sun shifts behind clouds again, dropping the temperature a few degrees. I'm cold and hungry, and I guess I can practice my fake relief from anywhere, and really, I don't know what exactly I thought being back in Stinson Beach was going to accomplish. Maybe Caden is right that you always think you can outrun your circumstances. I drive back home.

I go to Caden's when I get back to Los Gatos, and when he opens the door, he gathers me in a big hug. Something about that is so moving to me I tear up. I think it's how friendly he feels, how genuinely glad he seems to see me. I know instinctively he's not someone who hugs just for the hell of it, which, neither am I.

"I didn't think you were coming back this soon," he says as I follow him inside. We sit at his kitchen counter.

"Yeah," I say, "neither did I."

"Did something happen?"

The door flies open, and a blond woman in a loose white linen dress comes in. She looks startled at the sight of us. Caden says, "Mom, this is Honor."

I scramble to my feet. "Hi," I say. "It's nice to meet you."

"Oh, Caden, I didn't realize you were having anyone over. That's so nice. Honor, what a lovely name. Call me Madeleine." She has huge, searching eyes and is fragile looking and waifish but lovely still, ethereal really. "I'm so sorry—Caden probably didn't offer you anything to eat or drink. I haven't been to the store—I've been gone, and I hate that we don't have anything to offer—"

"Oh no," I say quickly, "don't worry about it, really."

"Do you like cookies?" Madeleine says. "I'll bake cookies. I think that would be really nice to have fresh cookies."

"You don't have to, Mom," Caden says.

"No, I want to. Honor, what's your favorite kind?"

"Any kind is great, Mom," Caden says gently. "Only if you have time, though. We'll be upstairs, okay?"

In his room, he shuts the door. It's strange being here in his room like this with his mother home. If we were at our house and our parents were home, they would never allow it. I say, "Your mom is nice."

"Mm."

"How's it going with her home?"

"The same. You know."

"She's not what I expected."

He looks amused. "No?"

I had imagined her, I guess, as imposing and harsh. But meeting her, I sense immediately that all her life, people have wanted to protect her. Have made excuses for her, have rushed to open doors for her and wanted to be a hero for her, have given her the benefit of the doubt and have let her believe always in her own innocence. I understand it, because I felt that exact same instinct stirring in myself. And I feel a deep, sudden sadness for all the women in our family who came before me. Who were not seen as delicate, who were never protected. Who had to be resilient and shrewd and hard. I wonder who they could have been otherwise. I wonder who I would have been. I say, "I guess you build someone up in your mind."

He cocks his head at me and smiles. "I'd think you of all people would know that people are always different when you know them, no?" •

"Yeah, you would think, I guess."

He clears some jackets off the back of his desk chair and slides it toward me so I can sit. "So how's your sister doing?" he says. "Is it a bad sign you're back home? I was kind of worried when I saw your text."

I freeze. Obviously, he can never know. "What kind of bad sign?"

"I don't know, didn't you say this was when you guys were having that appointment with your sister's results?"

"Oh. Right. No, I just needed to get out for a while."

"Did you guys have the appointment?"

I just have to grit my teeth and get through this one conversation, and then probably he'll never bring it up again. I can just avoid the topic. And I guess not talk about my family very much either, or all the ensuing fallout. "Yeah, actually, she said—"

I feel like I might choke. How would I feel if I knew he was lying to me about something this huge? If his mother weren't sick at all and he let me think otherwise, for instance. But then, what's the alternative? I ask him to carry this secret with me? It's a huge burden to put on another person, and also too much power to give. I'd forever worry he would tell someone. If he ever had a reason to want revenge, it would be too easy. And he could so easily decide we're too messed up and damaged for him to want anything to do with me.

I practice my smile from the beach. "She said everything looked really good. I think she's going into remission."

"Oh, what? That's amazing."

"I know."

"Are you happy?"

"Obviously."

He peers at me. "You seem kind of down, though. Am I imagining that?"

So much for my beach practice. I abandon the bad smile. "It's just all been a lot."

"Yeah, I bet. I guess sometimes it feels like you got the thing you were waiting for, or you got what you wanted, and then somehow still everything feels the same. Like your brain hasn't caught up yet."

"Yeah. Maybe."

"Or it's like a weird letdown, maybe. So are you guys done with Texas, then?"

I haven't thought that far ahead—some of my stuff is still there—but why would I go back? "I think so."

"Must be kind of weird," he says.

"Yeah."

"Your parents must be really relieved too."

Can we even have an actual relationship if I'm forever carrying around a secret this huge? What if he finds out somehow, someday?

I imagine walking away from this. Really, I've only known him for a few months. It shouldn't be that hard.

"I want to tell you something," I say impulsively, before I even realize I'm going to do it. "But if I do, you have to promise you won't tell anyone."

"Okay. It's not bad, right? You're not, like, being abused or anything."

"No, no." I hesitate. "I don't know—I'm not sure if it's fair to ask you to know this. Are you the type of person to feel guilty about things?"

He laughs. "Okay, are *you* abusing someone?"

"No. Okay, and this is, like, growth for me, I guess, or maybe I'm just being really stupid, because I'm trusting you here with something absolutely huge. This could destroy my family. You could get paid so much for this scoop. My sister was lying about having cancer."

All the air goes out of the room. Caden's smile disappears, and he blinks at me. "Wait, what? What do you mean she was lying?"

"She wasn't sick. She made it all up."

"What the hell? She made up having *cancer*? Why?"

"I still don't really understand why."

"Did you know about it?"

"No. None of us knew." It occurs to me that maybe he won't believe me, that he'll think all this time I was lying to him. "I swear I didn't know. I never would have gone along with it. We all thought—I mean, she had us talk to someone who said he was her doctor, and we dropped her off at the hospital, like, every day. And I mean, I'm happy she doesn't have this possibly terminal illness, but I just absolutely can't believe she would do this to us. Like, we all dropped everything to go be with her, and honestly, it's been incredibly traumatic watching her go through all this and thinking about her dying—" I reach up and wipe my eyes. "I honestly can't believe it."

"Yeah, that is—man. That is a trip." He widens his eyes at the floor. "What did everyone even say?"

"I'm still the only one who knows."

"Oh God, everyone else still thinks she's sick?"

"Skye thinks it would be selfish to tell them, because everyone's just happy her treatment worked, but I just—I don't know what to do."

"Wait, what? She wants you to just not tell your family? You're supposed to let them think she might be dying?"

"What do you think I should do?"

"What do I think you should *do*?" He squints at me. "Like, are you asking if I think you should keep pretending your sister has cancer?"

"I don't think it's that straightforward."

"Really?" he says. "Like, not trying to be a dick here, I'm genuinely asking. You don't think it's an obvious answer?"

"I mean, yes, it would be, like, a moral luxury to just wash my hands and be like, yeah, I'm not going to lie like this, but I do think she's right that it's going to destroy my family. Like, emotionally and professionally. So maybe Skye's right and it is actually selfish, because all I'd be doing is making myself feel better at the expense of everyone else feeling worse."

"Okay, but you would feel better? And for good reason? So—? I mean, that's not nothing."

"But that's one person versus everyone else."

344 • KELLY LOY GILBERT

"Can we call Victoria?" he says. "She'd probably have opinions here. If that's what you're looking for."

"Oh my God, no." I sit up straighter. "She lost someone to actual cancer. She's going to hate me."

"Why would she hate you? None of this is your fault."

"I feel so stupid, though. Like I should've seen the signs."

"I mean, why would it even be on your radar that she was *faking*? I think most people wouldn't have realized. Like, why would you even be suspicious? Victoria's not going to blame you."

I don't believe him. "Well, anyway, if she only ever liked me because we had this in common, we obviously don't now."

"What? No, that's not what she thinks."

"I don't know how I'm going to look her in the eye again. Ugh. Like when she asks about Skye or tells me about her grandfather— seriously. Please don't tell her, Caden. Or anyone. I know you can—I know I just handed you this huge thing and I can't stop you—"

"No, don't worry, Honor. I got you." He watches me a moment. "But just saying, I think if you can't imagine looking people in the eye, that kind of tells you something, doesn't it?"

"I don't think you understand my family."

Which, of course, he doesn't. Even Auntie JJ doesn't fully understand us. Our grandparents certainly didn't, and Andrew and Julie obviously don't. What are they doing right now? I imagine them all crowded around the dining table in the Waco house, except for Sonnet, who's probably ambling determinedly around everyone's legs. Probably they're celebrating still.

Sometimes things are clearer from far away, like how in the midst of an awful, turbulent flight you approach for a landing and

there's home beneath you, and seeing the place you know all minia-
turized and flattened that way, you feel such a deep affection for it;
you see it laid out in a clearer, somehow more obvious way.

Which is to say, I think I need to go back to Waco. I think the
choice here is clear.

I'm exhausted when I land, drenched in sweat. It was predawn when
I left home this morning, nighttime really, but we jumped forward
in time while flying, and now it's past noon, the light harsh. I didn't
tell anyone I was coming back, not even Atticus, and when I get to
the house, everyone is all together eating lunch in the dining room:
turkey, cranberry sauce, nuo mi fan. I'd completely forgotten today
was Thanksgiving. Skye's here. I thought maybe she wouldn't be.

"Honor," our mom says. "What are you doing here? Are you all
right? After Ava told me how you just left the other night, we were
worried something was wrong. Are you hungry? Elissa found some
decent sushi."

"It's good," Skye says brightly, pulling out the chair next to her.
"Come sit down."

"Um," I say, "actually, I have something I need to tell all of
you," I say. Skye looks alarmed. She tries to signal me with her eyes,
but I look away.

"Do you want to talk to me first?" Skye says. "I wanted to go
get coffee, actually. I think I'm done eating. Do you want to go
together?"

I waver. Should I warn Skye first? But then maybe she'll talk me
out of it. It would be so easy right now to find an excuse to back out.
Before I can, I say, "Skye isn't actually sick."

It's maybe the first time I've completely silenced our whole family—maybe the first time anything has. Our dad says, "Excuse me? What is that supposed to mean?"

Skye stands up. "Honor, stop."

"She's been lying to us about the cancer. She was never sick to begin with. The doctor we had the meeting with is someone she's seeing. He's an actor and not a doctor at all."

"This is the most selfish thing you've ever done," Skye says to me, low enough that maybe no one else hears, and then she shoves her chair against the table. She goes toward the hallway so fast it's almost a run, and a few moments later we hear her door slam.

Our mother has gone pale. "Honor," she says, "explain yourself."

It occurs to me halfway through my story that they might not believe me. Everyone listens, shocked. Jamison looks sick. I feel ill too, my chest crushing itself. When I tell them about following Skye to Dr. Bandley's, Wrangell says, "That is just straight-up sociopathic behavior. My God."

"So she made *all* of this up?" Jamison says slowly. "All the tests—all the results—that was all completely fake?"

"Atticus," our dad says, "go get your sister. We need to talk to her."

Atticus gets up and disappears down the hallway, then comes back into the living room, quickly, his feet pounding on the wood floors.

"Skye's gone," he says.

"What do you mean *gone*?" our dad says, jumping up.

"I mean she's not there and all her stuff is gone."

"How is she not there? We've been home the whole time. We heard her slam the door."

"She must have snuck out through the back while we weren't listening, then. She's not there. Her room's completely empty."

The table explodes in noise and movement, all of us talking at once.

"Should we call the police?" our mom says, panicked. "And report her missing?"

"She's an adult," Wrangell says sharply. "You can't report her missing when obviously she left on her own."

"We need to go find her," Jamison says. At the urgency in her voice my mind fills, immediately, with all the worst possibilities. She has run off with Dr. Bandley. They've made some awful Romeo and Juliet–esque pact. She's not with him but she can't bear the pressure of everyone knowing the truth. I can hardly breathe.

"It's okay," Jamison says, rubbing my shoulder. "Honor, take a deep breath. Let me give you some essential oils." She opens her purse and rolls something pungent and herbal from a glass tube onto my wrists. I am frantic enough that I don't bother pretending it works.

"Who can we call?" our mother says. "Who do you even call? I'll tell Ava to find a private investigator. Someone who can come immediately."

"We'll find her," Jamison says. "It's not a big city, and I doubt she knows her way around. Let's split up and have half of us go out and look and half of us stay here and see what we can figure out from her accounts."

"Yes," our dad says, "let's split up. Twins, Wrangell, you guys drive around and go to anywhere you think she could be. Melissa, ask Ava to get alerts for her phone and credit card activity also. Should we call TSA? I want to make sure she doesn't try to leave the country."

"What is she thinking?" our mom says. "I can't even imagine what she might do."

I go with Atticus. I drive because it's how we ended up in the car, and neither of us wants to waste the time switching seats. The only place I think she might have gone is to Dr. Bandley's apartment, and I don't remember exactly how to get there, so we drive to the hospital first so I can try to retrace my steps. I have zero sense of direction, and for the next hour and a half we take dozens of wrong turns, my blood pressure rising with each one. I am failing her. Atticus and I are both tense, snappish with each other. Our dad messages while we're driving that he's found investigators to come look for her right away. I have to pull over and put my head between my knees and inhale-exhale-inhale-exhale for several minutes before I stop feeling like I'm going to pass out.

"Do you think she's okay?" I say when we're back on the road. "I'm scared we'll never see her again."

"I have no idea. I obviously was really wrong about her. I don't know what she'll do."

I tell myself that this isn't the end, she's okay somewhere. She is walking around the wilderness preserve, trying to hold on to some kind of calm; she is huddled in one of the cafes, hungry. I can forgive her anything if I can just see her again. We can get past all of this.

We turn onto another street that I think looks familiar, but once we've driven a few blocks, it doesn't look familiar anymore. Maybe we're going up and down all these wrong streets, and by the time we actually find anything, it'll be too late.

Atticus takes out his phone to look at a map.

"Honor," he says. His voice is strange, and in that moment I live through all of the worst possibilities. "Pull over."

I do. He holds out his phone for me to see.

It's so disorienting it takes me several seconds to comprehend. It's Skye, livestreaming from her dorm room. She is composed and calm, doing an ad for a mineral deodorant company.

"What the fuck," Atticus says. "What in the absolute hell."

I can't breathe. I don't know what to say. Of all the possibilities I feared, this was not one of them.

"Also," Skye says on her stream, "I have an update to share with all of you about my health that I'm going to post in the grid right now."

She posts it within seconds—she must have had it ready to go. It's a black-and-white picture of her looking straight at the camera, not smiling, her hand cupping her cheek.

I wanted to share an important health update with you: I am officially in remission! It's going to take me a long time to get my strength back, but I could not have asked for better news. It has been such a grueling journey and I have traveled really to the depths of what I thought I could handle. I have been broken down and remolded. I have survived things I never believed I could survive.

I have been more grateful than I can say for all the support and good wishes and encouragement during these past weeks. There were so many times when I didn't think I was going to make it. Thank you for being a shining light to me and my family.

We sit on the side of the road like that, blinking in silence, for what feels like ten minutes.

"Do we just go back to the house?" I say finally. "Can you drive? I don't think I can drive anymore."

Atticus gets out and swaps with me, then slams the door behind him and turns the key violently in the ignition.

"I don't want to go back yet," he says. "Let's go find Dr. Bandley."

"Why do you still want to find Dr. Bandley?"

"Because I want to fucking talk to him face-to-face." He turns to me, out of breath. "Tell me where to go. Any road that looks even slightly right. I've got all fucking day."

It takes us another forty minutes, but we find the complex. He takes all the curves too hard and slams on the brakes whenever we have to stop. I don't know if I've ever seen him this angry in our lives.

"Do you know which apartment is his?" Atticus says.

"I don't know which one."

"Okay, well, should we knock on every door until we find it?"

"This complex is huge."

"Let's look him up online, then."

I am nothing if not good at stalking people online, but we can't find an address, even though I find his wife's profile on the hospital website and search under her name too.

Atticus unbuckles his seat belt and swings his door open. "Then we'll knock on every door," he says. "Or ask people. We'll go through the mailboxes. Someone's going to be able to tell us where he is."

"Atticus," I say, and he snaps, "What?"

"I don't think we need to find him."

"What do you mean we don't need to find him?"

"Like, probably we'll never see him again. It's not like she's going to bring him over. But I honestly think—he doesn't matter."

"He doesn't *matter*? He pretended to be a fucking *doctor*. He lied to our faces. He made us think Skye was going to die."

"Yes, but he's a bad person we're never going to see again. The world is full of those. The problem is Skye. That's what matters here."

"I just can't believe Skye would be behind this."

"Atticus—did I do the right thing?" My voice shakes. "I didn't mean to make everyone so miserable. She wanted me to keep it quiet forever and let everyone just be happy she was in remission. Should I have done that? Would it have been better? Please tell me if I did the right thing."

He closes his eyes, some of his anger evaporating.

"Of course you did the right thing," he mutters. "The problem is that sometimes the right thing feels like shit."

When we get back to the house, Wrangell's car is gone. I go into his room and find it totally cleared out, and I know in my bones I won't see him for a long time.

I go with Jamison to find Skye at her dorm. I don't even know what room she's in, but Jamison finds the Residential Life office and they tell us.

Atticus didn't want to come, and Jamison didn't tell our parents where we were going. I don't know what we're going to say to Skye.

The comments on her post have been pouring in. I have messages from Delancey and Victoria and Blythe, from Eloise and Lilith, from people I haven't talked to in forever. *I saw Skye's post!!! I am so happy for you and your family!!! Such good news!!*

She opens the door. She's wearing sweats—she's changed since her livestream. She doesn't look especially surprised to see us. She's been crying.

"Oh, Skye," Jamison says, and she wraps her arms around her. As soon as she does, Skye breaks down into deep, guttural sobs. Jamison strokes her hair, rubs her back. "A few years from now you won't even fully remember what this feels like," Jamison says. "We can figure it out. It's going to be okay."

Our parents barely look up when Jamison and I come home. They stay in the living room talking, going conspicuously quiet whenever one of us walks by. There's a familiarity in the way they're talking—the way it was always them against the world, a planet with its own gravity. It's long been dark by the time our dad announces we're going to sit down over dinner and have a family meeting, and also tells us, in a very deliberately casual way, that he's done with Brooklyn. He's going to move back to California, to the Los Gatos house with our mother. Our mother is quiet, happy, triumphant. She orders a huge spread of Thai food that no one especially wants to eat.

"All right," our dad says when we're all seated, spooning some green curry onto his plate. "This is going to be the biggest way we've ever come together as a family, so let's talk through some of our next steps here. So obviously, we're going to do some publicity to talk about Skye going into remission. My instinct tells me that's going to be a flash-in-the-pan story, going to come in with a bang but fade out and stabilize fairly quickly, but I think this is going to be an important chapter for us, so we're going to try to keep this momentum going."

Something goes cold around my heart. But really, I guess, what did I expect?

"We think it's important to consider how we can be most impactful here and center our narrative around that, so we're going to look into a cancer foundation to partner with. I'm going to look into a donation to the hospital. Honor, your mother and I think you in particular would be a great ambassador for some kind of cancer foundation, and we think that would be a good next step for you. It's a good place to carve out a stage for yourself and define your niche here."

"I think we should bring on someone specific to work on cancer org outreach," our mother says. "Lauren is already stretched and this is out of her wheelhouse. And if Honor's going to be involved, it would be good to get someone on the ground with her." She pauses. "Also, obviously, this stays between us. Lauren and Ava will not hear about this, nor will any new hires."

"Or your sister," our dad says to her.

Our mom hesitates. "Well—"

"I'm not comfortable with JJ coming on board here."

"You guys just got back together," Atticus protests. He looks ill. "You're going to lie to her about this?"

Some kind of small struggle plays out on our mother's face, but finally she says, "I suppose that's for the best. What about Wrangell? I don't think he'd say anything, but I can't say for sure."

"Wrangell's not stupid," our dad says. "He has quite a bit in the pipeline that he's not going to want to jeopardize."

She nods. Her eyes are red. "What about Julie? If they break up?"

Our dad winces, swears quietly. "We may need to look into an NDA."

"Jamison, what about Andrew?" our mom says. "Do you think we need to write up an NDA for him also?"

I feel like I'm in some bizarre nightmare, like the one where you're screaming at everyone there's a fire in the building but no one moves. "Skye's lying about all of it," I say. "She never had cancer to begin with, and you think we all should just literally keep up that lie forever?"

"What do you think she should do?" Jamison says, not ungently.

"I mean, I think she should tell the truth."

"I don't know that you understand the implications here," our mom says. "She would be utterly toxic to brands. Just absolutely radioactive. And not just her, either—that would impact all of us."

"But she's been lying to everyone for weeks now—and everyone's invested in this, and these are people who probably have actually lost people to cancer for real, or someone they love has had—"

"Honor, the *vast* majority of those people have never even met her," our mom says. "She's entertainment to them. She's content. So why would she owe them any truth about herself or her life? You're asking her to sabotage literally everything she's worked for, everything we've worked for, because you think a mass of strangers are entitled to know particular information about her? That's not how any of this works."

"Princess, I know you're trying to do the right thing here, but it's a little more complicated than you're making it out to be," our dad says. "This is a business decision, this isn't about relationships."

"It's about our relationship. She lied to all of us. And Auntie JJ and—"

"Yes, and that's a separate conversation we need to have," he says. "And we will. But for now, for the immediate concern, I want to make sure we're all on the same page here that this stays in the family. We're Los. This is about us. This is not for the outside world."

I am dizzy. They move on to more logistics, more talk of NDAs, but the room is spinning around me. We are signing up for a lifetime of this. I am being asked to choose this above whatever else, whoever else, may come.

I take out my phone and start typing. *My sister Skye has been lying about her illness. She does not have and has never had cancer. Her claims to have been sick were false.*

I post it. My heart is pounding so hard I can barely hear what anyone is saying. The edges of the room are wavering.

"Another thing we'll need to think about," our dad is saying, "is how much to dovetail this with questions people are inevitably going to have about relationship status."

"Yes," our mother says. "I think this is an opportunity to drill down and talk about finding what matters to us, really exploring personal and family values. You know, your daughter was sick, it made you realize—"

"Oh my God," Jamison gasps. She's staring at her phone, and she puts it down on the table and turns to me. She's pale. "Honor, what have you done?"

"What?" our mom says, sitting up straighter. "What is happening?"

Jamison opens her mouth, closes it again, tries to take a shaky breath. She slides her phone across the table, and our parents and Atticus all reach for it at the same time. Our dad wins. A look I've never seen goes across his face.

"How could you?" he says, staring at me. "Why would you *do* this to our family?"

"Don't talk to her like that," Atticus says, his voice low, leaning closer to me. "She's done literally everything a person could do for our family. I swear to God, you better not start anything with her."

Our mom's eyes are closed. When she opens them, she doesn't look at me, doesn't say anything to me. She stands up. Her hands are shaking.

"Call Skye," she says urgently. "We need to figure this out *right* now. We can't let this spiral. We're going to have to say Honor has been struggling—she's been struggling with the diagnosis—damn it, I need Lauren on this. Should we tell her? We need to tell her. I don't know what to do."

"Yes, we need to get someone on this," our dad says. His phone buzzes, and he checks the name and closes his eyes. "That's *People*."

Our mom sinks back down into her chair, holding her head in her hands. "I think I might faint," she says to no one in particular.

"Here," Jamison says, fumbling around in her purse and producing one of her essential oil rollers. "Put this on your wrist."

Our mom does, closing her eyes again and taking deep, shaky breaths. There's a long, etched silence like a canyon. No one will meet my gaze. Then the silence stops and our phones all buzz, a million times. No one moves to answer.

I inch myself closer to Atticus. I need to feel him solid and close.

"We can't keep doing this," I say. "We have to—"

"Don't say anything," our mom snaps, holding up her hands to stop me. "You've already said enough."

Atticus, our parents, and I share a town car to the airport, our parents hustling us into the car without time to pack and with barely enough time to say goodbye to Jamison and Andrew and Sonnet. Or Skye, who's not there anyway. The house is a mess. Someone will pack up our things and send them home, clean up after us. It's the next morning, although because none of us slept, it feels as if it's just been one long day.

On the drive, past the pawnshops and the HEB and the bridge over the green river, which are so familiar by now, our mom talks to Lauren. Lauren's quiet while our mom catches her up on everything, and when our mom explains the plan going forward, Lauren tells her she can't do that, and resigns. I think it's a bigger shock to our mother than when our dad moved out. She hangs up dazed and lost, and when I ask her if she's okay, she turns around without answering.

Lauren sends me and Atticus a message to tell us she's rooting for us in whatever we do. I cry. It feels like when the crew all left: people we naively thought would be part of our lives forever.

Our mother won't talk to me the whole flight back. Atticus is uncharacteristically quiet too, staring vacantly out the window most of the way. As we start to descend, I say, "Do you still think it was the right thing to do?"

"What?" he says blankly, turning back to me. "Yeah. I just don't know where all this goes from here."

I need him to tell me it'll all blow over, that nothing is as cataclysmic as it feels. But instead he says, "Does it feel like we just left her there?"

"Skye? She wasn't going to come home with us."

"You don't think so?"

"Atticus, I can't even fathom the next time she and I are going to *talk*. Like, what is there to say? Sorry you think I betrayed you? Except wait, you actually betrayed me? She's not going to come hang out in Los Gatos for family time."

"So what's she going to do all alone there, then?"

"I have no idea. But she knows where to find us."

"The thing I keep thinking," he says, "is, like—I don't actually trust that many people, but I trusted Skye. Without even thinking twice."

There are photographers and reporters waiting at our house. Our dad hurries our mom inside, and the picture that hits is of their backs disappearing through the front door while Atticus turns around and flips everyone off.

And actually, in the cascade of events over the next few hours, it's the least of our worries. Atticus turns off his phone and then shoves it in a drawer, because like mine, it's getting so many notifications it won't hold a charge. Wrangell tells reporters he's no longer in contact with any member of our family. Everything's in free fall. We hemorrhage sponsors; our mother's next book contract gets canceled. The stroller company Jamison was doing the collaboration with backs out. Hanna emails me: *Dear Honor: After careful consideration, we have decided not to move forward with your product launch at this time. Thank you.* I don't even have the mental bandwidth to be crushed, although I'm sure that will come later.

I keep instinctively wanting to message Skye about it all. Then I remember, and anyway, she's gone radio silent. And then, the next morning, after another mostly sleepless night for me, she posts.

There are some in my family who are spreading lies about me. I ask that you give them grace right now, as everyone handles trauma in different ways. We are all working to heal and everyone's journey and path toward wholeness will look different and take different amounts of time. Xo

Within seconds my notifications explode. I'm a lying bitch, I deserve to be orphaned and cut off from my family forever, I deserve to get cancer myself. I don't deserve a family. I should watch myself at night because everyone knows where I live.

Our parents, accompanied by a man I've never met before, find me in my room, staring at my phone. I put it away guiltily when they come in, I'm not sure why. Of course they've read everything. I realize I'm subconsciously waiting for some kind of message from Lauren.

"Honor, this is James Salwen," our dad says. "He's going to help us with some crisis PR here."

James is probably forty years old, with an easygoing smile and black joggers and expensive-looking Nikes.

"I saw Honor had something of a breakdown a few years ago when y'all went on your book tour. So that actually is lucky, because we're going to use that here to tweak this narrative."

Our mom blinks at him. "I'm not sure if—"

"So no one's going to get into the nitty-gritty here, nothing like that," James says. "In fact, no one even needs to answer those questions. We just need them to be asked. Easy peasy. So, Melissa, Nathan, you do an interview, they ask you, you know, is Honor stable right now? Because we know she had that unexplained incident a few years ago. Then you say, 'No comment,' and bam. That's all we need to do here. Just introduce this idea that Honor's not necessarily the most reliable witness. People will connect the dots."

I can't quite believe what I'm hearing. I think if I don't get out of this room right now, I won't be able to breathe.

"I don't know if this is the right avenue," our mother murmurs. She won't look at me. She still hasn't addressed me directly since Waco, and maybe she's still furious, but maybe, I hope, she'll stand up for me here. "Maybe we can discuss alternative—"

"We don't have time for that," our dad says sharply. "We're already late on this. Go check your email right now and see how many contracts just got blown up in the time it took us to have this conversation." He glances at me and his face softens.

"Princess, I want to be clear this is business," he says. "This is not personal. To get through this we're all going to have to—to stratify ourselves here and exist on two levels. Up here"—he holds his hand horizontally near his face—"we've got what people see, which is what we're saying, but down here"—he moves his hand midway down his chest—"down here we know the truth, which is that we're all Los and we love you very much and nothing will ever change that. It's unfortunate it has to be this way, but this is business only." He pauses. "Your mother and I aren't mad, Honor, we're just disappointed. And confused. Baffled, frankly."

James nods sagely. "So, Honor," he says, "all we're going to need from you, which is actually going to be very easy on your end, is just hang back for now. No posting, no talking to anyone, all right? Just hang tight and relax."

Atticus walks with me on the trail behind the house until I stop feeling like I'm going to crawl out of my skin. It's mountain lion territory up here, so I've always avoided it after dusk, but it's quiet and beautiful in the low light, our footsteps muffled by the redwood needles carpeting the ground.

Atticus tries calling Jamison, but it goes straight to voice mail. He tries calling Skye, too, and she ignores the call. He doesn't call Wrangell, and I don't think I'd want him to.

"Any member of our family who goes along with this, I'm never speaking to them again," he says. "You know how I feel about doing media, but I will talk to literally anyone to set the record straight. I'll call them myself. Seriously, bring it on."

"It doesn't matter," I say. "Then it's still just our word against theirs. People will decide what they'd rather believe. It doesn't matter if something's actually true. That just isn't how the world works." My skin still feels paper thin around my torso, like my heart could beat so hard it'll come out of my chest. I still feel nauseated.

I can breathe again, though. I stop and put my hands against the spongy bark of one of the redwoods, try to let its agelessness ground me. These forests saw our ancestors land and struggle and survive here. They will see me survive too. (*Get over yourself!* I imagine my ancestors saying, or whatever the equivalent would've been back then, in Chinese.)

"You don't deserve this," he says. "It's so beyond fucked up."

"Do you know what I wonder?" I say. "Do you think Mom and Dad actually think they're doing the right thing? Like, have they convinced themselves that this is, like, some moral path for the greater good here, or do you think they just only care about their image at this point?"

He's quiet for a while. Finally he says, "I genuinely don't know. Maybe to them that's the same."

"Do you think we're like that too?"

"What? No."

"No?" I'm still haunted by the fight I had with Wrangell. Maybe I'll always be trying to prove myself, trying to quiet that argument in my head. Maybe it's how our mom always feels about her own mother. "I don't know if it's as easy as that."

"Why isn't it as easy as that? I don't think we're anything like them."

"Maybe we aren't *like* them, but we're still, like—a product of them, so probably there's more of them in us than we realize. Or want to admit."

Wrangell may think he can neatly cleave himself, and that's where I think he's wrong. But then, we all tell ourselves different things to survive. Skye wanted to believe she could reinvent reality around her; our dad's always told himself he can recast and finesse the way other people perceive that reality. And I guess I told myself I could live with all that.

"Okay, well, we also semi had Wrangell and Jamie as parents," Atticus says. "Checkmate."

I roll my eyes. "That's not checkmate."

"That's totally checkmate."

"Atticus, no."

He grins. He slings his arm around me. "Honestly, I think it would've been better if we'd all been born a few generations back. Maybe we all would've been better people if we were orchardists. Or fishermen."

"You would not have lasted ten minutes after a shipwreck."

He laughs. "You never know. I could've pivoted. Maybe I have a special hidden talent for blasting holes into sheer rock."

"You could've been the first toothpaste model in history. Ahead of your time."

He makes a big show of removing his arm. "Yeah, shut up."

The last rays of light start to dim. It gets dark fast in the redwoods, a quiet sort of darkness. "I think we'll do better," I say. "Than our family. I don't think we're necessarily not like them, but I think we'll do better. I guess that's been true of every generation."

"I guess we get to focus on psychological survival instead of physical *and* psychological survival, so there's that."

"There is that," I say.

The trail forks, and we take the path leading back toward the house. "We should get an apartment," Atticus says.

"What do you mean, 'an apartment'?"

"We should move out. Do the emancipation thing."

"An apartment? That's a lot of Crest commercials."

"Yeah, shut up. I mean it, though. Like, what are you going to do? Like even tonight, you're going to go back and sleep in the house while they're fabricating your mental breakdown?"

"Tonight I think I'll call Victoria," I say, and I hadn't thought about it before, but as soon as I say it, I realize it's exactly what I want right now. "I'll ask to sleep at her house. You want to come? I bet she'd totally be up for a sleepover."

Actually, we sleep over at Caden's because Victoria's mom is not a sleepover person: me, Victoria, Delancey, and Blythe. Atticus stays home to keep an eye on things so I can turn off my phone and pretend nothing else exists in the world right now.

And it's fun, somehow. Victoria gives everyone elaborate facials, and we watch bad TV.

Except then I start crying during a commercial. It's a commercial for this room freshener we used to have a contract with when we were filming, so we used to always have it around even though our mom hated all the scents and we never turned it on. I hope no one will notice me crying, but of course immediately everyone does.

"Honor, you poor thing," Victoria says, folding me into a hug. "You've been through so much!"

"It'll get better than this," Caden says. When Victoria steps back, I lean against him, and he kisses me, very gently, on my forehead. Delancey holds up her phone to take a quick picture. I go cold.

"You're not going to do anything with that, right?" I say.

"What? No, of course not. I just thought you looked cute. I'll send it to you."

She does. She's right, we do look cute. Victoria asks if she can post it with some other pictures from the night, and probably that breaks James's embargo, but whatever. I say sure.

"How are you guys doing?" Delancey says. "I would be beyond upset. I don't even know."

"I just feel so stupid," I say. "And I feel so guilty—so many people, like you, Victoria, have been through this for real. I should've seen through it somehow. In retrospect, there's so much we should've wondered about. I'm so ashamed of all of us. I can't believe we all just went along with it."

"I think," Caden says carefully, "that you taking your sister at her word on something like this—that doesn't reflect badly on you at all. I think it's probably something good in you that made you not even wonder for a second if she might be lying to you."

When I go home the next morning, the house is quiet. Atticus is probably at volleyball, having immediately been reinstated to his team. I assume I'm alone in the house until our mother comes into my room, and I startle. She's wearing yoga pants and a matching jacket, her hair in a high ponytail. She hasn't spoken to me since Waco.

"Who's the boy in your picture?" she says by way of hello.

Victoria must have tagged me. "His name is Caden."

Our mother sighs. She sits down on my bed. "If I were you, Honor, I'd think about the optics of that. You just made a very serious accusation against your sister, publicly, and then in the immediate wake of that to be parading around a new boyfriend—I don't know how that's going to look to people."

A simmering anger in my chest. "I don't care how it looks."

"Yes, I suppose you don't." She looks around my room, her gaze hovering for a moment on my desk, where my half-finished order for Hanna is still scattered. "What happened to your contract? Do you need the lawyers to contact the boutique?"

"No. It got canceled."

"It got canceled? Well, we can have the lawyers—"

"No," I say again. "I think I want this to be something I keep for myself anyway." As soon as I say it, I realize it's true. I don't want to turn something I love into some optimized, perfectly marketed empire. I want it to be for me.

"Well, we all lost contracts," our mother says. "We'll have to work twice as hard to get them back. So who is Caden? Is he from your new school?"

"Yes."

"Is he kind to you?"

In spite of everything, I'm unexpectedly touched by the question—it's not where I expected the conversation to go. I don't often hear her worry about whether someone is being kind to us. "Yes, in his way."

"Well, that's good. You have to be careful with boys. They can break your heart beyond your wildest imagination."

I say nothing. I don't know what to say to that. Downstairs someone knocks on the door, and our mother stands up.

"I've fired James," she says. "And I don't think you're going to need to worry about what he said. A bigger story will crowd that out."

"What do you mean? What bigger story?"

She ignores that. "JJ said she's been trying to reach you."

"I turned off my phone."

"Yes, I figured. She wants you to know she's proud of you."

My eyes well up. "Oh."

At my doorway she turns back to me. "You know, I won't lie," she says, "I was shocked when you posted what you did about Skye. But at the same time, as soon as I saw that, I thought, well, it turns out Honor's strong. She's going to be all right in the world."

The *New York Times*

POWERHOUSE COUPLE BEHIND *LO AND BEHOLD* TO DIVORCE

LOS GATOS, CALIF.—Television personality and influencer Melissa Lo has filed for divorce from husband Nathan Lo. Citing allegations of infidelity and a desire to focus on their children, Ms. Lo, 49, has initiated divorce proceedings.

The pair's relationship, initially marked by a rapid ascension to celebrity and success, has recently been tumultuous. In June, the couple announced a separation, during which Mr. Lo, 50, claimed the two would work on themselves in order to strengthen their marriage. The couple said they were committed to their relationship. But during that time, Ms. Lo alleges, Mr. Lo began an affair with the host of HGTV's *Love the Listing*, Heather Young, 32.

"At this point in our lives I believe we have different and irreconcilable priorities," Ms. Lo said. "I am committed to the well-being of our children and that remains my first priority."

Mr. Lo could not be reached for comment.

EPILOGUE

Six months later

Wrangell has a last-minute change of heart and invites us all to his wedding, probably because Jamison talked him into it. We all go, of course. The wedding is at Pier 27 in San Francisco, a giant glass box of a building with views of the Bay Bridge. Sonnet is the flower girl. For a little while I think about bringing Caden as a date but realize I'd rather fill him in afterward.

"Don't think I can handle the full Lo family, huh?" he teases.

"I don't think *I* can," I say. I've been flying down every few weeks to visit Jamison and Andrew and Sonnet, and somewhat inexplicably, our dad decided to move back to California and is at the house for some reason or another probably four or five times a month. So I see that part of my family regularly. The wedding, though, will be the first time since Waco that I've seen either Wrangell or Skye. I am bracingly nervous.

"Relax," Atticus says to me on the ride over. "You'll barely talk to Wrangell anyway. He'll be so busy going to all the different tables and being all happy and all that."

"I can't imagine Wrangell married."

"I know, same."

"Are you nervous to see Skye?" I ask.

He makes a face. "Tiny bit."

"Just a tiny bit?"

"You know. Some mild terror."

"You all love each other so much," our mom says, looking up from her phone. "I'm sure you've missed each other."

Atticus rolls his eyes at me. To be fair, though, as far as I know, technically both those statements are true.

Our mother was right that for a long time news of the divorce eclipsed any coverage of me or of Skye. When the dust finally settled, it was only the hard-core followers still drilling down into the cancer story, going back and combing through all of Skye's posts for clues. It's only the most zealous who have taken a firm stand—Skye was definitely lying; I was definitely lying—and everyone else has adopted a sort of weary *Guess we'll never know* mentality, two sides to every story. Is anything true? Maybe things are only ever marketed better. By now I understand that Skye could go live tomorrow and corroborate my story, and it wouldn't matter; people would still hold on to whatever it is they want to believe, wielding all their little axes to chip away at any kind of shared objective reality.

At first I messaged her a lot because I was worried about her, I needed her to be okay, and maybe I couldn't help feeling guilty. She never answered, though. She unfollowed all my accounts. Atticus has spent the last months obsessively reading psych books and articles and studies, and every few weeks he has some different theory or idea about why. He and our dad talk them over, and our dad, surprisingly, has been the most consistent in reaching out to Skye, going to see her, making sure she has what she needs. Skye has mostly transitioned back to her normal content, except a few times a month she posts about cancer orgs. She left Waco and moved to LA. She bought a house, a pretty cottage near the beach. She got a cat. Once, in a reel she posted, I saw what looked like a pair of men's shoes by her front door. A month or so ago she did a livestream where she responded to people's questions, and one person asked, *Do you think you'll ever be able to forgive Honor?* I was watching, because I still watch most of her stuff, I'm not sure why. Atticus doesn't.

She blinked a few times. "Yeah," she said finally, and then she laughed. "Yeah, that's . . . a really good question."

There are probably 150 people at the wedding, most of whom I don't recognize. Wrangell and Julie are both radiant; Sonnet, solemn and protective of her flower basket, is adorable. Jamison shows me the little clay poke bowl tucked into the basket and tells me Sonnet won't put it down, bringing it to bed with her every night. Our mother and Auntie JJ murmur approval of Julie's simple, sheathlike gown. The seats are arranged in rows forming two semicircles that surround Wrangell and Julie in the middle, and we sit on one side, and Skye, wearing a tight gray dress, sits on the other. I spend the whole ceremony trying not to stare at her.

After the cocktail hour, which Atticus and I spend outside walking around with Sonnet, debating whether we should go talk to Skye, we go inside to find that the whole family, minus Wrangell, is seated at the same table for dinner. I end up next to Skye. I can feel my pulse in all my extremities.

"Hi," she says, and I say, "Hi."

She looks different in that way people do when you don't see them in a long time, that weird mix of heartbreaking familiarity and the slight evidence of all that time you missed out on, like seeing Auntie JJ again, or every time we see Sonnet. Skye looks healthy, though, not that that means anything.

"It's weird to see you," I say.

"I know."

"Um, so you moved to LA?"

She tucks her hair behind her ears and smiles one of her fake smiles. "Yeah, I did! I really like it there."

"I've never been an LA person, but in your pictures it always looks great."

"It's so great. The food is amazing."

She turns to talk to Jamison. I eat some grissini without tasting them. Our dad takes a picture with some mom from another table who comes up to talk to him. Skye takes a deep breath and turns back to me.

"I've been talking about this a lot with my therapist," she says more quietly. "And I wanted you to know that even after what you did to me, I do still love you and at some point would like to have, like, a relationship with you again. I miss you."

"After what *I* did to *you*?"

"I still have a lot to work through," she says, "but nothing I did was ever malicious or meant to hurt anyone. And I would've put you first, Honor. I never would've made you publicly go through what you put me through."

I don't know what to say to that. I am still searching for words when our dad says, his voice booming, probably four or five tables over, "Look, it's the man and woman of the hour!"

We look. Wrangell and Julie are approaching our table, the photographer in tow.

"The newest Lo!" Julie announces, lifting her bouquet in a cheer. "Well, not really, because I'm not changing my name, but in spirit! Yay!" She's flushed, happy. In her other hand she has a glass of champagne.

"You did it," Atticus says to Wrangell. "Happy for you, man."

Wrangell looks happy too, probably the happiest I've ever seen him. "I'm glad you guys could all come," he says. He gives me a hug. "You should meet Julie's family while you're here. They want to meet you."

"Can we all get together for a picture?" the photographer says, lifting his camera. "The bride and groom would love a shot with every table."

We get up and cluster together, and the photographer arranges us deftly. Wrangell drapes his arms across our shoulders, grinning hugely. We all match his smile. We are beautiful and poised. In the pictures, maybe to everyone watching us stand here together, we probably look like the perfect family.

ACKNOWLEDGMENTS

I am grateful to Adriann Ranta Zurhellen for being the constant first believer in each of my stories and finding them a home in the world. It was an honor to work again with Kendra Levin, whose enthusiasm and vision shaped and honed this story. I am also grateful to Amanda Ramirez, Alma Gomez Martinez, Amanda Brenner, and the whole team at Simon & Schuster BFYR for your efforts on this book and all the worlds and characters you bring to young readers.

I am thankful for the librarians, booksellers, writers, teachers, publishing professionals, parents, readers, and anyone else who is fighting hard for young people's freedom to read the stories they need and deserve.

This was my Pandemic Book, the one I started in the early days of shelter in place with two small children and a baby at home, and I am extremely grateful to Koo Koo Kanga Roo, *Mystery Doug*, and everyone behind *Frozen II* and *Floor Is Lava*—you got us through some rough days and gave me time to write. To my best friend, Anne Perez, it was a kind of gift to be writing our Pandemic Books together. I'm grateful for the support and community of the extended NorCal writing crew, always inspired by your work and brilliance, and ever thankful for the friends and group chats that kept me grounded these last few years.

I am grateful to my grandmothers, Marjorie Gilbert and Helen Loy, for the stories and memories they've passed down. I'm also deeply grateful to my great-aunt Mary (Junnie) Young for all the stories and family history she's shared with me, particularly about Ming Quong and local Asian American history.

I have been endlessly lucky to have the love and support of my parents, brother and sister-in-law, parents- and siblings-in-law, and many aunts and uncles and cousins and (honorary) nieces and nephews, and this book is my tribute to big, messy families—love you all. Here's to all the great things we've eaten together, the trips we've taken, the jokes and references only we know, and all the family legends and histories that've always captured my imagination.

And as always, to Jesse, Audrey, Zach, and Dash—grateful for everything, for all the new little worlds you open up for me and for each other, for all the things I've learned from you. Love you always.

ABOUT THE AUTHOR

Kelly Loy Gilbert believes deeply in the power of stories to illuminate a shared humanity and give voice to complex, broken people. She is the author of *Conviction*, a William C. Morris Award finalist, *Picture Us in the Light*, and *When We Were Infinite*, and lives in the San Francisco Bay Area. She would be thrilled to hear from you on Twitter (@KellyLoyGilbert) or at KellyLoyGilbert.com.